Eric came into the kitchen and elbowed Hank. "You missed all the excitement. Even before we knew you had taken off Mom was steamed because the Pughs had a Dead End sign put up the day you left, and she saw a bloody handprint on it yesterday morning. At first she thought it was us pulling a Halloween prank. Then, when she realized you were gone, she thought old Truman had done you in."

"Show me?" Hank demanded.

"Well...I can't. It's gone. Mom sent me to clean it up and there was zip. Creepy, huh?"

Not only didn't Hank reply, he ran to the dining-room window and stared after Sam disappearing into the shop. "Damn," he whispered at last.

Growing increasingly uneasy, Brette ignored the language. This was the second time he was reacting negatively to Sam. "What's wrong, Hank?"

Hank nodded to Sam's shop. "It's him. It's his doing."

She almost breathed a sigh of relief. "Sorry, pal, no way. It was a much smaller print on that sign. Hardly fits your hand, come to think of it, let alone a grown man's."

"Small like—like a woman's?"

Brette tensed anew. "Hank..."

"Have you seen Tracie Pugh since?"

She'd never seen him so serious. "I can't say I thought about her, hon. I was focused on you."

"But she was running to his house the night I left," Hank replied. "So if there was a print, I think it was hers. I think Sam Knight has killed her!"

HELEN R. MYERS

DEAD END

MIRA®

ISBN 1-55166-796-7

DEAD END

Copyright © 2001 by Helen R. Myers.

MIRA and the Star Colophon are trademarks used under license and registered in Australia, New Zealand, Philippines, United States Patent and Trademark Office and in other countries.

Visit us at www.mirabooks.com

Printed in U.S.A.

Although it was the sudden appearance
of the Dead End sign on our street that inspired this
story, the book couldn't have been written without
the kindness, time and enthusiastic support of the
Winnsboro Post Office, Winnsboro, Texas, particularly
the rural carriers I've come to know over the years:

Dolores Dugger
Mike Matthews
Cheryl Harris

Your dedication and caring for your customers is as
commendable as it is heartwarming. What's more,
no group has a healthier sense of humor about
themselves. Thank you for letting me share a bit of it.
Of course, any inaccuracies are strictly my error.

For additional moments of inspiration,
I'm indebted to Paula Henderson and Sam Perkins.
And for help and support—Linda Broday,
Linda Palmer, Dianne Moggy, Martha Keenan,
Ethan Ellenberg...and, of course, B.J. and Burt.

Anger is one of the sinews of the soul.
—Thomas Fuller

1

I always know when something is about to hit
the fan.
It happens just after I catch myself thinking,
'Hey, things are going pretty well...
—Journal Entry

Friday, October 29, 1999

Brette Barry hit the brakes so hard her stainless steel
thermos rolled from under the seat and struck the left
heel of her athletic shoe hard enough to remind her
of the arthritis developing in her knee. But what had
her really grimacing was the shocking sight before
her.

"Jeez. Oh, *jeez.*"

A handprint, a bloody handprint, was on the Dead
End sign that marked the end of the rural road and
the entrance to Pugh's Dairy Farm. At least the thing
looked like real dried blood. What had her suspecting
that her son Eric and his best friend Hank were probably behind the little surprise was the simplest of de-
ductions: first, this weekend was Halloween, and second, they lived only a few dozen yards up the road
from there. Aside from that, there were few other
houses on the rural street, and no other kids. In fact,

the next kid old or sharp enough to think up a prank like that was over two miles away, as a crow flies; closer to four if you were gauging by an odometer.

That is, if this is a joke.

She hated when her imagination did that to her.

It had to be a prank. The print was on the small side, larger than a grade-schooler's, but definitely not, say…a grown man's. What's more, Eric and Hank had the reputation to go along with this. Nothing serious, but they'd pulled a few such "surprises" in the last year or so that were the kind of things teen boys did. In fact, if it weren't a school day, she would have half expected them to be laughing their heads off in the woods at her openmouthed expression.

"Ten for cleverness, guys," she muttered. "But zero on the smart meter."

When had they managed this? By her best estimate, the sign was all of…a day old? It sure hadn't been there yesterday when she'd made her rounds. But the tight-lipped vandals-in-training hadn't said a word at dinner last night. In any case, if Truman Pugh saw this, he wouldn't "shit bricks"—Hank's expression when he thought she wasn't within hearing distance— he would go straight for the boys' hides. Only last month, after they'd been caught in the old shack down by the marsh, Truman had warned that if he found them on his land again or messing with his property, he would file charges with the sheriff's department. What were the chances that Farmer Frankenstein wouldn't remember that threat if he saw this?

Truman had been bugging the county for the sign, as well as the marker she'd already spotted back at the fork in the road, for months. He hadn't been content with the No Trespassing and No Soliciting signs he'd posted himself on either side of the cattle guard meant to keep out everything—from kids to Jehovah's Witnesses—but the giant milk and feed trucks that rumbled through his property. Rumor had it that even the county extension agent had to call ahead for permission to stop by.

Whatever had compelled the boys to disregard their promise to her? No matter, the important thing now was to get rid of it.

Thinking she would get the spray cleaner and roll of paper towels she kept in the camper of her red Chevy pickup to wipe the sign herself, Brette pulled off to the side of the oil-paved road. She didn't have much time. Under current regulations, her job as a Wood County, Texas, rural mail carrier allowed only a two-minute stop at each box, one minute at the cluster boxes, and she had already used up what little spare time she'd accumulated so far. That was not unusual. Several of her customers had wanted to chat about the gorgeous morning weather, to complain about the deluge of Christmas catalogs arriving daily, or to pass on some tidbit of news or gossip. As a rule, she enjoyed the people contact. For some, she was the only person they saw during the day aside from family members; for a few of the elderly, life could be even lonelier. But this was one time she should have resisted being so accessible.

Shutting off the pickup's engine, she opened the passenger door. However, no sooner did she begin to get out than she heard a vehicle approaching.

So much for bright ideas.

Scrambling back in, she tugged the door closed, and barely got the truck back on the road and up to the Pugh's mailbox when the familiar white flatbed came around the bend. A good move, she saw, recognizing who was behind the wheel. It was the head grouch himself.

Truman Pugh braked on his side of the cattle guard. A dour man at the best of times, this morning he looked like his best producing bovine had gone dry.

Could he have already seen the sign?

"You're late!" he barked as he climbed out of his vehicle. "This is my second trip up here."

"Sewer sludge," Brette murmured. Heck, yes, she wanted to say something more specific. But when you had a budding teenager and were responsible for another twice as challenging, you had a responsibility to choke earthy impulses whenever or wherever necessary so they didn't get to be a habit.

At somewhere between sixty and seventy, Truman was a square block of a man with the set features of someone who wasted nothing—time, energy, words or emotion. What remained of his snow-white hair grew mostly above his eyes like ice crystals in a blizzard; they tangled with his stubby eyelashes and made focusing on anything else a psychological test. The rest was a bit of bristle at the back of his neck and coming out of his ears. He wasn't an ugly man, rather a brittle, empty one. That's what got to Brette. She always wondered upon spotting him—if he had ever had a truly happy day, even one, in his life.

She managed a lukewarm smile. "Sorry, Mr. Pugh. Lots to deliver today."

"Huh." He rounded his paint-chipped, muddy vehicle. "Gossiping's more like it. I have better things to do than wait for you to get around to doing your job."

Wanting only to get away, Brette handed him his

small bundle of mail, as well as the larger one belonging to his son Albert. "Looks as though all the mail order companies are gearing up to vie for Tracie's holiday business."

He snatched the two bundles. "No wonder your boy is growing up to be a juvenile delinquent. You set no example, show no respect. No discipline!"

As fascinated as she was that he could practically bark like a German shepherd and yet barely move his lips, it didn't excuse his rudeness. "It would be fascinating to hear more, Mr. Pugh," she replied, "but as you've pointed out, I'm behind schedule. My regards to Elsie and the udders."

"You ridicule me, but I'm a father. I know!"

As he stomped back to his truck, it was all Brette could do not to choke. The man had the nerve to brag about his parentage? His thirty-something-year-old Albert was as big a bully as he was, as bad as anyone she'd ever met!

"Cretin." She scowled as he backed his vehicle onto the lush pasture and made a U-turn. But her annoyance turned to relief as she shifted into drive and continued on her way.

He hadn't seen it!

With a last glance at the sign, she sped back down the narrow road. As relieved as she was, though, the October woods—a kaleidoscope of amber and cranberry-red—no longer drew her attention. All her thoughts were on wanting to get hold of Eric and Hank.

It would be better that they clean up the sign themselves, she decided. Let them know what it was like to risk getting nabbed in the act. With luck they would have just enough time to get the job done after school before the evening milk truck arrived.

She accelerated on the rural oil road through the autumnal downpour of dogwood, sweet gum and oak leaves. And for a change she didn't fantasize as she passed Sam Knight's two-story relic. Nor did she spare a glance at her quaint pseudo-Cape Cod beside it with its domed side windows she'd had installed for plants. In fact, her thoughts so preoccupied her, she would probably have missed Keith Daggett if he hadn't been standing in the middle of the street flagging her down.

Brette braked hard, and for an instant wondered if she wasn't going to add manslaughter charges to her morning's offenses.

Keith ran a computer business out of his double-wide trailer. Although he looked like the stereotypical geek, with his blond hair cut ultrashort and wire-frame glasses too big for his narrow face, beneath that he was a doll, who also happened to be a genuinely nice guy. So decent, in fact, she'd tried to fix him up with Sally a few months ago. Unfortunately, her otherwise love-starved friend hadn't been impressed, and Keith had done a fast retreat like a whipped puppy.

He appeared not to be suffering any residual effects today and smiled warmly as he handed her an orange order envelope. "Thought I'd missed you. That's for a roll of stamps for tomorrow."

"Sure. You've got it."

As was often the case when he was on deadline, Keith's eyes were bloodshot. "You sound in a less than terrific mood."

"I have two words to explain why—Truman Pugh."

That won her an understanding nod from the lanky-built man. "What did he say the boys did now?"

This was why she liked him. He spoke her "short-hand." And despite Sally's scathing criticisms about his dating obtuseness, he remained concerned about Hank.

"Actually, nothing. Yet. Only because he didn't see it."

"Oh, goody." Keith hunched his shoulders and rubbed his hands like one of Dracula's trusty side-kicks. "A puzzle, mistress," he slurred. "I live for a puzzle." In his normal voice he added, "Let me see...what could 'it' be? It's almost Halloween— Ah! A glorious time for tossing rolls of toilet tissue over roofs and trees. Or how about tossing eggs atop grumpy farmers' roofs? No, wait! They painted one of Pugh's cows Great Pumpkin orange?"

"You're almost as bad as they are." But Brette smiled despite her mood. "They put a bloody hand-print on his new Dead End sign. He's the one who got the county to put it in—the one at the fork and the big one at his property line." When he merely stared back at her vacantly, she shook her head. "You don't have a clue as to what I'm talking about, do you? Well, you're excused in this case, Mr. Worka-holic, because the boys only put it there yesterday. They must've dreamed up the scheme last night be-fore I called them in to dinner."

Keith rubbed the corners of his mouth, clearly try-ing to repress his laughter. "Poor Brette. All things considered, though, it sounds like fairly tame Devil's Night humor to me."

"Exactly why you'd get an F in Baby-sitting 101. You have no appreciation for what it's like to have your heart bounce off the dashboard. You live a sheltered life lost in your program manuals and computer guts and whatnots.''

''And I should probably count my blessings, I know.''

''Seriously, Keith, Pugh could make sure the kids had a juvenile record that would follow them for years and haunt them forever. What college would want them? How do they explain that in an interview for some job requiring a security clearance?'' Brette chewed at her lower lip. ''I really should've stayed and wiped it clean. I intended to when I first saw it, but then Mr. Congeniality showed up.''

He nodded, more somber now. ''You couldn't risk it. You're sure he didn't see it?''

''Positive. He was more interested in criticizing my work ethic because I was late. But ask me which two boys are going to be chased out there with a pail and washrags as soon as they get off the bus this afternoon?''

''You get 'em, tiger.'' Keith saluted her like an intimidated recruit, but grinned as he stepped back from her vehicle. ''Guess I'd better not keep you so you can be here to catch them as soon as they get home.''

''Too true. I'll have your stamps in the morning. Thanks for letting me vent!''

2

By sunset Brette was in an even better frame of mind...somewhat. While it had irked her to hear Eric deny that he and Hank had been responsible for the print on the sign, he hadn't given her any trouble about getting out there to clean it off.

Now she was making the final preparations for dinner. Friday was Eric's turn to choose the menu, which always meant pizza, and she'd been experimenting with a recipe for a homemade vegetable one that the boys claimed to actually like.

After putting out fresh-grated Parmesan on the dining room table, she checked the oven and saw that the mozzarella was oozing, the crust was almost the right golden-brown. It was time to call to the other end of the house.

"Dinner! Wash up, please!"

She hadn't seen either boy since giving the cleanup order. That wasn't unusual; it was understood that homework came first, even on Fridays, and that rule applied to Hank, too. After all, he stayed there almost more than he did at his own house. It was also typical of Hank to hide in the background after instigating something until he saw how hot things got. Another law-of-the-land talk was due with the boy, so she'd spent the rest of the afternoon out back raking leaves and preparing the flowerbeds for spring bulbs, using the time to perfect what she wanted to say to make sure there were no misunderstandings as she again explained the "Gospel according to Barry."

But she couldn't help smiling as her son appeared around the corner. "You must be hungry. I only had to call once."

He still wore the Dallas Cowboy jersey he'd worn to school. Troy Aikman's number 8. A natural blond like her, Eric unfortunately also took after her in height and build, and more resembled a soccer player than football hunk. But then his father hadn't, either.

"Not really," he said.

Eric went straight to the refrigerator for the milk jug. He drank milk with everything and always had. Several years ago Brette had joked they could save money by keeping a dairy cow in the back as a pet, then regretted it when the boys tried to "borrow" one from the Pughs. A three-month-old calf they were certain no one would miss because it was so small. That had cured her of making statements that could be misconstrued as literal suggestions. And she'd been grateful the mother cow hadn't left a hoof mark on their skulls for stealing her baby.

"Finished with your schoolwork?" She sensed a tension in him and wondered if he was upset with her for making him do the right thing. She hoped not. Usually he was good about accepting responsibility for his actions. But he was thirteen now, and everyone had begun warning her that the big one-three could turn her child into an alien overnight.

"I wish. But Mrs. Durban got the school to link up with C-Span the way you and the rest of the PTA wanted, and now our history class has to do our own reports on the presidents. She pulled names today.''

''That's terrific! Who do you have?''

''John Adams.'' The name came out like a groan. ''I wanted Grant.''

''Adams will make a great subject. So would his wife, for that matter. He and Abigail had a terrific relationship. Very much partners.''

''I *wanted* Grant.''

Yes, there was definitely something wrong. ''Because of the Civil War aspect, right? And let me guess…Hank got him instead?''

''Uh-huh.''

''Is that why he's hiding? He's afraid I'll smack him with a pot holder for getting your guy, or worse yet, cut his ration of pizza?'' Despite her teasing tone, Brette was concerned. Maybe Eric and Hank had fought? That didn't happen often; they really were solid pals, despite Hank being one year older and having been left back a year in school.

Eric finished pouring his milk and put the jug back into the refrigerator. ''Hank's not here.''

That explained the quietness. Sally Jamison worked nights at a Tyler hospital and slept during the day. As a result, Hank spent virtually every waking moment he could at Brette's place. Of course, he probably would whether Sally had a day job or not, thanks to his uneven relationship with his mother.

''Did he have to run over to his house for something?'' she asked, careful not to jump to conclusions. ''He's coming back over, right? I'm taking you to that Halloween party at the school gym tonight?''

Eric took his seat at the rectangular glass-topped dinette table. ''Nah. Forget it.''

"But I thought you were looking forward to it?"

"That's before I heard it's gonna be mostly for little kids."

This couldn't be. The boys had gone last year and she'd seen young people of all ages there. But before she could ask about what was going on, the phone rang.

"Hello?" She slid her gaze to her son's somber profile, her thoughts remaining with him.

"Listen, do you think my kid wants to make an appearance and at least pretend to wish me a good night before I head to work, or what?"

"Sally...hey there." Brette frowned at Eric. Covering the phone she whispered, "Did I hear you right? Hank's not here?"

"Nope."

"Then where is he? His mother's looking for him."

Eric shrugged.

Everything about his body language spoke of repressed anger...or hurt. Something was definitely wrong.

"Could you expand on that, please?" she asked in a loud whisper. "How do I translate a shrug to Sally?"

"Brette? Hello?"

"Hang on, Sal." Brette covered the mouthpiece again. "Okay, out with it. What's going on? Where's Hank?"

"I don't *know*, Mom. I haven't seen him."

"Since...?"

He shrugged again. "He didn't go to school."

Out of nowhere a huge knot formed in Brette's stomach. "Why didn't you tell me?"

"Because you'd already left for work."

But he could have said something this afternoon when he'd first come home from school. No, there hadn't been time then, either, because of her. Because of that blasted sign.

"So what are you saying?" she continued. "He wasn't feeling well when he left here this morning?" It was an inane question. If Hank had stayed home due to illness, Sally shouldn't be calling. Unless... unless...

"He didn't spend the night," Eric said. "He went home after you turned in."

Brette pressed her hand against the mouthpiece even harder. "*Eric*. This doesn't make sense!"

"No kidding. He was in one of those moods, you know what I mean. And I'm tired of them. I told him if he didn't snap out of it, he should go take his attitude someplace else. He did."

"Ho-boy." Without taking her eyes off her son, Brette removed her hand from the mouthpiece. "Sally, uh...we'll be right over."

3

The Jamisons lived in the prefab house directly across the street. Dove gray, it was a long shoe box of a building with white trim, including some wheel-like adornment at the base that was the only part Hank cared for because he thought it made the place look like a Louisiana gambling boat. The vinyl siding kept it looking neat without being boring. Sally was allergic to everything with roots, and avoided gardens and grass like someone with a phobia. As a result, she'd covered the area directly in front with gravel. For color she relied on a few plastic pots at the base of the front stairs that, for most of the year, exhibited a bouquet of silk geraniums. In the fall they were replaced with silk chrysanthemums, and for Christmas she bought poinsettias. Sally liked color, which was why the flowers were always a shade too loud to seem real—not unlike Sally herself. One had to look over a hundred feet away for a glimpse of natural vegetation—pine, sweet gum, assorted oak, red maple and dogwood trees. In fact, their area was part of a dense but dwindling woodland that protected them from treacherous East Texas storms.

Sally stood behind the glass storm door, and Brette and Eric rushed to her. A divorcée since her son was in diapers, her method of coping with the world had been to "create her own reality" even before Hank's birth. Brette could only imagine what was going on in her mind now. A product of a broken home who never had a close relationship with either of her parents, Sally's opinion of herself was that she existed under a black cloud, a victim of bad luck, and that too often she gave ungrateful and unscrupulous people the benefit of the doubt. As a result, crises were frequent and all-consuming events in her life. When one was on the front burner, she could easily suck in everyone around her to feed it.

Befriending the woman, who at thirty-five was three years her senior, was tantamount to adopting a high-strung pet—not exactly what Brette had had in mind. Sally—and Hank for that matter—clearly needed professional help, while Brette's relationship with her parents had been healthy. Codependency wasn't in her realm of experiences, let alone something she yearned to experiment with. However, Sally was like coming across a dream house…in the desert…constructed on a fault line. In other words, she was a good person, kind, well-intentioned and often hilarious. She was also, as best as Brette could figure it, a manic-depressive. The condition had never been diagnosed, of course, and that was the problem. Sally might work in a hospital, but she avoided doctors with the same zeal she did bill collectors. However, after being a neighbor and friend for almost a decade, Brette had witnessed too much to doubt it.

Looking as though she'd done nothing since rising from bed except to grab the phone, Sally's makeup-free face was paler than usual, and her eggplant-tinted hair styled in a punk-rocker fashion resembled something seen on MTV—or in a cartoon. A fuschia

T-shirt and shorts hung on her undernourished body like dew-damp bathroom tissue on a leafless tree.

"What's wrong?" she demanded in lieu of a greeting. She looked around them for her son. "Where is he? Hank?"

"Sal, the one thing to remember is that this is nothing new, okay?" Brette hurried up the stairs and inside, reaching for the taller woman. "Hank's gotten upset before and punished you by hiding someplace, until he vented a bit."

Sally backed away. "What are you saying? He's run away?"

"We don't know that."

Sally focused on Eric, although her pale-green eyes didn't register a lot. "What did he tell you? Whatever it was, it's a lie!"

"Don't yell, Sal. Let's turn the TV off." Brette did that, adding, "And you need to understand that Eric is as confounded as you are."

"But you two were together at school," Sally continued. "He must've said something."

Eric shoved his hands deeper into his jeans. They were nothing like the oversize baggy things that Hank preferred to wear. "He didn't go to school, Mrs. Jamison."

Sally's facial muscles went slack; her skin seemed more translucent than ever. She turned back to Brette. "I don't—I don't get it. Why didn't anyone tell me? You should know what's going on in his life. You see him more than I do." She shot an angrier look at Eric. "You *had* to know. Why didn't you tell your mother?"

"Hank left our house after I'd gone to sleep," Brette said on his behalf.

That won her an indelicate snort. "Excuse me, he worships you. You're telling me he snuck out?"

Brette felt Eric twitch, and knew his reluctance to reply was out of respect for Hank's lifelong troubled relationship with his mother. But she also understood his natural reluctance to get into the middle of an argument.

"He'd been moody all day," he finally replied. "One minute he wanted to talk, the next he accused me of spying. For you."

"Well, that's a joke, isn't it?" Sally nervously patted her shorts pockets and then ended up tugging at the hair at her nape. "Like you'd tell me anything."

"By evening I finally had enough and told him to either tell me what was bothering him or to go home." At that Eric averted his gaze. "He left."

The admission sent Sally into another rush of indignation. "How could you do that to him? You're supposed to be his best friend! You're supposed—"

"Whoa." One thing Brette wouldn't allow, even from a friend, was anyone using her boy as an emotional punching bag. "I think Eric was clear that he'd tried to help. Hank made the decision to leave on his own. And don't forget, you're the one who gave him the freedom to do as he pleases. If you'd told me to make sure he stayed put, believe me, he would have. But you didn't…and you didn't give me a clue that something was wrong between you two."

"I told you, nothing was! Okay, okay." Sally rubbed her forehead with the force of someone in pain for some time. "Maybe things weren't perfect, but…they were normal. Not great, but we were still talking. We hadn't had what you'd call a *fight* fight in weeks. That's a pretty good stretch, isn't it?"

For them. But theirs wasn't an enviable partnership in the best of times. Her easygoing Eric had recently remarked how he couldn't think of living in the combustible atmosphere that was the Jamisons' home.

"You don't have the slightest clue as to whether leaving was his idea or...?"

"Or what?" Sally went from confused to horrified. "You think he was taken!" She backed into her living room. "That's it! He must've been and I just couldn't tell. I mean, look at this place...."

Brette did, although she would have preferred not to. The house always looked like a minitornado had swept through it. On Sally's bad days—and this looked to be one of them—it more resembled a ransacking. Who was she kidding? It always reminded her of the Roseanne Barr line, "I'm not going to vacuum 'til Sears makes one you can ride on."

"No, no, it doesn't make sense," Sally said before Brette could reply. "Who would come down this road, choose this house, *my* son? He's run away again. Brette, what do I do?"

The underlying angst beneath her surface panic was clear. Wood County Sheriff Chester "Cuddy" Cudahy had spoken plainly in regards to his people being called out there to resolve petty squabbles, or the boy's vengeful or stubborn behavior. He'd come himself after the last panic and had announced that the next time they called, he would personally do everything in his power to have the boy put into state custody.

"You know how you are when you first wake up," Brette said, hoping against hope. "Are you sure he's not hiding here somewhere playing a Halloween joke on you?"

"Hallo— No. No, I looked in his room, and he avoids the rest of the place like you do."

Not wanting to start on that subject, Brette told her, "We have to call this in. They'll put out bulletins on him."

"Cudahy won't authorize that. We're one step away from being trailer trash to him."

"The sheriff's not a ghoul, Sal. He has children and grandchildren of his own, and the only reason he said what he did last time was to scare Hank into behaving himself. Just because he believes in tough love doesn't mean he's not going to be sympathetic to your situation."

"You call. He likes you."

Only because she hadn't called him a cigar-addicted redneck, but Brette made the call. Naturally, the sheriff was already gone for the day and the dispatcher asked innumerable questions before assuring her someone would be out. After she hung up, she considered what they could do until a deputy arrived. Being a good twenty miles east-northeast from the county seat of Quitman, she knew it would take a minimum of thirty or forty minutes for them to reach there, and that was if someone was available. It was dark now, which meant the meager evening shift was on duty.

"Have you checked for a note?" she asked Sally.

"Why would I? I thought he was with you."

"Let's do that. Maybe it slipped off a table and got swept under the bed as you passed by or closed a door." Brette turned to Eric. "Go check his room, but don't touch anything you don't have to."

"My fingerprints are already all over the place,

Mom. If that's going to incriminate me, I might as well turn myself in as soon as they get here.''

If she was a fan of mysteries, her son was a budding detective. Bowing to his logic, she replied, ''I'm aware you're no stranger to his stuff. What I'm concerned about is you damaging someone else's print.''

He brightened somewhat. ''Hey, yeah.''

''Someone else? Who?'' Sally demanded. ''You know Hank doesn't have any real friends besides Eric. Truth is he's getting downright creepy, Brette. You don't think he planned something wild, do you?''

''Don't.'' Brette clasped her friend's hands. ''I'm only trying to think the way the deputy will once he arrives. Let's not look for trouble where there may be none.''

''What should I do?''

''Maybe we should stick together. Let's all go to Hank's room. With three pairs of eyes, we'll spot something faster.''

As Eric often pointed out, Hank's room was one of the neater places in the house. The door was fully open, but there was a computer generated Private Property Keep Out! sign over the knob. Inside, the twin-size bed was made and the desk was organized except for the stack of slightly askew schoolbooks. An unzipped gym bag lay open on the floor and the closet door stood ajar. Those were the only signs that someone had been in there—but who knew how long ago?

Brette put her arm around Eric. ''What do you think?''

''I'm trying not to.''

She rubbed his slim, tense back. ''I need you, pal. Give it a shot.''

Eric inspected the area some more, then sighed. "Seems to me that he was here only to get something, and left." He nodded to the gym bag. "That wouldn't have been there if he'd meant to go to school."

"Good point." Brette looked at Sally. "Right?"

Sally hung back at the doorway as though something in the room might attack her. "Well, he—he does get mad when I tell him he's still a child. I suppose he would have left it behind if he thought it would help him look older. But what if he's just hiding in the woods? That's what he did last time, remember?"

However, then he'd only been gone three hours, and it hadn't yet been dark. Just long enough to break through the floor at an abandoned cabin behind the Ponders', cut his leg enough for seven stitches and yell bloody murder until they found him. And when he'd been shown the boar tracks covering his by the laughing deputy, he'd humiliated himself further by wetting his pants.

"He wouldn't try that again, Mrs. J." Eric glanced around the closet door at them. "At least not while he's wearing his good shoes."

The Jamisons lived from paycheck to paycheck. Hank had learned to be careful with certain possessions, like the expensive shoes some celebrated athlete endorsed.

"That's good," Brette said to her son. Gently squeezing his shoulder, she added to Sally, "What other bag could he have taken?"

Before she could answer Eric said, "The denim duffel bag Mrs. J. got as a bonus for buying that cosmetic stuff. He really liked it." Eric looked expectantly at Sally.

She stared, dubious. "You're sure I had something like that?"

With maturity beyond his years, Eric said to Brette, "You may want to tell the cops. As for the rest, I'm not sure. He may not have changed...except for the shoes."

"So what do you think he's wearing?" Brette asked.

"His Dallas Cowboys shirt, the white version of mine."

The boys practically lived in the things and asked for a replacement each Christmas. Demanded in large sizes, they hung off both boys' shoulders, even though Hank had the stronger build, and almost down to Eric's knees and the middle of Hank's thighs. "Bless you, babe. And jeans, right?"

"The ones you hate."

She didn't reprimand him for exaggerating. "Hip-hop. Grunge big?"

"Yeah."

"Hat?"

Eric glanced around the room, then peered into the closet. "Maybe the blue one with the white star on it. Your fault, you told him it brings out the blue in his eyes."

Poor Hank. He craved compliments so much, he actually cared what she said about his strange eyes that went from fog gray to minimal blue.

"You're the best," she murmured with a smile. But it was short-lived. Glancing back, she met Sally's fearful gaze.

They now had something definite to tell the authorities.

4

It was almost thirty-five minutes before a white patrol car from the Wood County Sheriff's Department pulled into Sally's driveway. While Sally spouted epithets criticizing how long it had taken, Brette was grateful the deputy had arrived without flashing lights and shrill siren. Maybe they didn't live on a populated road, but there was no need to embarrass Sally in front of what neighbors she had.

She recognized the deputy as Roy Russell. From the photos she'd seen of him in the paper, she'd guessed him to be around fifty, but up close he looked a little younger. He was pleasant looking in a quiet way, but his somber eyes were skeptical as he sized them up.

"You the folks who called?"

"I'm Brette Barry," Brette said, stepping back to let him inside. "This is Sally Jamison, Hank's mother."

The lawman touched the brim of his hat. "Ma'am." He glanced around and to his credit managed to keep his face expressionless. "The dispatcher tells me this isn't the first time your son's given you some trouble."

Nothing like letting Sally know he thought she was

wasting his time. But before Brette could interject, her friend spoke up.

"It's the first time he's been gone overnight. Once he was found here in the woods. Before that he hid in a friend's car. He only tried the roads once and you people picked him up. Where were you this time?" Sally demanded, crossing her arms under braless breasts.

Deputy Russell flipped open his notebook. "What's the friend's name, ma'am?"

"What?"

"Keith Daggett," Brette said. "You passed his place coming in. It's the white double-wide on the left. He operates his own computer business from there. On the right is Clovis and Bertrice Ponder. She's retired from the phone company and takes care of Clovis full-time now. He suffered a stroke—what? Over a year ago, Sal?"

"I guess. I don't remember."

"The point we're making, Deputy Russell, is that this feels different than those other instances." Brette started ticking important details off the fingers of her left hand. "My son Eric says that Hank had been edgy all day, and yet he hadn't had a fight with his mother. Having said that, he waited until Sally left for work last night—"

"You work the night shift?" Russell asked Sally.

"No, I'm a hooker. My spot is up by the corner of—"

"Sally." Sending her a look, Brette entreated her to curb her sarcasm and not turn a bad situation into a full-blown scene. "These are necessary questions."

"Well, of course I work the night shift. What does he think, I'm out partying and ignoring my kid?

Okay, okay,'' Sally snapped at the blank-faced cop. "Yes, I work nights at Mother Frances in Tyler."

The man returned his focus to his notes. "Nurse?"

"Please, give me a burned macaroni-and-cheese pot to bedpans any day." She met his silent stare. "Cafeteria. Nights because it pays better than day work. Not that we don't earn our wages. You don't know what some people come in demanding at two in the morning."

"Oh, I reckon I do. My sister's second child took his time showing up and since her husband was overseas, I stepped in as the surrogate pacer. I spent some time down there driving the help nuts."

"Sweetie, I'm the night manager, not 'the help.'"

Clearing his throat, Russell said, "So when did you realize—" he checked his notes "—Hank...Hank was missing, Miss...Mrs. Jamison?"

"This is ridiculous." Sally made a beeline for the kitchen.

Going for her cigarettes, Brette surmised, hoping it wasn't for a drink.

"Actually, we realized it simultaneously," she said on behalf of her friend. "As Sally called my place wanting to say goodbye to Hank before leaving for work, my son was telling me that Hank hadn't been at school and had left here last night."

Russell pointed his pen from her to the kitchen. "You mean you hadn't been in touch with the boy you'd been sitting for?"

Brette grew uncomfortable with his phrasing as much as his tone. "Hank is a year older than my son. No one 'sits' for him. But he and Eric are best friends. We consider him family. He considers our place home when his mother is working. But sometimes he likes to be by himself, as does everyone.''

Without reacting to that, Russell shifted focus to study Eric. ''He left your house and you didn't tell your mother?''

''She'd just gone to bed. She's a mail carrier, she gets up early.''

''Did you two fight?'' Russell demanded.

''My mom and I don't fight.''

''Let me rephrase that. Had something happened to your friend at school?''

Eric shoved his hands into his pockets and tipped his head in a faint shrug. ''All I know is that something was up with him. Usually we can talk out his moods. But not last night.''

''He was moodier than usual?''

''He's a teenager for crying out loud!'' Sally snapped from the doorway of the kitchen.

They all turned to her. Indifferent, she leaned against the doorjamb and lit a cigarette.

Deputy Russell finally asked Eric, ''Could you expand on what you thought was wrong, son? Was he acting upset?''

Eric glanced at Sally as though waiting to see if she would erupt again. ''He tried to pick a fight with me a couple times during the day, then again when we got to my house. That wasn't...normal. He may have problems with people sometimes, but not with me. I guess I finally had enough. I told him to get lost until he figured out if he wanted to be a friend or to be a jerk. That was the last I saw of him.''

''And what time did this showdown happen?''

''About seven-fifteen. I remember now my mom's shower was running.''

Deputy Russell eyed his watch. "Pretty close to twenty-four hours. So you two didn't have a falling out over a girl or something?"

Eric bowed his head, his embarrassment evident. "No."

"He's only thirteen, Deputy." Brette wished she was standing closer so she could elbow him in the ribs for that one. Girls Eric's age were currently enthralled with upper classmen, especially the brawny jocks. They weren't noticing boys their own age.

"What about Hank?"

"Fourteen's still not old enough to go over the edge for a girl," Sally replied.

Deputy Russell's expression reflected skepticism. "These days lots of kids that age are sexually active. We recently had a case where two fifteen-year-olds had a suicide pact. Fortunately, a friend reported it. But it was a close call."

"So what are you suggesting, Deputy, that my son's shacked up with some bimbette in a cheap hotel room?" Sally raked a hand through her hair, doing nothing to improve its wild state. "What idiot has a death wish so bad he'd rent a room to a minor?"

"Kids today have a different view of what's romantic, ma'am. The back of a SUV will work fine for some."

As Sally vanished into the kitchen again, Brette drew a calming breath. "Deputy, please. We're talking about her only child."

"I appreciate that Mrs.—"

"Ms. Barry."

Russell pursed his lips, but all he said was, "Well, *Ms.* Barry, I can either hand out hankies and aspirin, or I can get a feeling of what's really going on. I mean no disrespect to you or Ms. Jamison, but we don't have an unlimited number of men available. Our time is valuable.''

"Mrs. Jamison."

This time the deputy stuck his tongue in his cheek. "Okay, let's put it this way. From what I understand from our records, this kid's had a few brushes with the law, and he's prone to pulling pranks. What makes you think this isn't another of his attempts to get attention, or to shake you up?"

"Because," came a deep voice from behind Brette, "he knew he didn't have to run again. He understood that if he had trouble, he could come to me."

5

Brette spun around. She couldn't have been more stunned if Hank's father had suddenly developed a conscience and come to see how his boy was doing. But it wasn't Henry Jamison Sr. who'd spoken. It was none other than Samuel Shane Knight, her neighbor since spring, and the object of her frustrations and fantasies, depending on how reclusive he was behaving.

What on earth was he doing here?

"I saw you and Eric run over earlier," he said directly to her. Gently placing his index finger under her chin, he closed her mouth. "When the patrol car showed up, I knew my hunch was right that something was wrong. I figured you might need help."

Since when? From the day she had baked a double-chocolate cake and brought it next door to welcome him to their neighborhood, such as it was, he'd made it clear that, unless the woods or her house were on fire, she could stay on her side of the property line. He hadn't been rude about it. On the contrary, he'd resembled a deer caught in headlights, but she'd gotten the message.

The next time she'd braved the invisible wall—after letting Sally convince her that she'd caught him in a bad moment—he'd politely turned down her offer to join them for a cookout, but his body language had screamed rejection. No pants-chaser she, Brette had gone back to pretending that the big two-story Texas Gothic monstrosity, which had stood uncompleted for nearly two years after the death of its builder, remained empty. Except when Mr. Gorgeous deigned it acceptable to nod as their paths crossed, or when she was working in the yard and caught him watching her from a window or from his workshop out back. That's when that annoying sexual energy she hadn't felt in years sprang to life with all the subtlety of a feline in her first heat.

"How...kind," she managed to mumble. "Sal...?" Desperate to break contact, she spun around looking for her friend, only to see she wasn't the only one having problems. Sally remained in the kitchen doorway, but the lengthening ashes on her cigarette were testament to her own dumbfounded state. "Sam's come to help."

Sally merely gaped, but there was plenty of reason to do so.

Her nickname for him in less than kind moments was Mr. Dead Below the Waist, but not because she didn't approve of him. What was not to like? He was strong-boned, long-legged and his shoulders looked capable of taking down one of their fifty-plus-foot pine trees without a chain saw. He also had the kind of face marketing people sought for guy ads like military posters—proud, capable and reliable. So what if there was a slight bump in his nose that announced he hadn't championed everything he'd tried? Not even his wary, sometimes-haunted gray eyes detracted from the overall appeal.

It was as depressing as it was disconcerting.

Right now, however, they were all being too quiet.

"Deputy Roy Russell, this is Sam Knight," Brette said to the lawman. "Sam is our neighbor in the white elephant across the street." No way was she letting Sam think he was getting away with anything. "He teaches Shop at Sandy Springs High."

"I can't help notice you seem surprised to see him, Ms. Barry," Russell replied.

"No, no. I'm only—"

"She didn't know that I would still be home," Sam supplied.

What the hell...? Brette thought.

Russell's gaze shifted between them before he nodded and jotted down something else. "No doubt seeing the boys in two different environments, you'd notice if something was unusual about their behavior, Mr. Knight?"

Brette especially wanted to hear the answer to that one.

"They're not quite old enough to be in any of my classes," Sam replied. "But we speak to each other in the halls."

It was all Brette could do not to drag her son outside and give him the third degree there and then. All she could do though was shoot him a covert glance, but he was fixated on Sam. If what Sam said was true, why had Eric hidden it from her? If not...if not she was going to break Knight's knees for not only using her child to lie, but doing it in front of him!

"Do you have any idea where the boy could be?" Russell continued.

"I'm afraid not. Hank seemed fine when we spoke yesterday. A little vague, but that's not unusual for him. School isn't his favorite place."

Russell grunted. "I had the same problem at his age. Was that the last time you saw him?"

"No. The last time was later last night when he left Mrs. Barry's house and went home."

It was all Brette could do not to gasp. He'd actually seen Hank leaving!

"Time?"

"I'm not sure about the exact minute. I'd say between eight and nine. Mrs. Jamison had already left. At least her car was gone."

"Where were you when you saw him?"

"Closing my workshop and heading for the house."

"Your workshop...so your point of view was clear? He was well lit so that you could tell it was actually him?"

"The streetlight between their houses was lit, yes. It was Hank."

"Good. You moonlight?"

"Pardon?"

"You were coming out of your shop."

Sam nodded briefly. "I have in the past, but right now my focus is on renovating my house. If you see it by day, you'll understand why Mrs. Barry calls it a white elephant."

"You mean *Ms.* Barry," Russell drawled, but he stayed on course. "What about Mrs. Knight? Any chance she might have seen something?"

"I'm divorced."

More news. When Brette had introduced herself and hinted about a "Mrs." Sam had merely said, "I'm not married." True, divorce was a fact of life these days, but it troubled her that he hadn't been more explicit. Such evasion triggered the suspicion that he'd wanted to hide the details. She didn't hold to Sally's philosophy that as long as a guy didn't look like Freddie of horror movie fame, he was worth checking out if only to give her vibrator a break; single, married or in-between, who cared? Brette worried about exposing her son to relationships that would color his own down the road.

Apparently his answer had Deputy Russell wondering, too, because he eyed Sam with renewed speculation.

"That's a pretty big house for a single guy."

"I agree. That's not against the law, though, is it?"

This was the Sam Knight Brette knew. Stare your opponent down with eyes as cool and tough as pewter in an enigmatic mask of a face that made Russell's attempt at it seem amateurish. Even though she wasn't the one being challenged, it brought back the off balance feeling she always experienced around him. At the same time, she had to admire him. He refused to be intimidated by the lawman's badge. It made her wonder what it would take to unnerve the man.

Clearing his throat, Deputy Russell turned to Sally. "Have you checked the house, ma'am? Did you notice anything to suggest your son has run away from home?"

"We'd begun looking when you arrived. Eric knows what he was wearing. Tell him," she directed.

Russell took down the information. "Well," he said at the end, "let me phone this in. My hunch is that, although we're right at the twenty-four-hour minimum for initiating a search, the sheriff will want us to check out the area first, make sure we're not sending everybody on a wild-goose chase."

"Sally," Brette said gently, "you'd better call the hospital and let them know what you're dealing with."

Sally's ashes fell forgotten to the carpet. "Oh, please. You call. I'll lose it the moment I try to explain."

But as Brette headed for the kitchen phone, she didn't miss how Sally had no problem using the opportunity to lean on Sam. As soon as Deputy Russell stepped outside she was all over their neighbor like a clothier fitting a suit. Poor Eric looked so rattled, he all but backed out the door. Oblivious, Sally let Sam take her cigarette butt and crush it out in the coffee table ashtray. Then she placed her hands on his chest and gazed up at him in a perfect pantomime of some tragic heroine in an old black-and-white movie.

Get bitchy, why don't you? You're supposed to be thinking about Hank!

Ashamed, Brette focused on the voice in her ear.

By the time she returned to the living room, the bathroom door was closing and Sam was exiting the house, too. Brette made a beeline for him.

"Hey!" Pausing on the top stair, she waited only long enough for him to reach the bottom and face her. "Exactly who do you think you're kidding?" she demanded.

6

"**K**idding? No one. My intention is to help."

Sam had been expecting that, had been preparing for it from the moment he'd abandoned the safety and darkness of his property and made his way over here. That didn't, however, ease the tension knotting and tearing at his gut. Nor did it help that Brette Barry was the kind of sunny, vibrant woman who made people smile. He had never been much of a smiler.

Her fine bones and natural blond hair that tempted the slightest of breezes made her a dead ringer for the popular TV sitcom actress who'd won several Emmys in a row, and recently an Oscar. But she wasn't looking remotely sunny at the moment. In fact, it was temper and suspicion that had her blue eyes sparkling like fireflies in July; and although he was an expert on both emotions, he didn't have a clue as to how to react to hers.

"You help?" she scoffed in a loud whisper. "Since when?"

He slipped his hands into the pockets of his denim jacket so he could curl his fingers into fists. "Everyone's entitled to change his mind."

Brette crossed her arms. Even her heavy denim shirt with the double pockets couldn't hide that she was built like those statues meant for indoors, sleek so water flowed, rather than splashed off them. The frustrated artist in him wanted to linger and appreciate nature's nuances. The veteran survivor overrode that to deal with her Mama Pit Bull demeanor.

"Would you be happier if I pretended I hadn't seen that patrol car pull in?"

"You have before."

"There was nothing to do last time. The police were bringing him home safe and sound."

Brette slowly shook her head. "Don't play games with me. I'm not Sally—or the boys for that matter, *if* what you said is true. You've made it clear since the day you moved in that you wanted us to keep our distance. We have. Why the sudden about-face in attitude?"

"I have my reasons."

"I'd love to hear them."

He remained silent.

He knew he had been a topic of discussion between her and Sally Jamison since he'd moved in last April. No telling what conclusions they'd come to, but he'd guessed well, and they'd been confirmed when Sally made a pass following the margarita party Brette threw her a short time later for her birthday....

"You're gay," the woman had accused after he'd turned down her clumsy advance in the middle of his shop. "Why else pass up a—a freebie? I'm not so bad, am I? Whatsa matter, not enough packaging? I may not be like those blow-up dolls on TV, but I got enough, and it's not saline or silicone. I also know how to satisfy a man. All those boy toys care about is their own orgasms.

"Brette thinks you've been sick," she'd added. "She thinks you have a...*problem.*"

He'd barely had time to catch her hands before she could check for herself. "None that I know of."

"AIDS?"

"Nope."

"Then whatsa matter?" she'd whined.

He hadn't told her because he had a standing rule never to reason with drunks. He didn't want to explain now because it would probably earn him a ride to the sheriff's office. But he understood his brief sojourn with privacy was, for all intents and purposes, over.

"You can reject my help if you want," he told Brette, "but you'd better know I'm going to look for him anyway. It will be a better use of everyone's time if we synchronize things and work together."

"I can't decide if you're talking out of guilt, or—" her gaze fixed on him "—are you trying to hide something?"

The bold jab didn't surprise him. This wasn't a rejected woman sniping the way Sally had. Brette cared about the kid. Sam had seen it over and over as he'd watched from the safety of his house or the crack between his shop doors. If she believed he'd hurt the boy in any way, she would go for his jugular as fast as if Hank had been her son.

"Feel better now that that's out of your system?"

Brette closed her eyes. "No. I feel like— I've never talked that way to a person in my life."

"Don't worry about it."

She studied him again. He saw a lot of curiosity, and a touch of temptation, but none of the spontaneous warmth that had illuminated her in those first days. He understood the reasons, but that didn't keep him from wanting it the way people craved a warm lit room after being lost in a blinding fog. Another reminder that he'd stepped into something more complicated and dangerous than he was prepared for.

"I guess another pair of eyes couldn't hurt," Brette said at last. The hint of reluctance in her voice was unmistakable. "But I have to know one thing first. Why did you say what you did about the boys knowing to come to you?"

"It was the truth."

Brette shot a look at her son. He was standing in the middle of the street, staring down the road like a lost puppy waiting for a sign that all would be well again.

"Eric has never given me a hint of anything like that." But her tone betrayed her lack of conviction.

"He's a teenager. It comes with the territory. Don't tell me you've forgotten?"

"As a matter of fact, I was one of those freaks of nature who was completely up-front with my parents, even when I knew they wouldn't agree with me."

"Lucky them."

"I'll ask him, you know."

Sam inclined his head. "Just remember it's not nice to take things out on the messenger afterward, okay?"

She stood her ground. "So what do you think has happened to Hank?"

"Hopefully nothing. But even from what little I've seen and heard, I sense this is turning into regular behavior for him."

"They didn't have a fight."

"Because, like you, Sally's track record with the truth is unrivaled?"

Brette started to speak, spun away, then faced him again pointing her finger. "I do not stab my friends in the back," she snapped. "Especially not when they're hurting."

"Facing reality isn't a betrayal."

"All right, so you're aware things aren't perfect, but Sally's ex had a little to do with that."

"What was Eric's relationship like with his father?"

Surprised, Brette took a moment to answer. "I thought you said you were all pals. Don't you know?"

"I said I was available to them, not that I was their personal confidant or counselor."

It was too dark to see if she was blushing. She had the skin for it.

"Eric's father's passion was skiing. He was killed in an avalanche before his son was born."

Now Sam had a better hunch as to why she insisted on being called *Ms.* He also had answers to questions he'd resisted asking her, had refused to ask Eric. "That's a tough break," he said, filing away the information to ruminate over later. "So, could Hank be with his old man?"

"I'd be more likely to believe he's hiding out with Elvis. Hank Sr. is, to be polite, indifferent. What bothers me most is that I've tried to make Hank feel we were his surrogate family. Apparently, I haven't been doing as good a job as I thought," she added, her voice fading.

"I don't think this situation is about you not doing enough. The boy's not Eric. He's pretty much a loner at heart. You're never going to know all that's going on inside him."

With a somber nod, Brette replied, "I'm aware of

that. The surprise is that you are, too. You *have* been keeping an eye on them.''

He found himself responding so strongly to her approval, his immediate impulse was to reject it. ''It's a small school, and they are my neighbors.''

Stung, she snapped, ''A fact that didn't come into the equation when I invited you to dinner.''

He let his gaze drop to her ringless hands. ''Or maybe it did.'' He knew the blurted admission triggered more questions than answers, but it was too late to take it back, just as it was too late to deny the bone-jarring chemistry that vibrated between them. ''Instead of being annoyed, you might be relieved, Brette. After all, you know nothing about me.''

''Remind me again,'' she purred, ''are you trying to talk me into or out of letting you help us?''

He felt an unfamiliar urge to smile, but deeper sadness and pain made it easy to resist. ''It's more about putting certain truths out on the table and letting you figure out the smart move for yourself.''

''Interesting phrasing. *Certain* truths, not *all* of them?''

''Look at it this way, that deputy would've liked any excuse to get out of here. He doesn't want to go into those woods tonight any more than you want Eric out there. But he'll have a harder time finding an out with me in his face laying a guilt trip on him.''

''That makes a lot of sense,'' she replied with a nod. ''Thank you. I keep having to wonder, though, why are you being so good to us?''

That was an easy one to answer. ''I'm not so old that I don't remember what it was like to be Hank's age.''

After a slight hesitation, Brette slowly descended

the stairs and touched his arm. "I'm sorry for being so suspicious. I guess I'm—"

Even through the thick material of denim and flannel, Sam felt a jolt. For the sake of his sanity, and her safety, he stepped back. "Let's find out where Russell wants to start, and collect what we need."

As he headed for the patrol car, he knew she was staring after him. He could only imagine what was going on in her mind, but whatever it was, it couldn't be helped. If he was to get through this, he needed a moment, and space.

7

Sam got the moment, but not the deputy. Fate, it seemed, was intervening.

Roy Russell was being called away. He'd been notified that there was a traffic accident on a county road not six miles from there that he had to respond to until the other deputy on night duty could reach this side of the county.

"I understand there are injuries," he explained, "so it might take some time. I'll be back as soon as possible."

"What about Sheriff Cudahy?" Sam asked as the shorter man climbed into his patrol car. "Wouldn't he be willing to bring more people on duty?"

"Headquarters is calling him right now. We'll see what happens. I'm sorry, folks. I've gotta move."

Even as he backed his car into the street, Brette was muttering under her breath. "I can't believe this. He's actually abandoning us."

"He said there were injuries." Sam said that for his own benefit as much as hers.

"I heard. I'm not being insensitive. I simply don't understand why there aren't more personnel on duty. It's ridiculous. This is a big county and the world doesn't shut off when it gets dark."

"A rural county for the most part, with a population to match."

"A boy is *missing*."

Sam held up his hand to calm her. "We'll start looking ourselves. Who else can we draft?" He pointed with his thumb over his shoulder. "What about that guy down the road? Didn't I see him over here a couple of times?"

"Keith Daggett in the double-wide. He and Sally dated briefly, and I suppose he would help if asked— but he has a deadline."

"He's a writer?"

"Not in the way you think, but I'd guess you could say he writes. He's a computer wiz. Creates his own programs, does freelance troubleshooting, that sort of thing."

"Uh-huh. And he's a corporate saboteur on the side, right?"

"Hilariously unoriginal. I'll pass it on to him. You'll cringe even more when you meet him. In fact, that's why things didn't work out between him and Sally. He liked her and Hank just fine, but she thought he didn't have enough of an edge for her tastes. Anyway, I'll give him a call. Across from him are the Ponders, Bertrice and Clovis."

"The Ponders I've met, which is why I didn't mention them. I was coming home one night and Mr. Ponder was standing in the middle of the road in his pajamas. Well, the tops anyway."

Brette sighed. "That's Clovis. Such a sweet man, but he had a stroke last year, and only weeks before that Bertrice said he'd begun showing signs of dementia."

"It wouldn't hurt to fill her in on the situation. No

need to scare her half to death when she sees lights in the woods. I'll do that while you use your charm to sweet-talk Daggett into getting his priorities straight. Then we can go see the Pughs.''

Brette coughed. ''Ah...maybe you'd better handle that one alone. You must have noticed they aren't overly fond of us.''

Yes, he'd seen enough to recognize that things were somewhat stressful between her and the dairy farmers. ''They need to be told to keep an eye out. Who knows, it might give you the opportunity to resolve some things,'' Sam added.

''You don't know how wrong you— Oh, my God!''

Sam stared as she clapped her hand to her mouth. ''What is it?''

''The sign! How could I forget the sign?''

Her soft keening tone had him clenching his hands in his pockets even harder. ''What sign?''

''Right outside the Pugh's property. There was a bloody handprint on the Dead End sign today.'' Brette slid her hand down to her throat. ''What if...oh, God, why didn't I remember to tell Deputy Russell about it? *What if it's Hank's print?*''

8

She couldn't get air into her lungs.

Horrified, the image of what she'd seen earlier that day materialized before her. "What have I done!"

Sam grasped her by her shoulders. "Brette, stop! *Stop it.*"

He shook her once, and her head snapped back, the action forcing her to gulp a deep breath and saving her from all-out panic. But weak-legged, she lowered herself to the second step. That's when she heard Eric.

"Mom? Mom, are you all right?"

He came running and stopped beside Sam. The vast differences between them made her boy look all the younger, and more vulnerable. The thought that it could as easily have been his blood she'd seen on that sign had her experiencing another wave of weakness. Horrified that she might really embarrass herself, she pressed her face between her knees and breathed hard.

"What's wrong, Mr. Knight?" Eric asked.

"That's what I'm trying to figure out."

As the world steadied again, Brette drew in another deep breath, then tried to make them understand. "The print. What if it was Hank's?"

Eric's expression went from realization to concern, to skepticism. "C'mon, Mom. I told you, there was nothing on it when I went over there."

"Which only means someone else saw it and washed it off!"

"Not the Pughs. They'd make a point to call the law first, take pictures for court and haul our butts over there to clean it up ourselves."

"Would someone please fill me in?" Sam asked.

"I just told you. I saw a handprint this morning while on my route. On the Dead End sign outside of Pugh's Dairy. I thought...I was convinced it was the boys' handiwork, what with it being Halloween weekend and all. Plus, there's no love lost between them and the Pugh family."

"Hey, we think Tracie's cool," Eric told her, his expression innocent.

Brette tried not to sound too dour. "That's because Tracie has the emotional maturity of a fifteen-year-old."

Eric shrugged, but for a moment he grinned sheepishly.

"Okay, I follow so far," Sam said. "But what makes you now think it's Hank's print?"

"Didn't you hear him?" She gestured at her son. "It wasn't there after school, and there's no sign of Hank!"

Sam frowned. "Who else have you told this to?"

"That's it. You and Eric."

Sam focused on the boy. "And you had no part in putting it there?"

"No, sir."

"Could Hank have done it after he left you?"

Eric grew thoughtful. "I guess. But the thing is, he's not big about being in the woods after dark. I like it tons better than he does, don't I, Mom?"

"You're a regular night owl in every sense of the word," she replied with a reluctant smile.

Sam glanced around. "This isn't exactly the middle of the woods. He could have stayed on the street."

"Yeah, but ever since the time we came home from Tyler when that cougar ran out of the woods in front of us and disappeared into the woods across the road, he's been easily spooked, right, Mom? That and all the boars everybody's seeing."

"Not spooked enough for him to leave home in the middle of the night," Sam replied.

Eric's eyes, no less blue than Brette's, widened. "Yeah, I guess you're right." He said to her, "But he's got to be okay, Mom. He just went somewhere to figure things out, that's all. He'll be back. Probably too soon for Sally to realize why he needed to go, but what else is new?"

Brette couldn't bear to hear him speak so cynically. Rising, she managed a fleeting smile and stroked his back. "You're right. I'm being a worrywart. Listen, it's getting damper and chillier by the minute and neither one of us is dressed for this. Why don't you go to the house and make yourself some hot chocolate and warm up."

"Where're you gonna be?" He glanced at Sam with a mixture of shyness and hope.

"With me. Are you okay with that?" Sam asked quietly. "We have to check the area."

"Shouldn't you wait until that deputy comes back?"

Once again Sam glanced around. "What if Hank's lying hurt somewhere?"

"Jeez, yeah. I should go with you."

That was the last thing Brette wanted. "Someone needs to man the phones. He has his cellular, right?"

"He always has it, same as me. That doesn't mean it's on. I've tried to call him."

"But when he's ready, he's likely to call our place first. Or he could e-mail you from somewhere."

"I get the hint. Okay, I'm going. You're taking your phone, though, right? So I can check on you?"

Brette nodded, her heart swelling with love and pride. This mutual concern was nothing new. He'd been worse than a B-movie interrogator the few times she'd dated. "My son the warden. Don't forget, though, the reception in the woods will probably be poor. Don't call in the National Guard if all you get is static."

Ignoring the lecture, Eric shot Sam a concerned look. "Stay away from the marsh, okay? He definitely wouldn't go down there because that's where the boars hang out the most."

"We'll be careful."

As soon as her son was out of earshot, she told Sam, "Thank you for letting the subject about the sign drop."

"I could tell that's what you wanted. Suits me since there's no way to prove it one way or another until we find Hank and question him about it."

True. Brette gestured after her departing son. "I'll be with you as soon as I make those calls and get a jacket and flashlight. Will you tell Sally what the plan is?"

He hesitated, but only briefly. "Will do. See you in a minute."

9

It was closer to a half hour before Brette and Sam were able to start on their search. The phone calls took a bit longer than expected, then Sally slowed things by insisting she was afraid to stay alone and wanted to join them. But typical of Sally, she hadn't made a move to change out of her shorts-pajama outfit. In fact, considering her half made-up face, she would have been late for work, too.

"Sally, think," Brette had entreated. "You need to be here to update Deputy Russell when he comes back."

"He's not coming back."

"He said he would. And even if he doesn't, what if Hank calls?"

"He'll contact Eric before he calls me. He really has to hate me to do something like this," she'd added, warming to a new wave of anxiety and self-pity. "I think I'd rather he was kidnapped than know that."

When they finally convinced Sally to stay put and set off, the first thing Sam said was, "She's getting worse."

Sad though it was, Brette knew he was right; nevertheless, she was reluctant to criticize her friend. "I would be incoherent if it was Eric we were searching for.''

"Eric is about as likely to pull a stunt like this as Sally is to voluntarily seek the help of a therapist.''

"What if none of this is Hank's idea?'' she murmured, haunted by that damned sign again.

"Don't obsess,'' Sam replied. "One thing you know for sure, you'd have heard from the Pughs if they'd seen the print and suspected it was made by anyone other than one of their own people. Maybe one of their Mexican laborers was returning from an errand run, stopped to get the mail or pick up something that had fallen off the truck and injured themselves.''

"A guy happens to cut his hand right there? That was a whole handprint, not just a palm.''

"Why does it have to have been blood? Couldn't it have been ketchup from eating French fries? Weird stuff happens. By the way, where's Daggett going to search? I want to make sure I stay away from him in case he's carrying a gun.''

"He's not going out. He said he could help starting in the morning. As I told you, he's tied up with a critical deadline.''

Sam stopped. "You're joking. He's putting his work ahead of a boy's welfare?''

"He's keeping his lights on and the blinds open, periodically checking outside in case he can hear something.''

"What a pal.''

The excuse did sound lame, but not if you knew Keith and understood his demanding clients. "Look, as I said, he would only be a hindrance out here at night. We'd probably end up having to search for him, too."

"Why the heck does he live where he does if he has no use for the woods?"

"The place was a steal. The original owners divorced and the wife wanted out fast so she could return to Alabama to be with her folks. Added to that, he was desperate for room, not to mention quiet surroundings for his work."

"I hear you," Sam muttered. "You're a fan."

She stared at his broad back wondering if she'd imagined something beyond condescension in his voice.

"He's a nice man," she ground out. "And for the record, he doesn't own a gun. You couldn't reasonably ask him to go into these woods alone without adequate protection."

They fell quiet after that, a seemingly mutual decision to avoid an all-out argument. They needed to focus on their surroundings anyway, adapt to the increasing darkness, as well as the terrain. The woods behind Sally's followed a natural incline eventually bottoming out at Little Cypress Creek, and Brette had to pay attention to the natural ruts and exposed roots as much as those brought on by fallen trees and scavenging animals.

They were following the Pughs' fence line, and when Sam's flashlight picked up what looked to be brownish-red hair, he stopped. It didn't need to be said that it was almost the right color of Hank's. Thankfully, it wasn't fine enough.

"Cow?" Brette knew better, but wanted to hear what Sam Knight would make of it.

He crouched for a closer look. "I'm no vet or

farmer, but...if it is, it's not theirs seeing those are black and white.''

"They're starting to mix their herd." But as she got closer, she saw her real guess was on target. "Too short for tail hair, and not coarse enough for feral hog. It's either a young deer or some canine. Perfect color for coyote." She nodded to herself as she directed the beam of her light on the smooth ground. There were no deep hoof marks, confirming her conclusion; although she couldn't be sure what she did see was coyote or dog, either. That could leave one more animal, and she didn't want to think of it any more than she did the hogs.

When they'd first moved out here, there'd been plenty of deer and coyotes, as well as the occasional night visits from raccoons and possums. The only thing you really had to worry about was the rare rattler, copperhead or cottonmouth, and mostly if it was a particularly wet season when they were apt to venture farther up from the marsh. But in the last few years things had grown downright busy in these woods. When people weren't tossing out unwanted dogs or cats on the roadside, some wealthy rancher was losing exotic game like cougars made available to business clients who liked to hunt. A few people were insisting they'd seen a black bear. None of that was given the attention that the drug labs were, though. And they still kept popping up as soon as another was shut down. Just this summer one of her customers had witnessed a whole posse of law enforcement people charging his fence line after a suspect who'd been trying to escape capture. With guns drawn, the cops and DEA personnel had literally dragged the man off the rancher's barbed-wire fence, hog-tied their suspect and hauled him away, scaring ten years off the older man's life. No, you never knew what you'd come across in the Pineywoods these days.

"You've learned a thing or two living out here, haven't you?"

Brette glanced over to find Sam watching her intently. "That's the idea, isn't it?"

"Just wanted to make sure you're not nervous. If you are, we can go back."

"Not for hair on barbed wire." But she gripped her heavy-duty flashlight tighter, and found herself a sturdy broken limb that could serve as both walking stick and club if necessary.

If Sam found her choice obvious and amusing, he kept it to himself. For his part, he carried a wicked-looking machete that he'd retrieved from his workshop.

After another minute or so he said over his shoulder, "Just a thought about the Pughs...being on the defensive isn't exactly the same thing as sounding guilty."

"I'm aware of that."

"Do you seriously think the old man is apt to pull something to hurt the boys?"

Brette took her time answering, stopped to shine her flashlight into a clump of brush. It looked like something had rested in there, but not recently—and nothing the size of a teenage boy. "He may be mean enough and Albert ornery enough, but hopefully neither one is that stupid."

"Sometimes excessive caution can make a person appear scary, too."

Brette stopped and waited for him to notice. "Have

the Pughs hired you to improve their public relations image or is there an intelligent point to this conversation?''

''Never mind. Unless reinforcements show, I think after we finish here, I'll definitely go down there next.''

Out on the marsh a wood duck complained about their intrusion on the calm night. Brette sympathized, feeling edgy, too.

''Be prepared for the worst. They operate twenty-two-hour days now that milk has become another commodity to wage political war over, and that hasn't enhanced their congeniality any. Good grief, a few years ago one of the game wardens almost got himself shot for not being more explicit in announcing his arrival. Well, if we're going down there, we'd better make better time here.''

'''We?'''

''I've changed my mind. If you're going, I'm going.''

''That doesn't sound like a vote of confidence. I've no intention of picking a fight with them, regardless of how they behave. You won't, either,'' he added, dropping his already sober baritone voice.

''Don't worry, I'm a real lady. I never take a swing at anyone unless they strike first.''

Sam made some guttural comment, but nothing decipherable. ''Do you take after your mother or father?'' he asked after a moment.

As he whacked at a thorny vine blocking their path, Brette paused and frowned at him.

Her prolonged silence had him glancing back at her again. ''I'm merely curious.''

''Since when?''

"If you don't want to answer me, say 'It's none of your business, Knight.'"

Exasperating man. "My sense of humor comes from my mother. I get my tenacity from my father."

"I've never seen them around. Do they live far away?"

"They were killed in a train accident in Canada right after Eric's third birthday."

"I wondered how you ended up out here."

No "I'm sorry to hear that" or "Sad." Well, at least he wasn't a hypocrite making empty sounds.

"Another question you didn't ask my son," she said, sugar in her voice.

He nodded as though answering his own question. "So that's it."

Now what? Brette wondered.

"You still don't believe I talk to the boys at school, do you?"

"He's never mentioned it to me." And one thing she knew was Eric's heart.

"Does he also not mention the miniature version of you he sometimes buys juice for after school while they're both waiting for the buses?"

The trail may as well have turned into a sheet of ice. Brette thought she did well to freeze without falling on her butt. "There is no—*my* Eric?"

"Don't worry. It hasn't gotten past the shy smile and brief, awkward conversation stage yet."

Brette had the strongest urge to run back up the hill and chase down her son for a full interrogation. It would, however, be the worst thing she could do to their relationship. A dozen questions for Sam sprang to her lips. She repressed them all, save one, and it came out more like a warning. "You'd better know what you're doing by ending the silent treatment.''

"To be honest, I don't. My first big mistake since moving here...well, second if you consider buying someone else's idea of a house. As for this...believe it or not, Brette, I saw a need and didn't give myself time to think about the consequences.''

She refused to be taken in by that home-on-the-range sincere drawl. "You'd better start, because I won't let you make Eric think you care, and then watch you break his heart.''

"Or yours?''

A forlorn coyote called in the distance. Something to their left rustled the fallen leaves. A swamp rabbit, Brette discovered as her beam caught the startled animal in fast retreat. But her heart continued to pound anyway, and she knew it wasn't because of the animal kingdom's interference.

Why was the man giving her the impression that he spent so much of his time trying to figure out her and her son? He'd made it clear he wanted no part of them.

"I'm not worried about me,'' she replied, her back stiff with resolve. "You burned any bridges to my dinner table months ago.''

Step after step a newly silent Sam led the way deeper into the woods. It wasn't dense tropical terrain, although things got progressively weedier because it was bottomland. It also wasn't dense pine acreage, either. The occasional loblolly competed for sky space, but the area was primarily where the sweet gum and black oak grew ten or fifteen stories high, hardwood territory that the beavers craved for nour-

ishment and construction material as they built their
ambitious dams.

"Are you seeing any prints?" Worse than having
to converse with him, Brette found having too much
time to think tougher.

"Not the human variety."

Suddenly something screamed down on the marsh.
The wetland lay another few dozen yards ahead, but
the tortured, horrible sound wrung an abrupt, invol-
untary gasp from Brette.

Sam backtracked and peered at her through the
darkness. "Are you okay?"

"Yeah, except for the burn marks when my heart
slid along my shoelaces. What the devil was that?"

"Something got a duck or crane."

"That didn't sound like any fowl I've ever heard."
Feeling a chill, Brette fastened another button on her
denim jacket.

"If a coyote or bobcat grabbed you by the neck,
or an alligator snuck up beneath you, you wouldn't
sound like yourself either."

The brutal image had her wincing. She loved
watching the ducks and geese fly south every fall, and
head back north at the first hint of warming temperatures. A good number of wood ducks and mallards
nested here year-round. So did the big gray cranes
that were about as graceful as a C-130. She preferred
to think of them all in a Norman Rockwellesque uto-
pia—safe and serene. This was a reminder that she
was still too idealistic for her own good.

"There's entirely too many flesh-eating critters in
these woods these days," she said.

"It's only nature."

"It's a trade-off and you know it."

"Can't have the country without dealing with the contents," Sam chided.

"If that's an alligator down there, it's not natural, it's the result of man's effect on his environment as much as the weather cycles. The same thing goes for the boars forced into new habitat. I just want people to think before they mess with what's around them."

Sam remained silent for a moment, then he offered, "If you've had enough, we can head back."

Is that what he wanted? Was he hoping she'd give in because his volunteering had been an empty gesture after all? To what end?

With new determination, she motioned him onward. "When we're finished."

He moved on, until they could go no farther due to the marsh. To the south was the fence, so they turned north. Every minute or two, Sam would call Hank's name, his rich baritone voice often winning a dog's angry bark some distance away, but no human reply.

Brette spotted the tree with the surveyor's ribbon that marked the north boundary of Sally's property. So had Sam, but he kept going. She had never gone this far even by day, and would have lost her bearings completely were it not for the marsh. She did, however, lose her balance.

Focusing more on keeping Sam in her sight, she didn't pay enough attention to the ground and edged too close to the cavernous hole from another felled tree. Overcompensating, she fell backward, in the process dropping her stick and scraping her right palm against a nail protruding from the massive tree behind her.

Crying out, she dropped her light and fell hard on

her butt, immediately pressing her hand between her thighs. "Damn, damn, damn," she ground out between clenched teeth as she fumbled with her good hand in pockets for a tissue, something to stop the bleeding.

Sam's light found her and he quickly ascertained what had happened. "Little fool," he muttered, lifting her like an empty sack. Leaning her against the tree, he gripped her wrist and directed his light on her palm. The cut was razor-fine and ran the full length of her palm. "Didn't you see the hole? It's only as big as a tank."

"Thank you for pointing out the obvious. I misjudged the edge, that's all."

"And probably earned yourself a nice case of blood poisoning if you don't get a tetanus shot right away."

"I had one last year when I stepped on a rusty piece of metal," she snapped back.

He swore, a softly spoken, one-word epithet. "You are a walking accident, aren't you?"

The observation exposed how well he knew her tendency to end up wearing a Band-Aid when working around the house or in the yard. To her way of thinking, she wasn't a klutz, as he'd suggested. She simply put her all into what she did. The point was how did he know? He had to have been paying close attention to notice such a little thing.

Brette stared up into his dark, enigmatic face.

His gaze locked with hers.

The night protected him somewhat, but not enough to hide some truths. Interesting ones. Nerve-jangling ones. Every feature of his face was taut with raw emotion—tension, secrets and...desire?

As her gaze dropped to his mouth, Sam sucked in a sharp breath.

"Damn it, *no*," he rasped.

Wholly expecting to feel his mouth, instead Brette was jarred by the bite of another hard tree, this one against her back.

Before she could begin to tell him what she thought of that and *him*, she heard a shrill cry.

"Sam? *Brette!*"

10

"That's Sally." Sam found himself more relieved than he thought possible to hear her voice. "Something must be up. We'd better get back."

"The sooner the better," Brette muttered.

As she resumed fumbling in her pockets with her uninjured hand, Sam pulled a minipacket of tissues from his jacket. "Here. This should help until we get back to the house where you can clean it properly."

"I have my own." Refusing to look at him, she clutched the already crushed mass in her bleeding hand. Then, snatching up the dropped flashlight, she started back the way they'd come.

"Brette..."

She pretended she didn't hear him.

He didn't blame her for being upset with him; his behavior was as off-the-wall as Sally's, and he didn't have the excuse of being on anything. Consequently, he didn't try to stop her again. It would be better this way, he told himself. Hell, considering the huge mistake he'd almost made, being treated like the Invisible Man was a gift.

He was in good shape, but so was Brette, and despite his longer legs, he had to move to keep up with her. When they were about halfway up the trail, he heard a male voice call to them. It could have been

Deputy Russell, but Sam didn't think so. And before he could call back to let everyone know they were on their way, Brette beat him to it.

"Coming!"

The first glimpse of back-porch lights through the trees broke his resolve, and he made another attempt to ease the tumultuous emotions he felt radiating from her.

"Will you give me a minute before we get up there?" he began.

"There's nothing to say."

"I owe you an apology."

"Not required, and I'm sure not interested in hearing it."

He lunged forward and grabbed her arm just above the elbow. Spinning her around to face him, he said, "Damn it, I need to know if I hurt you."

Brette shrugged off his hold with surprising force, but it was nothing compared to the temper in her eyes. "Don't confuse me with my son or Hank. I haven't been quite as innocent and gullible in some time. Keep your so-called concern and your hands to yourself."

"You're wrong about me. I wanted like hell to kiss you back there. But believe me, you'd have ended up regretting it."

"Finally, something we agree on. Now if you don't mind I'd like to get up there. They wouldn't be calling if they weren't eager for us to get back. I think they have Hank."

They didn't.

Brette actually ran the rest of the way, right up to Sheriff Chester "Cuddy" Cudahy. Sam's long strides ate up the ground fast enough to suit him. He hadn't expected a face-to-face with the man himself, not yet anyway, and he wasn't looking forward to it.

A big man by anyone's standards, the sheriff stood another hand over his own six foot two. Sam had read in the paper how the veteran lawman, and Wood County icon, had been through a rough year, what with resolving two murders in the nearby town of Split Creek. That had been followed by a slew of drug busts that had involved one of his people and a few law enforcement personnel from neighboring counties. The results showed. Sam had seen several news photos from earlier days, and the man who greeted Brette by politely tipping his trademark cowboy hat was a somewhat slimmed down and weary-looking version of that hearty attack dog. As Sam joined them he saw there were deepening lines on the man's face, too, particularly those running beside each side of his mouth, and that the corners of his mouth had a decided droop now. He also had that unlit cigar that had been in every picture. Sam watched as he removed it from between his clenched teeth as he addressed Brette and began rolling between his meaty fingers.

People said he had a big heart, but when Cudahy's gaze locked on him, Sam saw something in the older man's eyes that triggered a deep chill. A similar feeling to the one he used to get as a kid whenever he or his brother or mother had displeased his father.

"Sheriff Cudahy," Brette said, breathing hard and pressing her injured fist to her chest. "You mean he isn't back yet?"

"Sorry, ma'am." His deep voice resonated with fatigue as much as regret. "How are you, Ms. Barry?"

"Disappointed, of course."

"And what have you done to your hand?"

She shook her head dismissively. "Tripped, that's all. It's just a silly scratch."

"It's a bleeder, Sheriff," Sam interjected, "and she really should go inside and clean it."

Brette shot him a chilling look. "Thank you, but I'm fine. Sheriff Cudahy, this is Sam Knight, our neighbor."

The lawman's gaze slid immediately to Sam's machete. "Were you planning on cutting yourself a pork chop or two out there, Mr. Knight?"

"Only if forced to."

Recently he'd heard that the sheriff liked life simplified down to the smallest common denominator. "Puzzles and perverts," he'd been quoted as saying, "are for lawyers and other professional students with time to burn." Although clearly from the old school, he was not to be underestimated. His ability to see beneath the skin was considered close to psychic. That's what had Sam certain he would be sweating soon, despite the cool night air permeating his jacket.

"How's Sally?" Brette asked, drawing the man's attention again.

"She went back inside after we heard you were coming. She's pretty strung out, as I suspect you already know. Walk with me to the front, will you, folks? As I'm sure Deputy Russell explained, we're having a busy night, and I need to keep close to my radio."

Brette walked beside him, all but ignoring Sam. "We hate having to add to your troubles."

"It'll be sorted out. Your boy doing all right? Eric, isn't it?"

"You're good to remember. Yes, he's still on the Honor Roll and still too small to go out for football."

Cudahy's rusty laugh showed the effects of being a longtime smoker. "They're always in a hurry, aren't they?" At the front of the house, he stopped beside the second of the two cars parked on the road—the one with Sheriff marked clearly on the door. A cacophony of radio-speak blared from the open window. "Mr. Knight, I understand you've been the hero of the evening, coming to the ladies' aid."

"Hardly." And seeing him glance at the knife again, Sam set it against the rear tire of the lawman's vehicle.

"That's not what Mrs. Jamison says." Cudahy leaned against the driver's door and crossed his arms over his chest. He wore a khaki windbreaker over his usual khaki uniform, but it remained unzipped. "Guess you don't need me to tell you, not everyone would be willing to put aside his own responsibilities and interests to search for a boy who's showing a clear pattern of disrespect and disturbing behavior."

"Oh, Sheriff." Brette sighed. "Hank's not—"

Cudahy held up the cigar like a school guard with a traffic sign. "Allow me, ma'am. We'll get to young Jamison. The point I was making is Mr. Knight's generosity with his time after already putting in a full day with a whole passle of kids."

Sally had been talking. Sam tried to ignore the queasy feeling building in his gut and not worry about how badly she may have distorted the truth. "I just wish we were having better luck, Sheriff. Brette's right, though. Hank's got some things to work out, but I've met worse." Himself, for instance.

"Spoken like a dedicated teacher. You're at Sandy

Springs Junior-Senior High School, I understand. Shop, isn't it?''

"Guilty."

"On the contrary. I've seen too many kids who, after four years of college, can't hit their butts with both hands not to appreciate your service to our school system. We're living in a world where the next generation will have to be disposable everything because there'll be no one with a clue as to how to fix anything that breaks. No, I see yours as a vital as well as interesting choice of careers.''

Nice praise; nevertheless, it did nothing to ease Sam's dread. The man was playing bloodhound, no doubt thanks to Deputy Russell sharing his own gut hunches about him. And for all the compliments, he doubted Cudahy would hesitate reaching for that machete to get the answers he wanted.

"Glad to hear you approve." He had learned the hard way that it was civility and common sense that held real power, not aggression. But even though he believed the lesson, he still felt like a novice at putting it into practice.

Cudahy glanced over his shoulder. "And from the looks of that house I've been hearing about, you must also be the kind who likes to plant deep roots?''

"One can dream."

"Got your next five years of doing that *and* chores cut out for you, I'd say.''

Sam raised both of his eyebrows affecting dismay. "I wasn't planning on working *seven* days a week, Sheriff.''

Chuckling, Cudahy turned to Brette. "Ms. Barry, you're still with the Post office?''

"Ten years and still collecting jokes."

For the first time his rheumy eyes twinkled. "What's your favorite?"

She hesitated only briefly. "'What's it mean when you see the flag at half staff in front of the post office?'"

The sheriff leaned toward her. "I give up."

"'We're hiring.'"

Cudahy rubbed his big hand over his mouth, but his chest shook with silent laughter. "I'll have to remember that one." When he focused on Sam again, the twinkle in his eye had vanished. "What does Mrs. Knight do?"

Here we go. Sam swallowed as though he had a bucket of sand in his throat. "There is no Mrs. Knight."

"Right...my deputy did mention you're divorced." Once again he switched his attention to Brette, who suddenly looked as though she would like to be anywhere but there. "Confirm or correct a few facts for me, will you, Ms. Barry? You continue to keep Hank overnight at your place?"

"Yes. As I told Deputy Russell, that's the routine. He and my son are close friends," she added, "and with Sally's demanding schedule it makes more sense for him to sleep at our place than to trudge back and forth. Besides, these days everyone is saying you can't spend too much time with your children."

"I'm with you a hundred percent, Ms. Barry...and yet the boy left *your* house without your knowledge."

Sam had heard enough. "That's not fair, Sheriff. Eric told Deputy Russell that his mother was in the shower when Hank left. The boy obviously timed his leaving."

Looking tortured, Brette nodded. "Will you believe me if I tell you that he's never done that before?"

"If it's the truth, why wouldn't I?"

"It *is* the truth."

"But he has run away before."

"Gone off for a while, pretended to have run away. But it's never for long, and he's never actually gotten far. Okay, yes, I'm splitting hairs, but this time is different. There was no clue whatsoever that anything was wrong. That's why I'm more upset than ever about the print."

Sam closed his eyes. When he opened them again, Cudahy was watching him.

"What print?" the sheriff asked with seeming mildness.

"On the Dead End sign at the entrance to Pugh's Dairy Farm." Brette nodded down that way. "It was there earlier today. Now it's gone."

She proceeded to tell him her story. The sheriff listened with growing displeasure.

"You mean you destroyed possible evidence?" he asked when she'd finished.

"No! I told you, Eric said it was already gone. In any case, it's Halloween. I thought it was a hoax."

"With a boy missing?"

"I didn't know at the time. And why are you suddenly saying he's missing when you've been telling us he's run away?"

"Because I only know what I know," Cudahy replied with increased gravity. "Did it ever occur to you to call us?"

"We have called your department on several occasions, but to no avail. Your people take the information, but no one comes out here. Either you're shorthanded, or you don't believe the situation calls for your attention, let alone intervention. Or—and this is my favorite—it's *dark* and the deputy refuses to drive anywhere without backup.''

Cudahy scowled. ''It doesn't help to get condescending, Ms. Barry.''

''Condescending would be to tell you what I thought of that deputy's audacity,'' Brette replied without missing a beat. ''Look, Sheriff, I know your department is undermanned right now, but this isn't Beirut, Chechnya or Dallas's west side. What's more, we pay taxes, too! But we're lucky if we get your attention in the daylight!''

''Well, I'm here now, aren't I?'' he all but growled. ''Now let's get back to this print. Are you sure it was blood?''

She bowed her head. ''No. But it wasn't ketchup!'' she snapped, nodding at Sam.

Cudahy's cheeks filled before he purged a deep breath. ''And how long have you known about the print, Mr. Knight?''

''Only a short time.''

''What did it look like to you?''

Nice try, Sam thought. ''I didn't see it.''

''So you came over here by accident and intervened on the ladies' behalf on a lark? You wanted to borrow a cup of sugar? What?'' Cudahy pointed his cigar at him. ''I seem to recall Mrs. Jamison saying something about you not always being the social type. Exactly what changed your mind about becoming a concerned citizen this evening?''

As he had before, Sam decided Sally had bubble wrap for brains. And Russell was sharper than he'd given him credit for. With a flash of painful clarity

Sam saw his future—and it looked bleaker than when he'd left Houston.

"I suppose now that I've been here six months," he began with a studied calmness, "it's beginning to feel permanent. And having had the chance to get to know the boys at school, when I saw Ms. Barry and her son come running across the street looking upset, then your deputy arriving minutes later...it seemed the right thing to do."

Brette made a strangled sound. Seeing that it won Cudahy's attention, she covered it well by cupping her cut hand with her left.

"Let me see that," Cudahy demanded, taking hold of her wrist. Removing the crumpled tissues, he winced at what he saw. "I have a first aid kit in the trunk."

"Really, I'm all right, Sheriff. Could we just...get this done?"

"All right, then. Mr. Knight, did I hear correctly? You're from Houston?"

"The suburbs."

"You've always been a teacher?"

"I worked my way through school."

"What kind of jobs?"

"Construction, some metal fabricating, basically whatever I could do to also gain practical experience for what I was about to teach."

"So you have plenty of references."

"For what?"

The sheriff inspected the condition of his cigar. "Just making mental notes, getting to know the newest member of this little neighborhood."

"Fine. I'm easy to find if you need more."

Cudahy nodded to the woods behind Sally's.

"What about down there? Find anything at all interesting?"

"A lot of animal tracks," Brette replied before Sam could. "And as Eric reminded me, Hank isn't fond of the dark. So I don't think we have to worry about him being out there."

"I hope you're right." Like a master chess player, he immediately changed strategies. "This print you say you saw—"

"I did see it."

"Was it large, small...any one specific thing you noticed about it?"

"If you're asking if it could be Hank's, the answer is that I don't know. I can say it wasn't large, and yet it was too high for a child's reach. So could I at least describe it as a teenager's? Yes."

Cudahy nodded his approval. "That's the kind of observation we hope for, Ms. Barry. You aren't going for a P.I. license by any chance?"

"As a matter of fact, I am considering a change of jobs some time in the future, Sheriff. But that one isn't on the short list."

"Give me the benefit of your instincts and talent anyway. Who do you suspect cleaned the sign?"

Brette looked him straight in the eye. "I don't know."

"Can you appreciate that's a difficult answer for me to accept?"

After a brief pause Brette said, "I'd suggest you ask the Pughs."

"And why would they cause a situation like this right outside their own property?"

"You'll have to take up the matter with them."

Visibly unhappy, Cudahy checked his watch. "I'd

better get down to the farm before it gets much later.''
He eyed Brette again. "I'll want to talk to your son
on my way back.''

"I told you what he did and what he knows, which
is exactly what he told your deputy. He didn't see
Hank after he left our house.''

"Then it'll be a short, amicable visit all around.''
To Sam he added, "What are your plans?''

"To do whatever's needed.''

"I suggest y'all call it a night.''

Brette immediately became indignant. "How can
we?''

"Because right now somebody's lying and somebody else is guessing, which could mean the people
who need to know aren't getting the right information. We'd all be wasting valuable energy and re-
sources charging down blind roads of supposition, or
worse yet, getting in each other's way. Let me go talk
to the Pughs.''

"You're not going to mention the print, are you?''

"Any reason why I shouldn't? Maybe they can
back you up on it, and explain why it's not there
now.''

"Or, speaking of lying, they can deny any knowledge of it.''

Cudahy rubbed at his diaphragm. "Ms. Barry, I
wasn't in Mrs. Jamison's five minutes before I had a
flashback to the last time we were called here. I admire you trying to be a good friend to her. She's a
neighbor, and your sons are pals. But in your heart
of hearts, you know that woman is a seven on the
Richter scale of shaky. My deputy's conclusion probably wasn't far off. In all probability she and the boy
had words, and she's ashamed to admit it yet again.

"Now we have the pertinent data and Roy's in there getting a photo to initiate the paperwork for a missing persons report. But I have a hit-and-run that's a weakening heartbeat away from becoming manslaughter, as well as an arson case about twenty minutes old that I need to get out to. Does my presence here impress upon you how sincere I am to get you the assistance you want?"

Although she said nothing, Brette pressed her lips together and nodded.

"Good. As soon as I can possibly spare someone, he'll be in touch."

It felt odd to find himself respecting Cudahy, nevertheless Sam did. The man had the decency to be straight with them. On the other hand, there was no missing the blow this was to Brette. Sam could feel her struggle with renewed fear and frustration. But having destroyed any possibility to offer support or comfort because of his own stupid behavior, he stood there impotent.

As though on cue, Roy Russell emerged from the house. With a brief exchange of cryptic comments, the two men climbed into their vehicles. Sam snatched up the machete and the cars eased south toward the Pughs'.

Before they were out of sight, Brette turned on Sam.

"In case you're thinking you've gotten away with anything, don't."

"And what do you think I've gotten away with?" he replied.

"Both Sheriff Cudahy and Deputy Russell thought you were a little too good to be true, but for the moment they're giving you the benefit of the doubt. And so am I. So I'd suggest you don't do anything to make me tell them that may be a mistake.''

He hoped she was serious about not wanting to be a P.I.; her protective instincts outweighed her survival instincts. Wishing more than ever that he had kissed her, he continued to look his fill, waiting for her bravado to show cracks.

Finally, when she dropped her gaze he said softly, ''You're too honest a woman to do that, Brette.''

''What?''

''Lie.''

A frown created a tiny check mark between her eyebrows. ''I'm not even going to pretend to understand you.''

''I know. Another time, another place, maybe.'' Spotting Sally at the door, he started backing into the road. ''If Cudahy asks for me, tell him I've gone over to the school to check around there.''

''You know Hank skipped school. Why would he be there now?''

''Because no one expects it.''

11

"**W**here's he *going?*"

With a grunt of frustration and disgust, Sally plopped herself on the top step of her porch, sending the contents of her plastic tumbler sloshing over the rim. It was not, Brette discovered as she settled down beside her, iced tea.

"I found a bottle of wine and thought we could all have a drink while we regroup and decide what to do next."

Classic Sally. Brette chose to avoid her wounded look. "You already downed one of those Prozac samples you schmooze from the interns. Sal, you know better than to drink now."

"I'm not strong enough to endure this. I need something more." Sally offered her cup. "It's not as though there's a lot of this. Wanna swallow?" The victim was in her mode again. But at least she wasn't driving, and with luck, the combination of medication and alcohol would have her passing out before she did much more damage to herself. Before, Brette thought, she had to go across the street and be with Eric.

"No, thanks," she replied. "Sheriff Cudahy's gone to talk to Truman and Albert."

"Lotsa luck."

"As for Sam, he's gone to the school."

That got Sally's attention. "What the hell for?"

Brette cast her a sidelong look.

"Okay, fine. But I wish he would've waited a sec. I'd've gone with him." Sally took another sip of her drink, a speculative expression on her face.

That did it for Brette. Standing, she said, "It's getting too chilly for either of us to be out here, Sal. I'm going to go across the street a minute and tell Eric what's up."

"You'll come back, right?"

"Of course. But I do need at least an hour or two of sleep, or I won't make it through my route in the morning."

"Sam's been a total sweetheart, hasn't he?" Sally continued as though Brette hadn't spoken. "Kind and patient. Do you know that while you were getting your jacket and stuff he sat with me? Just sat and listened. When was the last time a man wanted to hear anything a woman had to say without expecting some sort of freebie in return? Not that I would mind if *he* asked."

Brette gripped the tissues that were decomposing fast in her hand and reminded herself that Sally retained nothing of these conversations. What was the point of holding a grudge against someone who had lost or never possessed a filter for her thought processes?

"Okay, so I come off as a bitch for not being fixated on Hank," Sally said, as though picking up on Brette's internal struggle. "But I have to be realistic. If I don't get my mind on something else, I won't make it. I'm not made for this kind of stress. I'm not strong like you."

"I understand." And Brette did. "I just don't think Sam Knight's the kind of person who wants or deserves to be put on a pedestal, let alone be on any woman's wish list."

Sally let her head fall back and gazed up at the sky. "I guess it's those shoulders. I'll bet he could tote each one of us under an arm and not break a sweat."

Deciding her wound wouldn't bleed anymore, Brette tucked the mess of sodden tissues into her pocket. "That's not my scene."

"Ha! Don't I know it. You wouldn't go to that male strip club with me in Dallas, no matter how far back in the pack I would've let you sit. Well, who would want to share a specimen like him anyway?" But a second later Sally frowned. "Hank's never said anything negative about him to you, has he? What about Eric?"

It was all Brette could do not to scream. The woman was serious about this. Gone was any memory of Sam's previous standoffishness, as well as Sally's oath after Keith to not get involved with neighbors again.

"Shit."

Jarred out of her brooding, Brette watched Sally rip apart her cigarette wrapper.

"This is my last one! Now what am I going to do?"

"Quit?" Brette drawled.

Ignoring her, Sally sprang to her feet and rushed inside, no doubt to search for another fix.

Left alone for the moment, Brette covered her face with her hands. She didn't know whether to laugh or cry, and wished Hank home with a new desperation.

How much longer could she keep listening to Sally and not think about her own moments with Sam?

Just then she heard an engine. Looking up, she saw his big Suburban backing onto the road. As he passed her, he nodded once. There was such intimacy in that subtle movement, she had to wrap her arms around her waist to keep from waving back. Only afterward did she understand what he'd achieved. Something she hadn't allowed herself to grasp earlier.

He'd made her his coconspirator. The question was, in what...and why?

From inside came the sound of Sally swearing and throwing something. Deciding she wouldn't be missed for another few minutes, Brette got up and crossed the street, to her place. She needed grounding and there was only one way to achieve that.

When she entered the house, Eric was pulling on the huge quilted flannel shirt they shared for quick dashes outdoors for firewood and putting out the trash. The front door opened directly into the living room framing him in the merry, refreshing whites, greens and yellows of the decor—a jarring contrast to her mood.

"Hey." Eric hesitated in buttoning up. "I saw you out there and I was coming over to see what's up. Mr. Knight left?"

"To look around the school, yes."

Brette found his expression a revelation, and nowhere close to a welcome one. "You wanted to go with him."

"Yea."

"To help look for Hank or to spend time with Mr. Knight?"

"Both. Does that hurt your feelings?"

She had brought him up to be as truthful and direct as her parents had raised her, but she'd never experienced the other side of its sting as profoundly as she did now. It bothered her for the moment, but she managed a fleeting smile. "I think I just experienced a pang of jealousy. Why didn't you tell me you liked him?"

With a sigh, Eric removed the shirt, and replaced it in the coat closet to his left. "Because you liked him, too. But then he kept refusing to come over, so…I decided not to make things harder on you."

"You were protecting my feelings?" she whispered.

He beamed. "I know how to be sensitive."

"Arrgh. Give me a hug, you." He was already her height, this personal miracle of hers, but once again she experienced the wonder she'd known the first time the nurse had placed him in her arms. "When did this great heart-to-heart with Mr. Knight happen?"

"After the last time you invited him to dinner. I could tell you were upset. So the next day at lunch, I went to his classroom and told him that I thought he was a real doofus."

"What?"

He burst into laughter and in one of those painful, yet beautiful flashes she saw a glimpse of his father at twenty and herself at sixteen. It was at times like this that she missed her parents most, wished they could see and share in her happiness and pride.

"Admit it, Mom. He could've been the one. It's been what, over a year since you went out on a date? And you never showed any real interest with that car dealer."

"I'm not comfortable when a man uses more hair products than I do. Sue me."

"And the one before him?"

"Wanted to put you in military school."

Eric's mouth dropped open. "You never told me that!"

"I was afraid you'd find a grub worm and put it in his beer can the way Hank did his mother's date at the time to get rid of him."

"Dang...military school. Brutal." Then he grew speculative again. "I'm beginning to like Mr. Knight more and more."

"Don't bother."

"I've seen you watching him."

Horrified to think that was true, Brette went to the kitchen and put on some water to boil. Hearing Eric behind her she said, "Please tell me you didn't share that with him, too? I swear, I'll never be able to face that man again."

"I'm young, not dumb, Mom. I've learned one or two things from you."

For instance, how to sweet-talk her out of half of her cheeseburger when he was extra hungry; how to give her space after talking Sally through one of her bouts of tears; and to keep quietly busy on Sunday morning, her one day to be lazy and to sleep in. But that didn't mean she wanted him intruding in her love life—or lack of one. Curiosity did, however, get the better of her.

"What did Mr. Knight say?" she demanded.

"He said he knew."

"Knew *what?*"

"That he'd hurt you. He said he could tell you were special and a lady."

Too pleased by the secondhand compliment, she pretended Eric had misunderstood. "I mean about you. What made you decide you like and trust him?"

"He didn't talk down to me," he said as she got a mug and the jar of instant coffee. "He was like you."

"How?"

"He didn't blow me off."

"Eric...*English*."

"He didn't give me pat answers to stuff he didn't want to talk about. And he seems to understand Hank as well as I do even though they haven't really talked the way we have."

Maybe. Either way Brette wasn't pleased. "So it wasn't true when he told Deputy Russell that *both* of you knew to come to him?"

"Sure it was. He told me to tell Hank. But you know Hank, he's not big on male authority, any authority, although he's better with you. Mr. Knight keeps an eye on him, though. Saved him from getting in trouble at least once already." Eric leaned his forearms on the counter as she spooned out coffee granules. "Maybe now that the secret's out, he'll be willing to come over once in a while."

This was exactly what she'd feared when Sam had first shocked them with his announcement. Expectations and dreams. But Eric hadn't experienced what she had down in the bottoms. Something was wrong with Sam Knight, and his kindness to her child couldn't be allowed to blind her to that.

"One thing at a time, okay?" She poured the boiling water into the large green leaf-print mug.

"Sure. But...Mom, was Dad built anything like Mr. Knight?"

Oh, God. Her baby wanted to be a junior Terminator.

She put the stirring spoon in the sink and cupped her son's face with her uninjured hand. "Your father was a terrific athlete, but as I've told you before, he skied, he ran, he rode a bicycle and surfed. He wasn't one of those tree-chewing, iron-bending behemoths with steroid-packed thighs."

As intended, Eric laughed. "Different muscles, I got it— Hey!" He caught sight of her right hand. "What happened?"

She hadn't paid the wound much attention, but now that Eric was fixated on it, she finally looked to see how bad it was.

Shaped like a crescent moon, it was unattractive, but not as deep as it felt. "I almost went into a hole in the bottoms," she told her son. "There are a lot of felled trees from that September windstorm we had. You know how shallow the sweet gum's roots are. It's no big deal."

"Yech." He watched over her shoulder as she washed the cut, then opened a drawer next to the sink for the peroxide and Band-Aids she kept there. "If that was my hand you'd tell me it needed stitches."

"It doesn't. And can we table the rest of this discussion until I get back?"

"When will that be?"

"Sooner than you think. Sheriff Cudahy wants to talk to you after he gets back from the farm."

"What for?"

She didn't blame him for the dread in his voice. "It's his way of doing things. You've heard me explain how thorough he is to Sally." Tossing the wrappers into the trash, she tested her work and decided the Band-Aids would hold for a while. Two aspirin would take care of the throbbing of the wound, as well as the one in her head. "Just let me go make sure Sally's not tearing apart the house to find another cigarette. Then I'll be right back."

Carrying her mug, she went to the main bathroom. "I take it there's been no phone calls whatsoever, not even any hang-up kind?"

"Nope. You might as well forget it," Eric added. "I've thought about it and thought about it. Hank isn't going to be in touch again until he's ready—if he ever is."

The confusion and hurt in his voice broke her heart. "Don't give up on him yet, babe. He's got to have a good reason for this."

Back at Sally's again, she was about to reach for the front door when Sally pushed through and joined her outside. In her absence her friend had added to her wardrobe somewhat. Now she wore strapless white-leather high heels on her bare feet, and had tugged on her white paper-thin windbreaker.

"Life can continue. Found half an old pack of menthols in my nightstand." Sally held it up for Brette to see before examining it herself. "Gotta be from before summer. What do you want to bet they taste like crap?"

"Maybe that'll inspire you to quit once and for all the way your son wants."

"Those in absentia don't get to vote." Sally finally noticed the mug. "Well, no wonder you didn't hear me when I yelled to you."

"I told you, I needed to warn Eric about Cudahy."

Her friend grunted as she lifted her refilled drink to her lips. "Don't mention that name around me more than you have to. I was asking if you know whether Sam has a phone with him? I thought maybe he could pick me up a couple packs of smokes.''

''I have no idea. I'd imagine not, though.''

But that only won her a delighted laugh from her friend. ''You're right! Hmm…maybe he'll be a sweetheart and offer to take me to get some when he gets back.''

''Sally—'' Brette struggled to find something un-critical to say ''—the man's got to be exhausted.''

''Nah, look at you. You were up before any of us and you're fine. And you have to work. It's not as though he has school tomorrow.'' But a moment later, Sally caught her brief look and blew smoke into the darkness. ''Hell, I'm sorry. I'm not getting any better at this, am I?''

Not knowing what to say that wouldn't sound bru-tal at a time like this, Brette simply patted her arm. ''Keep hanging on. That's all that matters. But you must be cold. Why don't you go inside?''

Before Sally could begin to reply lights appeared from the direction of the farm. As if someone had zapped her with a cattle prod, Sally bolted for the door.

''You're right, I'm freezing. Good luck with the Nazi.''

12

Brette met the sheriff as he parked in front of Sally's. This time Deputy Russell continued on by, only waving at her as he passed. Was that a good sign or a bad one? she wondered. At least Cudahy meant what he said about not lingering long with Eric.

"Any news, Sheriff?" She led the older man up the sidewalk. Unlike Sally's, her yard was full of flowerbeds and trees, and right now both sides of the walkway were lush with yellow and purple chrysanthemums.

"Nothing you'll be happy to hear. Mr. Pugh remains anything but a fan of the boys."

"Could you tell if he disliked them enough to do something about it?"

"He didn't know anything about the print."

She stopped, her hand on the storm door handle. "He had to."

"And why is that?"

"How else did it get washed off?"

"Maybe his son—" Cudahy motioned with his cigar as he grasped for a name "—Albert did it. I didn't get to speak with him. He and one of their two Mexican helpers were taking a break. But neither Pugh nor his other helper knew what I was talking about.

I consider myself a fair judge of character,'' Cudahy added, "and felt they were being straight with me.''

Not as far as Brette was concerned. "You haven't seen the anger in Truman's eyes when he confronts the boys. He sees them as some evil, out of proportion to what they truly are.''

"Which is…?''

"Kids. Sure they're adventurous, and occasionally mischievous. But in a humorous way, not nasty. They're definitely not vengeful.''

"Cutting fences and causing farmers to lose stock hardly sounds like simple fun to me.''

"That was not them!'' Brette would fight like a cougar to defend the boys on that one. "It was hunting season and it's not the first time some redneck frustrated with his shrinking space took it out on his boundaries. Did anyone point out to you that the cuts were made on their east border? The kids would've had to wade through a quarter mile of swamp to pull that off. And what about the cow that was shot later in the season? From the way they described it, the bullet also came from that vicinity. Another point, I don't own a gun. Neither does Sally. Yet who were the first to be blamed? Our boys.''

Cudahy's thick lower lip thrust out as he pondered that one. "He never reported any shot cow, at least not to me. Only a stolen one.''

This was news to her. "Well, I don't know about *that* one. And as far as I'm concerned, he could have made up both incidents!''

The weathered lawman scratched at his day's growth of whiskers. "People can and do say what they think will get them their best response, I'll give you that. Then again, there are old wells in these woods, and a cow could've gone down one. Or, if it got separated from the others, one of those runaway big cats from a game farm could have gotten it. Just because they didn't share that with you, doesn't mean it didn't happen.''

Brette opened the front door for him. ''Did he at least tell you when he admitted to last seeing Hank?''

''About a week ago.'' Cudahy motioned for her to precede him. ''He wasn't sure of the exact date.''

And it was clear Cudahy bought that. Resigned to their uphill battle, Brette closed the door after him and found Eric standing in the middle of the living room in an at-ease position. Amused as she was by this obvious reference to their earlier conversation, she was struck at how young he looked in his oversize jersey.

''Sheriff Cudahy, you remember my son Eric.''

The lawman extended his hand. ''How are you, young man?''

''Okay, sir.'' Eric dutifully shook his hand.

''I assume your mother's told you why I'm here?''

He nodded. ''But I've told my mother and Deputy Russell everything I know.''

''I understand. However, I've just come from the dairy farm and I talked to Mr. Pugh.''

''That shouldn't have anything to do with Hank.''

The remark won the sheriff's full attention. ''Why do you say that?''

''Because he's gone somewhere to do something,'' Eric replied without missing a beat.

''To do what?''

''Don't have a clue.''

''Are you sure? This isn't a matter of not breaking your word to a friend, is it?''

"My son doesn't lie, Sheriff Cudahy." Brette punctuated her remark with a look that left no mistake that she would not tolerate any questioning of her son's integrity. Eric had never given her reason to doubt him, and she would not abandon him to head games or bully tactics now.

If he was annoyed by her interference, Cudahy didn't let on any more than he had before. "What about your relationship with Hank?" he asked Eric. "Do you consider it as close as that of a brother?"

"I wouldn't know. I've never had a brother."

The sheriff's lips curved. "All right. So how good a friend is Hank?"

"My best friend."

"Even now?"

Eric glanced at Brette. "Yeah. He hasn't done anything to me."

"That's quite a mature outlook. A lot of adults can't reason that well."

The flattery had no effect on her son. He remained quiet and waiting. Brette had to press her lips together to keep back a grin.

"I'm not going to ask you to repeat things you've already told Deputy Russell," Cudahy continued. "But can you think of anything you haven't told him or your mom?"

"No, sir."

"Okay." Cudahy turned toward the door, then hesitated. "What about your good friend, Mr. Knight?"

That threw Brette. She could see it gave Eric pause, too.

"What do you mean?" he asked.

"I'm given to understand he's close to you boys.

So what do you guys do, work in his shop with him after school, go fishing…what?''

Looking less certain, Eric replied, ''No. We kinda like messing with computer stuff.''

''He hasn't offered to make you apprentices? A house that size, with so much to repair…seems like he could use the help, and boys your age always need cash.''

This time Eric shot Brette an anxious glance.

''Eric gets an allowance for chores around the house, Sheriff,'' Brette said quickly. ''And until now I've felt him a little young to take on the responsibility of a paying job.''

Cudahy nodded approvingly and once again started for the door. ''Just one more thing,'' he added, slowly turning back. ''Do you know if Hank knew how to get in touch with his father?''

Brette relaxed. ''Even if he did, he wouldn't,'' she replied. ''He might as well have been a test tube baby for all the connection there is between them.''

''A whole generation of children growing up with urban-city-like family units,'' the sheriff muttered. ''Helluva thing.''

''Better than domestic abuse.''

The aging lawman grunted. ''By the way, where is Mr. Knight. I noticed his vehicle's gone.''

''He went to check out the school,'' Brette said, wary again. Any reference to Sam Knight was best avoided.

''Thoughtful of him. Well, I need to be going.'' For the first time Cudahy glanced around the white-washed room with the domed windows on the south walls, and the cheerful, springlike white rattan furnishings adorning hardwood floors. ''You make an inviting home, Ms. Barry. No wonder Hank spends most of his time here.''

''Thank you.''

As he stepped outside, she shot Eric a relieved look before following Cudahy down the sidewalk.

They were halfway to his car when Sam drove up. He parked in his driveway and came over.

''Is there any news?'' he asked the waiting man.

''None. And I assume by your lack of passengers that you've had no success?''

Sam's compressed lips created dimples at the sides of his mouth. For a dejected expression it was oddly attractive, Brette thought.

''Afraid not.''

''It was a good idea anyway. I'll pass on the information to your principal first thing in the morning. I suspect he'll be grateful to you.''

''That's not necessary, Sheriff. I can do that myself.''

''No problem,'' Cudahy replied, the epitome of goodwill. ''I need to talk to him anyway.'' With another nod to Brette, he continued on to his car.

''When can I tell Mrs. Jamison she can expect to hear from you again?'' she called after him.

''As soon as there's something to report.''

She stood there next to Sam until the car pulled away. ''I can't believe this,'' she said under her breath.

''You might as well. It's only going to get worse.''

His cynical response had her considering his profile. ''Don't tell me that you kept information from him? Did you find something at the school after all?''

''No.''

Nevertheless Brette tasted his unease like a bitter

seed in her mouth and persisted. "Something happened between you two just now. What?"

"You're imagining things."

"No I'm not. I sensed something. When he said he'd talk to Principal Glick, you froze."

Sam kept his gaze somewhere beyond her right shoulder. "Tell Sally that I'm going to have to call it a night."

"Not if I'll be lying for you."

"It won't earn you a ticket to hell."

"I'm not sure I want to rely on your knowledge of geography—or fare rates."

For a brief instant his gaze locked with hers. "That's the smartest thing you've said tonight."

Feeling too much out of her depth to even understand how badly she'd been insulted, she ground out, "Exactly where will you be going?"

"Driving. Looking. I'm not sure yet. All I know is that I'd better not stay here."

It was a strange thing to say, Brette realized. "She'll hear you leave."

"So?"

She shook her head, not buying this macho I'll-do-what-I-want attitude any more than she did anything else about him. "You're rattled, and it's not Hank that's doing that. It's Cudahy. Why?"

13

Brette didn't get an answer that night. In fact, Sam literally walked away from her and drove off. She did return to Sally's for a while, but her friend had finished nearly the entire bottle of wine and, combined with the pills, soon passed out on the living room couch. Lingering only to grab the comforter off the bed to cover her, Brette locked up and returned home to urge Eric to go to bed, too. She didn't follow her own advice, though; she worked on the computer for hours making posters.

It was almost two by the time she turned off the lights, wrapped herself in a chenille throw and curled into the rattan rocker set between the front and side windows.

The next thing she knew the travel clock she'd put on the side table read 5:07. Dashing into the master bathroom, she took a quick shower. With no time to wash and dry her hair, she tugged the shoulder-blade-length mass into a ponytail and slipped on a red baseball cap. Red for determination and energy, she told herself as though repeating a mantra, not red for her bloodshot eyes. The rest of her autumnal outfit was jeans, a black turtleneck and a man's black cable-knit sweater that was long enough to wear as a dress—if you lived in L.A. or Miami.

After peeking in on Eric and making sure he slept soundly, she scrawled a note to him. Leaving it on the kitchen table, she snatched up her purse and the box of posters, and headed for town.

Outside, she inspected her surroundings with extra care. Things remained dark at Sally's, and her heart ached anew at the thought of all of them dealing with yet another day without answers. When she turned right toward her driveway, though, her thoughts took a ninety-degree turn.

Sam's Suburban was still gone!

She couldn't believe it. Sure, she'd known when he left that he would try to stay gone as long as they remained awake in order to escape her questions and Sally's relentless attentions, but this was going too far...wasn't it? Something must have happened. An accident? Cudahy?

The possibilities and implications haunted her all the way to Sandy Springs, the starless sky only adding to the sense of renewed depression and anger growing within her.

The Sandy Springs Post Office was nine miles to the northeast, in a small community of just over six hundred, not counting the rural residences the carriers serviced, which included her area. A struggling town that had lost its own police force during the last recession, the downtown was all of one block of buildings, most empty, with one or two looking ready to collapse. The rest were like those of other small communities in the area, appealing to the artistic and the collector, with one store portioned into stalls making it a minimall for budding craftsmen, and two other stores featuring antiques that had once graced the homes of the town's ancestors. A nonfranchise burger restaurant at the signal light disrupted the rustic look, but so did the gas station-convenience store across the street. The post office, located at the other end of the block, was relatively new, too, but still no hallmark of architectural beauty.

As Brette pulled in back of the one-story brick building and backed into her spot by the dock, she saw she was the last of the three rural drivers to arrive. Wally Cordell emerged from an overnight truck pushing a mail-laden cart, whistling one of the old spirituals he serenaded everyone with. She couldn't pause to catch up on the night's news with him, but waved as she rushed through the steel double doors to the sorting room. Good-natured calls greeted her.

"Nice you join us, blondie."

"Rough night, Barry? Finally! Give me his number, I'll thank him for all of us."

The last comment came from Tucker Rice, her best friend there, although she considered all of them like family. That she was closest to Tucker left everyone scratching their heads. At 51, the Vietnam vet had traveled extensively, worn through the good nature of four wives and had, for the last eleven years, called the post office his life. There was no reason for them to get along as well as they did. Lacking Brette's optimistic nature, it would take a blowtorch to the eyes for him to see a silver lining. He also wasn't wild about kids, was frequently reprimanded for threatening to bite people's pets and was the contender, so it was said, to be the author of the most irreverent post office jokes on record. But despite his dubious attitudes and inclinations, he was her biggest ally as she worked through single momhood. Tucker had been the one to teach Brette a few things about taking care of her truck, not to mention upgrading her expertise on basic plumbing and electrical repairs around the house. And it was Tucker who'd encouraged her and Eric to take some tae kwon do. The guy who had a difficult time caring about much cared about her and her boy; that's why she wasn't surprised when, upon taking a closer look at her, he held up a mallet-size hand to their counterpart Desiree Lauder, the Route 2 driver, signaling for silence.

"What's up?" he demanded.

Brette knew better than to deny anything. He might have a cherub's round face and a head of lush reddish-brown curls any angel would envy, but that button nose sniffed trouble faster than a mother knew it was diaper-changing time, and his big calf eyes might as well be an X-ray machine.

"Sally Jamison's boy Hank." she began. "He's missing."

Tucker and Desiree went wide-eyed.

"Again?"

"Since when?"

Reaching her station, Brette set down her bag and the posters. "Thursday night. But we didn't realize it until dinner yesterday. I know, I know…that sounds horrible."

"Heck, no. I pay my kid shut up dat long," Desiree replied in her usual broken English. Her second and current husband was a long-distance trucker whose eight-year-old daughter from a previous marriage had a mouth on her that made most DJs sound reticent.

Tucker grunted his agreement. "No wonder you look like you were left in a lye bath too long. You've been searching all night?"

"Most of it…and without the slightest results."

"Why didn't you call me?" he growled.

"You call police?" Desiree asked before she could answer. "Dey no help again?" The young woman had been born in Vietnam, a war baby to a Hispanic GI. She had her own history with authority.

"It took a while but they know. Trouble is, there was a hit-and-run and other trouble in the county last night. They can't give us much time at the moment."

"You should've called me," Tucker grumbled.

Brette patted his broad, slightly chunky back. "We thought we had things under control. By the time we realized we weren't going to resolve this as quickly as usual, it was so late. It's enough that I went without sleep. We all can't be driving around half-zonked."

Desiree tsked. "Poor Eric. How he taking it?"

"As you can imagine. He feels responsible in a way. Hurt, too."

"So he doesn't know anything?" Tucker asked.

Brette shook her head.

"What we do to help?" Desiree demanded. Despite her language challenges, she was no shrinking violet. She'd proven that by getting her job, as well as overcoming Tucker's unapologetic mistrust of anyone of Asian descent.

Brette showed them the posters she'd made and split the stack with them. "We'll be covering our area pretty well, but if you could tack these at major intersections in your area—"

"That means stay out of the rice paddies, comrade," Tucker said to Desiree.

As the tiny woman flung a string of Vietnamese at him, Brette gave him a reproving look. "Just keep an eye out, okay?"

"You betcha," Desiree replied.

But Tucker frowned. "Who's 'we?' Sally can't be in any condition to get behind a wheel."

Yes, he knew the people in her life as well as he did her route, having delivered there himself when she was on vacation.

"You're right, Sally's having to stick close to home. But Keith Daggett said he would be out at first light, and Sam Knight was up most of the night checking around town."

"The teacher?" Incredulous, Tucker's thick eyebrows almost vanished into the wild hair he had to be reminded to comb, let alone cut. He leaned over to Desiree again. "This guy makes the Terminator seem warm and cuddly."

"Eric seems to like him." Brette was careful to keep her tone neutral and her eyes on the job of sorting and bundling her route. "Apparently, he sees a side of Sam at school that the rest of us don't."

Tucker, who'd been to her place several times since Sam moved in and made a point of spying on him, didn't buy that. "Kids always like freaks and weirdos. It's part of the fun of terrifying your parents."

"Yeah!" echoed Desiree. "He crazy about Tucker!"

"You watch it." Tucker grabbed the scissors off his counter and made a swipe at her three-foot-long black braid. As she squealed and took off running, he turned on Brette. "And you watch it, too. Watch *him*."

She intended to.

Fortunately, the mail was light and they were all set to be on their way by eight. Supervisor E. J. Owens came by to clear them for release and before Brette left, she asked the soft-spoken man if he would put up one of the posters in the lobby. He agreed, although immediately began chewing at his salt-and-pepper mustache, signaling some anxiety. She knew he was very careful not to upset Postmaster Brenda Freese, who frowned upon displaying anything in their building that didn't come from Washington D.C. itself.

"Sure, okay. But you know if Brenda doesn't like it, it'll have to come down Monday?"

"I'm hoping we won't need it up that long, E.J."

"Oh, yeah. Sure." Adjusting his glasses, he patted her shoulder as stiffly as a first-time actor with stage fright. "Listen, get yourself something with caffeine, will you. You look ready to tip over and hibernate where you land."

She was wound enough without the extra caffeine, but grateful that the poster would go up, and did as he directed. Despite the tardy departure, she still made good time on her route so that she could afford to stop and put up more posters at several intersections. A few of her customers also came out to their boxes and, upon hearing her news, offered to help. One, a retired nurse, went so far as to offer to go stay with Sally. Brette thanked each one, and took down phone numbers of those she didn't have in her notebook in case more help was needed.

Things were far quieter on her street. She was grateful to see that Keith's black Grand Am was gone. As for the Ponders, their front door wasn't open yet— a sign that Bertrice could be late with feeding and bathing Clovis—and things remained locked up tight at Sally's and her place, too.

Then her gaze zeroed in on Sam's silver Suburban. He was back! In fact, she realized pulling up to his mailbox, he was standing at the front window, a mug of coffee in hand.

A glance at her clock told her that she'd used up most of her extra time, but she leaned over to shift into park anyway. The time would simply have to be made up elsewhere, she decided, grabbing his mail. And she wasn't going to let his state of undress unnerve her. It wasn't the first time she'd seen him in nothing more than jeans; the man had practically spent the entire summer that way, like some exhibitionist. Besides, she deserved answers and she meant to get them.

Before she made it to the top of the porch, he opened the ornate walnut-and-etched-glass door. He had the storm door pushed wide by the time she crossed the hardwood deck to him. That's when she noticed he was barefoot, too.

"It's cold so I won't keep you," she said, handing him the two pieces of bulk advertisement she knew would go straight into the trash. She tried hard to keep her eyes on his, but he put no such restriction on himself. His hair, still wet from a shower, looked almost black slicked back off his wide forehead, and that made his gray eyes that much darker and intense as they moved over her. "I was wondering, though. When I left this morning, you weren't home yet."

"I got in about fifteen minutes after you usually leave."

He'd *timed* himself? "I see. Well, you haven't had much sleep."

"As adorable as that hat is on you, it doesn't hide the fact that you haven't, either."

With effort she ignored the "adorable" reference.

It was easier when she focused on how he'd ignored her strong hint.

"I take it that means you aren't going to tell me?"

"The question is, what are you willing to hear?"

He rubbed his free hand over his chest, making it impossible for her to keep her eyes on his clean-shaven face. Wiping away the droplets of water still clinging to the matted hair brought new attention to what the biting nip in the air was doing to his—

"The truth," she managed to reply through dry lips.

"How much?"

Exhaustion and frustration got the best of her. "This is ridiculous. You want to play games, do it with someone in more desperate need of entertainment."

As she turned away, she heard a low, "Brette."

She stopped, but only glanced over her shoulder.

"If I'd come back," he said, "I would have come to you. Neither of us needed that."

Her pulse ringing in her ears, she replied, "What makes you think you'd have gotten anything more than what you have in your hand there?"

Slowly he shook his head. "Barry, there's a lot of the innocent left in you and that's good. You hold it tight. But know this—if these were different times and I was a different man, I'd be after you like a cowboy chasing down a prize filly. And I'd catch you."

Her mind all but smoked as she slammed on the intellectual brakes. This might be Texas, but no way in hell was a woman of her generation going to tolerate talk like that! The problem was, she couldn't think of what to say.

"Run, Brette. I'm feeling pretty rough around the edges and having a hard time remembering why I should give a damn about anything. So run while you still can."

She'd never thought herself a coward, but she did hightail it out of there. She also embarrassed herself further by first shifting into reverse instead of drive. But as soon as she had his place in her rearview mirror, she started fuming and berating herself for not putting him straight about a few things. Who did he think he was talking to anyway?

"Prize filly."

"Big horse's butt!"

Seeing the Dead End sign helped her resolve. But it also reminded her of the John Berry song with the line, "Going ninety miles an hour down a dead end road."

She couldn't afford to crash. Hank needed her help, as did Sally, and most of all, Eric. How could she risk the most important person in her life with a man who cast her away and reeled her in like a fisherman playing head games with his catch?

Fortunately there was no longer any sign of Sam by the time she returned from delivering the Pughs' mail. Not that she actually looked. But her eyes seemed to see anyway, just as her mind continued to work overtime to create trouble for her regardless of her determination to keep her thoughts elsewhere.

Last night's headache returned with a vengeance, but at least she had no trouble staying awake. For the rest of her route, when she wasn't filling boxes or looking for signs of Hank, she brooded over why Sam was intent on making hamburger out of her emotions now, of all times, when it was clear he had secrets he had no intention of sharing. And as a result maybe even deeper problems?

To make up for the time she spent putting up more posters, she skipped lunch—she wasn't hungry and just swallowed three aspirin with a bottle of apple juice—and managed to finish her route before two o'clock. Not surprisingly, though, the aspirin did little for her headache and her nerves were shot.

Upon returning to the post office, she quickly processed the mail and was relieved to be able to get away before the others returned.

She was within eyesight of her own street when she saw a delivery truck hit its brakes, then pull over. There wasn't enough of a shoulder for it because of the deep ditch, and Brette was forced to brake, too.

"Oh, come on," she moaned. "You couldn't have gone another hundred feet so I can turn?"

Her eyes burned as though she'd gotten Tabasco in them, and she was so tense, her neck and shoulder muscles screamed for a hot shower.

The trucker did stick his hand out of his window and motion it was safe for her to pass if she wanted to. But all of a sudden that was out of the question. Because the passenger door had opened...and someone jumped to the ground. Someone who had her beating on her horn with her fist.

14

"*Hank!*"

It was him all right, minus the tote bag Eric thought he'd taken, but wearing the outfit her son had described. Now that she had his attention, Brette quickly pulled in closer behind the truck.

Hank hesitated at first. Then, with a weak salute to the truck driver, he trudged toward her. Taller than Eric, and with a slightly more muscular build, he could have passed for Tucker's son, except that his reddish-brown hair wasn't curly. At the moment, however, he looked more like someone without a soul in the world.

As he dropped into the passenger's seat of her truck, she wanted badly to hug him. She settled for briefly running her hand down the length of his arm. "Welcome back, stranger."

"Thanks."

"Are you all right?"

"Good enough." His pale, unwashed face left him looking bruised and more vulnerable than usual. "Guess my mom's pretty upset, huh?"

"We all are. Eric included. We were imagining the worst."

He bowed his head and picked at the dirt beneath one broken fingernail.

"So? What gives?" She struggled to keep her tone soft and tender, while inside she raged to have answers immediately and to everything. "You look as though you've been living in those clothes."

"I have. I lost my bag."

"Uh-huh. Where?"

"Saint Louis."

It was worse than she'd guessed in her darkest moments. "Give me a second." She checked her mirrors, then proceeded to make a left turn into their street. Pointing at the poster on the utility pole, she made him get out and remove it. Then she passed the cabin on the corner and parked by the woods, just before the fork in the road. "I was preparing myself for Dallas or Houston," she said, braking again. "Why Saint Louis?" Before he could answer, though, she leaned over and gripped his hand. "Understand, I'm grateful you're safe. Truly."

"Thanks."

"And for the record, your mom will be, too. Once she gets over wanting to pin your ears to the wall and whip you raw. God, Hank, do you have the slightest clue as to how scared we were for you?"

"Probably no more than me."

"Oh, that sounds reassuring." Sighing, Brette pushed her hat back off her forehead. "Okay, lay it on me. Why'd you do it?"

He made a face and squirmed in his seat. "I don't suppose we could drive around awhile? I think I'm starting to lose my courage."

"If you think you're embarrassed now, wait until you face your mom and then have to deal with Sheriff Cudahy."

"Sh— Shoot. You called him."

This time Brette affectionately tapped the brim of his cap. "The moment we realized what was up, kiddo. How could we not? By the time we'd figured out your sneaky planning, you'd been gone longer than you ever had before. It seemed fairly obvious you were serious this time—or else something was dreadfully wrong."

Hank slumped deeper into the leather seat. "Maybe...could I tell you, then you could tell her for me?" He shot Brette a hopeful glance. "Truth is, I timed this. I was hoping to get here and catch you coming home from your route."

"Gee, I'm honored." But despite her droll reply, she was touched. This was more like the boy she couldn't believe would leave without warning; the boy she'd believed had come to care for her as much as she loved him. But as tempted as she was to be his ally and defender again, Brette knew it would teach him nothing to do all the work for him. "The problem is, friends don't do this to friends, pal. Not only did you betray my trust in you, you kept this secret from your *best* friend. And to add injury to insult, you compromised my relationship with your mom. Now you want me to keep her from crawling all over your back? What's wrong with this picture?"

Hank's already downcast expression grew even more vulnerable. "Sounds worse hearing you put it that way."

"It's the only way to put it. At the same time, I care too much about you to give up hoping that you've learned something from all this...and too curious to shut you down." At his weak smile, she reached into her bag and took out an energy bar.

"Here. It'll give your hands something to do. It's peanut butter, your favorite."

"Thanks. I haven't felt like eating in a while."

Brette watched him turn the thing over and over in his hands. His profile was softer against the dimming light of the afternoon, younger. "I should have already asked this, but...do I need to get you help, Hank? A doctor maybe?"

"Jeez. You did imagine the worst. Nah, I'm okay."

But there was something about the tone in his voice...and his hands shook as he ripped open the wrapper of the granola bar.

"Had a close call, though, huh?" she asked gently.

"Yeah. About as close as you can get."

That sent her heart plunging.

"Okay." She rubbed her hands against her jeans, the sting in her right hand reminding her that it was time to change the bandage. "The best thing to do is spill it out. For more reasons than one since virtually everyone around here knows about you and we won't have this privacy for long."

The bar stopped before Hank's mouth and he groaned. "Damn. That's something else I'll have on my conscience. Everyone who looked for me."

Brette chose to overlook the language. "People can be understanding."

"Not for stupidity."

"It's said that's what youth is for." Brette smiled. "I'm listening."

He shook his head. "It's embarrassing, Brette."

"Well, you have to be alive to be embarrassed."

"I guess." Finally he blurted out, "I met someone on the Internet."

"Someone?"

"A girl."

She wasn't going to pretend not to be relieved, despite what he'd admitted. It was just about a girl. "And she wasn't as cute as she said, is that it?" she asked with an understanding smile. "Or did she set you up with her homely cousin or something?"

"Worse. She wasn't a *she.*"

Brette couldn't keep from losing the smile, but took care not to show more. Inside, however, what was left of her nerves were short-circuiting. She'd heard things, horror stories, on the news. Who hadn't these days? She warned Eric all the time about avoiding chat rooms and certain Web sites. She monitored both boys' use of the Internet as much as she could without installing security devices that, to her, were a signal flag of distrust, and a challenge to kids to work around. No, she'd always believed communication was the key. Respect, too. And most of all, mutual love. That had worked with Eric, and she thought she'd made progress with Hank. Instead, a sick degenerate had toyed with the boy's heart.

"Oh, Hank." She touched her injured hand to the back of his neck. "That's a tough one. I'm so sorry."

"Me, too. Funny thing is, she—he—was the easiest person I'd talked to in my life, except maybe you and Eric."

"I believe it," she replied. "Otherwise you would never have left the way you did. So this—this person lives in Saint Louis?"

"Yeah."

"And how long has your online relationship been going on?"

"Two months."

That hardly seemed long enough to decide to run

away from home. But she'd read about how quickly intimacy could happen in chat rooms, and if you were lonely and troubled, faster yet.

"I know what you're thinking," he said sounding a little defensive. "Weren't you ever in love?"

It was a loaded question she was in no shape to deal with, even if they had had the time to pursue it. "The important thing is that you felt this relationship was real."

"Exactly."

"Hank, the guys who do these things aren't stupid. They know exactly how to play their victims." She moved her hand to his forearm and asked more urgently, "Are you sure you're all right? Please don't be embarrassed to admit if he touched you."

"No. I ran. We'd made plans to meet at a McDonald's and I was sent a map. I'd scanned my picture and e-mailed it. So did *she.*" Hank took a vicious bite of the granola bar. "Made it stinkin' easy for him to spot me. What a jerk, huh?"

"Don't say that. You were acting in good faith. But what did you think when it wasn't the girl you expected approaching you?"

"Oh, he was good. He said he was her uncle and that she had broken her leg and had confided in him about our plans to meet. He bought me lunch as an apology. Then, as we ate, he started suggesting I should come with him to her house and meet her, that he would tell her parents I was a classmate of hers he'd run into." Exhaling, Hank looked out the passenger window. "All the time he kept finding excuses to…you know, get near me. They were guy nudges, nothing-stuff at first. But then—" he swung around to face her "—it got to be too much. And then he moved next to me. He said he wanted to show me the pictures of her that he carried in his wallet. That's when I got totally grossed out because he—''

Poor boy. His heart broken and his psyche pushed to dangerous limits by a cunning predator. ''How did you get away?''

''I said I needed to use the bathroom before we went. Then I ran out the back door. He spotted me, but I hauled ass. Sorry. But I did, and he was an older guy with a gut. There wasn't much he could do, not without attracting attention.''

Brette sent up a prayer of thanks for that. ''Incredible. And how did you get all the way up to Saint Louis and back in such a short time?''

''I hitched rides part of the way. Took a bus the rest.''

''Where did you get the money?'' she asked slowly. She knew he got an allowance, but it wasn't that much.

''*She* said she was rich and sent me the ticket to come up.'' He made a face. ''At the bus station rest room on my way back somebody stole my bag and I had to hitch my way home. But I ran into this trucker from Oklahoma who was outstanding. Get this, he conducts all of his business on his laptop, and he hooked me up with a friend coming down here in another truck. I only had to hitch a ride from I-30 to here.''

Although he sounded almost excited by that part of the experience, she had to repress a shiver of dread. Didn't he realize anything could have happened to him doing that, as well? Could he be that naive, to think the sicko who'd conned him to Saint Louis was the only one? As he'd already learned, most looked like somebody's uncle!

"Hank." She moaned into her hands. "All you had to do was go to the police. They would have contacted us and *I* would have happily charged up there to get you home."

"Not my mother, huh?"

Brette knew that hurt. "Hon, she needed to be medicated."

"With margaritas or wine coolers?"

He knew Sally too well. To get him away from that subject she said, "We'd better move." She eased off the brake. "Sheriff Cudahy needs to tell the authorities up in Saint Louis. I wouldn't be surprised if the FBI will want to interview you."

"I was afraid you'd say that. Are they going to put my name and picture in the paper?"

"They can't. You're a minor. Which doesn't mean there won't be gossip," Brette added. "But one plus is that this happened over a weekend. I think everyone will be eager to keep this as quiet as possible. Except for your mother," she intoned, "who's going to be pretty vocal about how she feels."

"To tell you the truth, I don't care." He bit into his bar again. "I'm just relieved to be back."

"That's my boy." She picked up her cellular phone and handed it to him. "Ring Eric and tell him we're headed for your mom's."

15

Eric was waiting outside when Brette pulled into her driveway. He wore an oversize sweatshirt as usual, the white color of which only accented that he remained as pale as he had been when he went to bed. Yet he also looked relieved by the welcome news.

Brette watched fascinated and apprehensive as he approached them. The closer he came, the tighter he gripped his arms across his chest, and the more the skin stretched across his fine cheekbones. She ached for him as she did Hank, aware of the emotions he was trying to reconcile. The taste of betrayal had to be especially bitter for the young.

"How is she?" Hank asked him as he emerged from the truck. The nod in the direction of his house made it clear that he was referring to his mother.

"I think she stayed in bed all day," Eric replied. "Except for when the deputy stopped by."

His distant tone left no question as to his decision to reserve judgment about Hank for the moment. But his observation had Brette rushing around the truck.

"When? I phoned at noon. She said she'd called over there and they had no one available to talk to her."

"He came by about twenty minutes ago," Eric told

her. "And he didn't stay long. She slammed the door in his face."

"Terrific. Nothing like walking into a combustible scenario." Brette readjusted her hat in preparation for battle, not reassured that either of the boys had yet to make real eye contact. "Okay, let's get this done."

Placing a protective arm around Hank's shoulders and Eric's, she led them across the street. "No matter what, try to keep your cool," she recited. "If things get too rough, you two come to our house. And, please, do not antagonize her. No matter what you think she is or isn't guilty of, she did go through a terrible—"

"What's *he* want?"

Surprised by Hank's interruption, not to mention the venom in his voice, Brette followed his gaze to see Sam jogging toward them. At least he was fully dressed this time, she thought, stopping her group. Nevertheless, as she watched the man wearing a denim jacket over a blue flannel shirt and jeans, her insides did a crazy elevator plunge anyway.

"You're a welcome sight," Sam said to Hank as he halted before them. "Everything okay?"

The boy dropped his gaze. "What's it to you?"

"We're about to put his mom out of her misery," Eric added quickly. "I'm glad you're here. She's less likely to implode in front of you." To Hank he added, "Sam was out with my mom last night looking for you."

"Who asked him to?" Hank muttered under his breath.

Startled by his rudeness, Brette hugged the boy closer to her side. "Hey," she whispered to caution him.

Sam didn't let on one way or the other about how he felt about the remark. Before any of them could fill the inevitable silence, Sally opened the front door.

She spotted Hank straight off and clapped her hand to her mouth. In the next instant she dropped it to her chest. "I can't believe it…my baby!"

"Shit," Hank groaned from stiff lips. "It's Meryl Streep night."

While Eric struggled against laughing, Brette tried to figure out an appropriate response. She knew what Hank was referring to. Heaven only knew what was up with Sally—maybe her moon was in Leo or something—but she was a born actress and dramatized everything. When she wasn't playing Blanche DuBois for a guy who opened a door for her, she seemed to be prepping for the country playhouse rendition of *Gone with the Wind.* This was, however, the first time Brette had seen how much her theatrics upset the boy. Was it mere fatigue or embarrassment over Sam witnessing it?

"Are you all right?" Sally rushed down the stairs, a sight in her neon-green terry robe, purple socks and eggplant hair in punkish disarray. She crushed her boy to her. "Have you any *idea* what I've been through! Sam, bless you! Bless you for finding my child!"

Hank groaned up toward the cloudless sky. "Wrong speech, Mom. It was Brette."

After a split second pause, Sally laughed and pushed him to arm's length. "Isn't he incredible? After all he's been through, he has that same spunky sense of humor. Brette—" Sally dropped her voice an octave "—you again. Always proving to be my best friend, my sanity…."

Hank was right—the atmosphere was going from syrupy to suffocating. "Forget it, Sally. I'm just glad you have him back safe."

"Hmm." Sally's glowing smile lasted only long enough for her gaze to meet her son's. "So where were you?" she demanded.

Brette was eager to avoid a scene. "We need to call Sheriff Cudahy."

That initiated a new fire in her friend's pale green eyes. "I will not. He treated me like what sticks to those stinking cows' hooves!" she snapped, pointing toward the dairy farm. "If he wants to know how I am, he can call me. He has no idea what it's like to be a mother struggling on her own. Do you know his deputy was here only a while ago? Wanted to know what luck I'd had so far. *He's* the one who should have been searching! Then he had the audacity to remind me that I had to go to Quitman to sign the missing person's report."

As her face began to crinkle under the threat of tears, Hank uttered something indecipherable. Either unable or unwilling to take any more of it, he charged past her, straight into the house.

The slamming storm door had Eric exchanging weary looks with Brette and Sam. "Next?" he murmured.

Sniffing, Sally gestured after her son. "That's kids for you. I spend nine months in pregnancy hell, protect him from knowing how *utterly* useless his father was, and this is my reward."

"Sally, shut up." It was even too much for Brette; she lowered the reality boom on her friend. "Hasn't it occurred to you that for once this isn't about you? Hank has had a traumatic experience."

Opening her mouth to protest, Sally tugged her washed-limp robe tighter around her thin form and succumbed to a pout. "What do you mean? He looks fine. Doesn't appear to have gotten into a fight or anything. I suspect he wanted to punish me for the latest who-knows-what imagined offense, but—"

"Wrong," Brette replied. "Sal, he was targeted and conned."

Her friend stared, not only confused, but clearly not wanting to have this conversation. She kept glancing toward Sam, as though inviting him to give her an escape from the whole scenario.

He didn't offer one. "Duped how?" he asked instead.

"Someone got to him on the Internet."

That set Sally off anew. "I hate computers. I haven't had a day's peace since he got involved with those things. Now what did he do? So help me, Brette, I'm not taking out a loan to bail him out of trouble. I know you're all for this stuff, but you don't know that kid. I wouldn't be surprised if he bought Haiti. I swear, if the courts want him, they can have him!"

"You don't mean that." Sensing the worst was over, Brette focused on helping Sally find her pragmatic side. "You're more rational than you give yourself credit for and you know how exhausted and shaken he is. It was a scary experience."

"Should've been." She shot Brette a sidelong glance. "Where was he?"

"Saint Louis."

That silenced her friend a few more seconds. "So far," she murmured. "Why? How?"

"He can explain that to you later. The point is, he

was set up to believe he was having an online relationship with a girl, but he wasn't.''

''Come again?''

''Online flirtation...chat rooms...you know.''

Sally pressed her fingers to her lips. ''This is like the stuff they talk about on the news.''

''Exactly. He got caught up in it somehow, and this man behind it all tried to kidnap him.''

''I don't get it. Hank knows better than to trust strangers.''

Resisting a glance at Sam, Brette replied, ''This guy introduced himself as the girl's uncle. He had photos previously sent to Hank. This person knew how to play him. Look, I don't know all of the details myself yet, but from what I gather, it was a pedophile who won his trust by pretending to be both the teenage girl and the uncle.''

Sally immediately dismissed the idea. ''Please. You're telling me he didn't know a teenage girl from some old fart? I'd believe that of a younger kid, maybe, but not my kid. He's handing you a line of bull, Brette.''

An indignant blue jay shrieked somewhere to their left. Brette experienced a strong affinity for its frustration. ''I appreciate how unpleasant this is for you, Sally, but don't forget, I've known Hank almost as long as you have.''

''That's perfect. Throw in my face, in front of Sam, how you've been more of a mother to him than I have.''

''I'm doing nothing of the kind.'' Sensing things were not quite as in control as she thought, Brette spoke with a new entreaty. ''I've had the benefit of listening to him on any number of occasions, and I watched his face as he described what happened yesterday. I've never seen him so humiliated and crushed. He may be good at hiding that from you, Sally, but he's this close to being shattered.''

Not surprisingly, Sally's demeanor remained uncompromising. "Let's face it, I'll never be the perfect mother you are. So consider the message delivered. Mission accomplished. Give it a rest!''

It wasn't the first time her friend had sniped at her, but there was a new bitterness that suggested her hunch was accurate. After ten years, their friendship was beginning to show signs of having worn itself out. "Get him help, Sally,'' she entreated softly.

"I thought you said he wasn't hurt?''

"I mean therapy. A monster came close to destroying his life, someone who's still out there somewhere. Do you realize how vulnerable Hank must feel about that? Hopefully, the police will catch the pig, but—''

"I—can't—afford—it, Brette. As it is, I need to go in to work as soon as I can pull myself together.'' Sally began fussing with her hair and robe anew. "My car insurance is due next month, and I don't have *it* yet. How am I supposed to afford a shrink for the kid?''

"I'll lend you the money.'' There was no hesitation on her part to make the offer. Sure, she knew Sally had no problem finding the money for cigarettes and drinks—whatever her impulses craved to get her through the real and imagined hardships that were her life. But this wasn't about straightening out Sally. This was about the boy who'd barely begun to live and had spilled his guts to her a few minutes ago. This was about a near tragedy that could finish shutting him down and turn him into something she didn't even want to imagine.

Sally studied her, slowly shaking her head. "You know the sad thing in all this? It's not knowing I'm gonna let you get us out of this mess. It's knowing *I* can't, no matter what I do."

"That's not true," Brette intoned. She hated hearing the admission of defeat. "And you don't have to go it alone. Make the call to Cudahy. I'll be here."

Sally's gaze slid to Sam and with a hint of her old flirtatious self she asked, "Will you stay, too?"

"You don't need me at this stage," he replied. "Besides, Hank will feel uncomfortable enough having to tell his story to the law. Exposing all of that in front of me will only make it worse."

"Not if he knows you're here to make sure they don't humiliate him," Sally countered. "You saw how that deputy was trying to push us around until you stepped in." Sally massaged her scalp, her hair spiking skyward like psychedelic needles glistening in the afternoon sunlight. "Please, Sam. It would mean so much."

The strangest mix of emotions stirred in Brette as she watched Sam avoid Sally's gaze, hers, too, for that matter. A part of her wanted him to tell Sally his true feelings. Another part wanted him to get lost and never come back.

"All right," he said, relenting at last. "I'll do what I can."

"Great. I'd better get to it and clean myself up." She fingered the shaggy tendrils at her nape. "I'm embarrassed to admit it'll take a while. Brette…?"

The whole scene was so pitiful Brette wanted to laugh. But she couldn't do that in the face of broken

wings and cut-short dreams, so she simply nodded.
"Go. Do what you have to do. I'll get my car phone
from my truck and call Cudahy for you. I need to let
Keith and the Ponders know the coast is clear anyway. Also the gang at the post office."

But when the storm door closed after Sally, Brette
didn't head across the street right away. Instead, she
confronted Sam.

"Am I going to have to ask, or are you going to
tell me?" she asked.

"Now's not the time, Brette."

The only thing he had going for him was that he
looked ill himself. She didn't understand why, and
she didn't necessarily want to know. "You're running
out of time. And in case you think otherwise, I saw
that look Hank gave you. I want to know what's behind it, too. Before my son gets any more fond of
you."

16

Cudahy surprised them again by coming himself. "Got three deputies in the field working cases, one at the hospital awaiting the birth of her first grandbaby and the rest sleeping off last night," he said to Brette's blunt query. "I thought I'd wrap this up by my lonesome. Figured you'd prefer that, too."

Not Sam. While the others sounded relieved, he fought not to expose how unhappy he was at having Cudahy's personal attention. However, escape was impossible. Cudahy's covert but explicit look when he'd first arrived told Sam to stay put or the sheriff would come knocking on his door.

But first there was Hank's story. The veteran law-man listened quietly, taking concise notes. He had the boy go through the entire tale twice, jotting down where on the Internet Hank had met "Michelle," how often they had spoken, as well as the location for his meeting with "Uncle Mel."

At several points during the story Sally vanished into the house—Sam guessed for a cigarette break, or worse. Amazingly, Brette ignored those absences and, along with Eric, stayed close to provide the boy with encouraging smiles and hugs to sustain him through the ordeal. She challenged Cudahy when he pressed the kid for more details, and she ignored *him* entirely.

That allowed Sam to hang back from the group, and in all honesty, watching Brette handle Cudahy was damned fascinating to watch.

"It doesn't jive," the lawman muttered.

"Why not?" Brette demanded.

"You want me to believe a kid gullible enough to fall for what he did got through the experience with nothing more than a hand on the inside of his thigh?"

With all the warmth of a mama grizzly protecting her cub, Brette stepped between Hank and the sheriff. "You'll take the *facts* that you have, Sheriff, and you'll leave the boy alone. You know enough to understand the severity of what occurred. If more testimony needs to be given, it'll be done with a stenographer or into a recorder with a lawyer to protect *his* rights. He won't be subjected to repeating it ten or twenty times over to a bunch of suits who have yet to decide whether or not the story's sensational enough to put them on the front page of the newspaper!"

For a moment Cudahy looked as though he wanted to shove his cigar butt into her mouth, but he just clamped it between his teeth and growled, "Moving on…"

The whole interview couldn't have lasted more than twenty minutes, but it felt twice that, and Sam mentally echoed Hank's sigh of relief when Cudahy closed his notebook and tucked his pen back into his shirt. The kid was in luck, thanks to Brette. He would get a breather for a while.

"Is that it? I can go?" Hank asked, one foot on the stairs.

"God forbid we upset Ms. Barry any further," Cudahy replied. "Only tell me this, you do realize

you were one lucky kid? The odds were against you
making it back here.''

Hank shot a look at Brette and nodded.

''I hope it will make you think twice if you're
tempted to take off on some adventure like that in the
future. As the saying goes, if it seems too good to be
true, it usually is.''

''Yes, sir.''

Tears, no doubt from fatigue as much as humilia-
tion, glistened in his eyes. In the next instant Hank
launched himself up the stairs and into his house.
Brette had only to touch her son's shoulder and Eric
followed.

''I bow to your control of the situation, Ms.
Barry,'' Cudahy said with more admiration than re-
sentment.

''Come on, Sheriff. You know the boy has had
maybe—what? Two, three hours sleep in the last
forty-eight hours? He'll tell you what you need to
know, but not if he has to stand before an inquisition
and feel everyone's judging him.''

''Maybe when you make that job change you
should consider the counseling field.'' Cudahy
switched his attention to Sally, who was sitting on the
porch rail. ''Mrs. Jamison, good luck. It would appear
you and your son are getting a second chance. Use it
wisely.''

''You're going to search for this guy, right? You're
going to get him?''

There were new shadows under Cudahy's eyes that
spoke of increasing fatigue. He would retire soon,
Sam thought. But not soon enough.

''If possible. I'll pass this along to our detective.
He'll relay everything to the state offices and the FBI,

since this did involve luring a minor across state lines. But despite what appear to be good details, for all we know a lot of what Hank had been told could have been fake. Hank admits he never actually saw the man's driver's license, so he couldn't confirm the address or if Michelle Selby was actually Mel Selby. Only time will tell what's legit in all this and what helps.

"I would," he added, "keep his computer shut down for a while. At least until I get back to you."

"You mean the man may try to contact him again?" Sally asked, gnawing at a ragged thumbnail.

"There's always that. But I was thinking more of the boy being tempted to play detective himself. Or he might erase something he hasn't told us about out of embarrassment. Lock down the thing, Mrs. Jamison."

"I—I'll do it right away." A flustered Sally hurried inside.

Sam intercepted Cudahy's look. Here it comes, he thought, following the man's silent command to move toward the patrol car.

"Sheriff," Brette said following them. "You would tell us if you thought there was any danger, right?"

"How do you mean, Ms. Barry?"

"That man knows where Hank lives. What's to stop him from coming down here?"

Cudahy gave the question some thought before replying. "I think it's safe to say, you can rest easy. Pedophiles tend to be sneaky and secretive rather than boldly aggressive."

"You mean they're cowards."

"Never underestimate anyone, Ms. Barry. Unfortunately there are plenty of Hank Jamisons out there. It will be easier for our Uncle Mel to find another victim than to bother with the one that got away." His gaze shifted to Sam before adding, "Now, I don't mean to be rude, but Mr. Knight and I need to talk, and he does have a right to privacy."

Although he felt sick to his stomach, Sam heard himself say, "That's all right. You aren't going to bring up anything that isn't about to get spread all over the community. Am I right?"

As a startled Brette studied his profile, Cudahy compressed his lips into a grim line and nodded. "I wish I could say otherwise, but you may be correct. That said, if you had been up front with your employer, this conversation wouldn't be necessary."

"It was nobody's business but mine. You looked me up in your computers, didn't you?"

"What on earth is going on?" Brette demanded.

"All three of you were run through the system," Cudahy said, ignoring her. "I need reassurances, Mr. Knight."

Brette all but crawled into his face. "What do you mean, all three? You investigated Sally and me, too?"

"Ms. Barry, please." Easing Brette aside, Cudahy said to Sam, "You're a teacher working with young people, some of whom can be more unstable and impulsive than young Jamison. I don't like knowing that the person expected to be an authority figure, hell, a *mentor,* to these kids once tried to kill his own father."

For a moment the only sound was Brette's soft gasp.

"That was twenty years ago," Sam replied. "And it was self-defense."

"Yes, that's what it says in your file. Your father was being tried for killing your mother and younger brother."

"Be precise, Sheriff. He butchered them."

"And he made it clear he would have gotten you had he had the chance. But your bus was delayed. You were coming home on leave from the navy, and when you finally arrived, it was too late. Then when you testified against him, he attacked you and it took four men to subdue him, six to keep you from facing a trial of your own."

Sam saw no reason to comment on what had been written about, testified to and was a nightmare forever tattooed on his brain. He was, however, acutely aware of how still Brette had become, and this time he didn't have to will himself not to look at her. He couldn't bear to for fear of what he would see.

Cudahy sighed heavily. "Don't think I'm not sympathetic. Fact is, I don't understand how he's managed to postpone his execution date as long as he has."

Sam held his peace because he knew the "but" was coming.

"My concern, however, is about his surviving son, who nearly ten years later was arrested for almost killing *his* wife."

Damn Deirdre for this. "The charges were a lie and dropped."

"I spoke to her mother this morning. She said your wife—"

"Ex-wife."

"—only withdrew the charges because she was afraid of retaliation against herself and your son."

Sam had to swallow to keep down the bitter taste

of rage he'd struggled to contain since the day she'd filed. "My former mother-in-law is a vindictive, self-serving bitch," he said flatly, "who never asked Deirdre her opinion on anything and dictated to her relentlessly down to what brand of panties to wear. I would no more trust what she had to say than I would nominate her for Grandmother of the Year."

"That's quite a personality evaluation."

"I'm sure I was overly generous."

"That said, you do have an existing arrest report on file."

"I lost control *once* and rolled a liquor cart through sliding glass doors. It was in my house, it was *my* cart." Sam enunciated each word with cold precision. "Did you ask my ex-mother-in-law why I did it? Her latest version would be entertaining to hear. They seem to grow more colorful by the year. Whatever she said, though, understand this—I never touched my wife in anger, and my son wasn't home at the time."

"You say...and yet you ultimately signed the adoption papers, giving custody of the boy to your wife's current husband."

All energy drained out of Sam, leaving nothing but the barren landscape of ravaged dreams. "It was better that way. I didn't want my son raised in an unsettled environment, and my former in-laws made it clear that, if I didn't, they'd use their political connections to make sure I could never get a decent job in Houston again, let alone teach."

"This could be confirmed if I phoned your former employer?"

"Yes. And by calling my attorney down there, Paul Fain." Expecting Cudahy to take that down, he experienced a new wave of unease when that didn't happen. Nothing did. "I see. That's not what you're planning on doing, is it? You're planning on laying this in Principal Glick's lap."

"So I'm right—he's not familiar with your history?"

"*My* history, or my father's?" Sam drawled.

Cudahy nodded. "A fair point. One, I should add, I'm in no real position to argue against never mind yield to."

That won a smirk from Sam. He'd heard all this before. For example, immediately prior to his termination from that upscale design shop. His mother-in-law had helped that along, too, by making sure the company got a tidy little contract to do the exterior ironwork on the new symphony hall—once they'd met certain "security precautions."

"You'll do what you want, and the courts will support you," he said.

Although he didn't deny it, Cudahy looked more apologetic than determined. "Times are difficult, Mr. Knight. Kids are easily influenced and—"

Sam slowly shook his head. "Save the politically correct speech. Facts are facts, and my reputation as a summer school and substitute teacher is impeccable. No one's taking that away from me."

"Think of the dilemma the school faces. Your classes attract boys usually classified as discipline challenges. They're often prime drop-out candidates."

"Try poor and without much hope of getting a college education. Same as it was for me. The kids understand that. Do your records show I've never lost a student yet?"

Cudahy shifted uncomfortably and settled his hands on his hips. "The point is, you kept information away from people who had a right to know. Hell, you've seen the headlines in the last few years. Kids are turning into time bombs, and there's hardly any pattern to what is setting them off. Finding out they have a teacher who may be in worse psychological shape than they are—"

"That's enough."

If Cudahy missed the soft-spoken words, he couldn't have misinterpreted the steel in Sam's gaze.

"You're right. I'm out of line. I apologize."

It was a little late for that as far as Sam was concerned. "Just tell me this—are you going to tell Glick or not?"

"Things may go better for you if you do it."

He would have laughed if he could remember how. "In what way? Will they give me a glowing recommendation for my next teaching position—provided I can get an interview once it gets around why I left here? No, if you're intent on doing this, you do your own dirty work, Sheriff."

They stood there for several seconds. In the end Cudahy flexed his nostrils like a bull about to charge, then shook his head and climbed into his vehicle.

Sam waited until the car disappeared around the bend up the road before he forced himself to face Brette. She looked like someone had kicked her in the belly. He understood the feeling well.

"Your turn," he muttered.

"I don't know what to say."

"But your mind's going ninety to nothing."

"It's impossible not to think."

"I'm not like him," he ground out.

She didn't respond to that. She was lost in her own journey of revelation and revulsion. "It's a terrible story," she said at last. "Your mother *and* your brother...?"

"Kell was only eleven, small for his age, like Eric." Sam closed his eyes, but there was no escaping the scene he'd walked in on before the police could stop him. "The bastard had just been fired from his latest job. This time there would be repercussions because he'd struck his boss and the guy'd needed stitches. Instead of going home to warn my mother that he might be facing assault charges, as well as a lawsuit, he went to the nearest bar. By the time he was thrown out of there, he was primed to get even with everyone he imagined had tripped him up throughout his miserable life. No one was available, and if there is a God, He sure as hell didn't see fit to let him kill himself driving home."

17

Torn between wanting to run away and needing to understand the rest, Brette wrapped her arms around her waist. "What happened next?" she asked.

"As best as they could put it together from evidence at the scene, he came home determined to make sure no one survived who could ever say anything about him again." Sam's gaze turned inward. "He went after my mother first. That's when Kell must've come running into the kitchen, grabbed the meat mallet in the drainer and tried to knock him out with it. Not only didn't he hit him hard enough, he pissed him off more. My father took that mallet and—" Sam caught his breath and looked away.

Brette saw tears in his eyes. Her heart broke for him, and for what his brother and mother had endured that horrific day. The scene he'd described would have been brutal for a prepared mind. To Brette, who'd been raised to know only love and trust, it was a psychological assault that shot her into physical and mental retreat.

What she actually did, she had no idea. Take a step back? Do something he would see as more than rejection, but condemnation? She couldn't say. All she heard was his sudden "Goddamn it!"

The next thing she knew he was striding away from her, heading for his place.

She watched him, saw that rigid back, his fisted hands. Without thinking, she started after him, but quickly checked the impulse.

What are you doing?

What indeed. Hadn't she learned anything in the last forty-eight hours? Hank's close call, and now, thanks to Cudahy's strong nose for trouble, this.

Dazed, she entered Sally's house. Hearing talking in the kitchen, she went there first. Sally was just ending a call.

"No problem. See you shortly."

Brette hoped she'd heard wrong. "See who shortly?"

"Hey! Can you believe that?" Giggling like a flustered schoolgirl, Sally hung up the phone. "That was—" She glanced around Brette and dropped her voice. "What's the matter?"

"One thing at a time. You first."

"Where's Sam?"

"He had to go. Come on, Sally, what gives?"

"Just as well," her friend replied, grabbing her purse off a dinette chair. She checked its contents hurriedly. "I won't be here anyway."

No, Brette wasn't going to like this any more than anything else she'd heard in the last few minutes. "And where are you going?"

"Work. But don't worry. I talked to Keith a minute ago, and he's able and willing to stay with Hank or both boys tonight if you need a break. What a hoot, huh?" She squealed softly. "For months I couldn't even get a rise out of old Clovis, and now here are *two* guys sniffing around me! Boy, my luck is definitely changing.''

The inane prattle didn't help Brette's own nerves, but she tried to hang on. ''You can't go anywhere, Sally, not tonight.''

''But I just talked to them. They need me.''

''Hank needs you. Hank needs quiet time to come to terms with what happened to him.'' Another thought jarred her. ''Oh, God. You didn't...you didn't tell Keith *everything,* did you?'' Sally could justify virtually anything, including that, to earn sympathy for herself.

''Do you think I want to deal with another dose of Hank's attitude again?''

''Well, think about this. Hank holds a grudge against Keith for turning cold on you. What's more, Cudahy said to keep him off the Internet, and that's all Keith wants to do. How do you suppose the boys can avoid that and keep what happened under wraps?''

''Then you're going to have to watch him for me.'' Sally gestured toward her bedroom. ''Come talk to me while I dress.''

Brette followed but she wasn't happy. ''Sally.''

''When I first called the hospital, they said they only have two people working, one in the front and one in the kitchen. With luck I can almost make up for losing last night's paycheck.''

''Understood, but you haven't even had a second alone with Hank. You two need to talk. *He* needs to talk.''

''You do it. You're better than me with all the psychology anyway.''

Brette eyed the shut door across the hall. Sighing,

she closed Sally's. There was a message loud and clear, she thought with growing fatigue. It hadn't crossed her friend's mind that Hank might hear what she was saying. Sally was slipping farther and farther out of reach.

"Sal," she said softly, now that the two of them had a little privacy. "He's not my son. No matter how much I assure him that I love him—and I do—it's not the same as when you say it."

"Wanna bet?" Sally flung off her robe, then tugged open a dresser drawer and rummaged around. "In any case, I want him to know what it's like to wait and pace and wonder." Pulling out a black bra and panties, she wiggled into them. "Hey!" She snapped her fingers and spun around. "Sam can talk to Hank. He's making overtures, right? And kids are right up his ally. In fact, you don't even have to ask him. I can invite him for a drink tomorrow and—"

"Stop it!" Startled at her own sharpness, Brette pressed her fingers to her temples and struggled to regain her composure. How was it possible to feel so feverishly hot, while inside she was shivering with cold indignation. "Sal, I'm sorry. But Hank hasn't given any real indication that he feels close to Sam, has he?"

"Work on him, Brette." Sally grabbed a black shirtdress-type uniform from the closet and stepped into it, only to pause. "Wait—you're not interested in Sam for yourself, are you? You said after he acted so standoffish before that he'd really turned you off or you'd decided he wasn't your type or something."

Nothing quite that explicit, and it bothered Brette that her friend couldn't be more accurate about her feelings. "I said that it didn't matter, that the last thing I wanted was for any man to think I was chasing him.''

''Well, I don't mind if he knows I am. And while you're putting in a good word, make Hank like him, too. Please please please?''

Brette stared at the woman who blew kisses at her one second, then rushed into the bathroom and grabbed up a brush the next. It was obvious there would be no reasoning with her anymore tonight. Aware Sally was already mentally on her way to Tyler, Brette let herself out and knocked on Hank's door.

At the dull, ''Come in,'' she entered.

Hank lay on his bed. Eric sat on the floor, his back against the chest of drawers facing the bed. They looked relieved when they saw it was her.

''Bad news, hon,'' she said to Sally's son. ''Your mom's got a problem at work. She has to go in. I know she feels terrible about you two not having some time to—''

''Ease up, Ms. B.'' Hank spun his cap on his right index finger. ''More likely she called begging them to let her work *double* shifts if possible. However long it'll take you to do her dirty work for her.''

It upset her to hear such cynicism in one so young. ''There is no dirty work, Hank. I love talking to you. I love *you*.''

He eyed her briefly. ''Ditto, Mama Two,'' he mumbled gruffly using the nickname he saved for rare moments. Sitting upright, he slapped the hat on his head. ''So can we go to your place? The sooner I get out of here, the better.''

Brette saw Eric's relief and took that as a cue. ''That's the idea. How's it going between the two of you?''

"You mean, did I admit I was a jerk?" Hank grinned, although it was lopsided. "Yeah. Getting kinda smooth at it, too."

Eric rubbed his thumb over his pinky. "Know what that is? The world's smallest violin playing 'My Heart Bleeds for You.'"

Relieved that they could joke with one another—although she sensed some embarrassment lingering in Hank and some reserve in Eric—she motioned toward the door. "Get some clothes and let's move across the street. In fact, Hank, you'd better bring an extra change just in case." Now more than ever she didn't want either boy out of her sight longer than necessary.

"Uh-oh. Is there something more you're not telling me?"

"Huh? No, no. I was just thinking that if we decide to do something tomorrow, I don't want you to have to come here and wake your mom."

He nodded and quickly stuck some things in his schoolbag.

Eric, however, was more observant. "What's the matter, Mom? You look kinda—sick."

Rallying, she smiled but wrinkled her nose and pressed her hand to her stomach. "I just realized I haven't eaten anything yet today and I'm feeling a little queasy, that's all."

The boys accepted that well enough and headed out the door, tossing suggestions about dinner back and forth. Hank didn't say goodbye to his mother, and for once Brette didn't feel like reprimanding him.

But she stuck her head in the bedroom. Problems or no, she worried about Sally driving, not to mention working around hot grease, fire and the usual kitchen equipment.

"You will be careful?" she pleaded.

Sally groaned. "I only took one pill this morning."

"That's because you slept all day from what you ingested yesterday. You've been taking Prozac and heaven knows what other crap your friends at the hospital sneak for you."

"Hon, do you mind? I'm a little old for the nagging mother routine. I promise I will stay within eight miles of the speed limit, look both ways at intersections and not grab any pots without a towel at work. Now go work your magic on the kids."

Minutes later she heard more than saw Sally tear out of her driveway and down the road. Brette stopped beating an egg and bit her lip.

"She's only happy when she's looking at me in her rearview mirror," Hank said coming to stand beside her.

"That's not true." But increasingly, Brette wondered that herself. "Listen," she said, determined for all of them to at least have a pleasant dinner, "are you sure this is what you want? Smothered pork chops, mashed potatoes and salad?"

"If you don't mind." Hank swallowed. "It's what I kept thinking of coming back."

"Okay. Then, while I get these chops dipped and coated, wash your hands and collect the salad stuff out of the vegetable bin. Eric, you want cheese biscuits?"

"Yeah, but— There's Sam!" Eric stood at the dining room window and pointed to Sam walking to his shop. "Why don't we invite him to eat with us?"

"No way!" Hank groaned.

"We can't!" Brette said in the same instant.

Eric laughed, embarrassed. "Jeez. Gang up on me already."

"Sorry." Brette racked her brain for a justifiable reason. "I was only going to say I'm...more tired than I thought. You know, not really up to making small talk."

"Small wonder." Eric came into the kitchen and elbowed Hank. "You missed all the excitement. Even before we knew you had taken off she was steamed because the Pughs had a Dead End sign put up the day you left, and somebody pulled a stunt."

Instead of looking amused, Hank grew quiet. "What do you mean?"

"There's a new Dead End sign right outside the Pughs' place. Mom says she saw a bloody handprint on it yesterday morning. At first she thought it was us pulling a Halloween prank. Then, when we realized you were gone, she thought old Truman had done you in."

"Show me!" Hank demanded.

"Well...I can't. It's gone."

"It can't be...." Hank whispered.

"Ask Mom. She sent me to clean it up and there was zip. Creepy, huh?"

Not only didn't Hank reply, he ran to the dining room window and stared after Sam disappearing into the shop. "Damn," he whispered at last.

Growing increasingly uneasy, Brette ignored the language. This was the second time he was reacting negatively to Sam. "What's wrong, Hank?"

Hank nodded to Sam's shop. "It's him. It's his doing."

She almost breathed a sigh of relief. "Sorry, pal, no way. It was a much smaller print on that sign.

Hardly fits your hand, come to think of it, let alone a grown man's.''

"Small like—like a woman's?"

Brette tensed anew. "Hank..."

"Have you seen Tracie Pugh since?"

She'd never seen him so serious, so *sick,* not even when he'd sat in her car and spilled his heart out to her. "I can't say I thought about her, hon. I was focused on you."

"But she was running to his house the night I left," Hank replied. "So if there was a print, I think it was hers. I think Sam Knight has killed her!"

18

Sleep was an impossibility. Brette worked for it, though. Not only did she stuff the boys full of as much dinner as she could, but she made fresh fruit sundaes to keep them close and encourage them to talk. And for the first time since Sam had moved in next door, she wished she'd put miniblinds on the south windows.

She tried not to expose her own doubts and insecurities, but this was easier said than done in light of Hank's accusation. And although she and Eric pointed out that Sheriff Cudahy had been down to see the Pughs last night and no one there had claimed Tracie was missing, let alone filed a report on her, Hank remained suspicious of Sam.

"He's not like other teachers at school. He's like me, keeps to himself unless someone draws him out," Hank said. "I tell you, he has secrets."

That was an understatement. But Brette wasn't ready to share those secrets with the boys yet. Too much had happened in their young lives in the past two days. She wanted to let them have at least one night of easy sleep. They would have to be told before they went back to school and started hearing rumors on Monday, of course, but that was soon enough.

It was barely nine when the boys succumbed to

exhaustion, but by then Brette was ready to be alone. Needing time to think, she turned off all the lights and paced from window to window replaying Hank's words, Cudahy's—Sam's. He remained in his shop, the swing doors open, the lights on. Every once in a while she spotted a glimpse of him; he moved around a lot and she knew he was trying to stay busy. She wouldn't be able to rest, either, if she'd received the kind of blow he did today.

Would he lose his job over this once Cudahy informed Principal Glick? There was a strong possibility. School boards didn't like students who disrupted the flow. When a faculty member did— Only, she couldn't remember one ever doing that at Sandy Springs. There *was* that case in Split Creek last year where the principal had been forced to resign, as much because of his behavior with former students and employees of the school as the rest. Whether or not Sam Knight was a dangerous man would probably be of secondary importance to the board members. He'd been deceitful. On the other hand, who wouldn't try to keep something like that buried in the past? To ask him to present that with his résumé each time would be asking him to live with those horrors day in and day out. Who could do that without being driven over the edge?

The phone rang, jarring her out of her ruminations. As she dashed into the kitchen to pick up the portable phone, she saw on the stove clock that it was only nine-thirty.

"You all right over there?"

It was Tucker. She exhaled in relief. "Yeah, the boys gave it up about a half hour ago."

"How'd it go?"

"They're working through it. It's Sally I'm worried about. She went to work, Tucker."

"Not surprised. If you can't hide, run like hell. Was she at least coherent when she got behind the wheel?"

Yes, Tucker knew Sally well, not only from what Brette had shared with him, but what he'd concluded from the times he'd been here and sized her up himself. "That's the good news," she said sighing.

"So why aren't you in bed dreaming about Leonardo Di Caprio or chubby rural mail carriers?"

"Those are my options—puppies or wild men?"

"Beats the Terminator."

Brette had returned to the dining room window. As she watched the shop, she shivered at how much closer to the truth Tucker's nickname for Sam seemed tonight.

"Earth to Barry—what's going on, girl?"

"Sheriff Cudahy unearthed some information about Sam Knight and dropped his bomb this afternoon."

"I thought you sounded more uptight than you should have. So talk to Uncle Tucker, honeychile. What's the skinny?"

She knew she could trust Tucker, and she needed input. "Sam's father is on death row," she said softly. The words came out still echoing with shocked disbelief. "From what I gather, he was an abusive man. The very day Sam came home on leave, his father lost it and killed Sam's mother and brother. Tucker, the boy was only eleven."

"Christ."

"That's not all. Sam has an arrest record himself.

His wife—ex-wife—phoned 911 for a domestic dispute.''

"Did I not call this? Huh? Did I not tell you to be careful of this guy?''

"He says he never touched her," Brette added.

"And how long was her hospital stay?''

"There was no mention of that, and she dropped the charges. Sam says his ex was strongly influenced by her mother, who made no secret that she disapproved of the union. Different social backgrounds, if you catch my drift." As Tucker grunted in affirmation, Brette leaned her forehead against the glass pane. It felt refreshingly cool against her warm skin. "The thing is, he did give up custody of his son, Tucker. The woman's new husband adopted him.''

"No man gives up his flesh and blood to the new guy screwing his lady. He's guilty. You watch that cute tush of yours," Tucker ordered. "Hell, you're there in the jungle without even Dingbat Sally as phone backup. I'm coming over.''

"Tucker, the man's lived next door for six months and has been the poster boy for circumspect neighbors—neat, quiet and mostly invisible.''

"I believe that's the quote they used in the ad to rent Ted Bundy's old apartment—'Wanted, another neat, quiet and mostly invisible neighbor.'''

She could have done without the comparison. "Surely Sheriff Cudahy would have warned me or, more accurately, warned Sam if he thought he was dangerous. In any case, it doesn't look as though he'll be around much longer. Cudahy's going to inform Glick at school on Monday. You know what'll happen then.''

"Good. The sooner the better.''

Brette wished she could wholly share his enthusiasm. "There's one more thing."

Tucker's groan sounded like the wind picking up outside. "May I remind you it's Halloween, not April Fool's Day?"

"Hank said he saw Tracie Pugh going to Sam's the other night when he left."

"Now I know the guy's messed up. He chose Trashy Tracie over you?"

Embarrassing though it was, Brette had thought the same thing. "Tucker, that's not why I'm telling you this. What I didn't get around to sharing earlier was that I saw a bloody handprint on the Dead End sign at the Pughs' that same night. Hank seems to believe it's Tracie's."

"Holy sheep shit. I'm definitely coming over."

"It can't be hers, Tucker. Think! Cudahy went down there last night himself. Tracie wasn't missing."

"He saw her?"

"Well, I don't know. But Truman would have said something."

"Not if he knew she habitually caroused at night and was ashamed to let that little cat out of the bag." Tucker could be heard sitting up. "It'll only take me a few minutes to lock'n load and—"

"I'm serious. You can't come over, and you definitely are not bringing any weapons into this house. You know my feelings about that. Besides, you'll wake the boys, then what would I tell them? Are you planning to move in here with me until Sam puts his house on the market?"

"Why not? I like your cooking."

The truth was Tucker couldn't cohabit with anyone

for too long. Postmaster Brenda Freese had once observed of Tucker's friendship with Brette, "He treats her like an experimental pet gerbil. If she doesn't die on him, he may graduate to a dog or cat."

"Well, I've heard you snore out in my backyard, in the middle of a picnic," she said, letting him off the hook. "No way would anyone here get any rest with that racket in the house." She grew somber. "Seriously, Tucker, thank you, but I didn't tell you all this to put you in a panic. I just wanted your reactions."

"And you got 'em. I'm telling you that you need someone to watch you and the kids."

"I'm doing that. I have been all along."

Tucker sighed again. "I know it. So where is the bastard now?"

"Still in his shop."

"Where are you?"

"By the dining room window."

"What are you wearing?"

Brette chuckled softly. "Nice try."

"At least you can still laugh. Doors locked?"

"Of course."

"You realize I'm going to be checking on you regularly?"

"Don't you dare wake me. I'll call you first thing in the morning, okay?"

"You'd better. And you keep that phone by you at all times, right? I can be there in under ten minutes, which is a helluva lot faster than the law even if they stuck rocket launchers out of their asses. So, me first before 911, got it?"

"You're the best, friend."

Tucker grumbled something. "You just be careful, damn it."

The instant he disconnected, the lights went out in Sam's shop.

19

Afraid she would be spotted, Brette flattened herself in the tight spot between the window and the buffet. Pressing the phone to her pounding heart, she wondered if she'd been too slow, and how long before she could risk peeking again. One thing was for sure, tomorrow, while in Tyler, she would look into finding some miniblinds for these windows.

As she made mental notes to measure at first light, she heard a sharp crack. The wind! It sounded as though it had snapped a dead limb somewhere...in back? The resounding crash confirmed her guess.

Wincing, she peered around the edge of the window to see if she could spot it.

Sam had set the lock on his shop and he was looking in that direction, too. When he started walking that way, she scampered in her socks the long way around the table to peer out the Dutch-style, half glass door. It needed blinds, too.

She hated the very thought of closing herself in like that and closing out the reason she'd bought these ten acres. The catalyst making her a prisoner in her own home appeared from behind her tool shed and paused, hands on hips, to study the trellis crumbling under the weight of the branch. Her beautiful moonflowers would have nothing to climb on come spring!

Brette reached for the doorknob, and recoiled just as quickly.

What are you doing?

No, she couldn't go out there. Wasn't Cudahy's news today proof that she didn't know the man at all? And she had the boys to consider.

So she watched—watched as he examined the thing more closely and then returned to his place. Brette hurried to the side window again and saw him go in via the sunroom, where he left the growing lights on for the man-size lush tropicals.

She waited for lights to come on inside the house. It didn't happen. Was he going straight upstairs? That would be a relief. She still might not be able to sleep, but she would feel less—

Her phone rang.

Now what? she wondered, almost dropping the thing as she tried to turn it on. "Hello?"

"I'll replace it for you."

His voice was the last she expected to hear. Equally shocking was the realization that he knew she'd been watching him. He couldn't have looked up her number this fast, not in the dark.

"All right," she said, aware her voice wasn't quite steady. "You've made your point. You can frighten me. Satisfied now?"

He was very quiet a moment, then replied, "You think that's what I'm doing?"

"Aren't you?"

Instead of a reply, she heard the soft click of him replacing the handset in the phone's cradle. That, too, was as unnerving as the call.

What had he expected her to say? What did he want from her, one minute warning her away, the next drawing her in with those magnetic eyes and enigmatic comments?

She didn't understand him, and she certainly wasn't going to let him witness his hold on her one more second.

Shaking, with indignation as much as nerves, Brette retreated to her bedroom where she leaned on the door and turned on the light. Then she sprawled onto her queen-size bed and reached for her journal.

Her mother had been the one to introduce her to the ritual. In hindsight, Brette saw her mother was having a premonition. "I know you say and believe you share everything that's going on inside you," she'd said just before Brette's twenty-first birthday. "And in many ways you are the most honest person I've ever met. But I think you're mistakingly equating a clean conscience for a clear vision, darling. In any case, I won't always be here, and while I see you as someone who will always be surrounded by people who like you, the intimacy that only true friendships can share may not always be yours. Keep the journal, Brette. Let it help you find your way, but also to grow."

How wise her mother had been. Life did seem to be challenging her, and the journal acted as both mirror and therapist. Tonight she needed it to be her memory and confessor.

First she took pains to write down her discussion with the boys....

"Are you friends with Mr. Knight, Hank?"
"You're joking, right? He's a teacher!"
"But he said you would know to come to him if you needed help."

"Bull. I'm sorry, but no way."

"He didn't say that?"

"Not to me. He's just another voice telling me
what I'm doing wrong with my life. Who's he
to talk? Does he hang out with anyone? No. He's
a stiff with all these rules. And cross him just
once and you're out."

What did that mean? Had Hank offended or broken
a pack with Sam, too? Brette reread those words with
new worry. Eric had been stunned at some of those
comments, as well. There'd been several heated exchanges leading to Hank's final explosion....

*"Why are you defending him? We'd all be better
off if he left. I told you about Tracie. Do you want
your mother to be next?"*

They'd eventually calmed him down, but Brette realized what had transpired was more than the theatrics
of a frightened, embarrassed boy trying to get attention off himself. She had to examine her own behavior. There was a transition in her references to Sam.
Several times she sounded almost as though she were
defending him to Hank, and she knew why. She had
only to close her eyes to relive the moments down in
the woods behind Sally's, and earlier on Sam's front
porch. Her natural curiosity about the man had turned
into more than simple attraction. Somehow she'd
been wholly seduced.

"Oh, Brette, you're in trouble," she whispered to
herself. She sunk back against the pillows and stared
up at the ceiling. "You're in so much stinking trouble."

20

What is the truth? Is it what I see with my own eyes, hear with my own ears?
Dare I even trust my own instincts...or the accusations of others?
Everything I've ever believed is being challenged.
I feel so alone, and so responsible.
—Journal Entry

Sunday, October 31, 1999

The boys were still sleeping when Brette let herself out the front door to greet Sally. She'd already changed into fresh jeans and a fun black sweatshirt with a busy Halloween scene on the front. There were glittery pumpkins, a hissing cat with jeweled green eyes and a sheet-covered child who'd just fallen on his butt because he couldn't see thanks to a slipping costume. She'd bought it three years ago at the town's autumn festival, and, although she felt anything but celebratory, she knew the boys would notice if she didn't wear it.

As much as her eyes burned and her head ached from lack of sleep and too much writing, Sally looked worse. "I'm surprised you didn't take down a utility pole or two on your way in," she said as they met up by Sally's front steps. "You're beat."

"Almost fell asleep twice driving home." Sally yawned before patting her big canvas bag. "Did you see me close the car door on my purse? Probably broke my makeup mirror. Crap, just what I need—seven years of bad luck. But, heck, how will I notice, right?"

Brette chuckled despite herself. "That's the spirit. You want to come over and let me fix you some breakfast before you crash?"

"You'd have to chew it for me." She nodded over Brette's shoulder. "How'd it go?"

"He's going to be fine." At least he would if she had anything to do about it. For all of her inner conflict, that remained one of Brette's solid commitments, right after protecting Eric.

"Will I sound like a failure of a mother if I ask you to keep Hank until at least midafternoon?"

"Not a problem. That's why I came over. I'm taking them to a movie in Tyler."

"Great. Let me give you some money...."

Brette stopped her by staying Sally's hand. "My idea, my treat. "

Sally's smile grew wistful. "I don't deserve you. How's... Does he seem okay? More withdrawn? Sullen?"

"Not sullen, no. He's as well as can be expected for someone who's been scared silly and had his faith in humanity questioned. I don't think that's something a person can or should recover from too fast. He's learning hard lessons."

"Maybe he'll get most of them over with while

he's young, unlike his mother who's still working on hers.'' Sally's tired eyes darted down the street. ''Did Sam talk to him?''

''No.''

''Why not?''

''I suppose…he had other things to do. He did, after all, give up almost two days trying to find Hank. Maybe he fell behind in his work.''

''Cripes, what work? He's a shop teacher! Besides, he said—''

''He's an artist.'' Brette wanted to stop her before they got into that again. ''He is also renovating his house all by his lonesome.''

Nevertheless Sally pouted. ''But he said he would be there for the boys.''

''People say things, Sal. Let it go.''

She didn't mean to sound curt; nevertheless, Sally caught the shift in tone. She eyed her shrewdly.

''Is there something you aren't telling me?''

That one she wouldn't touch with the space shuttle's mechanical arms. ''You just take care of you. Do you have to go in tonight?'' Sunday was normally her one night off.

''No, but I need to sleep. I think I'm coming down with something.'' Sally rubbed her forehead. ''They say this year's flu is going to be extra bad and I think I'm going to be one of the first cases to prove it. Can I ask another favor? Keep Hank with you tonight, as well? This is probably only a twenty-four hour thing, but no sense exposing him. He can't afford to miss much more school.''

Brette repressed the suspicion that Sally was simply avoiding her son. ''Sure. But you know you can't put off being alone with him. You two need to talk.''

"Not before I find more patience than I have right now. Listen, I know I already owe you a lot."

"Friends don't have to keep track of things like that."

"It's better when I do. More than anyone, you know what a pity hog I can be."

Disturbed by the strong impulse to agree, Brette pretended to shiver and hugged herself. "If you're getting sick, you need to get inside. That little jacket's not warm enough for these cooler nights. Better make sure your pilot light's lit on your heater, too. I think it's going to get close to freezing tonight."

Sally huddled deeper into her paper-thin windbreaker. "Whatever it takes to keep troublemakers at home. I hate Halloween if it sends a Tweety bird to a cafeteria line with grandpa, while big brother is in Emergency getting stitches in his head thanks to some punks throwing beer bottles from a moving vehicle."

"Jeez, was that last night's highlight?" Brette's job showed her some of society's less attractive sides, too, but not on such a relentless basis. It took a more stable person than Sally to see such things day in and day out and not be affected. "Maybe you should try getting in at the cafeteria at school? It wouldn't pay as much, but what you'd lose there you'd save in gas and time on the road."

"There's a waiting list longer than your hair."

Grimacing, Brette reached up and fingered a handful like a worry stone. "Okay, soap-box ending for the day. Can I get you anything before I shoo you inside?"

"Put a good word in for me with Sam when you see him."

She didn't want to hear his name, let alone speak

of him. "I told you, I'm not planning on seeing him again anytime soon. I'm giving the boys a change of scenery."

"You know what I mean. If the opportunity arises. Jeez, even that floozy Tracie Pugh is liable to get at him before I get to see him again."

For a moment Brette wondered if she wasn't still in bed dreaming this. Why was Sally bringing up Tracie of all people? "What are you talking about?"

"I've seen her several times in town and over at Wally World in Mineola flaunting herself at everything with a working zipper. You've got to assume old Albert's not enough for her and she's got her sights on greener pastures—or hell, just more of it."

Something shifted in Brette, like a sunken ship slipping off a plateau of soft sand to a deeper, darker grave. The pressure, the depression, left her mute. Tracie was a busty, vivacious strawberry-blonde, and several years their junior. It was one thing to try to find a logical explanation for what Hank had said about Tracie and Sam. It was another when Sally had seen what she had.

"Men," she whispered.

"Yeah, they are," Sally replied with a rueful smile. "In my next life I'll swear off 'em. In the meantime help, okay?"

Brette supposed she made some kind of affirmative response. "Rest well, Sal," she added. "Talk to you tomorrow."

With that, she walked down Sally's sidewalk, but she didn't cross back to her house. Glancing back to make sure Sally had gone inside and wasn't at a window, she started down the road, past Sam's house, all the way to the sign before the Pughs' cattle guard.

The sign stood out like a yellow diamond in the gray chilliness of the morning. So clean—that's what struck Brette about it. It continued to look brand-new and pristine.

How could that be? She'd seen what she'd seen.

She ventured closer, determined as she checked the ground around it. Someone had been here. Therefore, there should be something left of that intrusion....

The ground was mostly sandy loam and treads showed from her own truck and also the Pughs' flatbed; she'd seen them too often not to recognize the different patterns. As for footprints, she couldn't be sure. There seemed to be something, but she'd driven over Eric's, which covered her own. Who else had stood here? she wondered, crouching down.

"What the hell are you doing?"

21

Caught off guard, Brette tried to pivot around and rise at the same time. Instead, she lost her balance, falling hard on her left hip. The force of her teeth connecting with her tongue stopped her shriek of surprise...and almost her ability to breathe.

Sam stood a mere three yards away towering over her like the huge black oak that dominated her front yard. She dropped her gaze to his size twelve or thirteen athletic shoes. So what if they were rubber-soled? How could a man with such large feet sneak up on her like that? How could she think when her stomach was roiling at the taste of blood?

"Let me see." He crouched before her. "Did you bite it clean through?"

With her bandaged hand against her mouth, she ran her tongue against her teeth, then shook her head.

"I'm sorry."

The two simple words—spoken with the weight of the world bearing down on them—were a humble and dramatic addition to Sam's bloodshot eyes and whisker-rough face. She felt that increasingly familiar wave of compassion—then was snapped back to reality as an image of Tracie in his arms formed in her mind's eye.

Waving away the apology, she gingerly got to her

feet and massaged the bruised hip. It would undoubtedly be black-and-blue by evening—another token to
remember him by.

"What do you want?" she muttered.

He straightened. "An answer to start. Why are you
over here?"

"Don't you have anything better to do than keep
watching me? I was walking, okay? Thinking."

Sam ignored her bitchy tone and eyed the sign.
"It's over, Brette. You should be getting some rest
instead of pacing half the night in the dark trying to
keep track of me." At her shocked look, something
warmed in the cold gray depths of his eyes. "If you're
going to live in a house without miniblinds or cur-
tains, you might remember that, even without any
lights on, your blond hair picks up the rays from the
security lamps outside."

A stronger blast of wind whipped at her hair sending several strands across her mouth. Before Brette
could drag them away, Sam did. His strong, callused
fingers were amazingly gentle as he tucked the fine
strands behind her ear.

It was too much intimacy. Shivering, Brette took a
step backward. "What are you doing?"

"The same thing you are," he replied, his tone
more sad than grim. "Trying to find my way. Being
tempted. Stumbling."

He spoke like no one she'd ever met. Was that the
allure? That strange, seductive, quasi-honesty that
never really answered a question or explained much,
but made you believe he had opened his soul to you?

"I'm beginning to wish you'd never moved here,"
she said before she could stop herself.

Sam nodded. "I understand. I'm not being fair to you or the boys."

"You can't go hot and cold with them...at least you won't get away with it with Eric. A person's word means something to him."

"I'm aware of that."

"As for Hank, he says you never said anything to him."

"I'm not surprised."

God. He was doing it again. "That's not an answer. Right now I don't care what *you* do or don't understand. *I* want to know what's going on."

"Because you believe Hank with the impeccable track record with honesty? Can't help you then. I don't argue with fourteen-year-old boys, Brette. Knowing me a little better than you did before, you should understand when I say that I strive to avoid arguing at all these days."

She waited for more, but when he failed to expand on that, frustration got the best of her. "And when was the last time you actually had a real conversation with anyone?"

"Anytime I'm around you it's pretty real."

He might be the silent type, but he had effective answers in his reservoir. "Does that technique work on Tracie?" she asked in self-defense.

That won her a startled look, soon replaced with a frown. "What do you mean?"

"Never mind. I think I've seen and heard enough."

She started back up the road, only to have Sam take hold of her arm.

He studied her through narrowed eyes. "You saw her come over the other night."

"Maybe."

"Or maybe not." His gaze bored into hers. "Maybe it was Eric or…Hank? Yes, Hank. Did he also tell you that she left within five minutes?"

How could he when he hadn't hung around to find out?

Sighing, Sam let her go. "We have a bad case going here, Barry."

She barely heard him. All Brette kept thinking was what he'd said. Tracie hadn't stayed.

"I'm only human," he continued gruffly. "You can't keep looking at me the way you do and not expect me to want to get closer to you."

"I know."

"Do you also know what it does to me to know on some level you're afraid of me? What you said on the phone earlier, your suspicion—"

"Is that why you hung up instead of answering me?"

"What's the point? There'll always be another question, more doubt. In the end, I am my father's son. I can tell you that I'm not like him, but you know that's not entirely true. In the end we're none of us free of our roots and ancestry.

"And in spite of having said all that," Sam said, his voice now barely a murmur, "I want you. Knowing you want me makes things even tougher. But we're not going to do anything about it because a surer bet is that I'm going to lose my job, and in the process you'll hear more rumors and allegations that will reinforce all the doubts you already have about me."

In any case, it was fast becoming more complicated than she wanted or needed it to be. What's more, no matter how much she wanted to give him the benefit of the trouble, she couldn't forget that handprint.

As though she'd spoken out loud, Sam's gaze shifted over her shoulder to the bright piece of yellow-and-black metal. Slowly his expression hardened. "Shit." He pointed to the sign. "That's why you brought up Tracie. Because you heard she was at my place, which means I did exactly what, Brette? Well?"

It was an insane moment, the kind where if you saw it on TV you yelled at the idiot actor to run. But how did you escape someone whose arm reach and stride outdistanced yours the way a cobra did an earthworm?

"I don't believe this." Sam took a step toward the Pugh farm, then spun around to face her. "Have you called the police yet?"

Thinking about tempers, head starts and, above all, the boys, Brette took a step backward. "You're jumping to conclusions."

"And you stop right there—" he pointed a finger at her "—and answer the question! Are you now suspecting me of murdering Tracie Pugh?"

"Don't be ridiculous!" Brette said with equal energy. "I suspect Albert would notice if his wife was missing."

"Maybe." Sam took a step toward her, then another. "There's just one complication. Tracie came to me the other night sporting a nasty bruise on her cheek and announced that she was leaving her husband."

22

"I—I don't know anything about that," Brette told Sam. Nor had she known anything about Tracie's plans to leave Albert.

"Right." Sam looked anything but convinced. "That's why you're playing Sherlock Holmes here, and why you nearly come out of your skin whenever I get near you, despite those longing looks. Guess I figured you wrong. Having a man lose sleep over you isn't enough. You want one who can't decide whether or not to break your neck after he screws you."

No one had ever spoken to her that way and he wasn't going to get away with being the first. As furious as she was hurt, Brette swung at him. But Sam, taller and stronger, had no difficulty in countering the move.

He caught her by her wrist, twisted it behind her body and locked her against him. "Thanks for easing my conscience," he muttered, and locked his mouth to hers.

Between the shock of their colliding bodies, the punishing pressure of his mouth and the sudden loss of ground beneath her feet, Brette was left fighting just to breathe. Then came the invasion, the hot, hard thrust of his tongue. Gone was any memory of the self-defense lessons she'd taken; she could only grab at whatever she could find—part shirt, part man—and hang on.

She'd never been kissed in anger before, not with *any* real passion to speak of. In fact, the only memorable experience had been a good one, the night Eric was conceived, but that hadn't been about passion, either. Far from it. It had been tender and nice, even a little fun. Nothing like this insanity.

He kissed her with an urgent hunger and she tasted blood again. With a deep groan, he filled his free hand with her hair and dragged back her head to expose her throat to him.

She thought she heard her name, as a prayer or curse, she wasn't sure. A freight train was suddenly roaring in her ears. Before the sound made sense it was on top of them adding a taunting blast of its horn.

Sam swept her to safety before letting her go and they watched the milk truck rumble past giving them another lighter tap of its horn. As wind whipped at her hair and clothing, Brette glimpsed the amused grin of the driver in the side view mirror. Belatedly, she felt the chill of fresh air on her skin and, embarrassed, tugged down her twisted sweatshirt over her exposed midriff.

When she saw Sam begin to speak, she raised her hand. "No. Don't say anything." She wiped the wetness from her lips and found it was fresh blood from her reopened cut. "Not another word."

The shaky warning served as her sole hold on dignity. How she managed to get home, she didn't know, but considered it a small victory to be still standing, albeit wobbly, as she locked the front door. Now all she had to do was get to her bedroom without the boys spotting her. She was in no condition to be seen, let alone to answer questions. Thankfully, there wasn't a peep from Eric's room. She eased shut her bedroom door, then made a beeline to the bathroom.

Upset enough to vomit, she sank down onto the vanity seat by the sink and fumbled with the washcloth and the cold water tap. All the while she tried to avoid her reflection in the wall-to-wall mirror before her. It reminded her of the night she got word that her parents' train had been swept off its tracks in an avalanche. Tears burned inside her. She knew if they came they could be explained by a lot of things, like the shock about Tracie or her fatigue and growing worry about Hank's future with Sally. But if she was being ruthlessly honest with herself, she knew they would be because of that damned kiss and Sam's utter loss of respect for her. She couldn't let it, him, matter so. There were things she had to do.

Think.

Dear God. Had that really been Tracie's blood on the sign? Cudahy needed to be notified.

Brette pressed the cool, dripping washcloth against her feverish face and was surprised steam didn't rise from the cloth. She repeated the process over and over. Afterward, she rinsed her mouth with cold water.

Back in control again, Brette returned to the bedroom, sat on the edge of the bed and phoned the sheriff's department.

Naturally Cudahy wasn't in. "Could you give me a number where he could be reached?" she asked. "It's important that I speak to him."

"Ma'am," the dispatcher replied without remorse. "That's impossible."

"He knows me. This is Brette Barry. I just saw

him yesterday regarding the search for a neighbor boy. Hank Jamison.''

''I'm familiar with your name, ma'am.''

The admission, combined with the pain in her tongue, only served to push Brette back toward shaky ground. ''Then you should understand why I need to talk to him,'' she replied, her voice not quite steady.

''Tell me where you can be reached, and I'll see he gets the message.''

''Is he coming into the office today?''

''He's the sheriff, ma'am. He's always in touch.''

The man sounded like a political announcement. ''I mean soon? I need to know how long.''

''Look, ma'am, this has been a busy few days for him. I'm not about to bother him unless you have a vanload of terrorists breaking in your front door or an airliner poking through your roof.''

Where would a possible murder fit into that scenario? Brette didn't have the energy to find out. ''All right, all right. Would you please give him my cellular phone number.'' She rattled it off for the officer.

''And this pertains to...?''

''He'll know.''

There was a heavy sigh on the other end of the line. ''May I have your home number, as well?''

''You already have it, Officer, but I won't be here.''

Having had enough, she hung up. Covering her face with her hands, she struggled to relax and slow the frantic beating of her heart. Had she done the right thing? How much should she tell Cudahy when he called?

What if he didn't?

She dropped her hands to her aching abdomen and

glanced out the front window to Sally's. Sally needed to know about Tracie. But by now she was fast asleep, and maybe she was safer that way. No, Brette decided, she wouldn't tell her or the boys anything until she had irrefutable information.

"Mom?" There was a tap on her door. "You still asleep?"

Brette drew in a deep breath and crossed over to open the door to her sleepy-eyed son. "Hi, sweetheart, sleep well?"

"Yeah. What're you doing in here? You're usually cooking up a storm by now."

True, but this was anything but a usual Sunday. "I was, ah…checking around the yard to see if the wind did any damage. The arch for the moonflowers is history."

"Wild. I never heard anything."

"You needed the rest. Hank still unconscious?"

"Believe it or not, he beat me to the bathroom. Think this is the start of him turning a new leaf?"

Brette liked his positive attitude. No matter what anyone said about her, he was living proof that she did some things right. "He's had a big enough scare," she told him, hoping herself.

"So what's for breakfast?"

Grinning with relative ease because neither of the boys ever stopped thinking of food for too long, Brette shared her brainstorm. "I was thinking…how about if we made a day of it, maybe go to IHOP then take in a movie and have a late lunch out, too?"

"Belgian waffles here I come. Do we get to pick the movie or is this Chick-Flick Day?"

She ruffled his hair. "Hey, you like some of my choices!"

"It was Mother's Day. It was against the law to hurt your feelings."

"Okay, Mr. Comedian, you pick...within reason."

"Do I need to tell Hank to call his mom?"

Brette shook her head. "I spoke to her when she got in a little while ago. Actually this was partly her idea. She's pretty beat."

Eric glanced over his shoulder at the closed bathroom door before replying softly, "Uh-oh...she didn't take more stuff, did she?"

Her cellular phone rang. "No, babe. Go have some juice. I'll be right with you."

Although she knew he'd think it strange, she shut the door in his face and ran to grab the phone.

"Hello?" She wasn't surprised to find herself almost as breathless as when she first got back to the house.

"Sheriff Cudahy here, Ms. Barry. My dispatcher called me with the news that you're disturbed about something."

Odds were, Brette thought, that he hadn't been so polite. "Thank you for returning my call." She kept her voice low in case Eric's curiosity got the best of him. "I'm sorry to intrude on your private time."

"If it makes you recant some of your strong accusations about me and my department, it may be worth it. Now what seems to be the problem? Did young Jamison remember something more useful about the guy in Saint Louis?"

"Ah...not exactly. It's about the mystery behind that bloody handprint on the sign."

There was only silence on the other end of the line.

"I know what you're thinking," she continued

quickly. "No one saw anything but me. However, I've been doing some additional checking—"

"That's not reassuring news to me, Ms. Barry."

"Something strange happened the night Hank slipped away to go to Saint Louis."

"I'm listening."

"Tracie Pugh was seen in the vicinity of the sign."

"So it was a Halloween prank after all."

Dumbfounded by his reaction, Brette enunciated, "I'm serious, Sheriff."

"And I'm not going to be happy about that, am I?" Cudahy sighed. "All right, I'll play—for a moment. By whom, Ms. Barry?"

Brette hesitated as the full impact of what she was about to initiate hit her.

"Ms. Barry, you're clearly intent on making allegations. But without facts to back them up, those allegations become nothing more than gossip."

"Can't we simply find out how Mrs. Pugh is? If she's at home safe, then I'll apologize and never bother you again."

Obviously not in the mood for hedged bets, Cudahy replied, "If I have to send a car out to collect you and bring you here for questioning, I will. Now what was so odd about Mrs. Pugh being seen at the entrance to her own property?"

What were her options? Brette thought fast. "Well, it all fits together, don't you see? And when I told Hank about the sign—"

"Excuse me?" Cudahy cleared his throat. "From all I've seen and heard, that kid plays as fast and loose with the truth as he does his respect for you, not to mention your trust in him. Why believe him? Don't you see this is a perfect opportunity for him to throw

attention away from himself and get out of the dog-
house with everyone?''

''That would be a valid point if Hank was the only
one who'd seen Tracie, and I hadn't seen what I did.
There's something terribly wrong here, Sheriff.''

''What's wrong is that you've forgotten that I
spoke to Mrs. Pugh's father-in-law last night. He
didn't give me a hint that she was missing. Remember
him? He's the guy you thought was behind Hank's
disappearance.''

Brette eyed the long red line along her right palm.
It no longer needed a bandage, but the starkness of
the wound reiterated what ramifications her information could have. But if she didn't give him more,
Cudahy would hang up on her—or make good his
threat to haul her in. Then Sam would be the one
brought in for questioning. As upset as she was with
him, would that be fair considering what he was already facing?

*Whatever he's facing is because he kept his secrets
from the wrong people.*

''Ms. Barry, I'm a patient man, but not when it's
apparent I'm dealing with a nickel slot gambler at a
high-dollar poker table. This is *not* your game, understand? So give me what you have before you or
someone you care about gets hurt.''

Brette closed her eyes. ''Sam Knight confirmed
that Tracie came to his house that night, just as Hank
said.''

After a slight pause, Cudahy murmured, ''Huh.''

''Now do you see why I'm concerned?''

''What I see is that I've done you a favor.''

''Pardon?''

''At the risk of embarrassing you, Ms. Barry, I

sensed something between you and Knight. I felt bad that you were involving yourself with someone who's carrying so much baggage, what with you raising a son on your own and all. It appeared you were following a straight path to heartbreak.''

"Wait a minute—you checked Sam's background because of some need to play surrogate godfather?''

"I ran a check on him because both my deputy and I agreed something didn't jive about the man, which, if you'd taken off the rose-colored glasses, you would have admitted yourself. And now you're telling me that, not only was the man seducing you, but he was seeing Mrs. Pugh, as well?''

"He was *not* seducing me," Brette snapped. "And we don't know that he was having an affair with Tracie, do we?''

"Of course, you're right. She was baking her husband his favorite buttermilk pie in the middle of the night, then realized she was short an unbaked pie shell and ran up to Knight's to borrow one!" Cudahy all but growled as he purged a deep breath. "Your instincts for self-preservation may not be too keen, Ms. Barry, but I'd suggest you wake up and realize the sooner you get him away from your boy, the better.''

He was making her sound worse than a nitwit. But what did she say that didn't prove she *had* made some mistakes in judgment?

With perfect timing, Cudahy asked, "By the way, Ms. Barry, exactly how did you get Mr. Knight to confess about Mrs. Pugh?''

"He— I confronted him with it.''

She heard a scraping sound and had a hunch Cudahy was rubbing a night's growth of whiskers as he tried not to turn the air blue with epithets.

"Let me get this straight," he began, a new edge in his voice. "Knowing the man has a father on death row, and his own police file, you still challenged him about a woman you think is missing?"

"It wasn't like that!" He made her sound so reckless Brette had no choice but to put him on the spot in return. "Maybe I have taken a chance or two, but only because you keep ignoring me about the print!"

"And you think that justifies risking your life, maybe even your son's?" Cudahy countered quietly. "Ms. Barry, we've just sent a man to Huntsville for not only murdering the woman he was living with, but her two preteen daughters just because she'd no longer wanted him around. Or maybe you saw this other case in the paper last week? A man shot his five-month pregnant ex-girlfriend in the belly because he heard she'd just gotten engaged to another man. And lest you think I'm only talking about a lower class of society, let's not forget what happened over in Split Creek last year."

"Do you think Sam Knight is a murderer, Sheriff?"

"You obviously don't."

"Just answer the question, please."

"I can't and I won't because I don't have a murder. I don't even have a missing person. Do I make myself clear, Ms. Barry?"

"Sam said she had a bruise on her cheek," Brette replied. "He said she was leaving Albert."

"If that's the case, and he did strike her, then good for her for getting out. Regardless, leaving a spouse isn't against the law."

"But the bruise—"

"Could have come from a fall, anything. Mr.

Knight could have made it up to add weight to his denial of their affair. You said she was leaving Albert Pugh? Did anyone mention her carrying luggage?"

"No. But maybe she'd just decided to while talking to Sam."

"And, about to unload a complication in his life, he kills her?"

"I was thinking about Albert when she told him."

Cudahy uttered a negative sound. "Listen to me, Ms. Barry. In cases of domestic abuse, there's characteristically a history of the law being called in numerous times before anything climactic happens. She didn't call *us*. Not once.

"Stick with the premise that Sam Knight wants badly to keep you as an ally," Cudahy added. "You're an attractive woman, clearly of a class above the norm. You'd make a credible reference down the road. People like him are always thinking two steps ahead and are careful about burning bridges. And if he needed your testimony in court, you and your son's clean-cut, innocent demeanor could be just the thing to push a jury toward believing whatever story he was selling."

Dear God, did he really see life as one ongoing corruption and lie? She liked puzzles and mysteries, but this...this was warped.

"I've depressed you," Cudahy said when she failed to reply. "I'm sorry, but when you're dealing with conspiracy theories, you need to understand the worst case scenarios. The good news is that I don't think you have that here."

Brette could hear what he was really saying. "You're not going to do anything."

"I told you yesterday, I'm swamped with real

cases. I'm shorthanded, and if I stick my nose in Albert Pugh's business without just cause, he could make a case of hemorrhoids a pleasure, if you'll excuse the indelicate analogy on this fine Sunday morning.

"Now I know you've had a difficult time and you're still under an inordinate amount of stress. But this is the last time I'm telling you, Ms. Barry—stick with delivering the mail and raising your fine son, and leave us to worry about the darker side of human nature. Good day."

She couldn't believe it.

"How?" Brette murmured as she listened to the click signaling he'd hung up. How was she supposed to have a good day when he was making it clear that if she wanted answers, she would need to find them herself?

23

I've never felt more alone. I don't know what
to do next.
And yet I know there's only one thing to do.
—Journal Entry

Monday, November 1, 1999

On Monday, Brette arrived at work with a troubled
mind and a heavy heart. She and the boys had stayed
in Tyler as long as possible, and then it had only been
Eric's reminder that his gym suit needed washing, that
had forced her home. Thanks to that task and the
compelling need to sit with her journal, it had been
nearly midnight by the time she'd gotten into bed.
She felt every minute of that lost sleep as she pushed
through the steel doors into the back of the post office.

"Uh-huh," Tucker grunted the instant she depos-
ited her purse at her station. "You didn't hear a word
I said yesterday, did you?"

She had called him while the boys had played a
few video games at the theater. Like Cudahy, he
hadn't been thrilled at all with her news about Tracie,
let alone how she'd found out.

"Please, Tucker," she said to the man wearing a green flannel shirt over a Hooters T-shirt. "We've already had this discussion."

"It doesn't seem to have done any good. You've been up all night plotting."

When she'd asked him for his help in determining whether Tracie was down at the farm or not by calling, he'd refused. "Ever hear of Caller ID?" he'd drawled. "I might as well go knock on her front door and wait for Albert to stick a double-barreled shotgun in my face."

"That's why I decided to call their number from Tyler," Brette told him.

He immediately came over, pretending to need help reading the box number on a handwritten envelope. "Is that a thirty-seven at the end or a twenty-two?" he said loud enough to be heard on the loading dock. Then he asked in a false whisper, "So what happened?"

Brette elbowed him in his meaty ribs. "I need help, not ridiculing."

"Keep holding your breath, it might loosen one of the clots in your brain. On this one I agree with Cuddly Cudahy. You're working overtime earning yourself either a trip to a padded cell or a lawsuit."

Ignoring the worst-case scenario, she told him as he returned to his own station, "I called their number three times from three different pay phones. I kept getting their answering machine."

"Lots of people prefer to screen their calls."

"*No one* answered in almost a ten-hour period. Who stays in a trailer and doesn't answer a ringing phone?"

"They probably thought you were a solicitation call and didn't want to bother."

"On a Sunday?"

"Well, cows don't stop producing milk on weekends and holidays, so that explains where Albert was. As for Tracie, she could've been at church and then cleaning daddy-in-law's place. Even I've heard her complain that she's used as a maid over there."

It was possible, but Brette needed to know for sure. There wouldn't be much opportunity to use pay phones today. They weren't exactly a common sight in the Pineywoods.

"You'd do better to worry about the grudge the Terminator's gonna have once he gets canned," Tucker added.

Yes, that was another thing on her mind. When they'd returned to the house last night, Sam's shop was closed and his house dark except for the growing lights in the sunroom. But even though she saw his Suburban in the driveway, there'd been no sign of life at the house. It had made her extremely self-conscious as she'd moved back and forth in front of the dinette window that gave him a direct view of her kitchen and the washroom. She told Tucker about that.

"What happened to those miniblinds you were going to get while you were in town?"

"I realized I'd have to take down the glass shelves to put them up." Both of the windows on that wall had several glass shelves where she displayed her collection of colored cut glass and her sun-loving plants. "It struck me that I'd be giving up something I really love to do what? Hide from someone who's trying to intimidate me. That's not a pattern I want to start.

Give an inch there, next thing I'll be afraid to unlock the front door let alone step outside.''

"Right. Better to let him watch you walking around in your nightie.''

She shot him a tolerant look because he knew a mother with two teenage boys in the house didn't wear anything transparent or otherwise overtly sexy. Her oversize T-shirts covered her to midthigh, and they were fast approaching the season when she added sweatpants to that uniform.

"What do I do?'' she asked, seeing Desiree was wheeling in the next cart of mail.

"Four tiny words of advice,'' Tucker replied in that same loud whisper. "Mind your own business.''

Easy for him to do. His nearest neighbors were the dearly departed at Cedar Cove Cemetery.

"I saw what I saw on that sign. Hank confided something in me and Sam confirmed it. I can't pretend that everything is okay when my gut says it isn't.''

"You still got trouble?'' Desiree asked, rubbing Brette's back in greeting and compassion.

Brette shot Tucker a cautioning look. "I'm still trying to figure out the mystery behind that print on the sign.''

Desiree tapped her index finger into her palm. "You call cops. Dey gotta help.''

"News flash, Eastern Peach,'' Tucker replied, lifting the last sacks of mail from the cart. "She has.''

As Desiree rolled the cart back to the rear of the building muttering under her breath, Tucker added, "I've got an idea for you, but if you tell anyone it came from me, I'll make the Terminator seem like the Easter Bunny.''

That said, he glanced around for E.J. and Wally. Then, with dramatic flair, he licked the tip of his right index finger, reached across her and into the slot for the Pughs' mail, flipped through it and tore the cover half off a fashion magazine.

"There! Now bag it and drive in there apologizing like crazy for the damage done in transit," he told her. "If that doesn't get you a glimpse of her, and put your mind at rest, I don't know what will."

Brette stared at the ugly cover. "You're scary, Tucker...but I love you for it. Only...you know all that's really necessary here is to stick this in the mailbox with that label explaining damage in transit. It's not required to present it personally."

"They don't know that. Just deliver the damned thing into her hot little hands and get this out of your mind, okay?"

He was right, Brette thought. And getting in would be easy now, thanks to him. Getting out could be another story. But what choice did she have?

24

One thing Brette didn't count on was the number of people who would stop her to ask about how things were going with Hank. Some didn't know yet that he was back and demanded a full recount of events. As a result, she was running late by the time she turned on to her street.

Keith ran out of his place when she pulled up to his mailbox.

"This needs to go Certified," he said, handing over a padded brown envelope with the proper form. "I should take it in myself, but—"

"You don't look good. What's wrong?"

"Aw, nothing more than a bug, I guess."

Although her own stomach was queasy, she knew that was for a different reason, and she summoned a warm smile for the soft-spoken man. "You never eat right when you're on one of those deadlines. What did you exist on this time?"

He pushed his glasses up his nose and, with a sheepish expression, replied, "Mostly popcorn doused with parmesan."

"That's it?"

"And Diet Dr Pepper as a chaser."

"I'm going to send Eric up later with a container

of my chicken vegetable soup with barley. All you have to do is defrost it.''

''Considering that my cupboard is virtually bare at the moment, I humbly accept. What can I do in return? Does Eric need any diskettes, a CD full of new fonts?''

''Stop. It is not necessary to repay a gesture with a gift every time.'' She indicated the envelope. ''I'll take care of it and have the receipt to you tomorrow.''

''How are things on your end? You look pretty good for someone who hasn't had much sleep in a couple of days.''

She'd purposely worn a powder-blue sweater over a white turtleneck with her jeans today to accent her hair and eyes. The theory was, she hoped, that even sour Truman Pugh wouldn't be too nasty to someone who looked harmless and soft. No need to have Keith laugh at her mini-psychology experiment, though.

''That's gratitude you're seeing. The boys are still friends, and things didn't turn out as bad as they could have in Saint Louis.''

''And how do things stand between Hank and his mom?''

''Like you, she says she's coming down with a bug. In her case, though, I think it's a way to avoid being with Hank too much. I'm afraid she's content to pretend this never happened,'' Brette said with a sad smile.

Keith whistled softly. ''Not good. And it puts too much responsibility on your shoulders.''

''Believe me, I don't mind. But I do agree with you that it's not healthy for either of them.''

''I sure wish I knew how to help.'' His expression softened. ''I miss the kid. He's bright, has potential.

But all that's going to get shut down without the right direction and influences in his life. Why does Sally think that just because we don't—well, you know. Why does that mean I can't help Hank?''

Brette didn't want to get in the middle of their argument, but she couldn't help it since she liked all parties involved. "Right now Hank thinks it's your fault that things didn't work out between you two. And you know Sal, she'd rather let someone stick with a misconception if it lets her avoid looking like the bad guy.'' She patted his hand resting on the car door. "Give it time. Between the two of us, we'll get through to him.'' She glanced down the road and added conversationally, "Listen, by chance did you see Tracie Pugh pass by?''

"What…this morning?''

"Yeah. I have something for her and I'd hate to go down there and get stuck facing one of the men.''

"Can't say I've paid much attention to traffic out here, until it was time for you.''

"No problem.'' She spotted movement behind him. "Speaking of traffic though, you'd better run if you want to avoid Clovis. He probably wants to corral you into taking him for a walk.''

"No can do yet.'' Keith glanced back and saw the aging man shuffling toward them with the help of a walker. "Whoa, he's getting stronger every day. I'm outta here before I let an attack of guilt cause me to miss a long-distance call I'm expecting. Thanks, Brette. Holler at me if…''

She waved him on, nodding at the open-ended invitation.

With a parting wave to Clovis, Keith ran back across the street and disappeared into his house.

Easing her truck back a few feet so she was directly in line with the Ponders' sidewalk, Brette shifted into park. Collecting their mail, she went to meet Clovis, who'd made it only midway down the long ramp that Brette had been stunned to learn Sam had built free of charge for the Ponders that summer. "How's it going, tough guy?"

She watched him struggle, his movements as unsteady as they could be for a man who'd suffered a stroke just after New Year's. Even so, she found it easy to smile at his progress, for as few as six weeks ago he could barely shift the aluminum walker without someone at each side to steady him. His steps weren't too confident yet, and sometimes he looked as though he were re-experiencing that life-changing explosion in his brain. The right side of his face retained the muscle damage that caused a drooping effect, but his fading eyes clung to hers as though following a prism's rainbow.

He tried to speak, the sound mostly a grunt and whine. She'd heard it enough times, though, to recognize it was her name.

"Good to see you, too, Clovis. Does Bertrice know you're out here?"

Instead of answering her, he released the walker long enough to gesture shakily toward Keith's.

"I know," she crooned. "He feels bad about having to run, but he had to dash back inside to catch a long-distance call. You know how busy he is." Brette had tucked the Ponders' mail in a plastic grocery bag she kept on hand so Clovis could carry it himself. "Here you go. Be sure to tell Bertrice hi for me, okay? Now Clovis, I have to get back to my route, and you should get back inside. You're only in your socks.''

Bertrice appeared wiping her hands on her apron. Pushing open the storm door she tsked. "I left him watching those tapes you made him of old Carol Burnett shows that he loves so much and was up to my wrists in bread dough. Next thing I hear the front door banging shut. I've got him now, dear. How are the boys?''

"Back at school today. Hopefully everything's back to normal.''

"That's the best we can all hope for, isn't it? Though how many of us are prepared for what 'normal' turns out to be?''

She had that right, Brette mused, watching the woman brush a stray strand of graying hair back from her round forehead before helping her husband. Just looking at the heavy bun at her nape made Brette's neck ache. Yet Bertrice was as strong as she was patient, and it was good to see her resolve, as well as her undeniable affection for Clovis, as she helped him back into the tiny, one-story frame house.

Making a mental note to stop by within the next day or two for a visit, Brette climbed back into her truck. The Ponders had no close relatives around here. Keith was attentive in cold or bad weather, but he tended to avoid Bertrice as much as he did Clovis the rest of the year due to Bertrice wanting to feed him as an excuse to talk his ear off. Unfortunately, the food was old-fashioned, peasant simple and rarely anything he found appetizing.

At her mailbox she dropped off a computer magazine for Eric and the phone and county tax bills for her. "Some trade-off," she murmured.

A glance across the street at the closed-up house told her Sally wasn't up yet. After putting her mail in her box, she eased down to Sam's. As usual, she had an acute awareness of what was in his bundle—his phone and tax bills, several advertisements from building supply companies and a manila envelope with a Houston law firm's return address on the mailing label. She'd seen that address before, in fact every month. It always followed a week after he mailed an envelope down to Houston. Her imagination usually worked overtime guessing what was inside. Today, however, her curiosity had to take a back seat to grimmer concerns.

A milk truck was leaving the Pughs'. As soon as it passed, she eased up to the cattle guard and braked. Once again she debated the wisdom of what she planned to do. Albert and Truman shared an ultrasensitive suspiciousness gene and were bound to see through her flimsy ploy if they caught her. But this was the fastest, most efficient way to get a glimpse of Tracie.

"Just do it," she commanded herself, and eased across the cattle guard. In five minutes she would be out of there. What was five minutes?

The Pugh farm was 111 acres of rolling pasture framed by a thin border of woods that protected them from view from the rest of the street. The farmhouse was half-hidden by one of the sloping pastures. Across from it, about three hundred feet closer to her, was the old hail-dented trailer where Albert had established wedded bliss with Tracie some five years before. The dairy was below the farmhouse, a yellowed brick building containing the tanks, pumps, compressors and other equipment—noisy as heck when everything was operating. Since the truck had only left moments ago, Brette hoped the washing up kept things equally noisy, as well as busy.

Beyond the brick building were the milking pens. Outside of them she noticed a number of black-and-white cows lingering like guests at a party who stubbornly ignored the hint that it was time to leave.

Brette parked close to the trailer's door. Keeping the engine running as she was required to do, she grabbed the damaged magazine and the rest of the mail, then proceeded to the front door and knocked. Her heartbeat echoed in her ears, but not loud enough to drown out something from inside. A curse...a *man* cursing. Before she could take a step back to her truck, the door swung open and Albert Pugh scowled down at her.

"What do you want?"

Square and coarse like his father, the younger farmer also had a lot more hair...everywhere. Admittedly, Brette found a well-developed chest with a generous bit of hair rather sexy. But thanks to Albert's unbuttoned shirt, she could see he could start his own donor program.

"Albert, hi. I...was looking for Tracie," she said regaining her composure.

He stared at her as though she'd spoken to him in some remote tribal tongue.

Feeling like the fraud she was, she held out the mail. "There seems to have been a problem in shipping and I wanted to let her know we're sorry her magazine got damaged."

"Bunch of incompetent jerks." He put out his hand. "Give it here."

Brette ignored the insult and glanced around his

legs to peer inside. "Oh, is she busy getting you a late breakfast? Sure smells good in there. Hi, Tracie! It's Brette!"

"She's not here." He wiggled his fingers impatiently. "Come on, come on, I'm burning my goddamn food."

"Sorry! Um...tell her that I'm sorry, too, okay? About the magazine, I mean."

With a thoroughly disgusted look, Albert grabbed the mail, threw it somewhere behind him and slammed the door.

Shaking and stunned, Brette returned to her truck. "I'm a jerk?" she muttered making a sharp U-turn. "*I'm* a jerk?"

Preoccupied, she drove straight into a pothole and her teeth came in contact with her bruised tongue.

"Ow—shit!"

Tears of pain and frustration blinded her vision as she drove out of the farm. All she understood was that she had nothing. No answers and no clue as to what to do next.

25

I need answers....
—Journal Entry

Wednesday, November 3, 1999

For the next two days Brette lived in limbo. Though Tucker encouraged her to take the experience at the trailer as proof positive that she was "barking up the wrong tree," she was haunted in her sleep by images of Tracie running through the woods, trying to find a safe place to hide. Despite her friend's advice, she made two more pay phone calls on Tuesday with the same results she'd had on the previous tries.

As for Hank, Sheriff Cudahy contacted Sally with the news that the FBI did, indeed, want to speak with the teen and an appointment was made down at the sheriff's office in Quitman for today. Sally kept insisting Brette go in her place, that she knew more about what had occurred. Finally, for Hank's sake, Brette had tried, but Cudahy had been adamant. "You aren't family and, while you may have power of attorney," he'd pointed out, "you know it wasn't awarded for something like this." Cudahy had assured her, however, that Hank would be treated with utmost care. He'd added that the authorities thought "Mel" fit some other cases they had pending and felt confident that with Hank's input they had a chance of catching this one.

Brette raced through her route on Wednesday and beat the school bus home that afternoon, only to find that Sally's maroon Ford Taurus was still not in her driveway. To add to her heightened anxiety, Sam's vehicle was—and he was still in it.

Something about the way he was sitting in the Suburban left her with the impression that he'd been there awhile. He tended to stick around school another half hour or so after the release bell sounded, and when he came home, he always moved from point A to point B like a man on a mission. This was unnatural behavior for him, and Brette suspected the repercussions of Cudahy's discovery had begun.

She collected her own mail and let herself into her house, casting frequent though covert glances his way. His trancelike state never altered.

Once inside she strode immediately to the dinette window, certain she would see him finally going into his place. After all, he'd made himself scarce on Monday and Tuesday.

He didn't budge.

Was he even breathing? Lord, she thought with growing concern, he hadn't gone and done something foolish like...?

She checked her sturdy sport watch and saw that Eric would be home within the hour. Knowing Eric, he would go over there. He'd been extremely upset and offended by the rumors that had begun to circulate at school.

"He's being tried and judged without anyone

knowing all the facts!'' he'd complained last night. ''The other teachers already avoid him as though he's got a contagious disease. They should fire him already. Anything would be better than this!''

Is that what had happened? she wondered.

Her decision made, Brette dug quickly into her bag for her pepper spray. In a way it felt a foolish gesture—and contradictory considering that she spent as much time remembering their kiss as she did everything else. But she stuffed the palm-size device in her jacket pocket and let herself out the front door again.

The leaves crunched loudly as she made her way from her yard to his, but not quite loud enough to muffle the din of migrating birds, the breeze rustling leaves and the bulldozer working a new trail for timberers somewhere to the west. If Sam heard any of that, he gave no indication. He didn't budge at all until she stopped before his truck.

He focused on her immediately, and they stared at each other through the windshield. She could only see him from the shoulders up, but his expression alone sent her imagination into overdrive. Were his hands on the gearshift, ready to shoot forward and pay her back for what he must believe was all her fault? Or on a gun that would not only blow a half-inch hole through the windshield, but leave the rest of it looking like bad ice on a lake and her—?

Before she lost her nerve, she continued to his side of the vehicle. Sam had stopped watching her.

She waited for several seconds. When he didn't respond, she tapped on the window. ''Are you okay?''

He ignored her.

She peered through the window and saw that his

hands were empty and resting on the base of the steering wheel. Somewhat reassured, she tried the door. It opened.

"Do you mind?" he intoned, continuing to stare straight ahead.

"I thought maybe— What's happened?"

Slowly he turned to fix her with a steely, mocking gaze.

Brette understood that he would tolerate no hedging from her. She supposed Eric could have shared with him that she was a member of the PTA and that they'd received a few calls from upset and curious parents wanting to know how much of the gossip was true and if she thought their kids were safe. She'd replied as fairly as she could saying, "He's been the model neighbor so far." But Eric had reported yesterday that two parents had pulled their sons from his classes.

"They didn't fire you, did they?" she asked instead. "They can't do that without a full meeting before the board of education. You have a right to be heard."

"Does it matter? The outcome will be the same." His gaze turned challenging. "What do you care anyway? This should be a relief to you."

She expected that one. "Maybe it will be if it turns out they're justified. But if not, you'll be owed a huge apology…and I'll lead the chorus."

Sam grunted. "That'll make it all better? And what about the next time a kid misbehaves in class, or I see a fight elsewhere in the school and step in to stop it? What's going to be the first question parents ask their kids? 'Was he rough with you?' 'What do you mean he said straighten up or else? Nobody threatens my son!'"

"That's your logic for giving up? Situations like that would come up no matter where you tried to teach."

"What makes you think I'm going to bother applying for another job like this?"

"Because you're good at it. Because you like it and the kids."

"Don't." He came out of the truck with surprising speed, forcing her to back up a step. His tan suede blazer gave him a clean-cut, professional look, but his bloodshot eyes and the shadows beneath them warned that there was much going on beneath his calm, controlled exterior. "Don't start pretending you're on my side now. It was a helluva lot easier to take when you thought I was only a wife beater and murderer in training. Since you've also come to believe I've turned Tracie Pugh into spaghetti sauce—"

"Stop it." She grimaced at the horrible image. "I'm not going to apologize for trying to find out what's going on around here."

"Nothing's going on." Sam pointed toward the farm. "She's down there!"

"No, she's not."

His look grew uncertain. "What do you mean."

"I have reason to believe she's not at the farm. I went down there Monday—"

Groaning he dropped back his head and said to the sky, "I don't believe this. What right did you have to stick your nose in the Pughs' affairs?"

"For your information, I was on post office business."

"What did you do, throw her mail in a creek so you'd have an excuse to apologize for its condition?"

He was so close to the truth, she felt her face heating. It was enough for Sam to utter something unintelligible as he slammed the door and start for his house. But after only three steps he swung around.

"Did you see her?" he demanded.

"No. Albert came to the door and took the mail."

"So you came to interrogate me again. That little performance, about being concerned, was just a psychological hand job, is that it?"

As intended, the crude remark stung, but Brette accepted how he could see things the way he did. Wholly on the defensive now, what choice did he have but to see everyone and everything working against him?

"You're the one who brought up Tracie." She spoke as calmly as her trembling voice allowed. "Who happens to be a customer on my route. I would be concerned for anyone after witnessing what I did." Seeing he didn't react negatively to that, Brette added, "Please, at least tell me this. That night…did you happen to notice anything wrong with her hand? That bruise you mentioned. Was the skin broken? Maybe there was more wrong than you first saw?"

Sam gave a slight, disbelieving shake of his head and began walking away again.

"Sam—please!"

"Call my lawyer," he flung over his shoulder.

26

"**W**hat's a three letter word for *depressed?*"

Hank studied the crossword puzzle in the Wednesday issue of the *Sandy Springs Signal* that Brette had brought home. As was their routine at least once a week, they each took a turn at the puzzle using a different colored pen. The person who completed the most not only got to choose dessert, but didn't have to help with the dishes.

"S-A-D." He pencilled in the word. "I hope."

"Try M-O-M," Eric offered drolly.

Brette paused in cutting out the coupon from the food section of the paper. "Excuse me? How do you figure that? I mean, yes, I'm sorry Hank may have to endure another of those monotonous interviews, but I'm hopeful, not sad. It sounds to me as though the authorities are being very thorough and are determined to catch this guy."

Sally had dropped off her son and dashed off to work a half hour after Eric's arrival. It was early, even for her, but understandable after Hank relayed the experience to them. While there had only been one agent from the FBI, the state had sent a field agent as well, and Wood County's detective John Box had asked to sit in. He'd also asked for a child-psychologist friend to observe. Clearly, it had been intimidating for Hank, and there had been several embarrassing moments, especially when the agents had pressed him for explicit details. But there was no missing how proud he was of himself, too. Surely a good sign for his self-esteem.

"I'm talking about what else is going on," Eric replied, pulling her back to the topic at hand.

Right before Hank's arrival, he'd filled her in about how it had spread around school that Sam was on leave without pay, as well as the wild range of speculation as to why. Eric had been indignant and had wanted to go next door to assure Sam that he wasn't one of those who were insisting they knew something was *different* about Mr. Knight. Brette convinced him otherwise. Privately, she was waiting for the phone to start ringing with the next deluge of PTA members who had heard of Eric's defense of him.

"I've caught you looking out the window at Mr. Knight when you thought we weren't paying attention," Eric added. "Even more than you did Monday and Tuesday."

Well, shoot. She thought she'd been more discreet. She *thought* the boys had been deep in conversation about that FBI agent.

"He's under a lot of stress," she replied, thinking fast. "And when you're working around the kind of tools he does, that can be dangerous."

"Lame, Mom."

"What do you care anyway?" Hank asked. He pushed away the puzzle. "Sounds to me like we had a close call. He could be another Hannibal Lecter or something. I think the sooner we're rid of him, the better."

Hank's vehemence came as no surprise, nor did his

mixing of reality and fiction. "You can't wish people away every time something happens that doesn't meet with your approval or affects you negatively. And for the record, Mr. Knight was forthcoming with Sheriff Cudahy about his past."

"Once he was found out."

"He hasn't run like someone with more to hide, has he?" Brette came to the table and sat in her chair. "Hank, his reputation at the school has been impeccable. Come on, even you didn't dislike him."

"Didn't love him, either. I always thought he was strange."

"Why?"

When he sat back in his chair and crossed him arms over his chest, Eric shot him a sidelong look. "You started it. Tell her. She won't say anything to your mom. What's the use anyway?"

Now what, Brette wondered.

Hank shifted forward, shoulders hunched. He fidgeted with the pencil. "I did something back in the beginning of the year. He caught me, but he didn't turn me in."

Brette glanced to Eric who pretended to be innocently tallying who'd won tonight's puzzle. A chip off the old block, she concluded, filing away the new insight. "Am I supposed to guess?"

"I let the air out of Mr. Glick's tires."

"Tires plural?"

Eric fought to repress a smile. "All of 'em."

She sent her one and only a quelling glance. "Why?" she asked Hank.

"He gave me detention for bashing a kid that had just kicked me in the...well, he kicked me."

"Did you try to explain to Principal Glick?"

Hank made a face. "He doesn't listen to me."

"It would appear Mr. Knight did. It sounds as though he was...very understanding."

"Exactly what he wanted you and me to think! I'd say he was trying to get something on me. Then he was going to make a move on my mom or you, and I couldn't stop him."

Eric snorted and gestured to Brette. "See what I have to deal with?"

"You're as gullible as she and my mom are," Hank snapped at Eric.

"*You're* the strange bird, pal," Eric shot back.

"Guys." Brette lowered her voice in warning. Then to Hank she said, "We'll overlook what you did to Principal Glick's car, and I'm touched by your protective instincts. But, Hank, do you hear what you just said? You're suspicious of a man who gave you a fair shake."

The boy wouldn't meet her eyes, but he also didn't look as adamant as before.

Guessing they needed a break, Brette turned to Eric "That puzzle looks finished. Who won?"

He did a quick tally. "Me. I want cinnamon buns and hot chocolate."

Brette made the refrigerator dough pastries while the boys inspected their video collection. She heard the first strains of the soundtrack to *Jaws* as she carried a tray with their treats to the living room coffee table.

"Somebody needs to make something like this about our boars," Eric told her, snatching up a bun.

"Write the screenplay."

Mussing his hair and squeezing a more silent Hank's shoulder, she returned to the kitchen. Intent on letting Hank off wash duty, too, she finished up what remained of their dinner dishes. It was in those last moments by the window that she saw Sam.

She had a sliver of a view. It was just a line of light in the dark between the door and shop wall, but it was enough to see him sitting there. He'd lowered his head in his hands, the model of a man without hope. Because of them. Because he'd tried to do the right thing.

Without stopping to think of his last cold words to her, she put two large buns on a plate, grabbed the mug of fresh coffee she'd made for herself and slipped out the back door.

By the time she made her way to his shop, Sam had shut off the main light. The smaller workstation one was still on, but it cast more shadows than light. She hesitated in the open doorway. That's when he spotted her.

"It...um, looked as though you'd be working late," she began shyly. His expression offered no encouragement. "I thought... How's your sweet tooth?"

He stared at her for a small eternity before dropping his hand from the last light switch. "What are you doing?"

"The truth? I'm not sure." She held out the offering. "These are fresh from the oven, though, and the coffee's hot if you like it black."

After hesitating a moment longer, he accepted the gift. "Smells good."

He sat on the stool and placed the mug on the bench beside him. He wrapped his hand around one of the frosted buns and closed his eyes as he took a deep breath. "Somehow food always smells and tastes better eaten outside."

Feeling less foolish than when she'd arrived, Brette crossed her arms and nodded. "That's what I loved about fall growing up. My father and I would rake leaves and bake potatoes for dinner in them. At least we tried. More often than not, we'd eat them before we got them inside—or we'd get too enthusiastic with the coals and burn everything but the very center to a crisp. But my mother always made a big deal of what we brought her." She smiled at the memory and at seeing how much Sam was enjoying the food.

Looking around, she saw he'd done a lot since the last time she had had a glimpse in here. There were several rows of railings, beautifully polished handrails with ornate iron rods, an unfinished weathervane and the beginning of what looked to be a baker's rack.

"You've been busy."

"I seem to have more and more free time."

Not wanting him to dwell on all of his sorrows and disappointments, she let that one pass. "Are the railings for inside?"

"That was the plan. What's there now is loose and cheap."

"They're going to be beautiful. But do you have enough? I'd thought—I've never been in there, but I've glimpsed through the windows and thought the stairs and balcony would be longer."

"They are. The plan was to duplicate this pattern."

What he left unsaid was, "If I'm still around."

Brette knew better than to bring that up again and continued to inspect her surroundings.

Sam finished the buns with a speed that suggested he'd skipped dinner and came over to where she stood in the far corner intrigued by a long piece of cypress root that looked more like a phallic symbol, but wondrous because it was old and natural.

"Thinking of using it in a dish cactus garden." He held the mug between his hands as though craving its warmth. "It was a gift."

Obviously from someone with a sense of humor as well as a person who'd meant something to him, she thought. A woman?

"Listen, thanks," Sam added more slowly. "For the gesture, as well as the food."

His softer tone appealed too much to her, and she found it safer to study a smaller piece of driftwood. "I expected you to throw it back at me."

"To know me is to know my stomach is in constant competition with my brain." He took another sip of the coffee and offered her the mug. "But maybe you should go now."

"Finish it."

"The boys will miss you."

"They're watching a movie." She moistened her lips. "Speaking of the boys, Hank told me about you saving his backside when he pulled that stunt with Glick's car."

Sam uttered a low sound deep in his throat. "Remind me never to be in an interrogation room with you."

"He's afraid you're only being nice to him to get at his mother."

"In her dreams."

Brette fought hard to repress a shiver of pleasure—and failed. She rubbed her arms, hoping he'd just think her chilled, although her white sweatshirt was as warm as it looked. "He's experienced so little real affection in his life, and he gets less and less of her time…''

''I don't want her, Brette. I don't want her because she could have all the time in the world and she wouldn't spend it with him.'' He put down the mug on another worktable and stepped closer.

Even in this dim light there was no missing the fact that her face was shiny from the scrubbing she'd given it before dinner, and her only scent was the cinnamon she had spilled on herself—proof that she truly hadn't come to seduce. But he was looking at her as though she could.

''Sally's a good person. She's just…''

''Unbalanced. Exactly what I need, right?''

His warm breath teased her hair, her left temple. ''You're right, I should go.''

But before she could move, he slipped his hand under her hair to cup the back of her neck staying her. ''Too late now. You should have gone while I had the willpower to let you.''

He drew her closer, closer, until all she saw was him, his mouth….

''I'm plum out,'' he murmured. ''Out of everything except need.''

She closed her eyes against the dizzying feeling that she was falling into the bottomless centers of his eyes. But that only intensified the sensations as his warm lips brushed against hers.

She was so ready. He drove his tongue into her mouth and sought hers, immediately picking up where the last kiss had left off as though they were longtime lovers reuniting. Relieved, Brette slid her arms around his neck. It was insane. So many questions and doubts remained, yet she wanted this, to taste the untamed hunger he stirred in her.

Groaning, Sam slid his hands down to her hips and lifted her, nestling his erection perfectly against her, letting her know how truthfully he'd spoken. Never mind that it wasn't supposed to happen this fast. In that instant Brette knew if he stretched her over the worktable behind him, she would only fight him if she thought she could get their clothes loosened faster.

Instead there was a sudden, sharp bang, and a voice yelled, ''You bastard!''

27

At the sound of Hank's outraged cry, Brette and Sam broke apart like guilty teenagers. There he stood, his fist against the metal door he'd struck and the worst look of hurt and betrayal on his young face.

"Oh, Hank." She started toward him, her every instinct to soothe. "What are you doing out here?"

Sam stayed her. "Let me. This is my fault."

"Damn straight," Hank replied. He dropped his hands to his sides only to fist both of them. Rage burned in his eyes. "You leave her alone."

Brette eased away from Sam and went to the upset boy. "I'm fine, Hank. I'm *fine*. And you mustn't call Mr. Knight awful names."

"Are you crazy? You know what he is! Do you want to be next?"

"That's enough!"

His expression crumpled, and he burst out, "Screw you. Screw both of you!"

Brette called after him as he ran away, but it was useless. He was heading back to her house and she knew what that meant.

"I have to go," she told Sam. "He's going to upset Eric."

"I'll come with you."

"Not a good idea." For the first time since hearing

Hank's shrill cry, she really looked at him. She saw the regret she'd heard in his voice, and saw the residual hunger. Her body still hummed with her own. Because no words could adequately relay what she felt in that instant, she briefly touched his cheek and ran.

When she came in through the back door, Hank was already on the phone. Although he had yet to say anything, it was clear who he was trying to get hold of. Brette went straight over, plucked the handset out of his grip and disconnected the call.

"You can't stop me," he sneered. "I'll use my own phone!"

Somewhat breathless and shaking, she held up her hand. "You are not calling your mother while she's working. Don't you know how you'd be upsetting her?"

"What do you care? You're no friend to her. Besides, you can't tell me when I can and can't use my own phone."

"Hey." Eric joined them, frowning at Hank. "Throttle it down, will ya? What's going on?"

"Ask *her*."

Brette crossed her arms, mimicking Hank's stance. "Hank, I appreciate that you've had a rough day, even a rough life, but none of that gives you free rein to behave the way you are. Now I'm sorry if what you saw upset you, but then, you shouldn't have snuck out there."

"I didn't sneak. I saw the back door open and you weren't around. I got worried. What a joke, huh?"

"Okay, poor choice of words. I apologize. At the same time, Mr. Knight and I are adults. You have no right to sound accusatory."

Eric's eyebrows shot upward. "What did you do?"

"They were about to go at it." He all but spat out the words.

"Excuse me." Brette knew she had to tread carefully, but she wasn't about to have him turn her actions into something dirty. "He saw Sam and I kiss."

Hank snorted. "He had his hands on her ass."

"Hank!" Brette had about had it with his mouth. "Remember me? I'm the one who's been fighting for you since day one. I was there to hold your hand when you had to get those seven stitches in your knee. I'm the one who helped you to the bathroom over and over the night you ate that earthworm sundae on a bet. Did I once call you a name? Did I once treat you with the disrespect you're showing me?"

"Who asked you to? You pretend to care and you act like you're so much better than my mother, but you aren't. At least she admits she's trash!"

"Knock it off!" Eric punched Hank in the shoulder.

Before Hank could reciprocate, Brette stepped between them and gripped each by the shoulder. "No way. Guys—chill out. *Now!*"

Aware there was no way to reason with Hank until he'd had some time to simmer down and think, she gestured toward the hallway. "Why don't you go lie down. We'll talk about this tomorrow."

"That's what you think," he muttered.

Brette caught his arm before he got out of reach. "If you try to leave here, I'm going to call Sheriff Cudahy and I'll let him have you. That's no threat, that's a promise."

He pulled free and disappeared around the corner.

Eric exhaled and shoved his hands in his back pocket. "What a jerk."

"He's feeling betrayed. It's hard to see the role models in your life as human beings."

"I didn't know you'd gone out. He got up to get something more to drink and the next thing I knew he was storming back into the house." He smiled sheepishly. "Were you really going at it hot and heavy with Sam?"

"I am *not* going to discuss that with you." Brette gestured helplessly. "Look, do me a favor and go be with him. Try to keep him from calling Sally. It's going to be bad enough when she hears, and neither of us needs that tonight."

"Sure." But he only took one step before he glanced back at her. "For the record, I don't mind."

As he, too, headed to his room, she covered her face with her hands. What else? she thought. It was a question that didn't need answering.

Sighing, she went to the dinette window. There she saw Sam standing by his back door looking over. Watching out for her. Touched, she shrugged to signal there was no telling how the rest of the night would go.

He pointed toward her backyard, then pantomimed drinking.

Understanding, Brette nodded and let herself out back. She found the coffee mug and a plate at the top of the stairs—another kind gesture from the man who was fast turning her world upside down and claiming more and more of her thoughts.

Inside the phone rang and with a parting wave, she hurried to get it.

Surely Hank hadn't had a chance to tell Sally yet? she thought, snatching up the handset.

"Brette? Monica Selby. What's this about Sam Knight? Why didn't you call and tell me?"

Not Sally, but almost as bad. Monica Selby was last year's president of the PTA and she had yet to act as though her term was over. The wife of the only dentist in Sandy Springs, she behaved as though his Dr. title was tantamount to that of Earl or Baron. As a result, Monica had an opinion about everything and honestly believed everyone wanted to hear it. That included her constant analysis of who should and shouldn't stay on the staff of Sandy Springs' school system.

"Tell you what?" Brette replied, buying time to get her nerves under control.

"Come on, sweetie. You live right next door to the man, and Eric must've filled you in on what's been going on at the school. How do you sleep at night? I'd be terrified."

"Sam Knight's been as conscientious a neighbor as he has been a teacher."

"So far. But Lillian Osgood in the office told me all about his family tree. I'm writing a petition tonight for the entire membership to sign and I plan to present it at the board hearing next week. Mr. Knight will learn fast that we don't need his kind here."

Brette covered her eyes with her free hand. "Monica, I'm not signing any petition."

"Why on earth not?"

"Because the man has a right to say his piece."

Monica sighed as though listening to the reasoning of a child. "Fine. Let him. But the end result is going to be the same, I promise you. Nobody who comes from the genetic pool he does is going to be within a mile of my Sawyer and Ashley.''

"Monica," Brette replied, "I have to go. My house is on fire and I need to dial 911."

She disconnected only to press the cool plastic handset against her warm forehead. "Oh, God, oh, God, oh, God," she whispered.

28

There's too much going on, and it's only going to get worse.
—Journal Entry

Thursday, November 4, 1999

"I'll trade with you."

Brette shook her head but sent Tucker a grateful smile as they loaded their trucks Thursday morning. "It's not my route I'm worried about. Sally will be sleeping by the time I get over there. It'll be later this afternoon that she's liable to make a scene."

She wouldn't have told Tucker of her expected trouble if he hadn't noticed earlier that the shadows under her eyes were worse not better. Even then she'd tried not to admit too much. But Tucker was nobody's fool and had put two and two together...and called her institutional. What she needed was a cap with a wider bill.

"In that case wait for me when you get done and I'll follow you home."

She appreciated the gesture, but she wouldn't hear of it. "She'll vent a bit and it will be noisy, but the sooner I face it, the sooner we'll get it behind us."

"This is the same drooling she-tiger who, when she saw all the tools and machinery the Terminator first unloaded into that tin barn of his, stuck a ribbon bow on a can of WD-40 and trotted over to introduce herself?"

"Thank you for helping to reassure me."

"Wait, I'm not done, because you've obviously ignored entirely how bad adding her kid to the mix is going to make things. His dream mama has realized that, unlike a Barbie doll, *all* of her parts work. It's vendetta time for him, babe. You might as well have eaten a bowl of fruit cereal with bad milk for breakfast to prepare for the kind of stomach cramps those two are gonna give you."

Brette never tired of listening to his colorful extrapolations; however, she had no plans to upgrade her minidrama into the circus he foresaw. "With these extra sixteen parcels, Eric should be there by the time I get back. And don't forget, Sam's home, too."

Tucker's chin doubled as he gaped. "How did an otherwise sharp little number like you miss the loading ramp for Survival Instincts R Us? I'll buy you your own inflatable boy-toy if it means you'll keep your distance from this dude. Have you forgotten you're supposed to be afraid of this sucker?"

She *was* afraid of Sam—afraid of how he made her feel, of how much her son liked him, afraid of how he managed to make none of what she knew about him subdue her own desire. Most of all she dreaded what she didn't know about him. But she could share none of that with Tucker. He lived just close enough to the edge that he would risk his job to protect her.

"All I'm saying is that Sally isn't about to lose it

in front of Sam,'' she replied to assure him. ''Besides, I haven't told her any of what I've told you because she has enough dealing with Hank. Now that he's undoubtedly filled her in, she's probably even a little relieved that things didn't work out the way she wanted.''

''*Sure.* She'll probably bake you a cake out of sheer gratitude. Only don't bite into it until you pull all of the razor blades out.'' Growling in disgust, Tucker plopped the last box of mail on the driver's seat of his Toyota and slammed the door hard enough to shake the vehicle. Glancing around and seeing that Desiree was already pulling out, he leaned toward Brette and said with aplomb, ''I saw Albert at the market yesterday.''

Brette almost hit her head as she put her carryall on the driver's side floorboard. Now *Tucker* was playing dirty. She didn't want to hear about Albert Pugh. She didn't want to think about Tracie or the sign. She wanted the whole experience to vanish as though it had been a bad dream.

''Stranger things have happened.'' But she frowned as her mind began to speculate.

Tucker nodded slowly, his eyes glowing with an inner satisfaction. ''Yup. He has every right in the world to buy a dozen frozen dinners, a box of laundry detergent and the closest thing you can get to a girlie magazine in a Baptist country grocery store. Nothing weird about that at all.''

''Jeez, Tucker, what did you do, follow him through the store like a bloodhound? He knows you.''

''Not as well as his old man or Tracie. He hasn't seen me in over a year. Before that it'd been almost another year. Besides, he was two people ahead in the express line. Also pissed and in a hurry. Never even looked at the cashier, let alone me.''

Brette massaged the ache building in the vicinity of her diaphragm. ''So maybe he had other business in town and did the odds-and-ends marketing for Tracie.''

Ducking, Tucker peered under the brim of her red baseball cap. ''Did your latest streak of self-injuries include a recent fall in the shower? First you tell me that you're baking for the Terminator, and—''

''I baked those buns for the boys.''

''—and now you're making excuses for Albert's suspicious behavior?''

''Wait a minute, you're the one who told me to give it a rest, that I was imagining things! Do you hear yourself? Not only have you done a 180 about Tracie, now you think Albert iced his wife, not Sam?''

''If he did, he did it because he found out the guy you're ready to let deflower you was poaching in his garden.''

''Tucker,'' she intoned, ''I have a thirteen-year-old son. I was deflowered a long time ago. What's more—''

He tapped the side of his head. ''Up here you're still a virgin. You think you're the first gal to have a kid with a guy she just liked?''

''Correction, I loved—''

''But you weren't *in* love with him. You've never been in love with anyone. That's what I mean.'' He glanced behind them to the dock. ''Better make tracks before E.J. starts in on us.'' He pulled his cellular phone from his belt and switched it on. ''Lock'n load, pard. Do it, Barry. I intend to check on you frequently today.''

Brette grumbled, but mostly because she knew he expected her to. In the end, she took out her phone from the breast pocket of her denim shirt. ''Okay, it's on.''

''One more thing.''

''What?''

''Albert didn't go straight home.''

''You *followed* him?''

''He went to the feed store and bought a couple hundred pounds of lime.''

''I'm not following you.''

''That's what they used in Nam to make the bodies decompose faster.''

29

It took Brette several miles to get over the feeling that she was going to be ill. She didn't want to believe Tucker was right about the lime, but the more she thought about it, the more she had to acknowledge that Albert had both a motive and the privacy to have done in his own wife. As for temperament, that barely required analysis at all. She had only to remember his expression when he'd opened the door the other day. He'd looked ready to take a bite out of her throat—and he only disliked her. What if he'd felt used and betrayed?

Sheriff Cudahy needed to be told about this. But no doubt he wouldn't see the correlation, even if Tucker were to phone in the information, and he wasn't about to do that. Tucker avoided people wearing badges and guns as much as he did ministers and women looking for engagement rings. No, Brette thought, she would have to tell the sheriff herself—or find out what Albert had done with the lime.

Lost in thought, Brette didn't see Sally until she was stopped at their boxes. Sally was clutching her short robe around her and half running, half gliding stiff-kneed around the front of the truck to her window. The expression on her face told Brette that Hank had filled his mother in on everything he'd seen last night. Even so, Brette smiled as she handed over her friend's mail.

"I thought you'd be fast asleep by now," she told her.

"You wish." Sally snatched the bundle wrapped around a sales catalog. "Exactly how am I supposed to sleep when my so-called best friend is stabbing me in the back?"

They were fighting words, but Brette knew better than to take the bait. "I don't think I've done that Sal."

"No? What do you call running next door to wiggle your fanny at Sam the minute I leave for work? What do you call making a spectacle of yourself in front of my son?"

"Excuse me, but Hank was in the house with Eric. I didn't know he'd followed me outside. And I didn't intend for what happened to happen, it just—"

"Spare me. Next you'll blame Sam. Everyone's always at fault except Miss Perfect."

The sneer was decidedly unbecoming, but what concerned Brette more was the rising note of hysteria in Sally's voice. "I'm saying it happened, that's all."

"If Hank had been a minute later, he would have witnessed an even bigger show, wouldn't he?" Sally paused only to suck in a quick breath. "You should be ashamed of yourself. I trusted you. Here I am spilling out my heart to you about Sam day after day—"

"Wait a minute." Now this was getting a little melodramatic. "Sally, you fantasize about everyone—Keith, the doctors at the hospital, even the UPS guy. It's not as though you two had a relationship."

"I was working on it!"

"I'm sorry. Truly." But even before that kiss, it

was obvious to everyone that Sam wasn't remotely interested in Sally.

"How sincere. Are you also sorry for breaking my son's heart? Do you know what a hypocrite you look like to him now?"

The dig was meant to hurt—and did. "Me? How?"

"By pretending to be something you're not. A lot of things you're not."

This was going to need time, the one thing Brette didn't have at the moment. "Why don't we talk later, after you've had some sleep and I'm finished with—"

"You have nothing to say that I want to hear. Everything has to be on your timetable. Everything can be explained away by *your* logic. Bullshit! I'm angry *now,* and you're the one with the problem if you don't get that!"

"Oh, I get it, Sal. I just have an obligation to deliver this mail. If you want to talk like a reasonable, mature adult after I get back, fine."

"You bitch! *I'm* immature?" Red with indignation, Sally began to screech. "How dare you attack me! You—always dressing like a tomboy and trying to play catch and basketball with the boys so they'll think you're more fun to be around than me. You're the one who should grow up! But, no, you have to have all the attention. No wonder I don't have a better relationship with my son. You work overtime to show me up."

Sally was definitely racing full throttle into one of her tantrums.

The first time Brette had witnessed one, she'd thought she would have to call 911 for an ambulance. Bizarre had been the only way to describe it. The experience had been as terrible as it had been darkly comedic. Sally could turn a conversation 180-degrees in the opposite direction as well as her position on any given subject, all the while emotionally unraveling. She became like a toy wound too tight, unable or unwilling to stop. Brette couldn't let things go that far, at least not now.

So she shook her head adamantly. "We're not doing this. Excuse me, Sal...Sally! I have work to do. We'll talk later."

With that she eased the truck down to Sam's mailbox. As she reached for the lid, she received a sharp blow on her forearm.

Gasping in pain, she recoiled. "Will you stop!"

"Bitch-bitch-bitch! Don't you *ever* drive away from me again. Who do you think you are?" Using both hands, Sally began to swing at her with the mail. "You coward! Miss Goody Two-shoes! Always out to make people feel sorry for you. Sweet little Brette Barry can do no wrong, and all the while you've been conniving and cheating to take what's mine. No more. *No more!*"

Over and over again she whacked at Brette, sometimes only striking the roof of the truck, other times succeeding in getting inside the window to connect a blow. And all the while screaming. It was all Brette could do to protect her face, let alone not lose control of the truck.

Just as she felt her foot slipping on the brake, the attack abruptly stopped. Brette pushed her cap up off her eyes to see Sam dragging a kicking and screaming Sally away from her

"What the hell's wrong with you, Sally?" he demanded. *"Sally!"*

"Ask your *girlfriend*. And get your hands off me."

She jerked free and crushed her damaged mail to her chest. The robe had opened, but Sally was oblivious to how ridiculous she looked standing there in her black bra and panties. "You prick," she seethed at Sam. "I'm glad you're losing your job. I'm glad you're ruined here and that you're going to lose everything. You're exactly what she deserves—trash!" She spun on Brette again. "And you...you stay away from my son."

"Come on, Sally," Brette entreated. "If you want to be angry, be angry with me. Don't involve the boys. Hank and Eric—"

"Are through. Hank's tired of being treated like a charity case. We don't need you, so keep away or I'll call Cudahy and tell him how you've been abusing my son."

Brette couldn't believe she'd sink that low. "That's ugly, Sally, and a damned lie!"

"Find out what it feels like to be on the receiving end for a change."

"All right, you've flapped your mouth enough," Sam told her. He gave her a light push to prompt her. "Go home now, or I'll be the one to call Cudahy. Then you'll be answering to a charge of assault."

"As if he'd believe anything you say." Head high, she stormed away, her short robe flapping behind her.

Brette slumped back against the seat and closed her eyes. She couldn't stop shaking, and she had the strongest urge to cry. But they would have been tears of outrage as much as hurt.

A light caress along her arm drew her attention.

"That arm's going to look like a mess in a few hours. Maybe you should go get it X-rayed," Sam murmured.

"Nah. It's just bruised and scratched."

"Then come inside and get some ice for it."

"Thanks, but I'm late as it is." Now that the lunacy was over, her arm hurt. A lot. But she still couldn't let it stop her.

"Brette, I'm sorry. This wouldn't have happened if it wasn't for me."

She shrugged. "Sally periodically needs to let the pressure off."

"Don't make excuses for her. You heard what she said—she's determined to hurt you by turning Hank against you."

She shot him a dry look. "It's pretty clear he won't need much prompting. He's furious with me, too."

"He has no right to be. You're the one hope that kid has of pulling his life together and making something of himself. He should get that by now."

Brette ducked her head. She heard the passion behind the words and knew how dangerously susceptible she'd become to him. She couldn't afford that anymore. Too much was happening.

"I have to go," she whispered hoarsely. "Thank you for what you did."

"Look at me, Brette."

The gruff murmur had the same effect as his touch. She wanted it, wanted him so badly that fresh tears burned in her eyes. She could only shut them tight and shake her head.

"All right, don't look, but listen," he continued. His tone was soothing, seductive. "I wish I could do more. I wish you could count on me. For as long as I'm here, believe that you can. Please."

What a relief that would be. Being the sole parent, the sole everything, had never bothered her until lately. Sam made her realize how good it would be to have a partner, someone to hold you in moments when everything seemed too hard and too hopeless. But before she could say anything she heard a vehicle.

She looked up and saw Albert Pugh coming toward them in his pickup.

30

Sam stiffened. Tracie's husband was coming at them and there was no way Sam could avoid being spotted. And then what? Was it too much to hope that Tracie hadn't talked about him the way she did everyone else?

Sure enough the white truck slowed as it approached them and Pugh gave him the kind of narrow-eyed stare that left nothing to the imagination.

Christ, she had said something, he realized.

Sweat broke out along his back. Sam bent lower to see Brette's reaction, only to find her staring at the man, too. Her expression of abject horror was equally disturbing.

Pugh then gunned the engine and roared away.

Exhaling shakily, Brette leaned forward to rest her head against the dashboard. When Sam realized she was hyperventilating, he placed his hand against the back of her neck and found it clammy.

"What is it? What's wrong?"

"Nothing. Just...a full morning, that's all."

"Brette, you're as rattled as I've ever seen you." Sam opened her door and, easing her back against the seat, reached across her to shift the truck into park. Then he brushed her flushed cheek with the backs of his fingers. "Tell me."

"It was seeing him again, so soon after—never mind. It's nothing. Silly."

"So soon after what?" Sam sensed it was something too important to let slide. And the look she shot him chilled his damp skin. "Brette, what happened? Did he pull something with you?"

"No. It was Tucker who saw him behaving... strangely."

The big hulk who came by occasionally to help Brette with large projects never failed to treat him as though he'd been caught urinating before a busload of little old ladies. "Your pal should invest in a mirror. He thinks everything and everybody but him is strange."

"He may be right this time. He said he saw Albert buying TV dinners and a man's magazine at the market."

"Uh-huh."

"See? I knew you wouldn't think it sounds like much. Neither did I at first. Then I thought about it. If you worked physically hard sixteen or more hours a day, would you be satisfied if your wife fed you TV dinners?"

"My ex could butcher a peanut butter sandwich, and something tells me that, even though she was no princess, Tracie wasn't any better," Sam replied. "Maybe the TV dinners were a treat for Albert."

"You don't have to pretend you're guessing. If you two were having an affair, it's none of my business."

"Isn't it?" When she continued to stare fixedly at the keyhole of the glove box, he sighed. "Your right, I shouldn't do that to you. You're emotions are being lambasted enough as it is. But Brette, c'mon. This doesn't make sense."

"It's not just his behavior at the market. Tucker said he also stopped and picked up a lot of lime."

"Lime?"

"From the farm supply store."

"I understand. But, again, I don't get it. I've just bought some, too." As she swung around to look at him, he gazed deeply into her eyes. "So what does that make me?"

31

His expression seemed sincerely puzzled, but Brette knew she'd delayed her departure long enough.

"I have to go." She leaned over and shifted into drive. "I'm so late Mrs. Petrie across from the country store will be phoning the office to see where I am." And that would trigger a chain reaction she didn't want to deal with.

Sam shut the door for her, only to lean inside the window again. "If you'd like to talk later—"

"I really have to work things out with Sally."

With that she murmured another "Thanks" and drove off.

He was gone by the time she delivered the Pughs' mail. She did see Sally watching at her doorway. There was no telling what conclusions she'd jumped to watching Sam linger to talk. But Brette was sure of one thing—it would provide more nails for the coffin of their relationship.

With that one cold certainty congealing in her chest, she focused on getting through the rest of her day.

Not surprisingly, Tucker was pacing along the dock when she finally got back to the office. After one glance, he insisted on unloading for her, but he didn't refrain from offering his unsolicited opinion of her appearance.

"You look like you were mauled by two women at a sample close-out sale. Look at that li'l ol' arm."

There was no need to explain what had happened because he'd called her minutes after she'd left her neighborhood. It was why he was still hanging around. Glad she didn't have to start from scratch, she only said, "I can't let her get away with it this time, Tucker. It's once too many."

"Then don't. It's about time the woman got her due."

"Wrong focus. If I give her the space she's demanding, it's as good as abandoning Hank."

"Like you have a choice? You think she's going to let you within a mile of the kid? She'd as soon see him in reform school. I know I'm only a guy, but that Sally strikes me as one vindictive bitch."

"Eric's going to suffer, too. They're best friends."

"Invite me to dinner and I'll keep his mind off that. About time he heard more of my war stories anyway."

"You don't like talking about them."

"So I'll make something up."

"I think, you just want to keep an eye on Sam," Brette intoned.

"That, too."

Immediately regretful, she pushed back her hat to massage her temples. "I should never have told you about the lime."

"Oh, sure. Better to let the cops find you planted under his azaleas six months from now, along with who knows how many other women."

''Whatever Sam is or isn't, no one is accusing him of being a serial killer.''

''Just keep the thought on a back burner and think about the way Albert looked at him.''

After the minimal amount of new mail had been cased and her electronic recorder turned in for the day's accounting, Tucker walked her back out to her truck.

''Sounds as though Albert knew about Tracie's affair with the Terminator, doesn't it?''

The thought that she had missed Tracie over at Sam's time and again irked Brette to no end. ''Maybe there wasn't an affair. Maybe the antagonism I sensed was from Tracie merely mentioning Sam once too often. Maybe she kept bringing up how good-looking he is. No man likes that being thrown in his face.''

''Oh, hell. He's not that good-looking.''

Brette smiled. ''So what am I supposed to feed you for dinner since it's clear I'm not going to convince you to go home?''

''Go light your grill. I'll stop and pick up some steaks. Have you got any fresh sweet potatoes?''

''At this time of year? Sure. Want them baked, mashed, in a casserole, what?''

''Baked, with all the trimmings.'' Tucker jingled his keys in his pants pocket. ''Afterward maybe I'll go down to see what's up in Pughville.''

''No way, Tucker. You so much as think that, you're officially uninvited.''

''You suggesting Fat Boy can't handle the mission?''

Brette checked her reply, recognizing that, beneath the teasing, Tucker was deadly serious. ''I simply refuse to lose any more friends this week. If you want to come, come to get Eric's mind off of Hank.''

''And yours off the Terminator?''

She would never underestimate him again. ''There's a sadistic streak in you that needs a hefty dose of some of grandmother's recipe, Tucker.''

''Pumpkin, all I'm saying is we're gonna cure you or quarter him. I promise you that.''

Not in one night he wasn't. ''I'm going home and putting on the sweet potatoes. If you plan on bringing beer, I'm giving you full warning, you're spending the night because I won't let you drink and drive.''

''Hot damn. I'm bringing a case.''

He brought a six-pack but didn't touch the first until the coals were hot and ready for the steaks. By then he'd interrogated Eric about Hank and school, and—no big surprise to Brette—Sam. Thanks to the continuing warm weather, she was able to listen with concern as well as unabashed curiosity from the open kitchen window.

As she had feared, Hank acted standoffish with Eric, no doubt due to getting an earful of fabricated injustices from his mother. Maybe it was just as well that he had left school early with Sally. The maroon Taurus was nowhere to be seen when she'd first come home, but it was back now. Had they been asked to go another round with the FBI? she wondered.

When Brette finished inside, she joined the guys outside to wait for the meat to cook, bringing a glass of wine for herself, a second beer for Tucker and a Dr Pepper for Eric. The sun was sinking fast, now only an orange glow coming through the dense woods. The long shadows were merging into an over-all duskiness.

As she listened to Tucker tell Eric of his latest experience with the rottweiler on his route that liked to chew on his tires, she glanced next door. Sam had been gone when she arrived home, and had yet to return.

"You didn't by chance see Mr. Knight at school today, did you?" she asked as soon as Tucker finished his story.

"No, but I was walking behind Mr. Glick and Coach Sandler in the hall just before seventh period, and overheard him say Sam was spotted walking into an attorney's office in town."

Standing guard over the grill, Tucker beamed. "Gee, I wonder why he needs one of those?"

"At the very least to find out what his rights are at school. Most likely to help look into suing to clear his name—"

"No doubt a short visit," Tucker drawled.

"—because if he doesn't, he'll be running for the rest of his life." Sitting beside her son on the picnic table bench, Brette shot her friend a look.

Beside her, Eric focused on linking the beads of moisture collecting on the outside of his can. "Has anyone seen Tracie around yet?"

Although Brette knew better than to be surprised at what Eric thought about when he grew quiet, she was. "I don't think so."

"If she was missing, someone would have said something, right? Albert Pugh for sure, huh?"

Beginning to follow his line of thinking, she nodded. "You'd think."

"So Hank was wrong to accuse Sam, right?"

"No doubt."

"Then why isn't Sheriff Cudahy going after Albert?" Eric demanded, finally turning to look at her.

Tucker hummed quietly as he flipped the steaks.

"No one's reported Tracie missing," Brette replied, trying to keep any emotion whatsoever out of her voice. It was important to her that Eric understand the facts and draw his own conclusions. "Thanks to his track record with the truth, as well as his behavior, Sheriff Cudahy isn't about to take Hank's word for anything. And Albert hasn't said anything about a missing wife. So for the moment, all Cudahy is interested in is that Sam didn't tell anyone about his past."

"But no one's seen Tracie! Doesn't anyone care?"

"Whoa, Sherlock." Brette shifted to rub his slender back. "Just because things appear one way, doesn't mean no one's paying attention. People are watching."

"Yeah, right. You, maybe. It'd take a satellite locked on the whole Pugh farm to tell what's going on down there. Why can't we sneak in and check if she's around?"

"There's a son a mother can be proud of," Tucker murmured.

Brette ignored him. "Eric, promise me that you'll avoid being anywhere in the vicinity of the Pughs or their place? We're talking lifetime grounding penalties here, pal."

"Okay, okay. Jeez, it was just wishful thinking." But, clearly upset, Eric worked his jaw. "It's not fair to Sam, though. Do you realize he'd be fine if it wasn't for Hank being stupid? If he'd had more time to prove what a neat guy he is, he wouldn't be going through this—this inquisition. Mom, when the Board meets next week, you're going to go...what do you call it? Testify for him, right?''

Here she was congratulating herself that her son didn't feel a need to indulge in the teenspeak so many of his peers used to confuse and aggravate their parents, and he had to blindside with a challenge to her ethics. ''I hadn't thought about it, hon.''

''That's a joke, right? You're the one with proof that he was helping search for Hank, and I know how he tried to work with him before and since. He's not the psycho they're making him out to be at school. I've never heard him yell or treat any kid rough. Know why? 'Cause he *knows* what anger can do. It's like you and guns, right Uncle Tucker? Because you've been to Nam, Mom says you're more respectful of guns than most people.''

''Watch how loud you say 'Uncle', kiddo.'' Tucker glanced around him as though there were spies lurking in the woods. ''You trying to ruin my reputation or something?''

It was, Brette thought, as smooth an avoidance as he could make to not defend Sam in any way. But just when she thought he had succeeded, headlights illuminated the area on their left as Sam's Suburban pulled into his driveway.

Delighted, Eric jumped up. ''Hey, Sam!'' he called and waved. Then he turned to Brette. ''Can he join us, Mom?''

32

"Oh, Eric—"

"We have plenty food."

"Of course, but maybe he doesn't want to."

"Sam!"

Eric ran to meet him where he hesitated in front of his truck. Brette watched in growing dismay as he put an arm around her son's shoulders and they headed back that way.

"There you go," Tucker drawled. "A pose perfect for a Father's Day card. He has balls, I'll give him that."

"Please behave," Brette whispered. "I know this isn't what you had in mind, but think of Eric's feelings."

Tucker spread his arms wide, his Miller Lite in one hand, the long grilling fork in the other. "Hey, am I complaining? This could be fun."

She couldn't respond because they were already within earshot, and then it was time to renew introductions. With that done, Brette politely assured Sam that he was welcome to stay.

"If you haven't eaten," she added. He was dressed more formally than usual. Although he'd removed his tie, the white shirt, navy blazer and gray slacks accented his fitness just as the outfit added a dignity and style that left her feeling untidy. Like Tucker, she still wore her work clothes. All she'd done was remove the cap and brushed her hair. "Maybe you already have?"

"No, I was tied up all afternoon."

He left it at that. After only the slightest awkward pause, Brette recovered. "Great. Then come on. There's plenty and it's ready, isn't it, Tucker?"

The rural mail carrier stabbed a burning steak. "As long as you don't want this baby that looks like a charcoal-crusted Angus. It's mine."

"Medium rare or medium is fine for me, thanks."

Tucker carried the steaks and Brette led the way opening the door for everyone. Sam brought up the rear and paused to whisper in her ear.

"Are you sure?"

He was so close, she could smell the lingering scent of his deodorant soap. "It's fine."

"How are you?"

"Fine."

They were inane responses to his sincere, almost gentle questions. She felt his disappointment like heat waves, but she couldn't help it. She wasn't prepared to see him again, to have him so close after what had happened that morning.

"What can I get you to drink?" she added quickly as she closed the door behind them.

He glanced at her barely touched Merlot. "A glass of that will work. Let me get it. You look as though you have enough to do."

His choice of wine reminded her that he'd once been married to a society princess. Why that bothered her, she didn't know. Her own family had been well respected, her father an executive vice president and one of the founders of a prominent Dallas bank, her mother a gifted gardener who ran her own exclusive nursery. As a result, class distinctions had never phased Brette. But as the unattractive *J*-word flittered through her mind, she decided to blame her disquiet on too many unanswered questions.

Thankfully, the next few minutes were filled with the business of final preparations, including adding a place setting to the table, which Eric did without being asked, and Brette pointing out the hutch to Sam, where her mother's wineglasses were kept.

"Your place looks even better on the inside," he said, returning to the counter to pour as she worked.

Brette removed the freshly browned dinner rolls to the serving basket and folded the linen napkin edges back over them. "Thanks. A lot of the ironwork and accessories came from my mother's shop. She specialized in custom decorating sunrooms as well as regular landscape design. She would have loved your addition to the house."

"You're welcome to a tour whenever you want one," he said quietly. Before she could reply, he continued in a normal voice, "So your mother was a professional gardener. That explains your green thumb."

At least that was a subject she could deal with. Brette smiled with pleasure. "It's a good thing I only have one kid to put through college, isn't it? Flowers…make me happy."

Sam merely stared at her.

"What?" she asked, immediately self-conscious.

"You're stunning when you smile."

Abruptly turning away, he joined the others at the

table. Brette had to grip the edge of the counter to wait for the room to fill with oxygen again.

"I noticed that Sally's car is still across the street," Sam said to Eric as he took the seat beside him. "Isn't she going to work tonight?"

"Guess not. She probably figures it's the only way to make sure Hank stays home." Eric had accepted the salad bowl from Tucker, filled his dish, and handed the bowl to Sam. A moment later Brette saw Eric and Sam reach for the same bottle of French salad dressing. It was a small thing, yet her heart skittered again as Eric grinned and withdrew his hand.

"Go ahead," he told Sam, then added, "His mom pulled him out of school early. Do you think the FBI wanted to talk to him some more?"

His eyes all but glowed with admiration. Consequently, her heart ached for the inevitable disappointment her son was apt to feel when things didn't turn out the way he hoped. Brette set the platter of corn on the cob and wrapped sweet potatoes on the table, then took her own seat between Sam and Tucker.

"It's feasible," Sam replied. "They're nothing if not thorough."

"You think?" Tucker interjected.

Hearing his note of sarcasm, Brette added quickly, "Maybe they'll recommend a therapist for him."

"And his mother." Eric's expression turned grim as he told Sam, "Did you see what she did to my mom's arm? Show him, Mom."

Flustered, Brette did well not to spill the salad she was spooning into her bowl. "He was there, dear. It was Sam who stopped her." She had told him the bare minimum of what had occurred after he'd noticed the bruising and scratches earlier.

The look Eric sent their neighbor reverberated with nothing less than hero worship. "Thanks."

"Anyone would have done the same thing."

"But you were there. If I'd been, I'd have wanted to flatten her."

"No you wouldn't." Sam passed the dinner rolls to Brette, holding her gaze. "Your mother raised you too well for that."

They might as well have been alone. She felt the caress of his eyes like a physical touch and knew if they had been alone, he would have kissed her. Dear God, why was he doing this to her now of all times?

Tucker cleared his throat and began to rise. "I've got a hangnail that's killing me. I think I need another brew."

"I'll get it," Brette said, glad for an excuse to get up.

"No, allow me."

Tucker followed her to the fridge. Hearing Eric begin to ask Sam something else, Brette whispered, "Don't be rude."

"Don't be stupid."

Things deteriorated from there. Although Tucker ate, he also chose to drink rather than converse. He didn't say anything else to Sam, and by the time Brette was serving the pear-and-custard tarts she'd made, he'd polished off the six-pack with such speed, he looked ready to topple out of his chair.

When Brette gave her son a pointed directive murmuring, "Homework," Eric reluctantly excused himself and retreated to his room.

Once he was out of sight, Brette's smile vanished and she started to rise, determined to take care of Tucker. Sam touched her arm.

''You want me to get him to the couch? Even if I can get him close to conscious, he's in no condition to drive.''

''He goes in his camper and I lock him in for the night.'' Brette knew that sounded hard-hearted and felt obliged to explain. ''Tucker's a sweet soul, but sometimes he has the instincts of a ten-year-old. He knows better than to do this to himself. He also knows if he gets in this condition, I won't let him use the guest room. I won't compromise Eric's safety or expose him to this kind of behavior. So the truck it is. I'll wake him in time to get home and shower before work.''

Sam's eyes warmed. ''You'd make a good drill instructor.''

''He's going to hate me like the original thing come morning.''

''Not likely. I suspect he'll remember it was his fault.'' Sam stood. ''You get the door, I'll get the train wreck.''

Tucker had to outweigh Sam by fifty pounds or more, but Sam got him to his truck and settled him on the sleeping bag the burly man kept there. Brette added a thick blanket she spotted under the bench seat, then locked up and pocketed his keys.

''You did that as though it's routine,'' Sam said, walking her back to her house.

''If it was routine, Tucker wouldn't be here at all and we probably wouldn't be friends. No, it was my letting you stay for dinner that convinced him getting soused was a good idea.''

Sam paused by her back stairs. ''Has it crossed your mind that he's in love with you?''

Brette shook her head, confident of that much. ''At

least not in the way you mean. War damaged Tucker. We're the closest to family he can handle right now. Maybe ever.''

"And I ruined things because I couldn't figure out a way to turn down Eric.''

"It meant a lot to him.''

Sam reached out and took her bruised hand. "It meant a lot to me, too.'' He unbuttoned the cuff of her denim shirt and, in the porch light, inspected the evidence of Sally's wrath. "I've often stood and watched you with the boys, watched you in there alone…envied what I saw. Thank you for not being too scared to let me experience it—once.'' He lifted her hand to his lips and kissed it, then buttoned the shirt back up.

"Why are you doing this now? Showing me this side of you?''

"I don't want you to remember only the bad when I'm gone.''

Despite being prepared for it, his admission jarred her. "So…you're leaving?''

"It doesn't look as though I'll have a choice.''

"You can fight. Isn't that why you went to that attorney today?''

Sam slowly let go of her hand. "Who told you?''

"Someone connected with the school saw you go into the law office. You know how small communities are. Nothing stays a secret for too long.'' Brette tilted her head trying to gauge what his closed expression hid. "So did you?''

"It doesn't look good. I'm too new. And Cudahy was right, I kept too much back.''

"Are you even going to show up to fight for yourself when the Board meets next week?''

He slipped his hands into his pockets. "Probably not."

"So that's it? You're going to forfeit everything you've begun to accomplish?"

Smoke hung like a dying breath in the air. In the distance a lone coyote called in the otherwise silent night.

"What do you want from me, Brette? One minute you can't get away from me fast enough, the next you're looking at me as though you can already imagine me inside you."

His brutal honesty came as a mixed blessing. The frankness brought yet another wave of heat to her face, but there was no denying that it allowed everything to be put on the table.

"Isn't that what you've done to me all along? From the day you moved in you've been giving me mixed signals. One day you can't bring yourself to say 'Good morning,' and the next you're turning on the charisma to scorch level."

Sam gave her the slightest of nods. "Guilty. You were my temptation, my gift to myself to reach for one more day. I used you to make myself keep trying to change, to evolve into the person I meant to be before—if my mother and Kell had lived.

"I lied to you about not being the man Cudahy described. After I lost my family, I did a downhill slide, a long and deep one. Even when I married, I was no prize. Oh, I worked hard. I got my degree, but that was just so I wouldn't have to sleep at night. Inside I was a volcano waiting to get another chance at the old man."

"What changed?" Brette asked, riveted.

"Putting that liquor cart through the glass door. In

that instant I knew I was only a step away from becoming my father's son in every sense of the word and it made me sick to my stomach. So I lost my son and my wife—though the truth is, I probably would have anyway thanks to the interference of her mother. But that's when I started trying to salvage what was left of my integrity.''

''I'd say you've done a pretty good job.''

''Then do yourself a favor and don't ask how often I've wanted to resolve a situation with my fists, like when Cudahy announced he was turning me in and when Glick looked down his anteater nose at me and acted as though I'd stolen money from the school district.''

''Anyone would have had that reaction.''

''Right. And they all come home and hammer the hell out of iron or wood to relieve their aggression.'' He shook his head. ''I can't beat it, Brette, so I'm going to stop wasting my time fighting for a job nobody wants me to have and give up the fantasy of you being my reward for keeping my head on straight.''

With the hint of a sad smile curving his lips, he reached over and, like the first time, put his finger under her chin to close her mouth.

''You like to do that, don't you?'' she managed to say though her throat was aching.

''Touch you? Very much.''

''I mean…never mind.''

''All right. I guess things were a lot simpler when you were just trying to keep me pigeonholed as your murderer.''

Blinded by tears, Brette reached back and gratefully grabbed on to the railing behind her. ''Damn you, Sam.''

33

"Did you sleep with him?"

"Shut up, Tucker."

Brette was angry. She'd managed not to cry herself to sleep after she'd walked away from Sam, but she didn't get any rest, either. Not even her journal could provide solace. In fact, she'd sat with it for over an hour before realizing she hadn't written a word.

"That's a nice way to talk to the guy who brought the steaks."

"If you hadn't gotten drunk, you'd have noticed that I repaid you and put the money in your jeans pocket. Check them before you throw them in the washing machine."

"Aw, what did you do that for? I wasn't complaining." He tried to take the load of parcels she was carrying out to her truck, but she brushed him off. "Hell, I'm the one with the hangover, what are you ticked about?"

"The fact that you got drunk without thinking of the impression you'd make on Eric. And that, had you been awake, maybe I wouldn't have had to listen to what I did."

Tucker followed her outside like a hound on a scent. "What? C'mon, Brette, what did you hear?

Holy—okay, okay," he mumbled at her sharp look. "I'll watch the language."

"Better yet, go handle your own deliveries. You won't finish before two-thirty, either, and that's if you're lucky."

Fridays were often busy for them, and with the holiday season cranking into gear, this one promised to be a full day. That's why she'd wakened Tucker at five instead of five-thirty to give him time to get home and shower. Even so he'd only just arrived.

"I want to know, did something happen? Knight tried to pull something, didn't he?"

Brette set the box on the edge of the dock, jumped down and carried it to her pickup. "I don't want to talk about it, Tucker."

She'd had it. In the span of one week she'd gone from being a happy mother and friend to a nervous wreck who was doubting herself on virtually everything important in her life. And why? For the two dumbest reasons on the planet: because she'd tried to do the right thing, and because she cared.

A lot of good any of that had done her.

Well, no more. She was going to become like the bulk of the population who minded their own business and didn't give a fig about anything but their own wallet. She would give that attention and energy to creating a great home for her son and herself. In fact, Eric had been asking to go skating. Maybe she would take him to the Galleria in Dallas after she got off tomorrow. They could get a room at the hotel there and take in a movie, too. Make a real weekend out of it.

And leave Hank out here by himself?

Groaning inwardly, Brette headed back inside.

There was no way she would abandon Hank, no matter how offended she was with Sally.

She returned inside to see Tucker had taken her advice and was hard at work.

Desiree approached her wheeling over the next cart full of parcels.

"More bad news," Desiree told her. "Dese all yours."

The gods were definitely in a mood, Brette thought. She was sure of it when she saw who the first one went to.

"Oh, no."

Tucker glanced over his shoulder. "Am I allowed to ask what's wrong?"

"This package is for Sally and it's C.O.D."

"Sorry."

But that wasn't the worst of it—there was another for Tracie Pugh.

"That does it," Tucker said when he leaned over and saw the shipping address. "I'm asking E.J. if we can switch routes today."

"Nope. I'm handling this all by myself and if someone doesn't like it, tough."

A new determination took hold of her. Maybe this was a sign that things were about to change for the better. Maybe yesterday had been that blackest moment before the upswing. Maybe today Sally's ice would crack a little and Tracie...Tracie would answer the door.

Brette warmed to the idea as she set off less than a half hour later. By the time she reached her street, she felt better than she had since leaving the post office the day before. When Bertrice rushed out flagging her down with a kitchen towel, she found it easy to smile back.

"Hi! Another gorgeous Indian Summer day, isn't it?" she said to the older woman.

Bertrice pressed the towel to her heaving chest. "If I get a second to enjoy it. Sweetie, would you by chance have a spare stamp on you? I plum forgot my telephone bill this month. Retired from the danged place and I forgot, can you believe it? I'm so embarrassed. It's due today."

"Give it here, I'll take care of it."

"Wait, I have the correct change right here in my—"

"Don't worry about it, Bertrice. It's my personal emergency stamp that I keep in my glove compartment for just these kinds of occasions. It'll be our secret."

"You're too good. Well, will you take this and bring me a book of twenty stamps tomorrow?"

Brette took the orange order envelope and nodded. "Sure. How're things going in there? Clovis watching TV?"

"No, he's practicing his speech therapy, can you believe it? For months I was trying to get him to work with the therapist and he acted like that old hound we used to have that insisted on lying over in the middle of the highway up yonder. Stubborn as anything. Now suddenly he wants to stop slurring and spitting on everything."

"That's great! So he's working with the tapes that last lady left him?"

"About to wear the things out—or my ears. I've gotta get back, sweetie pie. Have a carrot cake in the oven. Say, why don't you stop by on your way home and pick up half for you and that handsome boy of yours?''

"I have a better idea. Why don't we stop by after dinner tonight for a few games of Parcheesi and you can feed it to us then?''

"Oh, can you spare the time?'' Bertrice tucked the towel under her chin, and her dark eyes sparkled with excitement. "That will make Clovis's day when he hears.''

"It's been too long,'' Brette said in agreement. "Now maybe he'll save some of his energy and your eardrums.''

"Wait just a sec and I'll dash inside to give you money to get some ice cream to go with it.''

"Uh-uh. We'll bring it ourselves. Say six-thirty?''

"The lights'll be on and the door open. Oh, Brette, how *nice*.''

Yes, it would be nice, Brette thought as she waved goodbye and pulled away. Eric wouldn't mind, either. He missed having grandparents, and he was fond of Bertrice's baking as much as he was of Clovis who'd taken him fishing several times before the stroke.

See? she thought to herself. If you went with the flow and thought positive thoughts, you could effect a change.

Feeling increasingly hopeful, she drove down to Sally's and pulled into the driveway behind the maroon Taurus. She hoped this was one of those days when Sally was late going to bed, but a glance at her watch told her better; she hadn't left the post office until nearly eight-thirty.

There was no answer to the first ring of the doorbell, nor the second or third. Starting to worry that something was wrong, Brette knocked hard on the storm door. There was always the chance that Sally had taken something too strong.

"Sally! It's me. I have a delivery."

Finally she heard a crash and a curse. Then the locks turned and the door opened.

"Why couldn't you leave the damned thing?" Sally snapped even before she opened the storm door.

So much for positive thinking, Brette thought, her friendly smile waning. "Because it's C.O.D." She indicated the amount to her puffy-eyed neighbor. "It's $21.95."

"Shit."

Sally dropped the storm door and stumbled away. Hoping it was to look for her checkbook, Brette stayed put remembering the days when she would have happily delivered the box to her own house and written the check so that her friend could sleep. But there was no way she would risk that now. In Sally's current mood, she was apt to report Brette for not following instructions just out of spite.

Finally Sally returned, thrust the check at her without comment and grabbed the box.

"Listen," Brette said, handing over the pen and clipboard with the form requiring a signature. "Bertrice is having Eric and I over for dessert and a board game tonight. Would it be all right to take Hank with us?"

Her lips tightly pursed, Sally scrawled her name and slammed the door in her face.

"At least she didn't teach me a new four-letter word," Brette muttered under her breath.

Starting back to her truck, she spotted Sam. He stood in the doorway of his shop watching. When he saw she'd noticed him, he bowed his head and returned to his work.

"Old Warren was on target," she said to herself. She'd laughed and thought of Sally when she first read the quote in former President Harding's biography. The gist of it was about friends and enemies, the latter part ending with, "My damn friends. My goddamn friends. They're the ones that keep me walking the floor nights." She didn't much feel like laughing now.

After stuffing her mail in her box and delivering Sam's, she drew a deep breath and drove over the cattle guard into the Pughs', trying to let the view calm her. It was a gorgeous day and the farm reflected that, the pasture a jewel green, the surrounding woods a sea of pine greens and amber. The hardwoods weren't quite as richly toned as those in New England or Colorado, but the way things were going, East Texas would have its finest colors in years for the various autumn trail rides and festivals that were soon to start.

Brette noticed that there was no truck parked down by the trailer. Shifting into park, she scooped up Tracie's package and climbed out of her truck.

After knocking, she glanced around. The milking was over, of course. She could see the cows scattering in the southwest pasture. She could hear some machinery still running, but nothing as loud as the other day.

No one came to the door, so she knocked again...and began thinking of her options. She could leave a note advising Tracie that a delivery attempt had been made, advising that she would try again tomorrow, or that the package would be waiting at the post office. She could also drive down to the other house and see if Tracie was there.

None of those options appealed to her since all meant either missing an opportunity to see the woman herself, or worse yet, settling for Albert or Truman handling the matter. Opportunity, Brette decided, came when it came.

She reached for the doorknob and turned.

It was unlocked. She pulled the metal door open—and gasped.

What a mess! It wasn't your normal, sloppy-housekeeper type of mess. Tracie was a lot of things, but not that, as far as Brette could tell. This was the kind of disaster scene you made when moving. Boxes were stacked in the middle of the living room floor and the ones on top were filled to overflowing. That's when she realized the contents were all women's things—clothes, purses, shoes....

"What the hell do you think you're doing?"

With a yelp, Brette backed off the lowest step and almost lost her balance. But the momentum had the door swinging wide and banging against the outside of the trailer.

"I...sorry, Albert. I have this C.O.D for Tracie and—"

He slammed the door shut and snapped, "Take it back!"

"But—"

"Take the damned thing *back*. I don't want it."

"But Tracie ordered it."

"Tracie's not here."

"Okay." Brette tried not to visualize Albert phoning the office and reporting her infraction. "Well, I suppose I can hold it for her a day or two until she returns.''

''She won't.''

Lord almighty. Brette had to lock her knees to keep from backing toward the truck. ''I don't understand.''

''We've split. She's gone.''

''I...see. Do you by chance know—''

''Why the hell should I know, or care!'' Albert pointed to the box. ''I do know I don't want that. I ain't paying one more cent for her shit.''

''Okay, sure.'' Brette's heart pounded as she climbed into the truck. ''Ah...do you want me to bring you a change of address card for her other mail?''

''No.''

''But we can forward this and everything else that's in her name to her new address.''

''That's her problem.''

''Well, actually, it's yours, too, if I deliver mail addressed to her here and you accept it when she's no longer a resident. If you'll give me her family's address—''

''She didn't have no family. Now leave me the hell alone.''

''But Albert, by law—''

Glancing around, he suddenly picked up the cinderblock by the stairs and raised it over his head.

34

"**I**'ve never been so frightened in my life. Well, except for last week when I saw that print."

"So Albert and Tracie really have split," Tucker drawled on the other end of the connection.

"*He* says. What if he's lying?"

"He's packing her stuff in boxes, you said it yourself. Next Monday or Tuesday you'll see the UPS guy rambling down there to pick it all up to ship it to her. Where are her folks from? I forget."

"That's because she probably never told you or anyone. Albert says she has no family."

"Lucky bastard."

"Seems like it. Where is she, Tucker?"

"Ask Albert. Ask your boyfriend."

That had Brette gripping her cellular phone more tightly. "You want to hear dead air space?"

"No, let me think. Maybe you should call Cudahy."

"With what?"

"Albert admitted she's gone."

"And Cudahy's going to investigate a man divorcing his wife? I think not."

"Cripes! He threatened you with a stinking cinderblock!"

There was that. Then again, that was almost normal

behavior for Albert. Social he wasn't. Besides, she had snooped in his home without permission. Did she want Albert telling Cudahy about *that?*

"Let me sleep on it, Tucker. I only called you so that you'd know."

"Sure. Thanks for putting the burden of worrying about your butt again on me."

"He's not going to do anything." Brette brushed the crumbs from her sandwich off her lap. "I was there on authorized business. He knows all fingers would point to him if he did something."

"Yeah...unless he could compromise your neighbor. Remember that look Albert gave him. Knight must be lying about not having an affair with Tracie."

Brette thought of Sam's admission last night. If he had slept with Tracie, then he would have to be lying to *her,* and all her instincts told her that he wasn't. Maybe that made her gullible and a fool; certainly, she would never convince Tucker.

"You're awfully quiet, Barry."

"Ah...nothing. Listen, Eric and I will be out this evening. Just in case you planned to call. We're going to the Ponders' for a while. You behave and don't stir the pot until we talk some more, okay?"

"Not me. I'm picking up a pizza, going home and dropping my svelte self in bed."

Brette smiled, her annoyance with him forgotten. "Stop feeding my fantasies."

The rest of the day passed without incident and Brette returned home just as Eric and Hank were disembarking from their school bus. Neither boy acknowledged the presence of the other, but Hank did hesitate when he caught sight of her. Then he glanced over at his house and, seeing Sally at the door like a watchdog, continued home.

Interesting, Brette thought. At least he wanted this cold war to be over and wasn't totally buying into Sally's attitude.

"How'd it go?" she asked Eric as they entered the house.

"If you mean Hank, not so good. He's talking about leaving again."

"Not to go back to Saint Louis?"

"Nah."

"Well, his father doesn't want him. What's the plan?"

"He's just talking, Mom. He figures if I'm listening, you'll find out and convince Mrs. J. to let him back here again."

"For a guy who shares her blood, he doesn't know his mom too well." She stroked her son's soft hair suddenly missing the days when he was little and wanted long hugs. "You're developing a good insight into human nature, though."

He shrugged. "Common Sense 101."

"Aha." Setting the ice cream and mail on the counter, Brette faced him fully. "Well, 101, I have a combination proposition and request to throw your way concerning this evening."

"I'm not going next door to bring Hank a home-made dinner after Sally leaves. He knows where we are and what he has to do."

"Stop, you're scaring me with all this wisdom. How about a few rounds of Parcheesi with the Ponders? I told Bertrice we'd come by after dinner."

"That means I don't have to eat her raw liver. *Yes!*"

"Back in the old days when they didn't pump all kinds of steroids and whatnot into cattle, eating it rarer was healthier, my dear. You like your steak pink."

"But not bleeding. I take it she's making dessert?"

"Carrot cake. That's what this ice cream is for."

"I can handle that."

"Brave man."

"You have two sixes, Clovis. Go, darlin'."

Whining in his excitement, the elderly man took hold of his game piece and began to count the placements on the board. He needed to be corrected once, but he made it two steps into home base with that one. His other piece got within three spaces from home, putting him in the best shape of all of them.

As he raised his fists over his head à la *Rocky,* Bertrice chuckled. "Worse than a kid. I'm so glad you came tonight, Brette. You and Eric are better than any medicine."

"We're glad, too, aren't we, big guy?"

Eric pretended to scowl at Clovis as he scooped up the dice and shook them in his cupped hands. "I think he's cheating. I feel frosting on the dice."

As both women laughed, he threw the dice and howled when he, too, came up with twin sixes.

"See!"

It had been a nice evening, and Brette had enjoyed watching her son lap up the attention of both Ponders who wanted all the news from school and his other activities. She was also relieved to have a respite from thinking about everyone's troubles.

"Who wants another piece of cake?" Bertrice asked when the uproar died down.

"I'm stuffed, thanks," Brette replied. "Besides, it's getting late. I really do need to be getting home and to bed."

"Can I have a piece for breakfast, Mrs. B.?" Eric asked.

"Goes without saying, angel. I already—"

A knock at the front door stopped her. They all looked at each other in startled silence. It was almost ten o'clock—far too late for visitors.

Brette rose. "I'll get it."

As soon as Brette came around the corner of the dining room, she saw who stood on the other side of the storm door.

Sam. Her heart kicked into immediate overdrive, but she tried to tell herself it was because of his grim, troubling expression.

She unlocked and opened the door. "Is there something the matter?"

"I was just coming home and I saw your truck. Brette, do you know you have a flat tire?"

"That can't be. I just replaced all four of them last month."

"Well, the front driver's side is sitting on the rim." He lowered his voice. "Brette, it looks as though it's been slashed."

She rushed past him and raced down the incline he'd built for Clovis. He followed, but she was barely aware of him. All she was focused on was the word *slashed.*

Sam had his truck parked in the middle of the road beside hers and running to keep his headlights illuminating the area. Sure enough, she saw that the front left tire was a disaster.

"Of all the—" Her hands on her hips, she spun

away to look down the dark road and then back at her tire. "That stinking creep!"

"You know who did this?" Sam asked.

"Do I ever. Albert. It has to be. He got angry with me earlier today and this is exactly the kind of thing he would pull to let me know I should be afraid of him."

Sam's nostrils flared as he drew in a slow, deep breath, but he retained his cool. "What happened? I knew you'd gone down in there, but when I saw you leave a while later, I figured everything was okay."

"Hardly." She shared a brief recap of the experience.

"Why didn't you report that?" he demanded.

"To what end? He had me cold, Sam. My fingerprints were all over that doorknob. Wouldn't Cudahy love that one?"

Groaning, Sam rubbed his eyes with his hands. "What am I going to do with you?"

"Excuse me, but if memory serves, I am not your problem." He'd made that abundantly clear last night.

"Want to bet?"

Before she could reply, Eric came running out of the house. Bertrice and Clovis weren't far behind.

"What's up, Mom? Sam? Holy cow!" He gaped at the tire. "How'd that happen?"

"You don't want to know," Brette muttered.

"I'll change it for you," Sam said. "Where's your spare?"

"Actually I keep two. The easiest to reach is in the camper, but you don't have to—"

"I'm changing the damned tire, Brette."

She didn't want to argue in front of the others, and instead focused on Eric, who demanded to know why

Albert should be mad at her. She barely finished assuring him that it was no big deal when Keith came out of his house.

"Wow," he said frowning at the tire Sam was working on. "That was some nail you hit."

"It was a knife," Eric replied. "Albert Pugh is threatening Mom."

His anger left his young voice shaky. Keith put a reassuring arm around the boy, but his concern was directed at Brette. "You mean what you told me this morning got him that upset?"

She almost cringed when Sam shot her a sharp glance over his shoulder. It had been a harmless, unconnected moment. Keith had run out and caught her as she'd come back up the road meaning to give her yet another piece of mail. Seeing her pale face, he had pressed to know what had upset her. She'd forgotten the episode until now.

"You need to call the sheriff's department," Keith told her.

"I can't."

"Because...?"

She wasn't about to explain in front of the others. "Look, he's made his point and it's out of his system. If I call in the law, it'll just make him do something else. This is elementary school nonsense. You push me, I push you."

Keith pushed up his glasses, his expression rueful. "Well, you have the juvenile mentality bit right."

"I think it's awful," Bertrice cried. "This has always been such a nice quiet street. Why doesn't that awful man go away! I always thought it was him that ran over our Butterball."

Brette hugged her and urged her back to the house.

"You two don't need to be exposed to this humid air. See there? Sam's got this under control. He'll be finished in a minute and we'll be going."

Agreeing, Bertrice urged Eric to go inside with them to get his cake. Brette used the time to quietly interrogate Keith.

"Did you hear any vehicles drive by in the last few hours?"

"A couple, yeah."

"A diesel?" She knew that's what Albert drove.

Keith scrunched his shoulders in a movement not unlike a turtle. "Thanks, Brette. Go ahead and expose my vast knowledge of automotives. It could have been a diesel, but would I swear to it? Nope. I simply wasn't paying attention."

"While you're narrowing your field of suspects, don't forget one of those vehicles passing was me," Sam told them. "I ran over to Mineola to pick up more sanding pads and shellac for tomorrow. It's all in the front seat if you need confirmation."

His sarcasm was unmistakable and Keith was the first to reassure him. "I'm sure I heard more than one truck pass. Honest. Only...Brette, don't hate me for this, but have you considered maybe that Hank, well, you know..."

She didn't understand at first, but she caught on quick and wrapped her arms around herself, troubled by the idea. "Dear God, I don't want to believe he would pull something this...nasty. Besides, he didn't know where we were going when we left. He would have to have been out just wandering around, and Eric's right about him being afraid of the dark. There would have to be a strong motivation."

"You said yourself that he was thinking of running

again. What if—hey! You're shaking.'' Keith immediately put his arms around her and began rubbing her back. ''Hell, I'm sorry, Brette. That was tactless of me.''

''Smartest thing you've said yet,'' Sam muttered.

Having finished with the tire, he lowered the hydraulic lift he'd taken from his truck and returned everything to its proper place. By the time he put the ruined tire in the camper, Eric had returned.

Brette urged him into the truck and said good-night to Keith. ''I appreciate the good intentions, really.''

''I shouldn't have said anything.''

''No, you made me realize that I should check on Hank when I get back to the house. I had myself convinced that when he's talking it's just that. It's when he stops talking I usually worry. But situations change people.''

Keith kissed her cheek. ''Be careful. And call me if you need help.''

As he jogged back to his place, Brette steeled herself for Sam's criticism. To her amazement, he merely wiped his hands on an industrial hand towel he'd brought from his truck and said, ''I'll follow you and check around your house while you see about Hank.''

''I'm sure there's no need.''

''Unlike Daggett, I'm not content to wait for a phone call, all right?''

Crushing the towel into a ball, he strode to his truck leaving Brette to stare after him. Lord have mercy, she thought, he's jealous. But instead of being flattered, her heart wrenched painfully in her chest, because whether he was or not, he wouldn't let his feelings for her matter.

Mentally exhausted, Brette climbed in beside Eric and started home.

"What a bummer," he murmured.

"Won't argue with you there."

"And it had been fun tonight."

"I'm glad you thought so, babe. You remember that and try to overlook the rest."

"Do you really think Han— Yuck. Smell that?"

You couldn't miss it. The closer they got to the house, the stronger the smell grew. A skunk was in the vicinity.

"Jeez, I hope we don't come face-to-face with it on our way inside," Eric muttered.

Brette was grimacing by the time she pulled into their driveway and shut off the engine. Even though she'd left on the outside lights, she reached under her seat for her Halogen flashlight. "Here are the keys. Let yourself in and I'll see if flashing this thing around will scare it out of here."

"Smells as though he got run over in front of the house."

Eric launched himself out of the truck pinching his nose with his left hand and carrying the cake and keys in his right. As he ran, Sam came over from his yard scanning the area with his own flashlight.

"When it rains it pours, I guess," he drawled. "I haven't spotted anything yet, have you?"

"No, but it has to be close."

"Hopefully, we scared it off driving in."

No sooner did he say that than Eric came bursting out of the house. "Mom! Come quick!"

35

Eric ran to them gagging and coughing. Brette met him halfway.

"What's wrong?"

"It's in the house!"

"The skunk?"

"No, the smell. I mean it, it's worse in there than it is out here. It has to be inside."

Sam gripped Brette's arm. "Did you have your air conditioner on?"

"Yeah, it was too warm and muggy to leave the windows open. Why?"

"I don't hear it running. Maybe we've located the problem. You'd better keep back. I'm going to get some gloves and things. If it's still in there, it'll be bad enough if I get sprayed, I sure as heck don't want you two worrying about rabies."

It took Brette a moment to realize what he meant. The air conditioner—he thought the skunk was in the unit!

"Stay here," she told Eric, and took off after Sam.

"There's no other way," he said as soon as he saw her. He'd emerged from his shop with heavy gloves, an empty fertilizer bag and a long-handled shovel.

"It's my headache, Sam. I should do it—and can."

"I know, but you also have to go to work tomorrow, while I have all the time in the world to soak in tomato juice if need be.''

He had a point. ''Then please be careful.''

Nodding, he replied, ''You'd better collect what clothes you need for the next day or two, open all the windows and be prepared to switch the unit to Fan when I tell you.''

''Wait a minute, clothes—whatever for?''

''You heard Eric. If the skunk's in the unit, the odor's being carried throughout the house. You won't get any sleep. And where else are you going to go, Brette? To Sally's? The Ponders' or Mr. I-Feel-Your-Pain Daggett's?''

''There's no need to be rude.''

''Somebody attacked you tonight. I'm not exactly in the mood to practice my social skills. You're coming over to my place. Or am I still on your short list of suspects?''

She met his challenging look. ''If you think that, you don't know me at all.''

''Then get your things,'' he said more gently.

She did, and directed Eric to do the same. The smell in the house was as bad as Eric said. She opened every window, grabbed clothes and toiletries, and was nauseous by the time she got outside. Eric was already leaning against the truck. To her surprise, Hank was beside him.

''Hey, Mama Two,'' he murmured shyly. ''Sorry about the trouble. Eric told me.''

''Thanks, Hank. Are you sure you should risk being out here? I'm thinking your mom's liable to check on you.'' She knew that from past experience, not so much because Sally was worried about him, but because she didn't trust him.

"You're still mad at me, huh?"

"About the other night? No, I understand, believe me. But it's been a rough day, and the last thing I want to have facing me is another round with your mother."

"Eric says you're going to go stay with him." Hank nodded to Sam's place with his chin. "I think you should come over to our place. Mom won't need to know. You get up early anyway, and Eric can leave the same time you do."

"And go where?" Besides, she would have to do some serious housekeeping at Sally's before she felt comfortable letting her son or herself lie down anywhere over there. "Not a good idea, hon, but I do appreciate the thought. You didn't by chance see anyone around here earlier, did you?"

"You mean did I hear one of the Pughs go by? Sorry. I had my headphones on and was watching ESPN."

"Okay." She squeezed his shoulder. "Miss you, guy."

"Miss you, too." But Hank didn't leave. He clearly had something else to say. "I think...I think she's starting to feel sorry."

It wasn't much, but Brette smiled and gave him a hug. "Thanks."

With a reluctant look toward Sam, Hank added, "And I still don't like him."

The boy was nothing if not focused. "You know what's interesting, though? Under different circumstances, you probably would because you two have a lot in common."

Hank didn't respond to that, but he didn't seem

offended, either, and he returned to his house shortly thereafter.

Brette and Eric watched and waited for a sign from Sam. It seemed a small eternity, but finally he backed away from the air-conditioning unit, holding the bag with one hand and supporting the bottom with the blade of the shovel. He kept the thing as far in front of him as he could, his movements further hampered because the flashlight was in the same hand as the shovel and badly aimed. Nevertheless, he headed out back into the woods where she heard more than saw him dig a hole and bury the whole thing.

Once he returned, he paused by his shop to drop off his shovel.

Brette and Eric went to join him. "Where are your gloves?" Eric asked him.

"Had to bury them, too. That poor varmint didn't die pretty."

"Oh, barf," groaned Eric.

"It was a young one," Sam told Brette. "Got in through a dislodged panel in the housing and it was killed when the fan went on. I'll be able to tell more about damage in the morning."

"With everything going on I didn't think about that." Following Sam's lead, Brette and Eric started toward Sam's. Along the way she dealt with the realization that this could mean a whole new cooling unit. It was ten years old. Fortunately she could afford replacing it; however, it was one more thing than she wanted to deal with right now.

"Don't start worrying until you have to," Sam said when she remained quiet. He opened the door to the sunroom for them.

"All I want to think about is a shower and bed."

Eric sniffed once he stepped inside. "Boy, it smells a thousand per cent better in here, doesn't it, Mom?"

"Yes—and it's beautiful, Sam."

She wanted time to linger, to inspect everything and ask him about his own green thumb. For instance, had he bought that ficus that was at least ten feet tall, or had he grown it from something much smaller? And were the banana trees in a long wooden planter, some of which almost touched the top of the sloping glass ceiling, going to produce fruit? In between a dozen other specimens was a couch and a huge rocking chair. Against the wall by the door was a workbench with assorted tools. Most of the lighting in the room came from the growing lamps built on the backside of it. Several cactus were on the table.

"For the cactus garden?"

"If they adapt to this environment. I've lost a few already. They seem better suited to being outside, only I don't think they'd winter well out there." Once again Sam beckoned them through another door, this one wood and leaded glass, that led into the house.

"Cool," Eric said, inspecting his surroundings as avidly as Brette.

The outside still needed a lot of work, but the kitchen and dining area was gorgeous—as rich and intense as hers was light and airy. It was a huge room, yet the honey-toned wood cabinets, copper appliances and red tile floor created an intimate haven.

"I saw you bring this in," Brette said of the round wood dinette table surrounded by four straight-backed chairs. "It was in pieces and didn't look anything like this."

"Yeah, it was a steal. Slightly water damaged in a

fire—and heavy. I took it apart in order to get it here.''

He'd moved everything in by himself, except for the things that had been delivered from the furniture store in Tyler. That had been another reason she'd gone over to introduce herself. She'd thought she and Eric could help.

''I can't wait to see the rest of the place,'' she replied.

''Don't expect too much. Nothing's as finished as this, but the bedrooms upstairs are painted. Eric, why don't you take the guest room, first door on the left. It has a connecting bathroom. Brette, you can have the master bedroom at the end of the hall on the right.''

''Oh, no, I couldn't. Besides, I'm up early, and I don't want to wake you.''

''Most of my things are down here in the office. I tend to sleep in there or out with the plants.'' Winking at Eric's delighted expression, he led them beyond the stained-glass folding doors. The hallway went to the right. It was mostly a half wall that opened to a huge room with a stone fireplace at the far end. To the left was the stairway. ''Be careful going up. That old railing isn't reliable. Ah…there are fresh sheets on the beds, and essentials in the bathrooms. Feel free to hunt for whatever you need.''

''Sounds great to me,'' Eric said, stifling a yawn. ''See ya.''

He started up the stairs, but Brette lingered. ''You've been wonderful to us.'' She spoke quietly despite knowing her son tended to go deaf when he started yawning.

''You won't be nervous here?''

It was then that she realized the full extent to which she'd hurt him with her doubts and suspicion. "No, Sam."

He looked intent on saying more, but to her surprise only added, "Try to get some rest." Then he was gone.

It felt as though he took all the oxygen with him. Brette understood and knew it would only get worse to be around him and not imagine...more.

You'd better move or you won't make it out of bed in the morning.

Sam was right about the upstairs not being as finished but, considering that he'd only been living here for six months, she thought it remarkable that he'd accomplished as much as he had. Everything looked freshly painted a clean, soft white and the hardwood floors were waxed.

Brette knocked lightly on Eric's door. "Okay in there?"

He opened up and immediately pointed with his thumb over his shoulder to the window covered simply with white miniblinds. "I can see Hank's place for a change."

"Not when your eyes are closed."

She glanced around and saw that Sam wasn't being overly modest. Besides the lack of draperies, there was only a full-size bed and a nightstand with a wood-and-brass lamp she suspected he had made.

"Just kidding, Mom. Hey, what do I do tomorrow while you're on your route? Do you think our place will be okay by then?"

She didn't see how it could be, but she also didn't think Sam's generosity included watching over her son while she worked. "I may have to wake you and

take you with me. It might be the smarter idea anyway, what with Albert acting up the way he is.''

''Aw, Mom, it'll still be dark.''

''All the more reason to get to sleep. Night, babe.''

Brette closed the door behind her and carried her
tote down to the master bedroom. It was no more
personalized than the room Eric was in, but she loved
the spaciousness of it, the possibilities. The bed was
king-size, exactly what a man Sam's size needed. She,
however, would feel lost in there alone.

''Don't even go there,'' she muttered to herself and
went to take her shower.

Her hair was still dripping wet when Brette went
downstairs. She really had to talk to Sam.

Unfortunately, he wasn't in the kitchen and the
door leading to the sunroom was locked.

''Something wrong?''

She spun around. He was barely more than a silhouette in the dim light coming from the growing
lights through the half glass door, but she could tell
he'd already showered, too, and had slipped into fresh
jeans. Barely.

He did his share of staring, too, making her feel as
though the sleep shirt she was wearing was sorely
inadequate. She had to make a conscious effort not to
cross her arms over her breasts.

''Sam…I know I have no right to keep burdening
you with our problems, but I need help. I can't wake
Eric before daylight and haul him around with me on
my route. There's no room in the front and sticking
him in the camper isn't fair—virtually impossible if
I have a lot of packages to deliver. At the same time
you said the house would probably be uninhabitable

for a while. Is there any way he can stay with you? It's a lot to ask, I know, but despite what I said before, I am worried about Albert. It would give me great peace of mind if I knew you were keeping an eye on him."

"You'd trust me with him?"

She bowed her head. "I deserve that, but you did scare me at first. Sometimes I think intentionally." Slowly, she met his gaze again. "Yes, I trust you. More than I do anyone."

For a moment the only sound was the air conditioner cycling. Then Sam nodded. "He'll be safe here."

She had the craziest impulse to tear up again. Proof, she knew, of how much stress she'd been under lately. "Thanks."

There was no longer any excuse to linger, and yet she didn't budge. He didn't, either...and the silence lengthened, began to pulsate between them.

"Not a good idea," he said at last.

True. Both of them were in too vulnerable a place to do anything so foolish; nevertheless, she stayed put.

"Damn it, I didn't bring you here for this."

That, too, she understood. It was probably the real reason why he was making himself sleep downstairs and had placed her as far out of reach as possible.

It was the sigh that told her he'd decided. It reverberated of need as much as defeat.

Finally he murmured, "Come here, Brette."

36

Part command, part entreaty, the words left Brette feeling as though she'd just touched a bare wire. "You don't want this," she reminded Sam—and herself. This would be the riskiest thing she'd ever done…well, since deciding on Eric. "You've told me—"

"I know. Heaven help me, I do. So why do I feel as though I'll bleed to death if I don't kiss you again?" His chest expanded as he drew a deep breath, but as though he didn't trust himself to speak again, he simply extended his hand.

She launched herself across the room, then he took over, locking her against him. He took her mouth with the same precision, their kiss triggering an explosion of passion while their arms and hands clutched tighter and tighter as though trying to complete the fusing of their bodies that heat had begun.

As Brette felt every inch of her body begin to melt, Sam groaned and broke the kiss to bury his face against the side of her neck.

"Oh, God…I want you."

She could feel how much from the subtle tremor in his body, as well as the dampness she felt wherever she touched him. "Then don't stop," she whispered.

He leaned back to look deeply into her eyes. "Damn it, Brette, it can't change anything."

"Ssh." She brushed her lips against his. "No more of that tonight. Just make love to me."

Before the next kiss ended, he had her in his room and was lowering her onto the freshly turned down sofa bed. The only light came from a black-shaded desk lamp across the room. It provided enough for her to see the strain and intent on his face as he retreated to strip off his jeans.

She'd always thought him impressive. Seeing the rest of him only reinforced that and had her impatiently reaching for him. However, he had other plans—like undressing her and then exploring what he exposed.

"You're adorable," he murmured, running his hand along the full, slender length of her body.

Then he did it again with his mouth. Brette died a little as he lingered over her breast, and a little more when he slipped his fingers inside her.

But this had been too long a fantasy to delay the inevitable. Mere seconds after she closed her hand around him, Sam swore and broke away, murmuring, "Let me get something."

Then he was burying himself inside her. She wrapped herself around him in the welcoming embrace of a longtime lover. And the rest was a dizzying rush of need, utterances of pleasure and desire, and ultimately the breathlessness of completion.

Brette wanted nothing more than to keep her eyes closed and savor the sensations that continued to wash over her like the relentless tide. For years she'd believed there was something wrong with her. That, while capable of caring deeply, she somehow lacked the ability to feel real passion. Now she knew better. The revelation was a mixed blessing, though, for the discovery had come with a man who refused to fight for her, to fight for them.

"Regrets already?"

She thought he'd raised himself to one elbow out of consideration for his weight, but opening her eyes, she saw he'd caught her slight frown and had jumped to the worst of conclusions. She had to swallow to reply. Her throat was as dry as a desert; every ounce of moisture inside her seemed to be pooling in the hollow of her belly.

"Never."

"Sore? I wasn't as careful as I should have been."

An impish smile tugged at her lips. "I'll give you a chance to apologize in a minute."

She felt him spasm inside her, and the hand that caressed her moved with a renewed hunger. But when she forced herself to open her eyes again, he was frowning.

"What?" she murmured reluctantly.

"Will you tell me something that's been driving me nuts?"

"I'll try."

"Why didn't you marry Eric's father?"

Brette relaxed. "Several reasons. First, I wanted a baby, not a husband. I've always been unconventional like that," she explained when he raised his eyebrows. "Second, Adam was my best friend, and being my best friend, I knew better than anyone that he wasn't anywhere near ready to settle down. Third—" she sighed at the sad memory "—he died before I could tell him the experiment worked."

"Experiment?"

"Well, it wasn't exactly an affair. I loved him—I loved his spirit, his mind, the way he attacked life—but I wasn't *in* love with him. And neither of us were sure things would, um, *take* the first time, or that we were willing to go for successive tries."

Sam looked anything but pleased. "You're crazy. Why didn't you just go to one of those...clinics."

"Too cold."

"Would you have wanted him to be a part of Eric's life had he lived?"

"If he'd wanted to be. But Adam had just gone through a tough time. His father had died after a long illness, and his mother had abandoned him shortly before he'd been diagnosed to run off with another man. Adam wasn't big on family the way I was."

"Does Eric know?"

"Absolutely. And he's proud that his middle name is his father's, just as he understands I couldn't give him Adam's surname to protect him from his squirrelly paternal grandmother. That was Adam's one demand."

"Bet your *experiment* went over well with your folks."

Brette rather enjoyed his increasingly disgruntled tone. "You know, it didn't. My father broke his favorite pipe. My mother was more worried than disapproving, because she wanted me to be as happy as they were. But she ultimately trusted me to get there in my own way."

"And have you?"

It would have been a casual question, except for the tension in his body that betrayed him. "I used to think so. I still do to a large extent. Eric is..."

''Terrific.''

Brette touched his cheek liking the way his eyes warmed just saying her son's name. ''Yeah, thank you. And I love the home I've made for us, but...I've had to learn nothing is perfect.''

''Like having Sally as a neighbor.''

''Friend, neighbor, she would be a handful either way.''

''You only tolerate her because of Hank.''

''You'd like him more if you got to know him,'' Brette insisted.

''I like him fine. It's his mother I have the problem with—among other people.''

She knew he was thinking about what happened tonight. ''Sam, I'm not calling Cudahy.''

''Because of me,'' he said grim again. ''You think Albert's going to accuse me of being his wife's lover.''

''Sam.'' She took hold of the hand that had been slowly driving her crazy rediscovering the contours of her body. It was still trembling. ''Albert can accuse you of siring half his stock if he wants to, but—'' she pressed a kiss against his palm ''—I'm not ever going to believe you slept with Tracie.''

''But you do believe she's dead.''

Brette looked away. ''Don't ruin this.''

He bent low to nuzzle her breast. ''No, no more, because I can't make myself drive you away yet. Stay the night, Brette,'' he added, beginning to move inside her again. ''My sweet, idealistic, bright-eyed Brette.''

She wanted to tell him that she wasn't idealistic at

all, just determined, but decided he could learn that for himself. Instead, she simply urged him closer and whispered her answer against his lips.

"Yes."

37

Monday, November 8, 1999

Sam was almost relieved when Brette and Eric returned to their house. It was bad enough that on Saturday he'd found himself constantly tempted to check the time while he and Eric removed the old railing in the house and put in the new one. Later he'd become more pitiful, wondering if the boy would ever turn in so he could coerce Brette back into his bed. There'd been no denying it—in the space of twenty-four hours he'd turned himself into a full-fledged masochist. Today, however, would bring a reality check.

Tonight was the school board hearing and he'd put Brette on notice that she should stay away—precisely as he planned to do. The sooner he extricated himself from her life the better.

If only he'd had the decency to keep his hands off her, as well.

As he watched her leave for work in the stillness of the dark morning, his body reacted to the sight of her lithe form running to the truck. She did almost everything at Mach I speed. She was a moving violation waiting to happen—cutting corners too soon, doing too many things at once, in a hurry about everything. Everything but making love, that is.

As he had last night in his too empty bed, he relived their previous two nights together. It was incredible how focused and thorough she could be when she concentrated on one thing alone.

Moaning, he closed his eyes and pressed his forehead against the cooler living room window. How was he supposed to walk away from that?

How was he supposed to leave someone with such heart...and Eric, who could be his only other chance to try at fatherhood?

You damn well have to, that's all.

Somehow he had to find the strength to do it, for all of their sakes. Better for them to hurt a little now than to watch their love slowly turn into hate and fear as his mother's and Kell's had.

He felt more decisive as he watched to make sure Eric and Hank caught their bus a few minutes past seven, and again a few hours later as he reached for the phone to call the Realtor who'd sold him the house. Then he saw the milk truck rumble by and slammed down the receiver.

What if Brette was right and Tracie hadn't left to go live with family?

What if Pugh *was* more than a son of a bitch?

Leaving Brette and the kids to a couple guys with a nasty attitude was one thing. Leaving them to a guy who had to hide the results of a temper gone out of control was something else.

Sam didn't doubt that Tracie had been more successful elsewhere with cheating on her husband than she had been here. She'd just been too casual, too confident in her approach. That suggested to him that

Albert had to know about his wife's alley-cat ways. The look Albert gave him the other day sure suggested it. The question was, how much could he stand? To certain guys, any lay was better than none. Or had Tracie got fed up with her game and rubbed her indiscretions in his face?

Feeling trapped, he'd gone to the shop to take his frustration out on more iron and wood.

When he came inside at lunch, he found two messages on his machine. One was from Glick reminding him that the meeting would begin at seven-thirty and that he would be given time to speak, should he want it. Sam's blood curdled as he heard the underlying message: "Don't make this tougher than it needs to be."

The second call was no more helpful to his state of mind. Brette's soft, feminine voice seduced every nerve ending. "Hi Sam. Sorry I missed you earlier. Guess what? I just saw three turkeys behind the cluster boxes near the old church. Isn't that great? With all the coyotes and wild boars, I didn't think we'd have any left."

She loved the wildlife around here—with the exception of the venomous snakes and the boars. In fact, this weekend had been the opening of whitetail deer season, and she'd flinched at every gunshot she'd heard. He could just imagine how she'd enthusiastically share her sighting with Eric this afternoon. He wanted so much to be part of all those moments, both trivial and big, that he ached.

By the time he got her next call telling him that she would be done early and that she would have almost two hours before Eric got home, he was feeling as hunted as he was haunted. Coward that he was, he hauled ass.

He stayed away until seven-thirty had come and gone. In fact, to play it safe, he didn't pull into his driveway until just after eight. That's when he got the unpleasant surprise that her truck wasn't there.

She wouldn't, he told himself. But deep inside he knew she had.

Swearing under his breath, Sam shoved the gear-shift into reverse.

38

"That concludes our old business." Superintendent Jack Percy shot an expectant and somewhat nervous look toward Principal Glick. "Is there any new business?"

Sitting in the first row of the school cafeteria, Brette patted Eric's knee. In truth the reassuring gesture was to calm her as much as him. She hadn't seen so many people turn out for one of these meetings since the psychology teacher had done the survey in class to find out how many of his students had masturbated. There'd been virtually no discussion that night, and the vote hadn't taken more than a minute, either.

From the looks of the disgruntled group behind them, this wouldn't take much longer.

"The chair recognizes Principal Glick," gray-haired Percy said, striking his gavel for order.

The tall, long-nosed administrator sat forward in his chair, adjusted the papers before him and then his microphone. "Can everyone hear me?"

"Yeah, yeah. Get on with it," a sole respondent called back.

Embarrassed laughter sprinkled the room followed by embarrassed silence.

Glick cleared his throat. "As most of you know,

Wood County's Sheriff Cudahy has brought a matter to our attention, so serious in nature Superintendent Percy and I felt it warranted immediate attention.''

Eric wriggled in his seat, and Brette had to resist doing the same. She did, however, glance over her shoulder to look for Sam. Not that she expected him to come. He'd held on to his fatalistic attitude toward this meeting and had not only told her that she would be wasting her time being here, but he'd demanded she stay away.

Nobody made her decisions for her. In any case, how could she not come?

Glick proved to be long-winded, enjoying being the center of attention among adults for a change. That came as no huge revelation, either. The few times Brette had allowed him to corner her in conversation, he'd practically bored her into a coma.

When it finally came time for audience participation, Glick immediately suggested they give the people in the back a chance to be heard first.

''He's doing that on purpose,'' Eric grumbled. ''He knows you're going defend Sam.''

Surprisingly, despite the number in attendance, only a handful actually rose to speak. Unsurprisingly, Brette was the first to openly defend Sam—except for Rachel Durban, the History teacher, who argued that Sam's situation should be tabled so they could discuss approving her debate team's invitation to a nation-wide championship in Anaheim.

''One issue at a time, Ms. Durban,'' Glick told her with strained civility.

''I ain't spending my hard-earned money on a bunch of kids who are only gonna debate what ride to go on first at Disneyland,'' a man behind Brette muttered.

"Not a brilliant choice of locales,'' Brette whispered to Eric.

Before he could respond, Glick acknowledged her. "Ms. Barry, I believe you were next.''

It was almost nine, she was tired from her accumulated loss of sleep over the past week and people were leaving because they were satisfied with the way things were heading. Frustrated, Brette crumpled the speech she'd written in her hand and turned to face as much of the audience as possible.

"This is worse than wrong,'' she began. "This is embarrassing. Every one of us should be ashamed to have stayed and listened to the nonsense that's been spouted so far tonight.''

There were a few outraged gasps and a general murmur of disapproval.

"I'll wager that, up until tonight, most of you weren't even familiar with Sam Knight. Well, I am. He has been a model teacher and supportive neighbor in the short time he's lived here in our county. I'm not going to deny anything Principal Glick has brought up regarding Mr. Knight's family's tragedy. But if he wanted to be fair, he should have also pointed out how often Sam has voluntarily stayed behind class to supervise the bus loading and made himself accessible to students who might need more assistance with a project. He hasn't mentioned how Mr. Knight has already found part-time jobs for several of his seniors.'' This was information offered by Eric as recently as on the drive there that evening. "And how he strives to keep a connection with difficult students other teachers have written off.''

"He's bad seed!" someone called out from the back. "That's enough for me."

"You show me the data that proves people always grow up to be mirror reflections of their parents," she replied. "How many of you had parents who stayed married their entire lives? Well, looking around this room, I see more than half of you haven't done that."

"At least we tried," a woman drawled. "You didn't even bother."

Brette recognized the voice from an active PTA mother who was pushing her daughter to be a future Miss Texas. Ignoring her, she continued. "What I'm saying is that it would be criminal of us to try Sam Knight for his father's crime."

"What about that arrest Glick talked about?" a man called out.

Brette spotted Charlie Howard, a former precinct commissioner, and replied, "How about your DUI, Charlie?" She turned back to the rest of the group who appeared more tempered, but not convinced. "Okay, we're all tired and we want to go home and have this unpleasantness gone. But understand this, if you lose this teacher, it's your *children* who you'll be punishing. This is a gifted craftsman. He doesn't need to teach. He could make a far better living by going into business for himself. But he chose not to succumb to the very stereotypes you're trying to pin on him. He chose to change, and in changing give back. Don't let fear drive you into making a mistake your kids will have to pay for. Don't lose Sam Knight."

In the rumble of noise that followed, Brette saw only two things—her son applauding...and Sam walking out of the back of the building.

39

"Do you think he's going to be mad, Mom?"

Brette turned right on the main road leaving behind the bulk of traffic. "It's a good bet."

He was silent a moment. "I don't want to do business with him anymore."

Brette almost drove off the road doing a double take. "Sam?"

"No, Mr. Lemeki. There are other barbers. What he said about Sam being the next media-famous psychotic wasn't right, especially when he was just bragging last time I was in there about how the best thing his Cory had done was to take Shop."

Now Brette understood. "Well, Mr. Lemeki's having some serious problems with Cory and he's proof positive about how some people can make pretty large fools of themselves by aiming the floodlights elsewhere to try to hide that. At any rate, you've got it. If you want, we'll find you another barber who doesn't talk out of both sides of his mouth."

"The kids should've had a right to speak. Everybody I know was saying Sam was gonna end up with a bum deal and that it wasn't right."

Silently agreeing with him, Brette turned down their street. "I guess they could always ask their student council to send a letter of protest to Mr. Glick and the board. Listen, I need to go talk to Sam for a minute. You go on inside and I'll be there in a while, okay?''

"Maybe if I go with you, he won't get as mad.''

Her son was growing up fast. With a sad smile Brette reached over and squeezed his hand. "Bless you, but you need to get ready for bed. Tomorrow's another school day.''

There were no lights on in Sam's house when they pulled in, nor was the shop open, but the Suburban told her she shouldn't take any of that as a deterrent. Brette gave Eric the keys to their place and went over to the back of Sam's.

For once he didn't even have the growing lights on, and she had to lean close to the glass to avoid the reflection of the security lights on the glass doors. That's when she saw him sitting on the couch, arms folded, as though waiting for her.

She let herself in. "I hoped you'd change your mind,'' she said in lieu of a greeting.

"And I expected you to keep your word.''

Gone was the passionate yet tender man who'd made love to her tirelessly for two of the last three nights. So, too, was the civility. A cold stranger remained in his place, one she wasn't sure she wanted to deal with.

"I made no promises. How could you expect me to stand by and do nothing?''

"Because I asked you not to. I *told* you not to.''

If he was trying to upset her, he was going about it the right way. "Gosh. *Told me.* Well, I suppose I just assumed you'd know that most reasonable people don't demand the right to make decisions for another person.''

Sam rose and began pacing the length of the room like a caged animal. "Who do you think you are, poking your nose into my business?"

"Someone who cares." The reply came in quiet confidence because it was true. "Someone who hates the way you're standing by and letting this happen. I can't pretend to look the other way, Sam. It's not only about you anymore, it's about us!"

"There is no us."

Although his words were barely audible, his meaning couldn't have been more explicit, their intent more lethal. "You don't mean that."

"I told you, Brette. I said that our going to bed wouldn't make any difference. What made you think I didn't mean what I said? Having your first orgasm?"

She refused to strike back. His strategy was obvious and efficient, but she refused to participate in such bloodletting. If this was his choice—to run from life, and in doing that run from what was between them—she would not wound him back to help justify his stupidity.

"Good night," she whispered. "And goodbye, Sam."

How she got home without tripping over an exposed tree root, she didn't know, but she didn't see anything after getting herself out of there. That same determination that wouldn't allow her to lose control until she was able to lock herself in her room, and turn on the shower. She wouldn't sob herself empty if it meant upsetting Eric or humiliating herself.

She had gotten as far as the front steps when a car with the sheriff's department markings pulled up.

It was Deputy Russell.

Not now, she prayed, and immediately dealt with the hot rush of shame. It was probably Hank again. Why hadn't she gone to check on him before going to talk to Sam?

She tried to read the face of Roy Russell as he walked toward her, and the closer he came, the more unreal the moment grew. It shouldn't be possible for her heart to sink like the heaviest lead weight when Sam had just shattered it into so many tiny pieces. What now? she wondered. What else could possibly be added to this hideous day?

"Ms. Barry, I'm really sorry to disturb you, but is Hank Jamison with you?"

"No...no, he's not. Don't tell me he's run away again?"

"No, ma'am. It's his mother." Russell came closer. "She's been killed."

40

Sally dead? Brette covered her mouth with her hand and stared at the lawman who looked as though he would rather be anywhere but there.

"How?" she whispered.

"Car accident."

That couldn't be. There had to be a mistake. "She went to work three, almost four hours ago."

"A maroon Taurus went off the road on a wooded section of Highway 14 and down into a creek bed. About an hour ago somebody in a van had a flat in the same place and spotted it while the kids were messing with the flashlights. Otherwise, it would probably have been morning before it was spotted." Russell began to reach toward Brette. "Ms. Barry, maybe you'd better sit down."

Brette automatically shook her head. "I'm okay." But of course she wasn't. Her mind had had enough and like some out-of-control rocket shooting off into space, she saw only an endless darkness.

"Ms. Barry…"

She held up her hand, needing a moment, and took a deep breath, then another. The world came back into focus, perhaps too sharply, but she could see again. And think.

Poor Sally. Poor *Hank*.

"Wait. If she didn't make it to work, someone would have called the house." Then she remembered their conversation the other day. "Hank must have been wearing his earphones. Oh, no." She looked at her watch gauging how long it would be before he did get up and check the main phone. "God, if he hears them worrying about what's happened to her, it's going to be twice—"

The front door opened and an uncertain Eric asked, "Mom…?"

Too much must have shown on her face. As soon as he saw her, he hurried straight into her arms. "What is it?"

It felt so good to hold him. He was so beautiful, so alive. "This seems to be the night for it, babe. I need you to be strong, okay?"

"Just tell me. Is it…Hank?"

"No, it's Sally. She's gone, Eric." She leaned back to look into his young shocked face. "Her car went off the road. We need to go with Deputy Russell and tell Hank."

"Oh, man."

She rubbed his back, feeling him struggle for control. After a moment, she glanced over at the deputy who looked on sympathetically. "You realize, of course, Hank has no one else?"

"I remember. I've already talked to the sheriff. By law we need to try to locate his father, but Sheriff Cudahy thinks maybe if you can keep him for tonight, we'll hold off contacting Social Services about getting him into some kind of foster care until tomorrow."

"He's not going into any stranger's home. I have power of attorney, and I'm also the executrix for

Sally's will. She wanted Hank to live with us in the event...if something happened.'' And thank goodness, Brette thought. Who knew if it was a premonition or what, but she was so grateful that they'd made those arrangements two years ago. ''He *is* home, Deputy.''

She could only hope that Sally hadn't had time to change those plans—or that Hank wasn't in the frame of mind to insist none of that applied any longer.

They started across the street.

''Brette—wait!''

Sam ran over to them. His expression grew even more concerned when he saw their faces. ''What's happened?''

It was asking too much to speak to him at this point. She couldn't even bring herself to look at him and turned away.

Eric answered for her. ''Hank's mom is dead.''

Sam uttered a strange, brief sound that drew Brette's gaze, albeit reluctantly. She saw the dismay in his eyes—and the shame.

''What can I do?'' he asked gruffly.

''Leave us alone.''

With her arm around her son, Brette continued across the street. She felt sick to her stomach, but she knew what she had to do.

She put Sam in the back of her mind and knocked on the Jamisons' storm door. ''Hank? Hank, it's us,'' she called so that he wouldn't be afraid.

He opened up fast, his expression understandably as wary as it was curious. He, too, looked at them all, then locked his gaze on her. Why was it that when people were expecting bad news they focused on women? Did they believe it would come gentler that way? There was no gentle way to share this news.

"Mom...?" he murmured. When Brette nodded, he swallowed. "It's bad, huh?"

She simply opened her arms to him and he came at her like a lost Mastiff pup, all shaggy hair and clumsy movements, banging his elbow on the storm door.

"I'm so sorry," Brette crooned.

"It can't be true."

"I know. That's what I said, too. We'll sit down in a minute and Deputy Russell will explain it to you. I have questions myself."

Once the initial shock had passed, Brette suggested they return to their house. Roy Russell agreed. Hank had such a tight hold of her hand, he would probably follow her anywhere at that point.

"I do need to see the, um..." Russell left the rest of his request unspoken between them.

Grateful that he was trying to spare Hank's feelings, Brette nodded. "I have a copy of everything back at our place," she told him. Then she saw the blinking light back on the kitchen counter and indicated it to him. "Maybe you should listen to that. I think it would be best if we wait outside."

Unfortunately, Sam was also outside.

"Hank, I'm sorry," he said, approaching them again.

The boy turned his head away, but after a few seconds nodded.

"Maybe we'd better wait for Deputy Russell inside. Go on over, boys. I'll be right there," Brette said urging the boys forward. Only when she was certain they wouldn't overhear anything did she face Sam.

"Let me help," he said simply.

"Doing what? For how long?" She shook her head. "What's the old saying? 'Fool me once, shame on you. Fool me twice, shame on me.' I've learned my lesson well enough, Sam. Thanks, but no thanks."

When she caught up with the boys, she ushered them into her house, sat Hank on the couch and, as gently as possible, told him what she knew. He took the news in the same emotionless way Eric had described after the boy got accused of things in school. For all she knew, he wasn't even listening.

Knowing she needed to break that pattern, Brette put her arm around him and murmured, "Hank, it's all right. You're not alone."

The change didn't happen all at once. Hank had been keeping walls between himself and people for some time, and being denied this place, his most stable example of a family unit, had begun to have its effect on him, too. But fear, and the simple reassurance that she and Eric weren't holding any grudges, broke down those last barriers. Finally he collapsed sobbing in her arms.

That's how Deputy Russell found them. He let Brette know with a slight inclination of his head that he'd listened to the answering machine and that, as she suspected, the hospital had tried to contact Sally as to her whereabouts.

"Hank," she said, wanting to give the boy a moment to collect himself before they continued, "why don't you go splash some cool water on your face. Eric, this is going to be a busy night. Would you please put on a pot of coffee and get yourself and Hank a soda?''

The boys took off in opposite directions. As soon as the bathroom door closed behind Hank, Brette said to Russell, ''Was there anything else on there that would upset him?''

He shook his head. ''No, it was as you said, just agitated people wondering what was up. Nevertheless, I'd keep him out of there as much as possible for the next few days if you can. And stay with him when he goes to collect his things, of course.''

''I understand.''

Russell tilted his head toward the window in the direction of Sam's place. ''I am concerned about your reaction to Mr. Knight.''

''It's nothing.''

''I don't mean to embarrass you, Ms. Barry, but I'd feel the same even if I wasn't wearing this badge. Something's happened and if I need to know about it, I hope you understand I'm here to help you.''

She was touched by that, as well as with his discrete way of approaching the subject. ''It's been dealt with. Truly. But thank you.''

''All right then, but the gesture stands. Now about Mrs. Jamison—'' Russell glanced over his shoulder toward the hallway, then stepped closer to the couch. ''May I?''

She shifted over to make more room for him.

''The reason I'm trying to do this quietly is to prepare you. There may be problems down the road if there are matters of insurance to collect on behalf of the boy.''

Unless something had changed that Brette didn't know about, she doubted there was much. Sally could barely keep up with her homeowner's policy and car insurance. But she held her peace.

"What I'm saying is that there doesn't seem to be a reason for Mrs. Jamison to have gone off the road where she did. It was a fairly straight piece of road, obviously there wasn't any other traffic at the time, and she doesn't seem to have been speeding."

"You're saying she might have been either ill or under the influence of something, and you want me to confirm if I know anything about the latter?" Brette sighed knowing anything she said would be unflattering to Sally. But right now her concern was for Hank. "Sally was trying to take responsibility of Hank on her own," she said, reaching for diplomacy. "But the truth is that responsibility, personal responsibility, was always difficult for her. If you're asking me whether she had ingested something before she left, I can't tell you. I've been gone all evening and only returned home minutes before you arrived."

"Some medication was found in her purse—Zoloft, a diuretic, some blood pressure pills. They were all samples."

The first Brette recognized as an antidepressant Sally had been mooching since her Prozac and Valium supply had dried up. The blood pressure pills were no doubt new to offset her increased symptoms of stress, and the diuretics were for the weight gained from the drinking. Brette could only wonder what else was in her medicine cabinet and in what combinations Sally had been taking everything, especially when she'd left for work that evening.

"If you're looking for names of the staff at the hospital who gave her the pills, I can't," Brette replied. "I'd seen the samples before, and I tried repeatedly to warn her about self-medicating, so she avoided the subject with me.''

"There was also a flask with straight vodka in her purse. Full, I should add, which doesn't mean she hadn't had something at home.''

Brette heard Hank blowing his nose and said quickly, "Deputy, Hank isn't unaware that his mother had problems, but please don't hit him with this tonight.''

"We'll do our best not to make him deal with it at all," Russell replied. "I assure you, that wouldn't have been the case if another vehicle had been involved. But I do need to know her state of mind when she left the house.''

Hank returned then and Russell gave up his seat to him.

"What do I do now?" said the boy. "Do I have to go, you know, identify her?''

That would have been a nightmare. As it was, he looked ready to fall apart again. But Brette had seen enough accidents on her route over the years to know the body was on its way to Dallas for an autopsy, if it wasn't there already. "There'll be decisions to make for the funeral, sweetheart. But we'll talk about that tomorrow. Eric and I will be with you the whole time, or I can do it all for you. Whatever you like.''

The assurances seemed to relieve him.

"There are a few more questions I do have to ask," Deputy Russell said. He sat on the edge of the coffee table directly in front of the boy. "Hank, I know this is tough, but you're old enough to appreciate there are always reports to fill out. Can you tell me if you sensed anything different about your mom before she left for work?''

"No...uh, different how?"

Right then Brette knew he was lying. She had spent too many years with him not to read him as well as she did her own flesh and blood.

Fortunately, Eric appeared with a tray, and Brette could have hugged him for the care he'd taken with the preparations. He spilled some of the coffee as he set the tray down, which immediately drenched the napkins, but the coffee was steaming and smelled good, and he had even remembered teaspoons—although not the sugar or milk.

"Black's perfect," Russell assured her when she asked. There were also two Dr Peppers and the deputy handed one to Hank. "So everything was...normal when your mother left home this evening?"

"Yes, sir."

"And you two were getting along?"

"Yes."

"There weren't any upsetting phone calls or visits before she went to work?"

"No, sir."

Deputy Russell closed his notebook, took a few sips of coffee and shared a few more technicalities and procedures they would have to deal with in the coming days. Finally he indicated to Brette that he was ready to leave.

She quickly located the papers he wanted to verify. After he inspected them, she walked him outside. "Thank you for being gentle with Hank," she said.

"I knew he wasn't going to give me anything. They were still having a rough time of it, weren't they? Nothing had improved?"

"I'm afraid not."

His lips compressed, he nodded. "And now he's

your headache. This is a greater burden than you took on before. Are you sure you know what you're doing?''

Probably more than most people in this situation, Brette thought. Ironically, she could see the one positive that would come out of this sad experience. "The one thing I couldn't do, despite his half living here, was get him the professional help he needs. At least I can do that now.''

"So you're actually thinking of making this permanent?''

Brette gave him a rueful look. "Deputy, unless his father's had an epiphany, there's no way he's going to accept responsibility for the boy. The last time Sally heard from him, he denied Hank was his. We're all he has left. Of course I'm going to file for legal custody.''

Roy Russell let the professional demeanor slip long enough to smile warmly. "Then he's one lucky kid.''

Wishing her luck, he left. As Brette walked back to the house, she was aware of Sam watching her from a window. Just the knowledge of his interest triggered an inevitable surge in her pulse, but she couldn't allow herself to deal with any personal issues right now. There were more important hurts that needed her attention.

Inside she found Eric and Hank deep in conversation. They fell silent when she entered.

"Tell her,'' Eric demanded after an awkward moment.

Hank twisted the can of soda around his hands. "Me and Mom…? I lied about things being okay. I told her…I told her I was gonna leave if she didn't let me come over here. She left as bummed out as I'd ever seen her. Do you think... Is the accident my fault?''

''Oh, Hank.'' Brette sat down and drew him to her again. ''No. Get that out of your mind once and for all. If your mom was upset, it wasn't really about anything you two said to each other. It was more about her life and the bad choices she'd made. You know she wasn't happy with herself, and she knew she was slipping deeper and deeper into a rut. Even she recognized that getting out of it was going to take more discipline and energy than she had.

''Listen, there's going to be plenty of time for us to talk about all of that,'' she said with a reassuring squeeze. ''You've had the biggest blow a kid can experience. It's going to take time before you understand tonight and find a perspective about all this that you can live with. In fact, right now I think the biggest kindness you can do yourself would be to go lie down for a while.''

''Yeah. Do you—'' he shot Eric an apologetic look ''—do you think it would be okay if I used the other bedroom? It's not that I don't want to be around y'all...''

He wanted privacy to cry. Brette kissed his forehead, not at all surprised to find it overly warm. ''It's always been there for you whenever you were ready for your own space. Both you and Eric know that. Go. I need to make a few phone calls, but I'm here if you need anything, okay?''

He nodded and shuffled off. As soon as she heard the bedroom door close, Brette met her son's traumatized gaze. ''You all right?''

''I can't believe this whole night,'' he whispered. ''I thought what happened to Mr. Knight was bad, but Mrs. J. gone. And that way... Mom, I couldn't handle it if this was happening to me instead of Hank.''

His voice broke and his eyes filled. Brette went to him and held him close. ''I know, babe. I know. But I'm here and we're all going to get through this.

''Speaking of...for the time being, do yourself a favor and put on your stereo so you don't get more upset by what you might hear next door, okay?''

''Oh. Yeah, I get your point.''

''Just not house-shaking loud,'' she added with a smile. ''I do have to hear myself on the phone.''

He retreated to his room and Brette carried the tray back to the kitchen. As soon as she heard the stereo come on, she picked up the phone and dialed Tucker.

''Good God Almighty,'' he groaned when he heard the news. ''That is so flat-out weird. On the one hand, I've been expecting this for ages. On the other, I'm blown away.''

''That's exactly how I feel, believe me.''

''What can I do?''

''Call Brenda and E.J. for me, and let everybody who needs to know what's up. You'll also have to handle my route for me tomorrow. Actually, it may be wiser for me to go ahead and take a week's vacation. I'm still reeling and I already know there are a ton of things to sort out.''

''I'll handle everything on this end, that's one thing I don't want you worrying about. How's the kid?''

''Shell-shocked.''

''Imagine if he didn't have you and Eric. On the other hand,'' Tucker grumbled, ''I hate you getting stuck with that juvenile delinquent-in-training.''

''Hey, you know he's never shown any sign of that

kind of behavior around here. In any case, it's too late for that kind of talk. Maybe I wasn't fully prepared that this might happen when Sally first approached me about being his guardian, but believe me, it's been on the periphery of my mind in the last year as I've watched her unravel more and more.'' As she paced around the kitchen, Brette ran a hand through her hair. There were too many images running through her mind. ''I don't mean to cut you short, but I have more calls to make. We'll talk tomorrow, okay?''

''Wait a sec. What about the Terminator's meeting? How'd it go?''

He'd known she intended to attend, and hadn't much liked the idea. ''It went about as badly for him as you could expect. It's over,'' she said. In more ways than she would ever be able to tell Tucker.

''It's for the best. You hang in there.''

Brette disconnected, then phoned Bertrice and Keith before she let herself think about what Tucker had said at the end. Bertrice wept and Keith was deeply shaken. Both were also quick to offer support. Brette assured them that everything was under control for the moment, but knew both would be over in the morning with food or to offer assistance in one way or another.

She'd barely ended the call with Keith when the phone rang again.

''Don't hang up,'' Sam said without preamble.

She didn't, but she didn't say anything, either. She did, however, have to sit down at the dining room table, keeping her back to the window because, even with only the stove light on, he could probably see her.

"Brette...Brette, forgive me."

His voice was as deep as she'd ever heard it. He also sounded so strained, he was hoarse.

"If I'd known—" he continued.

"You'd have waited to insult me until after the funeral?"

She did disconnect then. By the time she set the phone back on the counter, the tears she'd been holding at bay finally flowed...for all of them.

41

Emily Dickinson wrote, "Death is a wild night and a new road." Sally found that wild night. I'm praying Hank can find that new road.
—Journal Entry

Friday, November 12, 1999

The funeral was held at ten o'clock Friday morning at the Cedar Cove Cemetery by Tucker's house. He hadn't been able to come, of course, nor had Desiree. But there was a wreath of red carnations from them and the rest of the people at the post office. In fact, few people attended the graveside service because Sally had no friends aside from Brette, and her employers at the hospital were deep into inquiries about the drugs that she'd been illegally obtaining. The only attendees were the people from the funeral home, the minister from Bertrice's church, Bertrice and Clovis, and Keith.

And someone else, too. She'd spotted him out of the corner of her eye, aware that he'd followed them all the way over there. Standing by a tree away from their small group was Sam.

Brette struggled not to think about him and to focus on what Pastor Martin was saying, but without much success. She was having too hard a time understanding why Sam was here. He'd seemed to get the message after that late-night call on Monday, and had been keeping his distance ever since. What's more, he'd never liked Sally, so what was the point of this gesture?

The point is his conscience is eating him up, and the way you're looking these days isn't helping.

True, she did look like a shadow of her former self, but then so did Hank. The difference was the demands of the week had kept her running and were taking their toll on her coloring and weight. The size-six black suit she wore hung on her almost as limply as it did the clothes hanger she'd taken it from earlier. Thank goodness the worst was now behind them.

As the service ended, the sun came out for the first time that morning. Brette still shivered. The temperature wasn't unpleasant, Indian Summer was lingering, but her body had been running on empty since midweek. Bertrice aimed to do something about that, though. She'd insisted on putting together a little buffet for all of them once they got back to Brette's.

Hank leaned toward her. "Now?"

She nodded and he stepped forward to place the pink rose he carried on the white casket. Eric did the same and she brought up the rear. Then Keith surprised her by stepping forward to take her arm.

"I'll walk you to the truck."

"I'm fine," she replied, giving his hand a squeeze. "You help Bertrice with Clovis."

Among other little considerations, he'd driven the

elderly couple here using their car, which was larger and more comfortable for Bertrice.

"Sure? I couldn't help notice who followed you in. This time I'll make sure I'm right behind you," Keith said, giving her a quick kiss on the cheek.

As he went back for the others, Brette and the boys passed the tree where Sam stood. Dressed in a navy blazer, gray slacks and a black turtleneck he cut a commanding figure, but there was no missing that he hadn't gotten much more sleep lately than she had.

"Hi, Sam," Eric said.

He had brought up the subject of Sam during the week when he'd noticed that she was avoiding him at all costs. She'd been forced to admit that things were difficult between them, and had begged off explaining. That might have been a mistake, she realized as her son continued.

"We'll see you at the house, right?"

Caught off guard, Brette looked up to find Sam watching her.

"That may not be a good idea," he replied.

"There's plenty of food. Too much," Eric insisted. "Mom and Mrs. Ponder set it all out before we left the house."

"Sounds great, but—"

"If it's because of what I did," Hank interjected, "I just want to say it would be okay with me."

Brette had been watching Hank struggle with his complicated feelings over the last several days. This was yet another sign that he was working through a good deal internally. But she wasn't as relieved or enthusiastic about this step. Before she could think of a way to counter it, though, Sam stepped forward and extended his hand to the awkward teen.

"I know I couldn't have shown that much class at your age. Thank you. And I'm sincerely sorry about your loss."

Brette touched each boy between the shoulder blades. "Go on to the truck. I'll be with you in a minute."

Since Monday, Sam had been like some archangel keeping watch, but never intruding. Although still too busy to revisit the hurt he'd inflicted, she could tell he was paying a price for what he'd done. That didn't, however, change what she recognized was as deep a problem in him as anything Hank had to deal with.

"It meant something to him that you came," she said, able to give him that much.

"I'd have done more, but I thought it would be disruptive rather than helpful."

"Every loss is different." She glanced back at the gravesite, the modest, quiet scene of pink, red and white flowers, and beyond where people hovered to do their business and get on with their next assignment. "You think because you've gone through it before that you know, you think you're prepared. But there's always something new to grab you by the nerve endings and shake you awake."

"And what did you learn this time?"

"How much time we waste on the things that don't matter, and the people who don't get it."

"Get what?"

"That anger and all the manifestations of it are *there*, a part of us, natural, inherent. Pick a word. I don't think we're wrong to feel anger, but I'm certain we're meant to use it better than we do."

"You're talking about both Sally and me."

"I'm talking about all of us." She looked back at

him. "You think in my life I haven't been ready to curse God and the universe? No one butchered my parents. They were wiped out by a big white wave of snow and ice that was no one's fault. It wasn't *personal,* but it damn sure felt that way at the time. My best friend refused to let the less experienced skiers in his group go down a questionable slope without first testing it himself. He'll never be found unless global warming turns Alaska into the next Key West. Why blame God for turning the guy I believed would figure out how to turn nuclear waste into the next millennium's harmless useful resource into an ice sculpture?"

"Brette, I love you."

"Don't you think I know that?"

She didn't mean to shout at him, and she couldn't bear to think what the people who'd overheard her were thinking, but she couldn't stop, either.

"What do you think I've been talking about? Look what you do with that love. You strike out and hurt because it's scary and hard. Well, it's all hard. It's all about skating on thin ice. So *what?* You do it anyway." She knew she was saying everything out of context and making no sense, but she pressed on. "You think I asked for you to love me? You think I want to love you? I liked my life the way it was— calm, focused and harmless. Isn't that what the great edict demands? Do no harm? I was a gold star student of that before I met you, damn it. Damn you—"

Brette covered her face with her hands. Pushed too far, worn out beyond tired, she began sobbing and couldn't stop. Then she felt Sam's arms come around her. Although she knew she should resist, and save what was left of her sanity, she didn't. As he lifted her in his arms, all she cared about was the relief of it, and the darkness that came from pressing her face against his chest.

42

The boys came bolting out of Brette's truck as Sam carried her past them. Pale and wide-eyed, they alternately called to her and entreated explanations from him. He didn't blame them. If he were their age and his life raft had sprung a leak, he would be freaking out, too. But it wasn't helping the situation.

"Boys, put a lid on it. Now, one of you open the back door of my Suburban, and the other one get her purse and keys out of the truck and lock it up. We'll worry about it later."

Eric opened the door and Sam placed Brette on the back seat, covering her with the blanket he kept for wrapping fragile objects. He was aware of the others hurrying toward them, but he waited only long enough for the boys to climb in beside him before taking off. Brette's choking sobs were his motivator. She needed solitude, the comfort of familiar things, and he'd fight hell itself before anyone stopped him from getting it for her, fast.

"What happened?" Eric whispered beside him. He kept glancing over the back of the seat.

"She's exhausted."

"It has to be more than that."

"Tell me that in twenty years." Sam heard the edge in his own voice and knew it was from the sheer terror of seeing one of the strongest women he'd ever met finding her breaking point. Purging a deep breath he tried again. "She's been handling everything, coping for all of you for a long time and these last weeks, hell, months, haven't exactly been a breeze. Some people feel so much responsibility they don't think they have a right to stop, so the mind or body forces them to."

They reached her house in less than twenty minutes and once again Sam sent the boys ahead, this time to unlock the doors. Then he carried Brette inside, and with the help of Eric's directions, found her room.

"Out," he said to the boys who followed as though attached by an umbilical cord. "And close the door."

"But Sam..." Eric began.

"Watch for the others. When Mrs. Ponder gets here, have her come in. But that's all, got it?"

"Yes, sir."

When the door closed, Sam eased the bedspread from beneath her, slipped off her high heels and began undoing the gold buttons on her suit jacket. She was anything but cooperative.

"Leave me alone."

Moaning, she tried to twist away. Fortunately, she had the strength of a moth that had been beating itself against a Halogen light half the night.

"You're home, Brette. Let's get you into bed. Then you can sleep."

The sound of his voice triggered the most intriguing contradiction. She grew calm and curled around him.

"Sam...?"

"Who else, angel?"

Her weight loss tugged at his heart, but also reminded him of how sweet it had been to watch her come apart in his arms. The other day he'd prayed never to be tempted by her again. Today he swore to himself that he would never be stupid enough to let her go. Brave thoughts for a guy who'd recently been stripped of his future. But what the hell, it fit. He'd been called a natural at a few things, but no one had ever bragged that he was a fast learner.

He had her down to her bra and panty hose and tucked under the bedspread when Bertrice rushed in.

"Sam, what on earth— You don't know what I thought when I saw you just dash off with her!"

Aspirin and water in hand, he switched sides of the bed for the hefty woman. "Sorry for the scare, Bertie, but there wasn't time to make press statements. She's had it."

"I was expecting this. I was telling Keith on the drive to the service that she was heading for a head-on collision with reality. But she's determined those boys know they're loved. Hello, darlin'," Bertrice crooned to Brette as Sam lifted her head for the tablets and water. "You take those like a good girl and then you sleep."

"The food—"

"Will be gobbled up, or it won't, don't you fret over that. You rest and I'll bring you a nice broth later."

"The boys need—"

"She's worse than a heifer with twin calves," Bertrice whispered to Sam. Then she said to Brette, "Those boys are fine, darlin'. Now, no more."

Brette curled toward Sam again.

"Right here." Pressing a kiss to her fever-dry lips, he added, "And I'll stay close. That's a promise."

But knowing that she needed a reprieve more than anything, and that Bertrice would be scandalized if he was the one to change her into a sleep shirt, he retreated from the room.

"Is she okay?" Keith asked, keeping watch in the hallway. He'd chucked the jacket and tie and had already downed most of the wine in the glass he held. "Do we need to call for an ambulance?"

"There's nothing they can do that a week in bed wouldn't fix faster." Sam glanced down the hall. "Where are the boys?"

"Trying to keep Clovis from eating the meringue off the chocolate pie. Are you sure Brette's okay? I've never seen her lose control like that."

"This must be your first funeral."

Keith blushed. "This isn't normal for her. I know. I've known her for years. We're friends."

"Then act like one and stop suggesting she's going around the bend."

Sam pushed past him and found the boys sitting at the table with Clovis. All three looked as though they were awaiting an execution.

"She's going to feel a lot worse if she comes out and sees nobody's touched all of this stuff," he said, nodding to the table.

"Is she coming out?" Eric brightened.

"Well, not for a while yet. But she will. Now how about making some dents in this food?"

He did his best at reassuring everyone, and even managed to get the kids to talk without a death-knell tone in their voice. Helping Clovis ingest more than he spilled on his shirt was another matter entirely.

"I guess I need to pay for your next cleaning bill,"

he told Bertrice when she joined them after a while with Keith in tow.

"Don't you worry about it. He looks content." She motioned to Keith. "I know you said you have to get back to work, so tell me what you like and I'll prepare you a platter to take home."

As she did that, Keith went to Hank. He whispered a few words and rubbed his back like Brette always did to the boys. Sam turned away from the scene, certain the gesture was meant as show for his sake. Hank didn't look all that thrilled.

Hearing Hank murmur, "Uh...no thanks," Sam had to keep his back turned not to expose his smug smile.

Shortly afterward Keith made a low-profile departure. Sam noted that no one seemed too disappointed about that, either.

After the boys cleaned their plates and had a second helping of dessert, they excused themselves and went out back.

"I should have told them to change out of their good clothes first," Sam said, watching them move the picnic table off the patio to prepare to shoot some hoops.

"Oh, I don't think they'll have too rough a game that you'll have to worry. If you'll fix yourself more than that bite you've eaten, I'll pack the rest of this away and see to putting Clovis down for his nap. I suspect the couch will do as well as anywhere else."

Sam looked up from the bowl of potato salad he was about to try. "Couch nothing. You're going home."

"Now Sam, the boys need watching."

"I'll be here."

Bertrice opened her mouth to protest, then she tilted her head and studied his face. "Well, I wondered when I first saw... Well, good. Good for you."

That remained to be seen. But Sam knew one thing—he'd seen hell twice so far in his life, and suspected that if he glimpsed it again, he would have to stay there permanently. Maybe the options scared him to death, too, but so be it. As Brette had said, it was all hard.

As Bertrice continued cleaning up, he went to check on Brette. She was out cold, sleeping so deeply she didn't appear to have budged from where Bertrice had tucked her in. The pastel purple color of her sleep shirt made her look younger than any thirty-two-year-old mother of a teen. Sleeping, she appeared far more fragile than when awake and in her whirling dervish mode. This should serve as a good warning to her. She would never know when to stop herself. Someone should be there to make her see reason.

It was as he stood there contemplating things that he heard a commotion outside. When he went to see what was going on, he found Hank sputtering to Bertrice.

"Eric's staying with him. He won't come. He just rocks back and forth and makes weird noises."

"What's going on now?" Sam asked upon joining them.

"Clovis wanted to be outside with the boys. Next thing they knew he'd wandered off. It's not their fault, Sam, so don't think about scolding. The dementia's getting worse, that's all. And now he's down the road and seen something that's triggered who knows what in his mind. Will you go get him for me, please?"

He didn't waste time answering. He ran with Hank

down the empty, oil-paved road to the entrance to the Pughs', slowing when he spotted Eric standing a few feet away from Clovis. Circling the scene, Sam saw the object of Clovis's attention was the oddest of fixations—a rural garbage container set on two wheels and with the long dollylike handle. As for the sounds he was making, they weren't really too scary. They sounded like a singer's warm-up exercises.

"He—ee—ee. Cee—ee—ee. Ga—aa—aa."

Sam had witnessed his share of bizarre moments, but this made absolutely no sense—until he saw the woman's high heel on the ground beside the canister.

43

Sam motioned the others to stay back and went over to the big vinyl receptacle. The lid was half off already, needing only a nudge with the back of his hand to shove it to where he could see the rest of the way inside.

No body—not that he actually expected one. The thing was, however, loaded with things that didn't ordinarily get thrown away, at least not in such good condition, like makeup, a blond hairpiece, magazines and a few other articles of clothing, including the matching half of the colorful open-back shoe that was on the ground.

"Well…?"

Glancing back, he saw that both boys and Clovis were watching him with rapt attention. What could he tell them that would make sense after Clovis's strange behavior?

"Looks as though she's moved after all."

"No way." Hank joined him at the bin and stared down into the chest-high container. "There's some useful stuff in there."

"Don't get any ideas."

"Not me. I mean, women don't throw this kind of stuff away even when they're moving, just like they don't pay attention to expiration dates on it. They take it all with them. Right, Eric? We went to the shore with our moms once, and my mom took the whole bathroom. She left nothing behind.''

''Yeah.'' Eric began to grin. ''We used half a dozen almost empty tubes of lipstick and bunch of other cream stuff to smear on doorknobs and benches before she missed anything.''

Terrorists in training, Sam thought in wry sympathy for Brette. It was a wonder she wasn't gray-headed. ''I believe you, but that's what Albert said to Eric's mom. Tracie moved.''

''Hey, y'all...?'' Eric's attention was drawn to Clovis. The elderly man was clasping his clenched hands to his chest and beginning to moan. ''I think he's definitely losing gravity, and fast.''

He had a point, thought Sam. ''Let's get him back to the house.''

Bertrice was standing guard at the front door, and immediately began fretting when they brought in Clovis. ''I was afraid going to the cemetery would be too emotional for him. Maybe we should call for an ambulance?''

''He seems to be settling down,'' Sam replied. ''I think it's only what he saw that got him upset.''

''What do you mean?''

''Well, you know there's talk that Albert and Tracie have split?''

''I seem to recall Brette saying something about it a while back...no, wait. She was just asking me if I'd seen her of late. But what does any of that have to do with this?''

''Albert appears to be in the midst of the great purge. You know, getting rid of the things she left behind. Female things. I'm guessing Clovis was fond of Tracie?''

Bertrice began to relax, even smile a little. ''There's no denying he's got an eye for a pretty form. Brette's his favorite, of course, but he enjoyed when Tracie stopped by to tease him. Keith told me about how she'd do so, mostly when he was taking a walk with Clovis for me. My hunch is that the girl was more interested in flirting with him. Truth is, I didn't care for her much. Her playful ways didn't seem all that playful to me, but Clovis did love the attention.''

Sam wasn't surprised that he'd pegged Tracie correctly in the first seconds of meeting her. ''Well, he saw a shoe that had fallen out. It looked rather suspicious at first, and who knows, he could have thought there was a body inside.''

''Oh. Oh, I see now.'' Bertrice pressed a hand to her bosom before embracing her husband. ''There, there, darlin'. It was nothing. You had a fright, that's all. I need to get you home so you can rest yourself. Stay put, I only need to do one or two more things.''

She rushed back to the kitchen, but despite Sam's efforts to assure her everything looked perfect, she wouldn't leave until she got things the way she wanted them. After that she started giving him and the boys a string of directions about when to eat dinner and where they could find everything.

Finally Sam was able to assist the tittering woman and her husband to their sedan.

''Now don't think I forgot that broth I promised Brette,'' Bertrice told Sam once she'd lowered the driver's window. ''I have a new batch in my fridge, so just send one of the boys over in a while—''

"Tomorrow will do," Sam replied. "Brette's tired enough to sleep through to morning, you know that."

"She should, that's true. All right, dear. It's ready when you need it."

Sam thanked her again and waved them off. When he returned inside, he saw that Hank and Eric were waiting for him, and if expressions were anything to go by, they weren't buying his explanation to Bertrice at all.

"We think," Eric began, "that Albert's getting rid of evidence."

Sam supposed there was some progress in that. At least Hank wasn't looking at him as though he were his prime suspect.

"Let's say he is. Isn't it kind of careless to do that by dumping the stuff right outside your front gate for the world to see? It would make more sense to leave it at some Goodwill drop-off site or even sneak it into a big industrial Dumpster miles away."

"I thought I read somewhere that things are easiest hidden in plain sight," Hank said.

"Sometimes, sure. But in this case Albert also knows Eric's mom is suspicious of him. She was just down there the other day trying to deliver something to Tracie and she asked questions, nosed around."

"Yeah, but the news about my mom's funeral was in the paper," Hank countered. "Also, he has to have seen Tucker handling the mail route. Perfect timing."

"Not when Tucker and Eric's mom have been playing Watson and Sherlock."

"But Albert doesn't know that," Eric said.

Sam was impressed, but unconvinced. "You two are sharp, but if you're hinting that I call in the calvary, forget it. Sheriff Cudahy and his people will only suspect I'm trying to cause trouble for someone else to get attention off of me.''

"One of us should call," Eric said to Hank.

"The 911 computers track numbers," drawled Sam.

"Besides," Hank added, "I'm the kid Cudahy thinks is most likely to wear matching ankle bracelets before I'm legal, so I can't call, either." Then he snapped his fingers. "Let's get some plastic bags and collect as much of the stuff as we can. Then we'll mail it to the cops so they can look for blood and stuff."

"Whoa." Sam's amusement ended there. "You're talking about tampering with private property."

"Evidence."

"If it is, your fingerprints would probably contaminate anything that's there."

"Mom keeps plastic gloves in the washroom cabinet." Eric launched himself to the utility room.

Even as he said that, the sound of a big truck passing caught their attention. Closest to the window, Hank leaned over to see what had gone by.

"Oh, no."

Sam and Eric joined him.

At the end of the street was a garbage collection truck.

44

When Brette opened her eyes, the room was dark, except for the glow seeping in past the drapes and miniblinds from the streetlight. She took a moment to assimilate herself...recognized the room, remembered the day. Stifling a yawn, she sat up and checked the time. It was almost one in the morning. She'd slept through an entire day and still felt as though she were the kick ball for a herd of elephants.

Questions began flooding her mind: How were the boys? What had happened to everyone? It was so quiet.

Gingerly testing her legs, she used the bathroom, cooled her face with a dampened washrag and got a long drink of cold water. Feeling more human, she padded barefoot across the hall to peer in on Eric, then Hank. Both were sleeping soundly, thank goodness.

Reassured, she headed for the kitchen.

"What are you doing up?"

Brette gasped and spun around. Thank goodness she recognized the voice, otherwise the dark silhouette rising off the couch would have frightened her. As it was, she was only self-conscious.

"What are you doing here?" she whispered.

"Voluntary guard duty."

More memories rushed to the front of her mind—
the scene at the cemetery, his confession. *Hers.*

She was tempted to beat a hasty retreat.

"Easy." Sam steadied her. "You don't have your
sea legs back yet."

"I'm fine." But she wasn't. Her body was reacting
to his touch, however objective, and her eyes were
noticing that he was stripped down to his slacks again.
She wasn't ready for any of this.

"You're weak from hunger as much as everything
else. Bertie packed a lot away in the freezer, but
there's plenty of sandwich stuff and salads in the
fridge."

"Bertie...?"

He shrugged. "It's the only way to get her to stop
giving orders like the War Department."

"Just don't try calling me Brettie."

"Want me to make you a sandwich...Barry?"

"I'll manage."

He was being entirely too appealing. She needed
space, time to find her equilibrium.

Of course he didn't give it to her.

"What can I get you to drink?"

He brushed past her so that her forearm slid across
his firm belly. She thought about telling him to go
away, that she couldn't think with him underfoot. But
the idea of being alone appealed even less.

"Brette, I can't help you if you don't speak to me
and tell me what you need."

"An explanation." She faced him. "Why are you
here? And don't start with the wisecracks again. I
mean, what's changed?"

She waited in expectant silence.

Finally he reached for the lighter on the center

counter and lit a fat vanilla candle with daisies imbedded inside. "I'll tell you, provided you sit down," he said pointing to one of the bar stools, "and let me make you something to eat."

Arguing, she decided, would only wake the boys. Besides, she didn't have the energy to survive another burst of emotion like the one she'd displayed that morning.

She sat...and frowned as he put on the kettle. "What are you doing?"

"Making you tea. It's getting cool outside again, and this way I can get some honey into you at the same time."

"I don't like honey, it's too sweet. Just the word gives me goose bumps."

"What it'll do is give you some quick energy. Don't worry, I'll add plenty of lemon, too. The boys had peppermint sticks in theirs."

She was feeling more and more a stranger in her own home. "The boys won't drink hot tea."

"Hank's getting a sore throat. My mother always used to ward off our colds with honey-lemon tea. She added Christmas candy canes to bribe us into drinking it. It worked on your two. They said it wasn't half-bad."

Maybe she was only dreaming she was sitting here...?

"Remind me to remind you in the morning that the phone jack is pulled in your room," Sam continued. "Messages are on the counter by the wireless. Just Tucker checking in and someone from the PTA who'll get back to you." He cleared his throat. "I think you'll hear a lot from her again. She recognized my voice."

Brette rested her elbows on the counter and buried her face in her hands.

As he moved around the kitchen, Sam continued to fill her in on the day she'd missed, keeping his voice low, the tone casual. He and the boys were going to watch a movie, but that would have been too loud, so they played poker instead. Hank had the makings of a genuine cardsharp, but Eric needed to stay out of Vegas and away from sailors on the prowl to part innocents from their paycheck.

A platter of cold cuts, vegetable sticks, cheeses and crackers appeared between her elbows. A moment later the steaming mug of tea was set beside it.

"Now eat." Sam poured himself a glass of wine from the bottle opened the other day and settled on the stool beside her.

She started to eat to keep her hands busy, and to avoid staring at him. He looked wonderful in the candlelight. On the other hand, she'd seen her reflection in the bathroom mirror and that was the best reason of all to keep her face averted.

"One more thing and then I'll stop bombarding you with jabber. You should know your friend Keith and I don't get along."

"Introverts rarely do, I suspect."

"I'm not an introvert, I'm particular. In any case, he got puffed because I wouldn't let him see you. Thought I'd tell you before you hear it from him with a different twist on things."

Brette swallowed her second minisandwich and considered reaching for his wine. But he was right about the temperature changing. Her toes were beginning to chill and her tender knee had begun throbbing. She wouldn't be able to hold the position long, but she curled her legs Indian fashion and reached for the tea.

"Give 'em here." In response to her questioning look, he patted his lap. "Your feet."

It seemed too intimate for here, now, and yet, she reminded herself, this was the man she'd made love with, the man who'd probably put the sleep shirt on her.

She stretched her legs and proceeded to take a sip of tea, only to choke.

"You're ticklish."

"I'm losing my mind." Brette put down the mug and shoved away the food.

"I can't do this. I'm trying, but I can't. Let me go, Sam," she said trying to free herself from his hold. "This isn't...I don't recognize you."

"Then try this...."

He plucked her off the stool and onto his lap, then angled his mouth over hers for a languid, thorough kiss that had her straining to get closer.

"Now am I familiar?" he asked, his voice thick.

"It's coming to me." But when she leaned back, her gaze was somber. "You're the guy I humiliated this morning in front of almost a dozen people including a preacher."

"We're going to have a problem if you're about to tell me you didn't mean it when you said you loved me."

He actually managed to say that with a touch of humor. Of course, his drilling gaze ruined the effort and had her wondering if he could see candlelight through her yet.

Brette sighed. "I meant it. Only, maybe letting you know isn't such a good idea, since I may be having

She carried it to the kitchen and inspected the clip-on earring in the candlelight. It wasn't hers. She made a point to only wear real gold because her ears were pierced, and she suffered allergic reactions when she tried to wear other metals. This was costume stuff, and pretty cheap, too. The pea-green and sallow-yellow colors with the brown speckles weren't even right for her.

What on earth had it been doing on her couch?

45

"**W**hen were you going to tell me?"

Brette followed Sam from his shop and into his kitchen. She'd left the boys raking leaves at Bertrice's precisely to have this conversation and she felt she deserved some answers.

"I told you, it was nothing. An old man having a sentimental moment and stirring the imagination of the kids."

"How can you say that? Albert is dumping Tracie's clothes, everything, into the trash, eradicating all evidence of her, and you call that 'nothing'?"

"They've split up. Not that I'm eager to bring up the matter of statistics, but have you noticed that the majority of couples don't make it these days? The Pughs are the norm, hardly front-page stuff."

"All the more reason for a woman like Tracie not to leave her plumage behind," Brette insisted. "A gal on the prowl never knows when she has to send out a new mating signal."

Sam placed the caulking gun on the counter. "Brette, I wish to heaven I could help you find an explanation for that handprint, but the fact is, we may never know. Want to hear my gut hunch, though? Hank did it. No, don't look at me that way. Say he just wanted to get a rise out of Eric, but once things started mushrooming, he lost the courage to tell anyone. Mark my words, someday when he's yanking out his hair over his own kids' antics, he'll admit to someone that once *he* pulled a real beaut.''

''But you said yourself that Clovis kept the earring because of Tracie.'' She and Sam had finally deduced he'd been the one to find the thing. Sam recalled Clovis's behavior down the road, the way he'd held his fisted hands to his chest. At least nothing else they'd come up with made sense.

Sam groaned up at the ceiling. ''Which isn't the same as saying she was his Lolita. I'm only saying— hell, the earring's funky and colorful. Maybe he just wanted to make a fishing lure out of it.''

He was trying to make her laugh, to focus on something other than the onslaught of bad news they'd been facing at every turn. And she should. After all, the weather, though cooler, was gorgeous, Hank's sore throat was better, and the boys had agreed to do something for the Ponders in gratitude for all of Bertrice's hard work. It also looked as though she and Sam would be spending more and more time together....

Brette *was* feeling better about a lot of things, partly thanks to Tucker who was finishing off the week by handling her route for one more day. But this, the story that the boys had told her and Bertrice had confirmed, was like a dark cloud appearing on the horizon. It threatened to ruin everything for them.

''What if I'm right, Sam? Fine, Tracie isn't the mayor's wife, or a national celebrity, or someone's beloved child. But she's a human being with hopes and dreams the same as us. We can't let Albert get away with this.''

Sam rested his palms on the latte-colored tile counter and hung his head. "Leave it to you to remind me what a self-serving bastard I can be.''

"No, I didn't mean—''

"I know it, but that's what I am. So okay, if you want to imagine worst case scenarios, have you considered the possibly that it's not junior, but senior behind this?''

Brette made a silent, O. Truman! It had never crossed her mind.

"Whoa," he added upon seeing her expression. "We're talking hypotheticals only, okay?''

"Absolutely. You think...? His daughter-in-law?''

"He wouldn't be the first old fart to have watched a hot-blooded young thing drive his boy nuts year in and year out. To top it all off, there's no sign of heirs in sight. Maybe she's even been toying with *him*.''

"Now you're going too far. The only toying Tracie was apt to do with Truman was put Milk of Magnesia in his oatmeal.''

"You're not seeing it from the right angle. You said yourself they're both misogynists. Dysfunction makes people close, too. Trust me, I've lived there. Even if they despise each other, Truman and Albert understand one another. That's a powerful bond.''

"That's terrifying.''

"All the more reason to keep your distance," he said with a level look.

But Brette's mind was already wrapping around the idea. "I'm going to mention this to Cudahy. He called to ask if Hank could come over and look at some pictures the FBI faxed from their known pedophile files to see if this Mel creep is among them.''

With a brief shake of his head, Sam headed out of the kitchen and turned down the hallway. ''You'll make him sorry he called you,'' he said over his shoulder.

Brette followed. ''I'll stick to the facts. I won't broach the subject until Hank's busy studying mug shots, either. Discretion is one of my assets, you—oh!''

The instant she reached the doorway, Sam tugged her into his office, shut the door and kept her against it with his body.

''I'm well aware of your assets,'' he murmured, lightly scoring his teeth along the length of her throat. ''But discretion's not my favorite.''

There was an urgency in him, a readiness confirmed by the arousal he pressed against her womb, a hunger that was contagious and had her moaning into his mouth as he took hers. She had wondered when they could be together again; the likelihood hadn't seemed great for the near future. But here they were, and he was proving their time was now.

Releasing her hands, he ran his palms along her sides, over the outer swell of her breasts and over them, clearly entranced with the discovery that she wore no bra, until soon her nipples thrust hard against the stiff denim of her shirt. Then, with a restless sound, he popped open the snap enclosures and spread the material wide.

''Damn, you're pretty.''

He bent to taste and suckle, not satisfied with the tremulous sigh he won from her, not satisfied until she was gripping his hair and arching into his mouth.

What she wouldn't give for the luxury of time. But there was so little.

"Sam..."

"I know." His breathing shallow, he straightened and gazed down into her eyes. "Can't we be selfish for...ten minutes? Give us ten minutes."

Ten minutes didn't allow for a lot of things—not slow undressing or lingered caressing. But there was no denying its power to excite.

With a wide-mouthed kiss, Sam drew her onto his bed. By the time he had her matching the rhythm of his tongue with the thrust of her hips, he had her shirt almost off and her jeans and panties down.

Brette helped get his belt loose, and she alone opened his jeans. He was busy watching her, stroking her hair, slipping his thumb into her mouth.

"Take me in your hand. Hold me tight."

He surged inside the vise of her fingers, his face a mask of concentration and pleasure. "The table...can you reach...?"

The one condom they hadn't used the other night. She managed, barely, and as she put it on him, his hand ventured down between her thighs to explore the delicate, moist folds, and deeper to the heat within.

Desire and her imagination were working against her though, and instead of relaxing and letting herself flow with the sensations, she tightened against her own body's betrayal. "I think I'm too far ahead of you."

"No." Shifting he buried himself inside her with one, smooth stroke. "You're perfect. Perfect."

She peaked simply from the pulsating pressure of him, only to be driven higher yet by his urgent thrusts.

That dragged a sharp groan from him; then, rendered momentarily still, the two of them drifted down together.

Panting, Sam spread a series of kisses over her face. "Forgive me," he murmured, his voice a dry rasp.

"For what?"

"For needing this, you, too much."

"I'd rather just love you for all you are."

"Don't stop." Sam buried his face in her hair. "For God's sake, never stop."

46

One of the Greeks said the two things you can't
hide are being drunk and being in love. I don't
want to hide what I feel for Sam, I just want the
chance to experience it fully. But I can't do that
if I do what he's asking. Turn my back on something I feel is so malevolent and close? I need
to find the answer to the riddle that's Tracie,
otherwise I don't think any of us will ever know
real happiness again.
—Journal Entry

Monday, November 15, 1999

As they approached Quitman and the sheriff's office,
Hank grew increasingly quiet. He'd seemed happy to
see her when she'd picked him up earlier as arranged
with the office. He'd all but run to her truck. They'd
had a good weekend—no laughing or anything like
that, it was too soon for those kinds of expectations.
But with Sam's help, they'd moved his computer and
things he wanted to keep from across the street. Then
Brette had taken him to Tyler to choose some accessories for his room. He'd surprised her by asking to
forgo the drapes she'd suggested and requested a

small aquarium instead. The rest of what he chose was all in shades of blue, and the calming colors and the aquarium already seemed to have had a soothing influence on him. It sure would come in handy now.

"Nervous?" she asked when he'd shifted for the third time in less than a minute.

"Yeah. I guess."

"Maybe I should have gotten Eric out of school, too, to keep you company."

"Nah. He's looking forward to getting home and seeing what Sam's up to."

"Do you mind? I mean, his wanting to learn how to use his hands and make things?"

"Uh-uh. Do you?"

Brette didn't quite follow. "His being drawn to what Sam does?"

"Aw, if Sam was into raising rabbits, Eric would ask you for a bunny cage."

It was a surprisingly cynical reply for a kid his age, but Brette was careful not to criticize. "There's something to be grateful for. I have a feeling we'd have twice the coyote population if we had to deal with them. So what are you telling me? You think Eric's only doing this because he thinks it'll please Sam?"

"Maybe not. They do seem to be hitting it off pretty well."

"And how about you? Do you dislike him any less than you did?"

Hank slid her a sidelong look. "Are you figuring out a way to tell me you two are getting married?"

One thing she had to say for him, he didn't mince words. Brette replied with as much honesty as she could. "He hasn't asked me, and even if he did, I think it's a little soon."

"Because of my mother dying?"

"That, and a number of things."

Hank was quiet for a moment. "He'll ask you."

"And...? You still haven't told me how you'd feel about that?"

"I guess if he treats you okay, he's not as bad as I thought."

Well, Brette thought, it wasn't a standing ovation, but it wasn't the prelude to Armageddon, either.

Degrees happier than she expected to be this afternoon, she added, "By the way, I asked Keith about that computer cable you said you were having trouble with. He's getting you a replacement and said he'll come over to hook it up when it arrives."

"I know how to hook up a dumb old cable."

"Of course, but he said this one can be touchy because the connector part...sorry, I forget. Most things about computers still confuse me."

"You forgot because what he said is crap."

"Hank, that's cold. What's your problem with Keith? He's been great to you."

"So he says, but then he's a legend in his own mind. Truth is, he's a jerk."

"Since when?"

"Since I grew up."

Brette didn't know how to respond to that one.

"Tracie was right," he continued, his venom all but uncontrollable now. "He's a fag."

"*Hank.*" They could no longer pretend otherwise that his experience up in Saint Louis would make it more and more difficult for him to respond to men with anything but antagonism. Tomorrow, Brette promised herself, tomorrow she would start the search for a good therapist. In the meantime she had to put some kind of signal flag out there for him to understand how deeply he'd been out of line.

"Tracie didn't know Keith well at all, and she had no right to use derogatory language about him to you."

"She knew him well enough to tell my mother she was wasting her time with him. And she was right." Then Hank grimaced. "Do you hear us? We're talking about her as though we know for sure that she's gone."

"You're right, I'm sorry."

But he was wrong about Sally and Keith. They hadn't clicked because Keith couldn't respond to Sally's crassness, or to her addictive nature. Hadn't he made it clear to *her* afterward that he would have liked to go out with her? But by then Sam had moved in next door....

As they arrived at the station, they saw that Sheriff Cudahy was returning from somewhere himself. He waited at the front door for them to catch up and opened it for them.

"Appreciate you coming Ms. Barry, Hank. How's it going?" he added to the teen.

"I've been better."

"It's been a bad streak, yes. I'm sorry about your loss."

"Thanks."

Cudahy laid his big paw of a hand on Hank's shoulder and directed him past the dispatcher-reception desk behind a bulletproof window, to a door marked Detective John Box.

"John's working out in the field, but he left this folder of mug shots faxed down from Saint Louis and another compiled from Texas agencies for you to look at. There are quite a few, which should tell you that we're not doing as well on the visual ID of the guy as the Feds are in tracking him online. So don't feel bad if, after a while, all the faces start looking alike to you.''

Cudahy brought the file to a small conference room with a glass window. ''You're welcome to sit with him, Ms. Barry.''

''I will in a minute. First I'd like to talk to you, Sheriff, if you have time?''

Cudahy checked his watch. ''The DA's coming by at three, but I'm yours until then.''

Brette stepped across the hall and waited until he closed the door and joined her.

''That's a fairly soundproof environment,'' he said, pointing with his thumb over his shoulder.

''It's just that Hank has enough to worry about right now, he doesn't need me adding tonnage.''

Cudahy's expression didn't change, except for a warming of his relentlessly bloodshot eyes. ''You look as though you could use a week with a different view yourself. And a banana split or two.''

Brette was grateful for the gentle teasing. ''I'll be fine. If I can get Hank the right people he needs around him, and on the road he's wanting to travel, that will mean more to me than a vacation, Sheriff. What I want to talk to you about is Tracie Pugh.''

Cudahy's chin dug into the collar of his starched khaki shirt. ''I was afraid this would be that same old dog and bone.''

''It's not, Sheriff. Do you know she and Albert have split?''

''Hmm…Mrs. Cudahy must have missed that one in the paper.''

"Go ahead and make jokes, but this isn't so amusing. We don't have a forwarding notice for her."

"You're now speaking for the United States Post Office?"

"Don't you find that odd?"

"Not if there was nothing she wanted, and no one she wanted following her to her new destination."

"In which case, she would have already taken everything that's hers, correct?"

"I can tell you're dying to share something with me."

Brette would have preferred he phrase that differently but she nodded. "Albert's throwing away her things."

Cudahy's expression remained impassive. "Like?"

"Her *things*—clothes, personal items, makeup...all still good. She would have taken it all with her."

A rumbling sound rose from his chest making him sound like a great old alligator. "And how do you know all this?"

This wasn't her favorite part, but with some reluctance she repeated the story the boys had told her after Sam went home the other morning.

The corners of Cudahy's mouth were on a downhill slide. "You're going through the people's trash?"

"Not me. But the lid was off, and no one took anything...except, well, Clovis."

"Placing blame on that poor sick soul isn't going to win high marks from me, Ms. Barry. If I find your prints on anything, or Knight's—and I shouldn't have to remind you he's the last person seen in the company of the so-called *missing* woman—you're the first people I'm coming to see."

"Why? Sam's not the one trashing her property."

"No, but it sounds as though her husband has cause— Damn." Cudahy ran his hands over his face. "Where's everything now?"

"Gone."

"To?"

Brette shrugged meekly. "The garbage truck came and took it. Everything, that is, except what Clovis had in his...well, this." Brette held up the plastic baggy with the earring.

Looking as though he could teach her a string of new words that even a marine drill instructor hadn't heard of yet, Cudahy plucked the bag from her and squinted at it. After several seconds, he tugged his glasses from his shirt pocket and slipped them on. The more he looked, the more his chest swelled and his face discolored.

"Who all's touched this?" he demanded. But before she could respond, he motioned her to wait. A uniformed man was passing. "Avery, get somebody to check this out pronto. I need to know if what's on there is what I think."

"Yes, sir."

As the man dashed away, Brette wrapped her arms around herself feeling a distinct coldness settling around her. "Why? What did you see?"

"Blood. Now answer my question. Who had possession of that earring?"

She had virtually no time to gauge her options. "Me...and Clovis, of course."

"Who *else?*"

She could see it in his eyes. He wasn't going to leave her alone until she said it.

"Sam."

47

"**I** tried, really. I wanted to see him in those mug shots," Hank said as they drove home. "It would have been a relief for something good to happen for a change."

Brette gripped the steering wheel willing herself to keep from panicking. She was terrified, and she didn't know how she was going to face Sam.

"What's wrong?" Hank leaned forward studying her. "You've been awful quiet since I finished with those files. I thought you were looking kinda flushed, but now you're more grayish-green. What did Cudahy do, feed you bad coffee?"

She couldn't tell him, not until she spoke to Sam. It wouldn't be right. "Something's come up. I'll explain later."

"Something I did?"

"No." She reached over and patted his shoulder. "This is definitely not about you."

Hank tried to initiate conversation several times on the way home and grew progressively more quiet, in the end only watching her. When they got to the house, she simply sat there behind the wheel.

"Aren't you getting out?" he asked.

She nodded toward Sam's shop. "They're over

there. I need to talk to Sam, so Eric will be returning to the house shortly.''

''You're acting weird.''

She supposed she was, but there was good reason.

Leaving her purse in her car, she headed for the shop. As she drew nearer, she heard laughing. It struck her that she hadn't heard Eric sounding happy in weeks. And she was about to put an end to that.

He spotted her first. ''Hey, Mom, I made my first corner joint. A real one with wooden plugs, look. Cool, huh?''

Brette stared at the two pieces of scrap wood fastened by a piece of circular wood, but her mind saw Cudahy's face as she'd left the sheriff's office.

''Mom? You don't look good.''

''I guess not. Honey, I need you to do me a big favor and go be with Hank at the house. Sam and I need some time.''

''But I'm in the middle of this.''

''Eric.'' Sam had been observing them, withholding any comment, but now he simply nodded to the boy.

Looking contrite, Eric murmured, ''Sorry,'' and started to leave. After a few steps he paused. ''Is Hank okay? Did he see the guy or something?''

Brette shook her head. ''No. He didn't have any luck.''

As her son disappeared around the shop door, Brette exhaled shakily and buried her face in her hands. She heard Sam approach her, and his strong hands gently grip her shoulders from behind.

''Eric's not the only one wondering. What's wrong?''

She loved the way he spoke to her now. Since he'd

lowered the barriers between them, every word, every look or touch, was underscored with such sensitivity and caring. It was the height of selfishness to delay answering so as not to lose that, but she knew the world was going to be a much colder place in a few moments.

"Hey..." He turned her and framed her face with those same careful, work-rough hands. "You aren't keeping something about Hank from Eric, are you? Brette, this isn't like you."

"I've made a terrible mistake." She forced herself to meet his concerned gaze. "And you need to know straight off how terribly, terribly sorry I am because you're about to hate me and there may not be an opportunity to say it then."

"I love you. You can say anything."

"No, Sam. You don't know what you're saying. You see...I told Cudahy about what was in the trash and what Clovis found."

While not overjoyed by the news, his expression didn't turn cold, and he didn't push her away, either. "You as much as said you would. So now what? He's angry with you for messing in people's private property and for continuing to play detective, right? Probably told you that you were lucky to get away with a slashed tire for your nosing around."

"He doesn't buy that Albert cut my tire."

"Well, hell. Even after you told him about what happened to you down at the farm earlier that day?"

"It gets worse. I showed him the earring."

"Accused you of planting it, right?"

"No, he thinks there's...he's sent it for testing, Sam."

Realization dawned on his face and he relaxed.

"You're worried about fingerprints. On something that small that at least three of us touched? I don't think so, angel."

"For blood."

"What blood?"

"He saw...those speckles aren't merely tasteless art, Sam. He thinks some of that's blood."

A slight frown appeared between his dark eyebrows. "No wonder you're turning different colors. You can't help imagine how it got on there. Wait. You think it's— Babe, I didn't bleed when I laid on the thing. I just scraped myself a bit." Although he looked less confident than before, Sam stroked her hair. "It'll be all right."

"No, it won't be. Listen to me. If there's blood on the earring and it's not yours, it's hers, isn't it? And even if you didn't bleed, chances are there's minute skin residue on it. Yours, Sam."

"Jesus."

He slowly let go of her and began backing away, stepping deeper into the shadows. It was so much like before when he had locked himself from her, from virtually everything. Brette couldn't bear it and covered her eyes again.

Silence stretched between them, until suddenly Sam demanded, "Look at me."

She didn't want to.

"Do it."

She dropped her hands.

"Hell. That look is back in your eyes."

What on earth...? "No."

"After all we've shared?" Pain underscored the words as much as disbelief.

"I'm not afraid of you. I'm afraid *for* you."

But he didn't believe her. His mind was manifesting what he feared most to see—her rejection of him.

"Did Cudahy tell you when he's coming for me?" he continued with growing sarcasm. "Or am I expected to turn myself in like the nice law-abiding citizen that I'm supposed to be when I'm not being a psychotic killer?"

"Don't." She went to him. He held up his hands to ward her off, but she pushed them aside and wrapped her arms around him. "I'm sorry. I'm so sorry. It never crossed my mind that he would jump to that of all conclusions. If I'd known, I never would have shown him the earring. Never."

"You protect a killer? I don't think so."

"You're no murderer, Sam."

But his expression was becoming more resigned, and when he freed himself, the intimacy that had begun to characterize his touches no longer existed.

"I can't do this again," he said as though talking to himself. "Go under a microscope, live morning, noon and night at the beck and call of the police, hunted by a media hungry for anything that smells like a story." He shot her a harsh look. "Do you know what it's like to come face-to-face on the street with a neighbor kid you taught to apply calculus, to see form out of a bunch of numbers and lines, to create with these?" He held up his hands. "Ask me what it's like when none of that's there anymore, when there's only sheer terror on his face? Or how about when a cop draws his gun on you because you're holding your child after a court says you can't?" He dropped his hands. "Not again."

"We'll get through this," Brette pleaded. "This time things are different."

"Hell, they are. I've lost my job because an entire school is afraid of me. I was the last person to see Tracie alive. *I'm* the one who first noticed your tire was slashed. You'd have to set me up to make me look guiltier."

"But you're not alone this time. There are people who believe in you."

"You, exactly one-point-five of your kids, and an old lady who's got her hands so full caring for a sick and senile husband, she believes anyone who gives her the time of day may be one of those visiting angels out of Hebrews?" Sam taunted. "Cudahy's probably calling together a team to come and get me as we speak. Go home, Brette."

"No."

"Don't you get it? *It's over.*"

As he headed for his workbench and reached for the switch to turn off the lights, she went after him. Grabbing his arm, she pulled him around. "Don't you dare quit on me, Sam Knight! I believe in you. I believe in *us.* Now, I created this mess, and I'm going to see that the real guilty party gets what they deserve. For my money that's Albert Pugh."

"You stay away from him, his father, too, for that matter." For the first time since she'd told him, there was torment in his eyes as he looked at her. "I don't want you on my conscience on top of everything else."

"I'm already there. Here, too," she added laying her hand against his heart. "Gripe about it if you want to, but you're stuck with me."

At first he looked apt to argue with her; however, in the next instant he was swearing under his breath and crushing her against him. "Oh, God, Brette," he groaned against her hair. "I can't lose you."

"You won't."

"Kiss me."

He needed reassuring, to feel the promise of life, of hope. She could give him that.

She put her heart and soul into that moment, holding him as tightly as he held her, so tight her bones, not just her muscles, ached. Her kiss was a promise. Everything would be all right. They had innocence on their side. And after they proved Cudahy wrong, they would begin convincing everyone else that he was a good man.

When Sam broke the kiss to simply hold her against his pounding heart, Brette knew it was time to get him out of there and into the light. She didn't want fear getting its hold on him again.

"Let's close up and go to the house," she told him. "I'll make us all some dinner. The boys need us."

She helped him swing shut the doors and he locked up.

As they were walking toward her place, their arms around each other, a white vehicle with the telltale strobe lights on the roof drove by.

"It's going to the Pughs'," Brette murmured. "Could you tell who was inside?"

Sam's arm tightened around her. "Cudahy was in the passenger seat. It's too soon to have any information from a lab. That means he's on a fishing expedition. What do you want to bet I'm his target for the next cast?"

48

"They've *invited* him to come down to the station this morning and tell his side of things." Brette could barely slot her mail, she was so upset. "What do you want to bet if he'd declined they would have cuffed him right in front of the boys and hauled him off to jail? I swear, if Cudahy doesn't retire after this term is over—"

"We draft Tucker for sheriff," Desiree called over from her side of the room. "Den I get my brodder in California to take Tucker's route."

Her attempt at humor didn't go over well with him. "Here's a new one for you, Miss Rice Cake. If you take an Oriental person and spin him around a couple times, does he become dis*orientated?*"

"You steal dat off Internet, Tucker?"

"You're trying to steal my job." Answering her stuck-out tongue with a goofy pantomime of his own, he turned back to Brette. "That'll keep her talking for a while. So Cudahy doesn't think Albert did your tire? Hard core."

"He thinks it's suspicious that Sam just happened

to be coming home at a convenient time to play the hero."

"Hell, in that case, it could have been the Keyboard Kid."

"I'm sure Keith will be interrogated next." Brette indicated a registered letter on the corner of her table. "That's his, so at least I get to warn him—and ask him to inform Cudahy that he'd heard more than one truck drive by that night."

"While you're lining up witnesses for your honey, you might ask Bertrice to check with her doctor about Clovis's ability to testify."

"Oh, jeez, Tucker, add to my day why don't you." Brette couldn't see how he could. "Even if anyone could understand what he said, his memory is starting to come and go so sporadically, he could do more damage than good on a witness stand."

"The handwriting's on the wall, sugar. Cudahy doesn't have a corpse yet, and he's serious about sticking your boy with a murder charge. Old Clov better have a lucid moment, 'cuz right now he's the only thing that'll keep the Terminator from rooming with his old man down in Huntsville."

Brette winced at the horrible thought. "There has to be something I can do."

"Did he call his lawyer?"

"Yes. And that brings up more cheerful news. If he has to put him on retainer, that'll mean getting a second note on his house or putting it up on the market."

"I hope to heaven you didn't offer to hand that boy your wallet."

"I know you're not wholly convinced he's innocent, Tucker, but if I did offer to help him out, he would have turned me down. That's the kind of noble person he is.''

''Bull. Slick's going to make you *insist* he takes your money.''

''Damn you, Tucker.''

Brette refused to speak to him the rest of the morning. He'd so upset her that her mind wasn't on her driving and she almost got herself killed an hour later when she failed to stop at an intersection. The eighteen-wheeler that blasted its horn at her raced by, leaving her to break out in a cold sweat. Since the temperatures had dropped back to more seasonal temperatures, she ended up shivering hard enough to make her teeth chatter.

''Another moment of brilliance, Barry. You're going to be a ton of help to Sam dead.''

She wished she could see him. But by now he was over in Quitman. There hadn't been an opportunity to wish him luck or kiss him one last time. Sure, she'd done all that last night as he'd left to go home; however, he needed all the moral support he could get.

When she reached the Ponders', she was dismayed to see that their inner door was shut and the miniblinds were down on the picture window. Of course she understood; Bertrice was probably still exhausted from helping with the funeral.

It was just as well, Brette decided. This way she didn't have to split her time between them and Keith and, as a result, rush explanations about Sam's situation. There would be plenty of time to fill Bertrice in later.

She pulled into Keith's driveway and parked. The registered letter was all he was getting today, and she saw that the side door to the kitchen was open. Thinking he was probably in there making himself a late breakfast, she headed for it rather than the front door.

"Keith?" She knocked on the glass.

He appeared wearing a white T-shirt and navy sweatpants.

"Have a Registered for you." She held up the white envelope.

Looking bleary-eyed and somewhat preoccupied, he fumbled with the door's lock. "Now I remember why I hate using this door. How's it going?"

"Don't ask. Here, let me give you my pen so you can sign the card. By the *X* as usual."

He accepted the pen and letter, but his focus was on her. "Either you haven't downloaded yet from the stress of last week, or those kids are wearing you out."

Self-consciously, Brette smoothed her wind-mussed hair. She supposed she should have clipped it back or worn a hat, but after tossing and turning all night, she'd accidentally hit the snooze button and almost overslept this morning. There had barely been time to brush her teeth let alone worry about anything else.

"Look that bad, huh?"

He smiled. "You never look bad. You look fragile."

"I don't know about that, but I'm definitely concerned. Cudahy called Sam in this morning. It turns out that, after you left our place the other day, Clovis wandered off and found an earring."

"Huh. Hope there's a big diamond in it."

"Hardly. We're pretty sure it belonged to Tracie. To make a long story short, I'm more certain than ever that Albert's killed her. Sheriff Cudahy's found blood on the thing, but instead of hauling Albert in for questioning, Cudahy's fixated on Sam. In fact, he's over at the station this minute.''

"Why Sam?''

"Because he was the last one to see Tracie the night she vanished. She stopped at his house for a minute wanting a lift to a bus station. She was apparently leaving. From my perspective, a husband's more apt to turn violent over abandonment than a neighbor is just because he's being hit up for a ride.''

"It doesn't sound like the good sheriff's in his usual form, does it?''

Brette accepted the letter and pen back from Keith only to drop the pen. "Now you know how much of a wreck I am today.''

"Let me get that for you.''

"No, I'll get my act together in a second.'' First she ripped off the green card that had to be returned, but in the process of handing the letter to Keith, she dropped it. "Hell. This is turning into a farce.''

She went down two steps and plucked the card from the top of one of the dying azalea bushes. "These need water.''

"Yes, Mommy.''

She was less successful in locating her pen. "It's got to be here. C'mon, c'mon...oh, I'd forget about the darned thing if it wasn't the only one I have left.''

"I can give you—''

"Aha!'' She spotted a brief flash in a small pocket of sunlight angling through the plants. "There it is.''

But she was wrong. It wasn't the pen, it was...an earring.

Brette stared, her mind wanting to reject that it was

there, what that meant. The problem was, this earring was clearly covered with blood.

"Oh, God."

The survivor's voice inside her yelled, "Run!," but Keith's reflexes were faster. Before she knew it, he had a handful of her oversize sweater and was hauling her backward.

"No!"

Literally yanked off her feet, the backs of her calves hit the concrete stairs. She cried out in pain and terror. He was taking her into the house.

"No—please!"

Abandoning her attempt to right herself, she tried to break free. In the commotion of flailing hands and limbs, she saw something coming at her—shiny, metallic. It struck, delivering a pain that blinded her with its white light. And then she was falling…falling into a black, cold sea.

49

The unbearable pain was returning. Only now it wasn't merely threatening to burst her head wide-open, it had spread throughout her entire body. Brette felt as though she'd been dropped off of Reunion Tower in Dallas and, for good measure, fallen in front of a passing Amtrak train.

Wave after wave of agony assaulted her, bringing a nausea that soon had her gagging. She was going to throw up, but she couldn't get to the bathroom because she was bound. Worse, she couldn't open her mouth.

Suddenly a brutal hand grabbed a handful of her hair jerking her head back. Through a new flash of pain, she stared up at Keith's face as he reached down and ripped the wide piece of tape off of her mouth.

"Breathe. Do it. And don't think of screaming. You scream and I'll have to hit you again."

Brette gulped at air, grateful when it succeeded in stopping the hideous rush of bile threatening to suffocate her. Only then did she see clearly enough to notice Keith's expression of disgust as he wiped blood off his hand with a tissue. Her blood. She could feel it seeping down the back of her head.

She took more gulps to repress the mounting panic

inside her. At the same time she tried to determine where she was.

There was office furniture, and machinery—no computers. Keith's house. That explained the humming, clicking and whirring sounds. But what she had trouble believing was the image on the screen directly before her.

Disgusted, she averted her gaze, but it was too late. In her mind's eye she still saw the naked young boy lying on the cot, his hands on his genitalia.

"Some line of work you're in." Unfortunately, she couldn't emote the proper loathing; her voice was barely a croak.

"It's just a hobby."

"One that's going to put you in prison."

"I don't think so. You said yourself, fate was kind in providing me with your good neighbor Sam to draw attention away from me. And if by chance the authorities disappoint by smartening up, I'm making arrangements for your nemesis Albert to be caught with something of yours in his possession."

Brette struggled to stay calm, to not fight the duct tape that bound her hands behind her back and her ankles, but Keith's pleasant, matter-of-fact tone was as unnerving as the realization of who he was and what he'd done. "You won't get away with it this time, Keith. Someone's going to see my truck outside."

"It's not outside. Hasn't been for hours."

Hours? Despite the searing pain in her head, she looked around for a clock. She finally found one on the desk nearest her head and saw it was nearly three. Sam should be home by now wondering what was keeping her. He had probably already tried to call her on her cellular. The boys would be arriving within a half hour. Tucker and the others would be wondering what on earth had happened to her. All was not lost; she had to believe that. There was hope as long as she kept thinking and planning.

She licked her burning lips. "What do you mean my truck's not outside? Where is it?"

"Back at your place. That's why I had to hit you so hard. I'm sorry about that, but I needed to be sure you'd stay out cold until I could move it and get back again without being seen."

The frightening thing was that he actually sounded apologetic. "You're all heart. But you made a mistake, you know. Sam will take one look at all the mail in my truck and realize something is seriously wrong—and he'll have the best of alibis. So much for your thorough planning."

Keith shrugged. "I told you, there's always Albert. After it gets dark I'll see that enough evidence is planted to get the job done."

"The way you *saw* that my anger at Albert stayed high by slashing my tire?"

"You kept feeding me these delicious opportunities to keep myself out of the picture." Keith's grin was boyish and delighted. "How could I resist?"

How could she have been so wrong about him?

"So where did Tracie fit in all of this?" she asked, trying to piece it all together.

"Like you, she made a mistake."

But he didn't sound sorry like he had when he'd talked about her blunder. "Why didn't you like her? As undiscriminating as she was, she could have given you more cover."

"Please. She proved there was a class below trailer

trash.'' He smiled at his own rhyme. ''You know that
country definition of a low-life person? 'If a snake
farted, it would blow dust in her eyes.' That was Tracie. That slut thought all she had to do was shake her
booty and guys would swarm around her. Of course,
in a way they did—like flies to a garbage dump. Albert won't ever know, but he owes me a big thank
you for alleviating him of *that* problem.''

Ignoring her roiling insides, Brette forced herself
to learn more. ''She found out you were a homosex-
ual, didn't she?''

He came out of his chair as though from an ejection
seat. ''I'm *not* gay, got it?''

Brette shrank away from the arm he raised to back-
hand her. ''Okay, okay. Reset the fuses, why don't
you?''

Tight-lipped, Keith punched the monitor button and
the offending screen went blank. ''I didn't ask her to
come here.'' Agitated, he paced the length of the
room and back again. ''But after your boyfriend shut
the door in her face, she came up here trying to con-
nive me into taking her to a bus depot. She even offered to reward me, if you catch my drift—as though
I'd dirty myself on her. When I said I had work to
do, she whined some more and then demanded a drink
before she would leave. I was so ready to get rid of
her I made it. But the minute I turned my back, she
started wandering around the house. I found her in
here. That's when she called me a—''

Brette watched in horrified fascination as he
stopped before the window and looked out, clenching
and unclenching his hands. She could only imagine
what he was seeing.

''She laughed at me. And she was going to blackmail me. Oh, I got to see the survivor in Tracie come to life. She was so desperate to get away from the misery of her own making, she didn't care if she hurt me, ruined me.''

''So she would have spewed some gossip,'' Brette said. ''Who ever took Tracie seriously? As for Albert, he knew what he had in her. He would have been more upset that she came to you than worried about any, um, hobby she claimed you had.''

He turned to stare at her. ''You're laughing at me, too.''

''No.''

''You are. And you'd spread stories. I'm right about this,'' he said as though assuring himself. ''It would never end.''

In that instant she knew there was no way she could talk him out of killing her. To think this was someone who'd been in her home, who she'd trusted to be with her son and Hank. He'd been wise to tie her up because in that instant she knew if she was free, she'd tear him apart.

The rumble of an engine drew Keith's attention and he stepped out of the room. Brette used the time to twist around to see how securely her hands were tied. It looked as though he'd judged her on her size and sex; there were only two layers of tape. If she could find something sharp...

Her gaze locked on the staple remover on the desk by the window. Its sharp teeth could be sufficient. Duct tape wouldn't give easily, and the more you twisted, the more it became like rope, but if you managed to puncture it, get it to begin tearing, things changed considerably.

But as she tried to struggle to her knees Keith

stepped back into the room. He grabbed up the role of tape and ripped off a new piece, which he quickly pressed against her mouth.

"The school bus just passed," he said. "Time to start moving."

50

The sun had begun its slide past the first tier of pines when Sam pulled into his street. The clock on his dash told him that the boys and Brette should be home by now. In fact, he'd passed the empty school bus about three miles back. They were going to be eager to hear how things went. But as relieved as he was to be coming home, he wasn't looking forward to sharing the news.

Cudahy was definitely eyeing him as his number one suspect, the logic being that Sam had more motive than anyone to get Tracie out of the way now that he had seduced Brette. All Tracie had to offer was a divorce settlement. But, the sheriff reasoned, if Sam played his cards right, he was within reach of Brette's inheritance, as well as control of Eric's trust fund, not to mention whatever Sally's estate brought once her will was probated. Afterward, he could move Brette and the kids away from the area, maybe out of state, and within a few months easily dispose of them, too. Who would know if they vanished off the face of the earth? And he, the grieving widower-stepfather, would be set for life—or more likely, until the next meal ticket came along. Yeah, Cudahy had sounded as though he was writing the DA's opening argument for him.

The boys were outside circling Brette's truck when he passed. Although beat, he waved back at them and pulled into his driveway, belatedly realizing as they chased after him that they hadn't been greeting him at all, but trying to signal him to stop sooner. Something was wrong.

"Sam, come quick!" Eric almost yanked the door out of his grasp in his eagerness to rush him.

More unsettling than the panic in the boy's voice was the desperation in his and Hank's faces. "Is it Brette?"

"She's gone."

"Gone where?" Confused, he looked at her truck.

"Missing," Hank supplied. "We got here maybe ten minutes before you and that's what we found."

Eric urged Sam closer to the truck. "Look inside— the mail is all there. She didn't deliver it. And she's not in the house. It was locked up and everything was the way we left it this morning."

This was so unlike the devoted and efficient woman he knew that Sam found himself hoping it was some kind of joke. He would be pissed for sure, but once he got over explaining that a coronary tended to be fatal, he would grudgingly admit they'd succeeded in getting his mind off the hours he'd spent in interrogation.

"What about your place, Hank? Did you check in there? How about the backyard? You know how she is about the deer. Maybe she saw an injured one and—" He caught Eric's look. "Right. Not even she would leave the mail undelivered and risk her job that way."

"There's a bunch of messages on the machine in the house. One's from her supervisor and two are

from Tucker,'' Eric said. ''There's even a couple
from customers because Mom's like family to them.
They're all as freaked as we are. What do we do?''

Sam didn't answer right away for the simple reason
that he couldn't. He needed a moment. He took it by
leaning into the open passenger window looking for
some clue of normalcy or, God forbid, a lack of it.
But he couldn't really tell without opening the truck,
and he was in enough trouble without adding his
prints to his list of alleged sins.

As he straightened again, another vehicle approached. It was Tucker.

''Boy, this had better be good, Barry,'' the red-
faced man roared as he charged toward Brette's truck.
''Because I'm about to call the—'' Tucker ducked
once, then a second time to look into the open passenger window before giving Sam a dumbfounded
look. ''Where is she?''

''That's what we're trying to determine.''

''What the hell does that mean? She's gotta be
around. Have you checked all of the houses? The
sheds?''

''Hey. I only just got here myself,'' Sam replied,
''and the boys ten minutes prior to that. You're seeing
what we saw.''

''Oh, damn. Damn it to hell. I should have taken
her more seriously.'' Tucker struck the top of her cab
with his fist. ''Why the hell didn't she keep that little
tush in the fucking truck.''

Sam backed him away from the vehicle and the
boys. ''You listen to me because I'm only going to
say this once. I want to swear, too. I'm scared shitless.
But you keep the language down in front of the kids

and you hold the Rambo talk for when it's just you and me.''

The wild-eyed man wiped at his mouth and beard and nodded. ''Sorry. I'm okay. Have you called Cudahy? Yeah, yeah, I know you spent the day with him, but this is federal property,'' he said pointing inside the truck. ''And last I heard, my boss was about to phone himself, so call him.''

Sam went inside and started to dial Cudahy's number, then disconnected and used the memory dial to get Bertrice.

He tried not to upset her, but there was no getting around it. ''Bertie, it's Sam. Have you seen Brette?''

''Why no, darlin'. Is she supposed to be coming over?''

''Not exactly. Did you receive your mail this morning?''

''That's a strange question. Of course I have, as have you.''

''Not exactly.''

''What do you mean?''

Because of time pressures, Sam gave her the briefest of explanations. ''We're just groping in the dark, Bertie, and I know this will sound strange and scary to you, but keep your wits about you, all right? Stay inside, stay off the phone, and please don't panic if you see a lot of police vehicles arriving.''

''I'm already panicking. Sam, you have to find her.''

''I'll get back to you.''

His hands were beginning to shake, but he found Daggett's number in Brette's address book. This time the phone rang a few times before he got a machine recording.

"This is Keith. I'm here but tied up for the moment. Leave a message."

"Keith, this is Sam Knight. If you're there it's imperative that you pick up. Hello? Daggett?"

Sam disconnected, ready to cut his losses. The guy was probably useless anyway. Hadn't Brette said he didn't like the woods after dark any more than young Hank did? He supposed the guy lived in front of his machines so much, thieves could steal his house from under him and he probably wouldn't notice.

Wound tighter than when he had left the station, Sam finally dialed Cudahy's number. Not surprisingly, he got some screener.

"This is Sam Knight. I left the sheriff less than an hour ago and I need to speak with him."

"He's in a meeting. What's this about?"

"An emergency."

"Dial 911."

"Listen, pal. Because of him Brette Barry's missing. You tell him I said that and get him on this phone."

Cudahy was on the line within seconds. "What's this about Brette?"

"She's been taken, Sheriff." He gave him a slightly more graphic account of what he'd found. "Are you taking us seriously yet? I'm stuck in your stinking office all day and come home to find she's *gone*. Now I want men and dogs here fast or I'm going down to that dairy farm and I'm going to stuff Albert's head into some milk tanks and hold him there until he either talks or there are no more bubbles."

"That's real sharp, Sam. Start making threats." Cudahy sighed. "Where are the boys?"

"Here."

"Keep it that way, and yourself. We're on our way."

Sam hung up and dropped his head back to gaze at the ceiling. The house was abysmally quiet, and yet so full of her.

"Oh, baby...where are you?"

"Sam?" Eric came in. "Any luck?"

He could only shake his head. "The sheriff's on his way, though."

"You mean we have to wait longer yet to set out looking for her?"

Sam didn't blame him; he was frustrated himself. Nevertheless, he made himself say, "If we don't synchronize things, we'll end up duplicating our efforts."

"Tucker thinks Albert's got her."

"Tucker is—" Sam checked his words "—feeling guilty like I am that he didn't believe your mom sooner." He didn't want the boy to be torn between them and redirected his focus. "Can you remember anything, anything at all that she might have said to explain this?"

"There is no explaining this. She wanted to finish her route quick to get home and be here when you got back. She was worried about you."

Worried about him. And now he was losing his mind over her.

"Her purse isn't there," Eric offered. "That's a good sign."

"How so?"

"Isn't there some kind of law that women don't leave their purses behind?"

Sam laid a reassuring hand on the top of his head. "I don't think Congress has voted on that one yet."

"But she must've been okay when she left here because she took it with her."

And left her keys behind? Sam didn't buy it, but he wouldn't say that to Brette's son. "Keep at it. That's the whole idea. Maybe one of us will hit on the right thing. In the meantime, let's go outside to wait for the sheriff."

In actuality, he wanted to keep an eye on Tucker, and to intervene in his influence with Hank. The other boy was pointing out the places they'd searched when he and Eric rejoined them.

"I've been thinking," Tucker said to Sam. "This is where the truck's been all along, right? Right here?"

Sam considered the vehicle parked at the farthest end of the driveway. "Yes."

"Tell you what, then. She wasn't the one who parked it there."

"Why is that?"

"See that pine between your properties? It's a drippy old sucker. Brette loves the tree, the shape and all, so she won't take it down, but she hates the mess it makes. There's a pine by the post office and she has a baby cow when she gets stuck with the slot beneath it. So whoever parked that truck there—"

"Was someone who didn't know that." It wasn't much, Sam thought, but it was something.

"Maybe more important, it was someone who wanted to implicate someone else," Tucker added.

"Me."

Tucker nodded, encouraging him to keep going with the idea with a motion of his hand. "But you were in Quitman all day. Who all knew that?"

"The boys. You."

"What about…?" He directed his index fingers in opposite directions up and down the road.

"I just spoke to Bertrice Ponder. She was clueless. All she knows is that she received her mail as usual today. As for Daggett, I can't say yet. I tried to call him and got his machine. It says he's down there, but he's not picking up." And there was something about that that bugged him more and more.

"And the boys in Pughville?" asked Tucker. His smile grew cunning.

"You don't exactly expect me to phone them, do you?"

Tucker hoisted his jeans higher over his belly. "No, I think we should pay them the courtesy of a personal visit. I have a .12 gauge in my camper. What have you got?"

"A bad enough reputation to know not to own one." Sam turned to the boys. "You didn't hear any of this, right?"

"Yes, sir," they replied in unison.

Minutes later two patrol cars and a SUV arrived. Cudahy and another uniformed man came out of the first, Deputy Russell out of the second and the detective Sam was introduced to earlier, John Box, emerged from the four-wheel drive vehicle. After brief introductions John Box immediately returned to the back of his vehicle and brought out a black case the size of a piece of weekend luggage.

"So now what?" asked Sam when he'd obliged Cudahy and repeated everything he knew and had done since coming home. "And don't say sit tight and wait, because that's not going to happen."

"My men and I are about to go down to the Pugh place and have a more frank discussion with Truman and Albert than we had yesterday, as well as another look around.''

''Then I'm going up the road to finish talking to Brette's other friend.'' He intercepted the anxious glances of the boys. ''And taking my men with me.''

Neither his wit nor his intention impressed Cudahy. ''Isn't that a waste of your time?''

''The Pughs are Brette's suspects.'' He gave a final glance at her truck. ''I think I'll keep my options open.''

51

They were almost running, but Brette was cold, adrenaline doing nothing for her at this point. The sun was sinking fast. Down here in the bottoms that meant hardly any light was getting through the dense canopy of vegetation. She loved the woods in autumn, with the rainfall of colored leaves, the aroma of harvest and smoked food in the air and the various woods smells. But all she could think about now was that she'd heard of two new sightings of boar herds in the bottoms.

"You're lagging, move it."

Keith gave her a mighty push that almost sent her headlong into a tree. Brette stumbled several yards beyond it before regaining her balance.

He had removed the tape around her ankles so he wouldn't have to carry her. He said he'd "learned his lesson" with Tracie. Which was also why she was still conscious. As far as Brette was concerned, it was a gift to her more than himself. If she was to live, these were the little things that would save her.

She grunted from behind her taped mouth and bent at the waist, hoping her face would get red enough for him to worry that she was getting nauseated again.

"Stop it," he demanded. "I didn't push you that hard."

She whimpered and coughed harder to indicate that he had, until the coughing stopped being a performance.

"Shit." Keith pushed her against the nearest tree and ripped off the tape without any compassion for her increasingly tender skin. Pointing the two-foot length of pipe he carried into her face, he snarled, "Now shut up."

Brette wrenched to the side to cough in peace, ultimately slumping to her knees. Exhausted, dizzy, she rested her forehead against a young dogwood and wondered if Sam and the boys had any clue yet.

"Get up. We're not even halfway there."

"I won't make it the way you're treating me." She shifted to rub her runny nose and dirt-and-blood-smeared face on the knee of her jeans as best she could. The bleeding seemed to have slowed, but the pain was, if anything, more intense. "In case you've forgotten, I buried a friend recently and have barely eaten or slept in over a week. This little marathon of yours is asking a bit much." She thought she heard her words slurring—not a good sign.

"It'll be dark soon. We can't slow down."

"What's the rush? It all ends the same anyway, doesn't it?"

Just then she spotted the tree she wanted and let herself slump toward it. Groaning, she pretended to struggle with the ability to right herself, finally sitting with her back to the pine tree stump. It was perfect— wide, with lots of sharp edges from when the force of another tree snapped it close to the base.

"You'd better give me a minute, or you will have to carry me."

She wasn't going to insult him by adding that she

didn't think he was up to the job even in the condition she was in. She needed concessions at this point.

Grumbling, he lowered himself onto a long polished tree that had gone down in a storm two summers ago. "Two minutes. No more."

Two minutes…and no doubt his method of keeping time would be fast. Brette knew she couldn't just begin sawing her arms against the sharp wood, so she continued annoying him by whining.

"God, my back hurts. I must have struck my spine against one of your steps."

He looked away. Brette knew he was preparing himself for what was to come by refusing to get emotionally involved with her. Good news in that she could give a hard slice or two against the pointed pine. But on the third try she slipped and it cost her a jab into her flesh that sent a knifelike pain through her.

Pretending another coughing fit to cover her blunder, Brette frantically sought a way to buy herself more time and to get her mind off her various injuries.

"Just out of curiosity, are you…are you going to grant the prisoner a last wish?" she asked.

Emotions of unease and amusement flickered behind his neat little glasses. "You should be quiet and catch your breath. You're starting to sound drunk."

"Hey, it's my murder," she said with false bravado. "I'll die how I want to. What are you so uncomfortable about? I'm curious about how it went for Tracie. It's going to really bug me not knowing how her print ended up on that stupid sign. Wasn't she at your place when you knocked the holy heck out of her?"

Keith shrugged, looked away again and then murmured, "She came to."

"She what?"

"She came to too soon," he snapped. "I thought I'd hit her hard enough. I mean, she was unconscious and all. But when I went to find a blanket to wrap her body in, she was gone."

"You mean she ran all the way up the street passing the Ponders, our house, *Sam's* and she didn't scream for help? Boy, she must have had a worse concussion than I do."

"She kept to the woods because she heard me coming after her. But she was losing a lot of blood. I guess that's when she came out to the road and tried to steady herself on the sign. I didn't catch up with her until she was about a hundred yards from the house. That's also why I didn't know about the print on the sign until you told me."

The mystery was over. He'd been the one to sneak through the woods and wash the sign clean, coming dangerously close to Sally's house, assured that she was sleeping.

Brette had to bite her cheek to keep from exposing her horror for Tracie, too. She'd come so close. She'd almost made it.

Blinking back tears of rage as much as sorrow, she gave another try at the tape and felt it give somewhat.

"Then you had to carry her all the way back?" she asked quickly.

"No, down to their part of the marsh." Keith looked south to where the property line was almost visible, the same wire fence she and Sam had walked along looking for Hank only two and a half weeks ago. "It was only by accident I discovered that's where the boar activity has been especially intense. I think it's partly because the Pughs put their dead cows there. They're very strange people. You can get a few dollars even for diseased or fallen cattle, but Tracie said they didn't want anyone to know theirs had died, as though someone would think the milk the cattle produced wasn't any good. Anyway, that's where I put her and she was right. In three days there were only bones left, which, of course, eventually get eaten, too, by squirrels and other varmints.''

He rose. ''That's where we're going.''

52

They were losing daylight fast, and the boys were as aware of it as Sam was. As they drove up the street to Daggett's, they leaned over from the back seat like a couple of anxious six-year-olds.

"Tucker sure didn't want to stay behind." Eric watched Sam in the rearview mirror. Like Hank, he wore the fluorescent orange hat Brette had bought, insisting the pair wear them during hunting season, as well as another layer of sweaters and jackets.

Yes, Sam knew. However, Tucker was—to put it less kindly than Brette—a loose cannon who needed to be kept under close supervision. Sam figured Box was the best man for that job. He wasn't about to tell the boys that, though.

"I understand," he replied, "but even if Detective Box doesn't need any help or information, someone has to be there to answer the phone. And ultimately, that mail in your mom's truck needs to either be delivered or returned to town. He's the obvious choice."

"C'mon. You went cold when he told you he'd brought that .12 gauge, that's the real reason," Hank said.

Sam glanced over his shoulder at the boy. Whatever happened, he mused, Hank was going to require someone's total mental abilities to keep one step ahead of him. The kid wasn't a handful because he was slow or lazy, but because he needed to be adequately challenged. Neither his mother nor his teachers had taken the time to figure that out yet. Sam bet Brette knew, and he would talk to her about it when—

God, let there be a when.

Clearing his throat, Sam replied as fairly as he could. "You're right, but don't assume that means I'm antigun. They're wrong for Tucker, and they're definitely wrong for this situation. We'll be continually crossing each other's paths. With this being hunting season, and all the land on the east side of the marsh being leased, there's enough to worry about without a stray bullet coming from there."

Hank nodded, seeming to accept that as a solid explanation, and a relieved Sam turned into Keith Daggett's driveway. His sports coupe was in the driveway, but there were no lights on inside the house that Sam could see. Brette had said Keith could lose himself in his work, but surely he would have turned on something by now?

"You guys stay here for a sec." And for reasons he could attribute to intuition alone, he left the engine running.

"Suits me," Hank said. "The less I see of him the better."

Sam would have liked to question Hank about his increasingly cool attitude toward Daggett, but this wasn't the time. Besides, Eric was opening his door despite his directive.

"I didn't come to sit in any car," he began.

"Eric, I could use a little cooperation here."

"What if he tells you something that you don't get but I would?"

"I understand English."

"But you don't know her route. I know the names, I know her routine as well as she does."

He was his mother's son, all right, Sam thought. And although he still didn't like it, he relented. "Make sure you stay well behind me," he insisted.

The front door was shut, but the side door looked open. Sam chose to stay on the first step and stretch to knock.

"Seeing it's Mom, he'll probably want to come with us," Eric whispered.

If he tried, Sam intended to shut him down fast.

He knocked again.

Seconds stretched closer to a minute. Sam was ready to check and see if the door was locked, but he hesitated. It wasn't the legality issue, he just didn't like the vibes he was getting. Maybe it was sheer paranoia setting in, but the place felt as "off" as the scene back at Brette's truck.

"Tell you what," he said to Eric. "Go stand by the truck. I'm going to circle the house to check for some sign of light or activity inside."

His caution didn't sit well with Eric. "Why can't we just see if the door is unlocked and go in? Keith comes into our place without knocking. He's probably fallen asleep, that's all."

"Could be." Sam shot him a look he knew would rattle the kid. "But his answering machine says he's here and he's not picking up. Considering the scene we've come from, you should be assuming nothing, and suspecting everything and everyone."

Just then the phone rang inside and Sam touched his index finger to his lips. The answering machine immediately clicked on and Sam heard the same message he'd gotten when he called. The caller didn't leave a message and the system reset and shut off.

Sam glanced back at Eric, and the boy returned to the car without comment.

Wondering what the heck was going on, Sam started around the back of the house. One thing was for sure, Daggett was an all-show guy. That revelation came as he aimed his flashlight around. The yard was a mess, and totally unlike the neat front yard. Wading through thigh-high grass and stepping between empty and decomposing shipping boxes and empty plastic containers, he had to shine his light on where he would next step as often as he did on the windows. It made Sam wish he'd taken the stronger Halogen light. He didn't understand the bagged trash, either. Where was the necessity of that considering they had regular service twice a week? But most compelling was that there were no lights on whatsoever in the house.

By the time he was coming across the tree-filled front of the house, Sam had decided he was going in. About to tell the boys, he noticed a bulky silhouette approaching from across the street.

"Yoo-hoo, Sam? Sam is that you? Wait!"

Bertrice. Hoping she wasn't going to insist on helping, too, he hurried down the drive to her. "Sorry if the flashlight made you nervous, Bertie. I thought you'd recognize my truck."

"Oh, I do. It's Clovis—I can't get him to calm down."

Didn't she realize they didn't have time for this? "Bertie, Keith's car is here, but he doesn't come to the door. I don't have time to—"

"That's what I mean. Clovis thinks something is

wrong, too. He's been staring out the front window and pacing and going on all day. Usually I can make out some of what he says, but I don't have a clue about this.'' She glanced back at her place and uttered a tsking sound. ''Well, now see? The old fool's bound and determined to get over here.''

Sure enough, Clovis was making his way across the street—at a snail's pace, but determined nonetheless.

Following the growing hunch that the old timer had seen something important, Sam ran to him. ''What is it, Clovis?''

He lifted a withered shaking hand and pointed. ''Hee—hee—hee.''

Not that again, Sam thought.

''Hee—Baat—*Baat.*''

A chill shot through him. Maybe he was nuts, but as far as he was concerned ''Bat'' sure came close to sounding like ''Brette.''

His inside churning, Sam launched himself back to the house and up the stairs. The storm door turned out to be unlocked. Not giving a damn if what he was doing was kosher or not, he stepped inside.

''Hello! Keith? Daggett, are you in there?'' He found the switch for the kitchen light and turned it on.

The place looked normal enough for someone who didn't use his kitchen. The only appliance seemed to be the answering machine. And the only other thing in the room was a roll of duct tape on the counter.

Mr. Fixit, Sam though with a smirk. He moved on.

There was no one in the living room, either. Small wonder. There was no TV, stereo or even furniture.

The guy gave new meaning to the term "computer nerd." His whole life must be tied up in his office.

Sam was about to enter the master's domain when he heard Eric call his name. This was followed by more voices. No doubt a worried Bertrice had overridden his order to Eric and suggested they all check on him.

Sam was reluctantly impressed by Daggett's setup. There were machines humming and cranking away all around him, but all of the monitors were shut off. About to click on the one nearest him, Sam saw a green piece of paper on the floor and stooped to pick it up.

Eric and Hank entered. "Maybe you'd better come," Hank said. "Clovis is getting worse."

"Is this not a cool setup?" Eric asked. "He never shuts any of it down, except when it's storming, of course. You have to be careful around here even if you have monster surge protectors like these because of our sand getting wet and being such a good conductor of electricity. He told me and Hank all about it, and how he should sell the pine trees to the timber company because they draw lightning, too, but he doesn't want to lose the shade."

Sam barely heard him; he was more intrigued by the paper, which turned out to be a postcard. A registered mail receipt to be specific. It had been signed and dated by Daggett. So why was it here?

"Wonder what he's working on."

Before Sam could reprimand him, Eric turned on the first monitor, and in front of all of their stunned gazes a naked young boy materialized.

A feminine gasp filled the stunned silence. Sam spun around to see Bertrice standing in the doorway.

He shut the thing off and wondered what to say to everyone. He didn't want to think what it meant, but Hank didn't suffer the same problem.

"That prick," Hank whispered. He looked at Eric. "Didn't I tell you?"

Eric remained rooted in place. Sam gently gripped his shoulder and gave him a subtle shake. "We can't dwell on this right now. This card tells me your mom was here. The fact that she didn't take it with her tells me maybe she wasn't given the opportunity. We have to go get the sheriff."

Bertrice let the children pass so that she could get closer to Sam. "Why on earth would Keith have something like that on his computer?" Bertrice asked, her hand pressed to her bosom. "Oh, this is awful. And after I was so pleased that he had begun a relationship."

"Relationship?"

"Well, he must have. I almost fell slipping on this earring. There must be someone he— Why, Sam!"

Sam grabbed her hand. In her palm was the twin of the earring now in possession of the Wood County Sheriff's Department. Daggett...Daggett was the one behind Tracie's disappearance, and if the card in his hand was the evidence he believed, the bastard had Brette.

Where? Dear God, where?

Grim and silent, they checked the rest of the house for more clues, but came up empty. Outside, though, they received another shock. Clovis was gone.

"Mercy, not now," moaned Bertrice. "I do hope he went home. He's only wearing slippers and that sweater he has on isn't—"

"There he is!"

They all looked to where Hank was pointing. Indeed, half-hidden by the tall grass and shrubs at the perimeter of the woods, was Clovis. It was obvious he wanted to go after something.

Sam told the others to stay put and caught up with him. "What is it? What did you see? You did, didn't you?"

As before, the old man pointed and whined.

"Was it Keith?"

Clovis looked at him vacantly.

"Okay, okay, that's all right that the name means nothing to you. How about Brette? Remember Brette? Did you see Brette?"

"Baat."

"Yes, Brette. We'll get Brette. Come on back now. It'll be okay."

As he urged the man to turn around, he signaled the others to come help.

"Bertie," he said when the hyperventilating and upset woman reached him. "You have to calm down. We'll take it from here. Get him home before he catches pneumonia." He quickly kissed her cheek and moved on to Eric and Hank. "Come with me. Eric, can you get a signal on your phone?" At the Suburban he retrieved a hatchet from the back.

The boy tried. "Not a good one. I can use the phone inside. Want me to call the sheriff?"

"It'll be faster if I run," Hank told them.

Eric nodded to Sam. "He's fast."

"Then fly, son." Even as he took off, Sam slammed the door on the truck and headed toward the woods again. "Okay, Eric, this is what you have to do. Stay here and watch me as long as you can, and when the others get here, show them where I went."

"What if Keith has a gun?"

"We can't risk waiting. Look, it may not be me who comes out. If it's Daggett, you get across the street, lock the door and call for help."

Eric nodded, but his look was that of a scared child. "Do you think you can find her, Sam?"

"I won't stop until I do."

53

As Keith stood up, Brette understood her time was almost up. With growing desperation, she attacked the sharp stump edges, sawing the tape against them. She felt the material give a bit more, but just when she thought she had it this time, a shard of wood broke and what felt like a nail pierced her right wrist.

She cried out.

Keith had bent to pick up his pipe and the loud cry snapped him to attention. "Stop it!"

"My…my…oh, damn." He was going to know. He was going to see. "It's another spasm," she managed to explain. She took several deep breaths fighting the urge to faint. "I'm all right now. I'm sorry. I'll get up. It's okay."

She would say anything to keep him from looking behind her at this point. But her wrist hurt so badly she wasn't sure she could bear the pain of trying a final time to break through the rest of the tape.

You have to. If animals caught in traps and barbed wire are able to chew off their limbs, you can damn well handle a big splinter.

But as she felt a warm oozing run down into her cupped hand, she knew she had more than a splinter in her flesh. What if she'd severed a vein?

"Then get up already." Keith moved with a new deliberateness as he came toward her.

Before she could summon the strength to move, he grabbed hold of a handful of her sweater and hauled her to her feet. The momentum jerked her arm and ripped the rest of the tape, but not without causing Brette another dizzying lash of pain. The blood pooling in her cupped hand was beginning to seep through her fingers. It became her new fixation to hold on to it as long as she could.

Every step became trickier. Keith's light wasn't as strong as the ones she and Sam had used.

"Your battery's getting weak." She was grimly pleased. "It won't last for you to make it back."

"I don't want to talk anymore."

"I understand." Neither did she, but she would do it anyway to work on him as much as to stay conscious. She had to get more personal. Wasn't that a key point with psychotics—if in fact Keith was one? If he got away with this, he would be on his way to becoming a...she didn't want to face what. Personal was her one defense, she told herself. She had to keep it personal.

"I guess you're starting to feel bad about w-what you think you have to do. But you don't have to do it."

"Be quiet."

Brette's focus wavered, the evening grew darker.

"Killing me will affect you. You won't forget. Maybe you think you handled Tracie pretty well—I mean, I never suspected you—but that was because she'd hurt you. But you and I are friends and I care about you. How are you going to go to b-bed night after night with that on your conscience? You won't, you know. I'll be the first thing you think of in the morning. The last at night. When you go somewhere and pass a w-window seeing a reflection, you'll think I'm behind you. And I will be.''

Keith spun around and rammed his forearm against her throat, driving her backward into a nearby oak. ''Shut up! Just shut the fuck up!''

Brette was almost grateful for the adrenaline surge. It made her realize if she was going to make her move it had to be now. Any later and she would be too weak.

''What are you going to do, hit me, Keith? Knock me out because you're angry with yourself? How will you get me across that fence then? I always felt a little sorry for you because I knew you were sensitive about your slight build, but I guess I should be grateful now, huh? Because you won't be able to do it. You'll leave fibers on the barbed wire. They'll track you down by that, Keith.''

He raised his pipe to strike. ''You—''

She gasped. ''What's that?''

He looked behind him. When he turned back to her, she had her hands free and shoved the hand with her blood across his face, smearing his glasses and wiping it across his mouth.

He gasped and choked, then spit and screamed in disgust and outrage.

All Brette cared was that he'd backed up a step— just enough for her. Taking a deep breath, she drove her knee into his groin with all of her might.

As he crumpled to the ground, she took off up the hill shouting.

''Help me!''

Without a light she was at the mercy of every bush

and dip in the ground, every stump and thorn-riddled vine. Her sweater caught on one and she had to rip it loose, further cutting her hands. A few steps farther and a broken branch raked at her from the other side.

If she could only get as far as the back of Sally's she was sure someone would hear her. They had to be outside looking for her by now.

"Sam!"

About to shout again, she was hit from behind. She went flying face first toward the ground. The only reason she didn't break her nose was that she landed on her hands, but the new blow to her wrist tore an anguished sob from her. There was no chance to come to terms with the pain, though. Before she could catch her breath, Keith was grabbing her by her hair and dragging her back down the hill.

He was merciless, and the situation became a battle of wills. Unable to keep her feet under her, Brette began wishing her hair would come out in his hand, if only for a moment's relief. It didn't...and they were getting closer and closer to the water.

She heard animal sounds and realized they were coming from her as she clawed at his hands. Unfortunately, she didn't have any nails to speak of, and her palms were slick from the blood. She tried to punch and pummel him in the kidneys, but she kept missing or hurting herself by striking his hipbone.

The mud and the first few inches of water brought a strange mix of relief and new terror. A few steps in Keith slipped and dropped to his knees. That brought some relief to her head, but also drenched the back half of her body—a taste of what was to come.

With a final surge of strength, Brette struggled to beat him getting up. Gripping her least-injured wrist and using it as a sledgehammer, she swung at him. While he ducked, suffering only a glancing blow, she lost her balance.

Down she went. He pushed her deeper into the black swill that stank of decay and chilled her to the bone. Then he hauled her up and farther out into the water.

"No!" she sobbed between coughs.

On he went. The water rose...to her knees...to her thighs. She felt the muck take one of her athletic shoes and try for her whole leg. She stumbled into what by day were giant clumps of swamp grass sitting on pillars of clay that flooding had carved. In warmer weather they served as sunning spots for water moccasins and the occasional alligator that wandered up the numerous tributaries. As Brette grabbed hold of it, she didn't care about snakes. She thought only of staying above the black death rising around her. Keith, however, would have none of that.

He pulled hard, overestimating her remaining strength and dragging her free. The momentum sent them both under.

Her mouth and nose filled with water. Death became a presence reaching for her. She pushed it away, clawed frantically at his face, his eyes....

Miraculously, he pushed her away and she burst to the surface. He rose, too, no longer Death, but Keith again. He'd lost his glasses and he was gasping for breath as desperately as she was.

She let him come. Then, with all the anger and outrage inside her, she jammed her palm against his nose. Her aim was poor, but as the blow struck him in the cheekbone, it cost him his balance and propelled him back. All of a sudden he vanished altogether.

Brette waited. Not able to trust the peace, she began backing to dry ground.

Suddenly he surfaced, his arms flailing. "Help me. Brette, it's *quicksand.*"

It wasn't, but it felt like it. He'd found a sinkhole, or more accurately, a natural spring. So deep it seemed to have no bottom. And if she went out there, he would take her down with him.

"Help me!"

"Goodbye, Keith," she whispered.

He went under again…and this time he didn't resurface.

The night grew still and serenely quiet. Stunned to still be alive, but unable to feel anything, not even her limbs, Brette sunk to the ground.

She thought she heard her name. For a terrible moment she thought it came from the water, but it wasn't Keith's voice. It was Sam's. Her Sam. She wanted to get up, to go to him, but she couldn't budge or take her eyes off the water. That was all right, though. Sam came to her.

He sank to his knees and began to reach for her only to stop and stare. "Brette…my God, Brette. What did he do to you?" Swallowing he ground out, "Where is he?"

She lifted the only limb she could move to indicate the water, then whispered, "Sam?"

"Yeah, love?"

"I think I'm running out of blood. Can you get me out of here?"

54

Can't write. Sam's doing this for me. So much to put down. Most he wants me to forget. I don't. You can't change if you forget. And you can't grow.
—Journal Entry

Friday, November 19, 1999

Brette lay against a pile of pillows watching the convoy pass her bedroom window. Some were from the sheriff's department, the state, and the parks and wildlife department. There was also one ambulance. Eight vehicles in all heading for the Pugh farm to see what they could locate of the remains of Tracie Pugh. The consensus was that they would try to find Keith next.

It was a sad sight. Brette knew that's why Sam had turned from the window to sit beside her. He didn't want her to see this, had tried to talk her out of opening the miniblinds when they'd heard what was scheduled. He hadn't wanted her to write in her journal, either. Or rather, he didn't want to write the few lines she'd asked him to put down for her until later. But for her this was the final chapter…and closure was a good thing.

"You promised the doctor you'd rest," he said, brushing his thumb across her lower lip.

It was about the only part of her that wasn't bruised, sutured, scraped raw or concussed. She'd cried when she first saw herself in a mirror, until Sam reminded her that the first time he'd seen her she had had a bump on her forehead and scratches on her knees.

"Well, you must think I'm ravishing now," she'd sobbed.

"I do," he'd told her.

And the way his eyes had glistened, she believed him.

His eyes were getting that look again.

"You slept better last night."

"No nightmares."

Her first night in the hospital she'd dreamed of Keith rising out of the water like that final scene in *Deliverance* to drag her out of her bed. The second night she'd dreamed of the boars. They'd come out of the darkness, only those yellow eyes and razor-sharp tusks visible, grinding their teeth in characteristic fashion, ready for a meal because Sam had not come, and she hadn't had the strength to move anymore. She'd woken in Sam's arms, but the greasy, rancid smell of them had lingered in her nostrils for hours afterward.

Right then and there she'd decided hospitals were a hazard to her health and she'd ordered the doctor to release her. Not that she took her injuries lightly. That's why Sam wouldn't leave her and the boys had slept camp-out style on the Ponders' floor for two nights—and robbed Clovis out of every penny in his jelly jar playing poker. She'd lost a lot of blood, and there was still concern of infection in her right wrist, not to mention her concussion. But dizzy spells and headaches were a small price to pay for the sight of her son and Hank charging off the school bus to plop on her bed and compete with each other about who at school had found the grossest joke on the Internet.

She supposed the thought of computers changed her expression because Sam immediately asked, "What?"

"I was so wrong."

"About what?"

"The Pughs...Keith. My God, I was even afraid of *you*."

Sam shifted, his movements guilty. "I gave you cause. A part of me wanted you to stay away so I could be near you without doing the work."

"And why not? It's what you'd been trained to do all your life. The important thing is that you changed the pattern."

"*You* changed it. You're too damned honest for your own good."

That wasn't true. "I've been hiding, taking life for granted. I thought I was fine, that my job was to take care of other people. And one day I wake up to find that nothing works anymore, all of the systems are failing me." She laughed briefly. "Sounds as though I had a hard-drive crash, doesn't it?"

"You keep coming back to Daggett."

She knew he would prefer if she didn't, but she needed to make him understand. "I know you can't ever hope to answer all of life's mysteries, but I think we're obligated to try."

''He was no mystery, he was a worm.''

Brette had mixed feelings about that. Granted, she was in no state yet to forgive him for what he'd done. The thought of how he'd inveigled himself into her and Sally's lives... Why? To get closer to their sons? Sheriff Cudahy had told her that Keith's computer room would prove to be a windfall of information about the psyche of the pedophile. But even Cudahy had admitted Keith hadn't qualified as a ''charter'' member of the club. He had been building himself up to finding the courage to do something personally, so the Internet had been like a giant birthday present to him.

Could he have changed, stopped the downward spiral with the right help? They were going to try to find out. Keith's past was proving difficult to unearth, though. He'd been an orphan. He'd stayed at two homes, enjoying rather privileged conditions for some time, but neither had provided the close nurturing and monitoring that he'd needed. And then, sometime midway through college, he'd vanished—and shown up here a few years ago. It was those missing years the agents and doctors would be trying to uncover.

''What decided things for him?'' she murmured.

''What?''

She looked up and saw she'd left Sam behind again. She reached for his hand, although she could only feel him with her fingertips because of all the bandages.

''It's all about choice, I think. The strangest thing happened to me when I was with him.''

''Brette, you're doing to drive yourself crazy going over and over it.''

"No, I'm facing myself and understanding it. Sam...I could have been you."

He frowned. "In what way?"

"I experienced true anger, rage. It was there inside me, waiting. Me. The post office's answer to the hospital candy striper."

Sam's jaw began working and he fingered her bandages. "It's not a bad thing."

"No. I'm not going to apologize for it. I've loved my life, but I still feel like this fountain in the middle of a flowerbed."

"You are."

Her answering gaze was all seriousness. "Maybe the fountain still works, but there's a little mud in the water."

Sam shook his head. "I know what you're going to say. We've talked about this, Brette. Why won't you let it go?"

"Why won't you let me speak!"

A truck pulled up outside. It was Tucker. They'd known he was going to stop by, just as he had yesterday.

Using the excuse that he needed to answer the door, Sam left the room.

Brette waited, listening to the brief exchanges. At least they weren't throwing punches.

"Hey, Mummy-gal."

Tucker entered the room like a hot West Texas wind. He held an armful of cards, tiny stuffed animals and jarred goodies that he eased onto the bed.

"Gifts from your fans. Now you'll have something to do this afternoon besides envy me while I'm dodging timber haulers and blind old bats in vintage Cadillacs the size of nuclear subs.''

Brette laughed. She had to hold her head, but it felt wonderful to hear his nonsense nonetheless.

''I can't believe it. More.'' Her room was fast becoming the equivalent of a local Hallmark store. ''This is so nice of everyone. I hope they've all put their names on everything so I can thank them properly.''

''Heal fast so I can get credit for your first-class postage.''

She cast him a suspicious look. ''You aren't blackmailing my customers to do this, are you?''

''Hell, no. But I've gotta admit, seeing this haul tempts me to get this route back. Shoot, I told Mrs. Zimmer down yo ways that I had a bellyache for two days and you know what she made me? Homemade chicken'n dumplings. Almost gave me an orgasm.''

''Okay, stop. Laughing still hurts.''

He grew immediately serious. ''Field Marshall Knight tells me the snoops'n spooks are down rummaging in the bottoms, passing here like a parade of Roman chariots going to see what the lions left. You shouldn't be here while that's going on.''

''It's fine, Tucker. They have a job I don't envy, and they have reason to take pride in their work.''

''Well, aren't you all sweetness and cream this morning. Guess it helps that Cudahy came by to apologize.''

It did. He'd been gracious and humble, too, acknowledging that he'd fallen into a trap he'd sworn never to do—to undervalue the needs and validity of his rural constituents.

"Anything new with the Pugh boys?"

"No. Nor do I expect it. Cudahy says there was minimal reaction to the news about Tracie. Isn't that sad? Like someone yelling 'Lockdown' in a penitentiary. I don't expect miracles, I just hope we can all go on with our lives. Did Sam tell you what the FBI discovered over at Keith's?"

Tucker lowered his head to give her one of his "Get real" looks. "Barry, the Terminator thinks he's doing me a favor letting me in here to see you."

Brette knew that, as a result, Tucker remained nervous about coming, a condition she hoped he'd adjust to in time. "They've discovered that Keith knew Mel. You know Hank's Saint Louis Michelle?"

Tucker's eyes grew wide. "Holy sheep—uh—no kidding?"

"When Sally got frustrated with Keith for his lack of...well, lack of passion let's say, Keith was embarrassed, more so than we realized. He paid her back by giving one of his Internet soul mates Hank's e-mail address and a lot of personal information that fooled Hank into believing he'd found the girl of his dreams."

"The prick."

"Yeah. Hank was pretty shaken when he heard. But this morning he came to me and said he felt like a load had been lifted off him. Sam sat him down last night and explained what the sheriff had told us, how there's this whole secret networking for those people. The poor kid didn't stand a chance with them conniving against him."

"But you're still gonna nudge him toward getting help, right?"

"As much as he wants, although I'll tell you this, he's also going to join the track team and that requires disciplined attendance, too."

"Aha. He's told you about that."

She smiled proudly thinking of Hank's personal discovery. "When he was running to get help for me? Yeah. He said he'd never wanted anything more or felt stronger about anything as much. Pretty cool, huh?"

"I think you're worse than the soap operas." Nevertheless, he was grinning as he headed toward the door. "My time's up. Knowing you, you'll call in and report me."

"Hey," Brette replied. "Do you know I've almost died and you've still never even kissed me on the cheek?"

He turned yet another shade of red and pulled on his nose. "The next addition to the family, I promise. A big noisy one. But for your sake, I hope he doesn't arrive eating what the other three do."

Sam took a while to return. Brette knew it was because he was afraid she would want to pick up where they'd left off. She did. It was unfinished business, and she would get out of this bed much faster if she didn't have to tiptoe around topics he was ashamed of.

He arrived with a cup of his nefarious honey-lemon tea. After obliging him with a sip while he cleaned her loot off the bed, Brette studied him.

"You don't have to accept Cudahy's offer to help get your teaching job back," she began. "And you don't ever have to talk about your father to me again if you don't want to. But, Sam, you have to let me be honest.''

He looked dumbfounded. ''What the hell are you talking about? When have I denied you that?''

''When you refuse to listen to me say that I let a man die.''

Sam frowned down at the stuffed basset hound in his hands. ''He went into a spring. You can swim out of those things, you know, just as you can get out of quicksand if you don't panic.''

''Keith couldn't swim. I knew that. I could have found him a long branch, I didn't.''

''Stop it.''

''I might have been able to give him a hand out.''

''You were bleeding to death, Brette. Enough.''

''No. I was *angry* with him. In that instant I wanted him to die for the pain and suffering he'd caused. Don't you see, Sam? I can't be something you put on a pedestal to worship or win. I love you. But I'm only capable of loving you because I understand you and what you've been through. Really understand.''

''And I hate that you had to learn.'' His eyes burned with emotion. ''I'm not an idealist, Brette. I'm never going to expect sunshine after three days of rain because it's only fair. But I have been lucky enough to come across a few precious things in my life.

''You,'' he said, growing calmer, ''are one of those. Can you live with that? Being cherished whether you think you deserve to be or not?''

This man—he still needed so much healing. They all did. Thankfully, although she didn't know what else their future held, she did know they were going to be given a chance.

"I can live with it a lot better than I can live with my thin walls," she told him.

The beginnings of a smile curved his lips as he leaned close to kiss her. "Thin walls. Admit it, it's my sunroom you're after."

"Believe what you want," she murmured, easing her bandaged arm around his neck. "As long as I get you."

The spellbinding story of a man and woman who
journey through hell to arrive at a place in their
hearts that offers the promise of heaven.

THE DEVIL'S OWN

In a terrifying race to save nine children from the threat
of war-torn Central America, Kerry Bishop prepared for
the fight of her life. But she wasn't prepared for a passion
almost as dangerous as the mission she had undertaken.

Dependent on a stranger, Kerry refused to let unexpected
desire complicate their mission. Survival was all they could
think about. But if they succeeded, what then?

NEW YORK TIMES BESTSELLING AUTHOR

SANDRA
BROWN

Available March 2001
wherever hardcovers are sold!

Visit us at www.mirabooks.com

MIRA®

MSB793

New York Times Bestselling Author

JOAN JOHNSTON

Abigail Dayton has a job to do—trap and relocate a wolf that is
threatening local ranches, in an effort to save the species from
extinction. Abby knows the breed well: powerful, strong and lean.
As rare as it is beautiful. Aggressive when challenged. A predator.

But the description fits both the endangered species she's
sworn to protect…and a man she's determined to avoid.
Local rancher Luke Granger is a lone wolf, the kind of man who
doesn't tame or trust easily. The kind of man who tempts
a woman to risk everything….

Never Tease a Wolf

Available April 2001 wherever paperbacks are sold!

A gripping novel of psychological suspense
from the bestselling author of *Sacred Trust*

MEG O'BRIEN
GATHERING
LIES

Six women have come to Thornberry, a writers' colony on a tiny
island off the coast of Seattle, each hoping to work on her own
writing at this secluded resort. But they have also come to hide.
Each harbors her own secret—until a devastating earthquake
shatters the haven these women have found. Suddenly the resort
is partly in ruin, communication has been cut off from the
mainland and the women are forced to rely on each other for
basic survival.

Then a man washes up on shore. Is he the salvation they've
been looking for...or an even greater threat to their survival?

Available April 2001, wherever paperbacks are sold!

HELEN R. MYERS

66572	LOST	__ $5.99 U.S. __ $6.99 CAN.
66504	MORE THAN	
	YOU KNOW	__ $5.99 U.S. __ $6.99 CAN.
66436	COME SUNDOWN	__ $5.99 U.S. __ $6.99 CAN.

(limited quantities available)

TOTAL AMOUNT	$_____
POSTAGE & HANDLING	$_____
($1.00 for one book; 50¢ for each additional)	
APPLICABLE TAXES*	$_____
TOTAL PAYABLE	$_____

(check or money order—please do not send cash)

To order, complete this form and send it, along with a check or money order for the total above, payable to MIRA Books®, to: **In the U.S.:** 3010 Walden Avenue, P.O. Box 9077, Buffalo, NY 14269-9077; **In Canada:** P.O. Box 636, Fort Erie, Ontario L2A 5X3.

Name:_____

Address:_____ City:_____

State/Prov.:_____ Zip/Postal Code:_____

Account Number (if applicable):_____

075 CSAS

*New York residents remit applicable sales taxes.
Canadian residents remit applicable GST and provincial taxes.

MIRA®